BLUE AGAINST A BLACK LOOMING NIGHT

A NOVEL BY

John Michael Whitten

Copyright

***** The story, all names, characters, and incidents portrayed in this production are fictitious. No identification with actual persons (living or deceased), places, buildings, corporations or businesses, political parties, and/or products are intended or should be inferred. *****

MerryJohn Publishing   Merryjohn4850@gmail.com

WEBSITE: blueagainstnight.com

EDITING: **Yanah G. Cook.**

Ordering Information: Quantity sales. Special discounts are available on quantity purchases by corporations, associations, and others. For details, contact the publisher at the email above. Orders by U.S. trade bookstores and wholesalers. Please contact Merryjohn Publishing: Tel: 360 894 0657
First Printing, 2023

9798218320676 ISBN

Printed in the United States of America

DEDICATION

To all the children in the world and in particular my Grandchildren. My abject, humble apologies for the world we are leaving you. If I leave you any advice it is this: Learn to Adapt.

You are the future and I love you all: Phoenix, Andrew, Alexis, Nicholas, and the irrepressible Neala, my wonderful grandchildren who are bright, creative, strong, and hopeful. If any can survive, they will.

**

I want to dedicate this to Yanah G. Cook, my editor, and my friend. She is the 1960's flower child fully grown and holding fiercely to the principles of egalitarianism, compassion, empathy, and generosity. Yana represents the 'Age of Aquarius', living the belief that we have a responsibility to each other; helping others in need. Her beliefs and her dedication to making a positive difference in this world are humbling.

We owe a deep, fundamental debt of gratitude to former Vice President Albert Arnold Gore, Jr. Mr. Gore sacrificed his own dreams of the Presidency in order to preserve and protect our union at a time in which partisan politics sabotaged the people's will. We will never know what kind of President Mr. Gore would have made but we do know this: If moral fortitude, compassionate integrity, and prescient intelligence count, he would have been outstanding.
**

**

Once again, this work is for my MERRY, there are not enough words to tell you how much you are loved, you are my world. You have led me to love. In this world and the next.

SPECIAL DEDICATION

"Dogs have given us their absolute all. We are the center of their universe. We are the focus of their love and faith and trust. They serve us in return for scraps. It is without a doubt the best deal man has ever made." Roger A. Caras

Of course, mention must be made of our beloved Bodhi, our companion, and our friend. Bodhi, another in line of wonderful canine beings who have taught us the nature of love and loyalty.

CHAPTER ONE

"But man is a part of nature, and his war against nature is inevitably a war against himself. Rachel Carson.

September 15, 2028

At 2:30 PM on a drizzling afternoon, a young black man named Kenny Johns was closing the Beautee' Nail Salon shop for his wife, Brenda. Six months pregnant, Brenda Johns often asked Kenny to help her because Kenny's job as a Lyft driver gave him some latitude with his day. Also, Kenny loved to help her. Best friends in MLK high school they married right after graduation and were inseparable. Their third child was due in three months to join with Sheria and Julia, their other daughters.

That afternoon, just as Kenny was bringing out office equipment from the back of the store to put in his car an Olympia Sheriff's cruiser pulled up.

Sergeant Ted Bubonky, a fifteen-year veteran, irritated because it was raining again, had been assigned crowd control, which meant standing in the rain. What made it worse, the protestors were Liberals. Bubonky thought Liberals to be stupid at best and Communists at worst.

All at once, he saw a young, black man carrying something out the back door of a store, Sgt. Bubonky immediately hit lights and siren. Quickly exiting the vehicle Bubonky gave a short, sharp command to the black man to drop what he was carrying and get against the wall.

Bubonky, recognized the man as a mongrel he'd ticketed a few days ago. By now he was just a few feet away and had a hand on his service weapon.

Kenny, carrying a brand-new copy machine looked down at the damp pavement, puddled from an earlier rainstorm.

"Sir," Kenny, slightly nervous because he recognized Bubonky, but still comfortable in his innocence, smiled and held out the machine. He knew he was doing no wrong and this was no problem. "Officer, if I drop it I might…" Kenny wanted to explain that dropping it might damage the machine, plus the pavement was wet, and was about to say: "…just set it down, where it's dry?"

Kenny never got that far.

Sgt. Bubonky heard all he needed to, pulled his service weapon, a 500 Smith & Wesson Magnum, and shot Kenny twice in the face and twice in the chest.

The young black father of two-year-old twins, newly accepted into Montpelier University graduate program to study Social Work, died instantly.

The brand-new Epson copier crashed to the wet pavement just seconds before his lifeless body.

Thick gobbets of bright, red blood, tissue, and meat splattered everywhere because Bubonky's S&W handgun fired a monster 440 grain bullet, generating 1700-foot pounds of energy, effectively obliterating the human body.

Bubonky cursed. "Oh man, too fast, too fast," he scolded himself, realizing he had reacted too quickly again. This was going to get hot real fast, so he quickly called in a '10-33' code for 'Officer involved shooting', which means immediate backup. Bubonky paced up and down the alley furious at himself because the Brass might think this was premeditated.

Bubonky wasn't sure himself; it had all happened so fast.

A month ago, Kenny Johns lodged a harassment complaint against Sergeant Bubonky for a traffic stop, claiming the Sergeant was rude and offensive. Bubonky was warned to be more professional by Sheriff Orwell, a rebuke that infuriated him. He had said some pretty inflammatory things about Johns around the station and he worried many would believe he was here to get even.

Fortunately, within minutes of his call, he could hear the sirens of officers rushing to his aid to protect him from possible citizen retaliation.

In times past, if an officer gunned down someone and the shoot might not be totally 'righteous' the cop could throw down a gun, and pretend it was the victims': "He pulled a gun." But he didn't need a charade these days. Sgt. Bubonky had no fear of legal jeopardy at all, his largest concern was being attacked by citizens, because under the present political administration, the shooting of colored people wasn't a problem; some would say it was even encouraged.

But Bubonky knew the protestors wouldn't understand so he needed to get surrounded by cops and taken away to safety. *Those protestors surely heard the shot, and those damned Liberals would probably blame me.*

Two blocks to the west, protestors had angrily gathered to protest a recent Homeland Security Directive that all Democrats must register with the Homeland Security Office, Liberal Control Division, to turn in their passports.

As Bubonky predicted, despite their noise, the protestors heard gunfire echoing off the buildings. A witness to the shooting used his phone and word quickly spread that another black man had been gunned down. The crowd wheeled as one, leaving the City Hall to race down a side street to the scene of the shooting.
**

Deputy Tomas Two Hawks cooped behind the Dollar Store read a recent FOXE NEWS Poll: "Republican voters were heavily in favor of martial law and shoot to-kill orders for looters; a term synonymous for Liberal Protestors". Tomas thought this was a little extreme.

The FOXE poll completely ignored the actual cause of the incident; a black, six-year-old girl gunned down by a white, off duty cop.

This kind of outrage is what brings people out of their warm, comfortable homes and into the streets. Tomas thought the cause of the protest was vital to the reaction; some protests were necessary. *When citizens feel powerless against a perceived wrong and they have no way to settle it, they go into the streets to demand change.* Other protests, however, were just political theater.

The cause of their protest mattered; Tomas firmly believed. *Because people don't riot for the hell of it. Most people don't want to be bothered; they want to live their lives with no hassle. For normal humans to rush into the streets takes an extraordinary event, something so compelling, so powerful they cannot stay home. As authority, I think cops need to understand this.* Tomas reasoned, *A violent response to a peaceful citizen protest is more about oppression then crowd control.*

Two Hawks heard the radio call out, "Officer-involved shooting", shifted into drive and pulling out of the parking lot he headed to answer Sgt. Bubonky's call for assistance.

Two blocks later, Two Hawks pulled into the alley just as the first of the protesters also arrived on scene. Already, Sgt. Bubonky surrounded by several uniformed officers was being escorted to a squad car.

Ambulance Medics bent over the victim, working hard, trying to get a pulse back, bloody 4x4s and gauze lay all around on the wet pavement.

To Tomas's surprise, the paramedics abruptly stopped their efforts, and then placing the dead man on a gurney wheeled him to the ambulance.

"Wait a minute!" Tomas called out. "This is an active crime scene; you can't pull the victim out of here yet! We need to investigate the shooting!"

That brought Sgt. Bubonky out of the squad vehicle.

"No sir, no sir, you back off, you Indian motherfucker!" Bubonky literally screamed. "You read the Homeland Security, Memo #23-5. The latest MAGA DOJ Crowd Control Directive?"

"What are you bitching about?"

Just then the first of the protestors came around the nearest corner and the level of noise went up incredibly.

A thin line of cops moved to intercept.

"Deputy Two Hawks, we are ordered to clear all shooting scenes immediately. This is to prevent further citizen injuries," Sgt. Bubonky shouted to be heard over the growing, raucous crowd.

Two Hawks gave Bubonky a confused look. "What?" He shook his head because this didn't make any sense to Tomas.

"Common sense," Bubonky said self-importantly with a knowing smirk. "When there is a shooting, crowds gather and with more people there is always more violence. So, we resolve it by eliminating the scene, eliminating the public, and doing our investigation in private where it belongs. If there are criminal actions we'll get the bad guy, the rest of the mutts don't need to know shit!"

Two Hawks was a lawman who believed he worked for the citizens to keep them safe. *Cops are part of the community; we're guard dogs keeping them safe from the wolves.* But he felt he was in a shrinking minority. Others in law enforcement believed citizens were sheep and cops were the wolves; being paid to be polite as long as the sheep didn't stray across the lines designed by those who control the wolves.

The ambulance moved slowly away, no lights, no siren. But the protestors had seen the bloody body of a young black man placed in that ambulance and there came a collective outcry of rage.

Tomas continued to stare at Bubonky, once again perplexed by the seemingly irrational world he lived in. Then another squad car pulls up, the officers, fully dressed in riot gear, got out forming a line against the crowd.

"What are you looking at asshole?" Bubonky snarled. He and Tomas were not friends. "Fucking prairie nigger giving me the eye! It was a righteous shoot, motherfucker," Bubonky screamed at Tomas, as he was pulled back into the squad car for a ride to their station.

Tomas, frowning deeply, had learned long ago that silence was generally best around bigots and bothersome degenerates. It never seemed to dull his anger though. Cops could be your best friend or your worst enemy and Tomas had no doubt where Bubonky stood.

As he watched Bubonky being driven safely away, Two Hawks, a Potawatomi Nation Native thought; *Discrimination in this Nation is rampant, this has been proven repeatedly.* He knew it personally, from infancy to the present.

Almost daily, Tomas read about mass shootings. So far this year, America was on course for the worst record of all: over two thousand people killed this year from gun violence and year's end was still months off.

Nationally, the killing of minorities by law enforcement was escalating with no apparent reason for it other than skin color. *Racism in the Nation is growing exponentially by official sanction,* Tomas thought. Of course, not every shooting was racial. The streets of bankrupt and impoverished American neighborhoods dealt with violence daily and weapons were ubiquitous.

As a cop he dealt with this professionally but as a Native man he knew it personally. Two Hawks grew up on a Reservation and knew firsthand the violence of poverty and the viciousness of racism. *Some of us managed to break free completely while others escaped to drugs, or alcohol, or suicide. Many souls left on the Rez were exhausted, hopeless and bitter, marginalized by society, punished by extreme poverty and prejudice for being Native.* He also knew many carried weapons because that is what desperate people do when they are overwhelmed and scared.

The increase of guns and gunplay in America's economic distressed areas have made law enforcement a hair trigger duty whether it is over the barren acres within a Native Reservation or on the deadly streets of The Hilltop in Tacoma. It seems as if anyone and everyone has some kind of weapon. Tomas had begun his career in Law Enforcement as a Tribal Police Officer on the Rez, and it seemed as if Olympia, Washington wasn't that different.

As the death tolls mounted, protesters around the Nation became increasingly more violent which, in turn, increased calls for 'Law and Order' by frightened citizens. The more the people protested in reaction to the police brutality the more intense the demand for additional police. It was a vicious, horrific circle that no one seemed to understand or be able to change.

A large man in the crowd yelled: "Hey Cops, you kill another unarmed black man?" The protestors still gathered in the ally were hostile and frightened. Many joined in, yelling at the police: "You kill another black man today?"

Tomas could see several local reporters in the crowd, and everybody had their phones recording everything. Tomas understood the media exploited such incidents. Media pundits take hours studying and criticizing a situation in which the police officer has only seconds to make a life-or-death decision. Nobody truly knows what goes down except the cop and the victims on scene.

"Murderer!" Someone shouted. "No justice, no peace!"

Other voices in the crowd were shouting "Why did you shoot him?" and "Fuck you, cops!"

There are a lot of guns out there in private hands and every single person we meet could open fire on us. Tomas could understand how a person would overreact to the perceived threats out there. It was a real balancing act for him as well. He had no idea who in this crowd might be armed but he had to assume at least quarter were packing weapons.

"This is another Detroit!"

"Yeah, why you killing black folks?"

**

A huge protest in Detroit a year ago turned deadly as seventeen were killed, fifty-five wounded when BlackThorn LLC, a private militia-army owned by a teen-age Oligarch, took command away from the local police authorities and opened fire without warning. Two Hawks shook his head. *Innocent people killed trying to protest a government decision. Protest only happens when there is no other choice.* Worse still, these citizens were killed by a private army, owned by a member of the ruling elite, Peter Popper, eldest son of the newly elected President, Barthalamew J. Popper, leader of the Make America Grow Awesome (MAGA) wing of the Republican Party.

America was changing much faster than he could believe. *No wonder people are acting so weird, they're scared, and they need someone to blame. They know this society is broken; they just don't know what to do about it because this place is essentially leaderless.*

In 2024, Republican interference in national elections became so persistent and intrusive the Presidential Election was declared a stalemate. Although the Democrats declared, with indisputable proof, they had won the election by forty million votes, the MAGA Republicans, holding a majority power in State

Legislatures across America, were able to manipulate the Electoral College giving the victory to Republican Barthalamew J. Popper. The Supreme Court loaded with MAGA Republican Judges, then ruled 7 to 2 in favor of Popper as the next President of the United States.

There was uproar across the Nation, calls for fraud investigations into the Electoral College process for US President reached a fever pitch, as did death threats against Congress. So, to ensure a solid and unshakable Republican victory, and save their lives, the Republican Congress interpreted the 12th Amendment to the US Constitution and called for a 'Contingent Election' in which each state legislature would vote for President: One State: One Vote.

Tomas had never heard of such a thing, but the Republicans had.

The American Lutheran Exchange Council, ALEC, a dedicated organization of MAGA Republican lawyers and Conservative Christian zealots traveling state to state assisting lawmakers by writing legislation favorable to Conservative Christian causes, made it all possible. Through ALEC's message coordination and skillful re-writing of state laws, Republicans, in secretive, midnight sessions, gained dominion over State legislatures in forty eight of the fifty States. Giving the Presidency to Popper in 2024 was a simple matter.

When Popper became the 47th President of the United States, losing by tens of millions of votes, citizen protests surged and spread exponentially across the Nation. There were riots and massive protests in every major city, put down with vicious, bloody efficiency by BlackThorn LLC and selected units of the US Military.

A chilly fall drizzle was quickly making the crowd calm down. As Tomas watched the agitated protestor's mill about, this kind of weather made it difficult to maintain outrage; the need to get warm and dry could be far more compelling than protesting.

"Listen up! Another black man died today. What are we going to do about it?" To the right of Tomas somebody had a bullhorn chanting, "No Justice, No Peace!" attempting to rally the crowd, some stopped leaving to listen and a crowd reformed.

In spite of the cool dampness, tempers were still heated.

**

They were being surrounded by angry citizens.

"Oh, shit." While Tomas had been woolgathering about politics, things changed. "Where did the other guys go?"

Deputy Sheriff Perry Werden gave Two Hawks a scornful glance. "What are you, blind? They had a call out over the Eastside, some kind of armed robbery."

Only Two Hawks and one other deputy were here, everyone else had left: the ambulance gone, shooter gone, victim gone, all the other police gone.

"Nobody here but us, boss," Werden moved out to confront the crowd.

Two Hawks keyed his mike, "Capital, 12, 10-44, send help."

CHAPTER TWO

"Tolerance is the only real test of civilization." Arthur Helps

Within minutes a two-and-one-half-ton truck, marked 'Olympia Sheriff Department' pulled up and the cops dressed in battle armor began unloading a massive piece of machinery, similar to a satellite dish, but thicker and more ponderous.

They quickly set up the dish facing the protestors, attached wires and cables to a control box, and then paused, staring at the control box dials for a few minutes before one stood up and flipped a switch.

Tomas heard a loud humming, a ripple formed in the air, a sharp scent of ozone pierced his nose, and he watched as the citizens reacted; within seconds the protesters were screaming in pain.

An older man cried out, "Ah God those hurts!"

A young woman screamed, "The bastards turned a laser weapon on us!"

"Hey, look out, run for your lives or you'll get burned!"

A heavy odor of ozone permeated the area, as shrieks of pain and surprise echoed off the walls of downtown Olympia buildings.

Tomas had read about this weapon but hadn't seen it; a crowd control device shooting microwaves like an oven. It was a violent weapon that caused agonizing skin damage if the human didn't move fast enough; old, disabled people would be cooked.

Tomas's mind flashed to tribes he knew on reservations fighting oil pipelines because the pipelines were certain to leak, certain to foul their drinking water. The human mantra of "Water is Life" appeared to mean nothing to the global corporate pipeline operators. These innocent Native people were also burned, tortured, and traumatized by this microwave weapon. The protesting people were forcibly dispersed with crowd-control cannons shooting freezing water, they were beaten, abused, and arrested for trying to stop the poisoning of their land. All because no one would listen to them; no court of justice would hear their pleas.

Tomas watched as the crowd was rapidly subdued; beginning to disperse. Clearly protesters realized they couldn't directly fight these merciless government weapons, so the people were scattering to continue their protests in a more random manner, away from the crowd control devices.

Deputy Tomas Two Hawks had no illusions about America. *There are many forms of 'justice' in this Nation: Rich man justice v poor man; white man v black man; man v woman. America, founded by wealthy, white men, was still ruled by them.*

The crowd dispersal weapon made a loud, irritating pulsing noise through the dampening of the heavy drizzle.

Tomas hated what he was seeing. He told the other deputy, "These people didn't do anything. They were protesting, but they didn't do any damage. People have a right to protest when they perceive a wrong."

Deputy Sheriff Werden didn't like hearing that. "Fuck that! Those are fucking Liberals, chief. If we don't shut those assholes down, we won't have our jobs. Those assholes wanted to defund the police! Can you believe that shit? Fuck 'em. We need to use live rounds."

Tomas said nothing, turned and went to his cruiser, started up, and pulled out without acknowledging anything the man had said.

It was building, he could feel it. The tensions in the squad room were intense; some officers saw themselves not as lawmen, but as super patriotic defenders of the US Constitution.

Deputy Tomas Two Hawks was a lawman, and believed he was a good lawman.

As he moved cautiously up 4th Street, in Olympia, a one-way road lined with restaurants, bike shops, pet stores, and small boutique venues for soap, flowers, art and books he drove carefully. The streets were lined with people going about routine activities, which sometimes meant abrupt attempts to cross the street in front of traffic. Because Olympia is a town in which pedestrians have ultimate rights, hard braking from irritated drivers was not uncommon.

He was alert as he drove down the crowded street, so Tomas noticed something very odd: A dark blue, 1966 Pontiac Firebird was sitting, idling at the curb, in front of a Hispanic falafel stand called; 'The Moroccan Taco'. Of course, the restaurant was what first caught his attention, but the real eye catcher was that car: *A Firebird?* He braked, slowly passing the muscle car. *A 1966 Pontiac Firebird, man, that was my first car!*

Eighteen years ago, Tomas, newly graduated from Mayetta High School, in Kansas, had purchased a 1966 Pontiac Firebird with money earned from wheat harvesting and dance contests at Pow Wow's. He loved that beast, racing it on the Potawatomi Reservation every chance. Those Prairie Band Indian boys were hell on wheels and betting their last nickel on who was fastest.

Tomas's car was also deep dark blue just like this one, but his windows were never as dark as this Pontiac. He could not see the inhabitants of the car. That made him curious.

As the Pontiac Firebird sat at the curb, waiting, a plume of exhaust billowed into the darkening afternoon sky, Tomas drove past, turning right at the next corner, onto Adams St., then did a U-turn to face back at 4th. St.

Pulling to the curb he waited, watching and wondering if he was wasting time on a hunch.

More rain threatened, there were fears of another massive rainfall like the one the area suffered two weeks ago; fifteen inches of rain in twenty-four hours. It had been a microburst flooding most of Thurston County, even areas that had never known flood before; Lake Lawrence had overflowed its banks inundating several lake side homes.

Because flooding also affected adjoining counties, all emergency services were fanned out across South Puget Sound.

Over three days of nonstop effort, Tomas searched for, found, argued with, and ultimately rescued eighteen people and their pets from the raging waters. He was only just now beginning to recover some energy from that exertion. He hoped tonight would be a quiet shift, then back home, nice dinner and bed.

He thought of Blue, waiting patiently at home and he couldn't help but grin. I'll be home soon, Blue. Tomas thought with pleasure. He was going to pick up new dog food tonight on the way home. Good dog food with prime ingredients, he knew Blue would love it. That dog never met a meal he didn't love.

From puppyhood to two years of age, Golden Retrievers will eat anything-anything. *So, the major task of raising a Golden is to keep them safe from what they eat; like loveable, tender hearted furry crocodiles.* Tomas grinned. Now over two years old he could finally trust Blue not to eat chicken meal or plant fertilizer.

He couldn't wait to see his Blue.

All at once, a black SUV, windows darkened, passed him and proceeded up 4th St. at a slow pace.

The Firebird pulled out and was right behind it.

"Car 12?" The radio broke the silence.

"Go."

"Lt. Strum wants you on crowd control ASAP."

"They were quiet, dispersing, no need. I have moved on, now 4th St. and Adams, street patrol."

There was silence for a moment.

Then Lieutenant Brenda Strum, his supervisor came on the line, her voice was strident and demanding as usual. "You will immediately return to the scene and supervise the protestors! That is a direct order, Two Hawks!"

But there are no protestors, Tomas thought. What is the point of this? They were all dispersing.

"10-4", was all he said and hung up the microphone. But he had no intention of doing as ordered and he was not going to argue this over open air.

Tomas pulled out, turning right on 4th St. discreetly tailing the SUV and the Firebird as they are heading east.

Something about these vehicles bothered him; his gut was telling him they were wrong somehow. He couldn't help it; his cop instincts had kicked in and he was following a hunch.

It had worked for him many times. US Army Rangers, Fallujah, Iraq, and later in Pesewa valley, Afghanistan, narrow moments of intense combat when he chose a course of action that probably made no sense to others but seemed right. Two Bronze Stars with V device for combat, backed his decisions.

However, the Purple Heart awards from his wounds proved his decisions weren't always accurate.

He quickly caught up with the SUV Pontiac combo but stayed well back in his squad car. They were speeding, 40-45 in 35 MPH zones, and he could have stopped them, but something told him to wait and see where they were going in such a hurry.

They took a quick right onto Jefferson, then just past the Capital building, another right on 14th Ave, catching the on-ramp to I-5 South for a few miles, then off that highway to Black Lake Blvd, where Tomas's curiosity took a real jolt.

CHAPTER THREE

Planetary Tipping point Report:

"GREENLAND ICE SHEET COLLAPSES":

Dr. Bobb Snow, Ph.D. Bioenvironmental Physics, Chief Scientist, Council on Global Climate, United Nations

Report to Science Summit, United Nations General Assembly UNGC#3334.

It was getting toward evening and the September air seemed to be moving swiftly from fall into early, freezing winter. The weather turned to an intermittent drumbeat of icy rain, and then quieted to a freezing fog. The air smelled of car exhaust and ozone.

As he followed the Black SUV and the Pontiac Tomas could tell they were headed someplace specific, they had a mission of some kind.

"Capital, 12." Deputy Tomas Two Hawks radioed HQ.

"Capital. Go 12."

"Capital, vehicle check request." Tomas was staring at the darkened SUV. He glanced at the useless onboard computer in the squad car. Normally he had this information right there. Unfortunately, once again, Tomas had been given a defective computer.

"Capital, 12, Go."

"Chevy Tahoe, SUV, Black, license 353 356 SA"

"Wait one." While he waited, he watched the SUV. Tomas knew he was disobeying his orders but attacking legitimate protestors wasn't the same as stopping crime and his instincts told Tomas this SUV was trouble. *When Lt. Strum hears about this, she'll scorch the air waves.* Tomas thought.

"12?"

"Go," he responded.

"Vehicle belongs to Feds. This is official business. Stand down. Leave it alone."

"10-4." Deputy Two Hawks pulled over to the curb and parked. Official business? Fine, he had other concerns. He was about to U-turn when a raspy, harsh familiar voice erupted from the speaker.

"Car 12!" Lt. Strums histrionic grunt, burst from the speaker.

Tomas almost laughed. *Okay, here it comes.* He really did not want to keep making her angry; it's just that street duty and desk bullshit don't always agree.

"Deputy Two Hawks!" she shrieked. "What are you doing? Where are you? You are to do what you are told to do, got that? You are there to observe and help in crowd control! That is all you are going to do, understand? No bullshit. Just do your job! Do not, I repeat, do not, interact with that SUV. Do you understand?"

What the fuck is that about? This is insulting. Tomas knew he was evil incarnate to Lt. Brenda Strum, his ex-sister-in-law. Even his ex-wife wasn't as angry with him as Brenda Strum, and he couldn't figure why the extremely heated animosity.

"Acknowledge 12!" She demanded.

Doing this over the open radio channel was meant to be humiliating for him and she knew it.

Tomas, in defiant reply, double-clicked the microphone without answering.

"Fuck her." Putting his cruiser in gear he accelerated away from the curb, quickly turning right, fairly certain he could catch up to the 'Official Business SUV'.

He had little doubt this was going to get him suspended at best.

Tomas liked being a cop. Listening to his instincts and constant training was what made him good at his job.

Something about these two vehicles told him trouble was near. "I guess this is one of those better to beg for forgiveness then ask permission," he asked himself, as he followed. There had been a lot of that in his life, not often well tolerated.

He had no idea how right he was, once again.

Ten minutes later, he caught up with the SUV, just as it was turning into the Governor's Mansion parking lot heading toward the Mansion driveway.

The Pontiac Firebird just kept on rolling past the Mansion and on down the city street. But curiosity led him to follow the SUV right onto the Mansion grounds of the Governor of Washington State.

CHAPTER FOUR

His curiosity even more aroused when the SUV rolled passed the Guard Station to the State of Washington Governor's Mansion without pause. The guard did not appear outside his little darkened glass shack as they swiftly past him.

What the hell! Tomas thought. The rules say 'check with guard' before entering.

Several nearly successful assassination attempts of Democrat Governors across the Nation had prompted tightened security over all seated Democrat Politicians, down to county levels. County Commissioners traveled with armed guards. Two weeks ago, a Mason County Court Recorder was strangled outside her courthouse by an enraged citizen. Tomas was puzzled; *How could anyone be pissed at a court recorder? They type. That's all. They don't even type their own words. What is there to hate so badly you must kill them?*

Tomas wasn't surprised at the animosity toward government workers. The Republicans have vilified government for decades so by now citizens had a Pavlovian hatred toward it. Of course, Tomas was curious to see how the Republicans would spin this one. *Now that they are totally in charge, who are they going to blame for their failures?*

Then the darkened SUV slammed to a stop at the front steps to the Mansion, scattering white rocks from the parking lot. Immediately all four doors opened, and four men leapt from the vehicle, each carrying an AR-15 Assault weapon, they raced up the steps and into the Mansion.

"Oh Fuck! What is this? FBI? Secret Service? Who?" Tomas couldn't identify them; they had no agency patches on their black uniforms. That bothered him. *But maybe I just didn't see the patches, they went in there so fast.* Tomas hoped he had made the right call. *Should I stay or should I go?*

But the lack of patches was too much to ignore. *Legitimate law enforcement identify themselves,* in Tomas opinion. *Secretive, unidentified Government Agents carrying weapons with permission to arrest and detain are a cardinal sign of totalitarian societies. If Law Enforcement is not transparent it becomes an occupying army because they are no longer accountable to the community.* Tomas believed the only people that should fear him are the law breakers, not the citizens.

The Mansion security guard, a Washington State Highway Patrol Officer, unexpectedly appeared outside of the guard shack. He was staring at Tomas.

"It's now or never, I'd better check this out," Tomas told himself. *Those guys with guns mean business and they were in a hurry, maybe I should be too.*

Tomas was going to have a tough time explaining to Strum why he disobeyed a direct order and left crowd control. But also, Tomas was growing tired of following orders that made no sense or were contrary to how he felt law enforcement should operate.

Tomas had the distinct feeling his days in law enforcement might be numbered anyway.

He skidded to a stop about twenty feet in front of the guard shack, not up to the shack itself; something told him not to trust this guard.

Getting out of the squad car, he grabbed his AR-15. If these masked guys were the enemy Tomas needed firepower to match them.

His boots crunched on the round parking lot stones made slippery from the rains, as he came around his vehicle and faced the guard. However, as soon as Tomas cleared his squad car, moving about ten feet into the open, there were two loud shots, simultaneously something plucked his right sleeve.

The cop shot at me!

Tomas flinched, ducking to make a lower silhouette, but he was in the open and had no cover. To turn back to the vehicle now would mean a shot in the back.

This was no place for defense, only offense.

Tomas steadied himself, knowing the guard still had his gun lined up on him, he heard another shot. With regret, he accepted the fact he'd probably take a bullet here, but he had no choice; it was kill or be killed. He was in the open so attack was all he could do.

Tomas calmed himself, sighted and fired twice.

Tomas had been under fire before; when weapons are drawn, bullets flying, death immediate as a moment, he knew how to handle the explosion of adrenaline and fear.

Tomas Two Hawks was back at war and good at it.

The guard shouting in pain, dropped immediately.

For a moment, Tomas hesitated; cognizant of what just happened; *gunning down a Washington State Highway Patrol guard at the Governor's Mansion while disobeying a direct order was going to be a bitch to explain. The fact the guard fired first might be a moot point in his defense.*

Just then, gunfire from inside the Governor's Mansion; loud pops of single fire, followed by a magazine burst decided for him.

"Shots fired! Shots fired!!" Tomas shouted into the microphone attached to his shoulder. "Governor's Mansion! Shots fired!"

"Say again, 12?"

Tomas spoke urgently into his mike. "10-44, officer needs help, 10-944, shots fired. Governor's Mansion. Officer down, repeat officer down, ambulance, now!" He shouted in staccato words. "I am going in, I need back up, now!"

Tomas, not waiting for a reply, especially from Strum, raced into the grounds and past the SUV which had been left running, the doors wide open, and the vehicle empty.

Someone, a male, screamed from inside the Mansion.

Tomas raced into the Mansion, but as he did so, out of the corner of his eye, the dark blue Firebird glided into the parking lot and stopped, motor running. He did not hesitate in his duties but he itched to get to the mystery of that 1966 Pontiac Firebird.

CHAPTER FIVE

More gunfire shattered the quiet and Tomas could hear glass breaking.

The Governor of the State of Washington lived in a well-restored historic Mansion built in 1908; an elegant multistory mansion of bay windows, red brick, and sculpted gardens, reflecting wealth and sophistication from the early part of the twentieth century. It had been modernized to a ten-bedroom luxury estate with tennis courts, a swimming pool, gardens, and an entryway chandelier that weighed over 2,000 lbs.

Tomas Two Hawks quickly, but quietly approached the Mansion, trying to look in the massive windows without being seen.

He caught movement inside, men moving back and forth, and shouting, then more gunshots. Then more silence; Tomas figured it was either all over or at a standstill.

He saw an entrance to the house through the garage and took it.

"Get him, for Christ's fucking sake!" A man screamed in the other room. *Probably the kitchen*, Tomas thought, *I'm on the first floor.*

"Where the hell is he?" The second man asked.

Tomas froze, not sure who they meant. He had moved up a short hallway, checked the kitchen but it was vacant. The next room was the formal dining room, the sliding doors closed.

Two men were in that closed room as far as he could tell. Tomas moved cautiously to the doorway, through a crack he peered into a large, ornate dining room, well-lit by another massive crystal chandelier, gun smoke swirling around it. The room reeked of gunpowder from recent gunfire. Both men dressed in woodland camouflage, carrying AR15s, were standing face to face yelling at each other in the middle of the room.

"Fuck you; I'm not taking your orders!"

"We're in the middle of an operation you asshole, do what you are told!"

"I am a Patriot Warrior; we don't take orders! We are free men!"

"Well, the rest of us have a revolution to win! We're here to kill the Democrat

Governor; you think you can help us out with that, 'free man'?" That was all

Tomas needed to hear.

He was going to take down the two in front, but, just as he was about to move, gunfire erupted from upstairs; a long, full magazine burst on full auto. The two men turned and raced up the stairs. Someone was screaming, a male voice. Tomas had no idea who.

Just then, movement caught his eye. Tomas looked to his left, in another room behind a floral settee, a young woman with bright red hair and brilliant green eyes waved to him frantically.

Tomas moved swiftly across the room to the delicate couch and the girl.

"You a cop?" She asked, fear shining from her eyes. "I'm Bree Myerson. My dad's upstairs…. the Governor. Can you help us?" Her voice was low and trembled. "Please, please, you have to help him!" She clutched at his arm. "Please, he's in danger!"

"How many are there?" Now that Tomas was kneeling, he felt dizzy again for a moment. He shook it off.

"You're hurt?" She removed her hand from his blood-stained left arm. Tomas looked down and sure enough, blood had soaked his sleeve down to the elbow. But it didn't seem to hurt.

The man upstairs screamed again, and Tomas jumped. He had to get up there. *Where the hell was backup?* He heard no sirens. *Where is backup?* He thought. *Can't wait any longer.*

"There are four; I'm sure, four of them." She told him with a trembling voice.

"Good, thank you. Now, I need you to get out of here!" He whispered forcefully.

He pointed at the door.

"Go now, while the bad guys are distracted."

She hesitated. "But my dad? I'm not gonna leave my dad!"

"Look, I understand," Tomas said earnestly. He admired her courage. "You want to save him, I get it. but that's my job. Leave that to me. You staying here isn't going to make this better, only worse. Understand? Now, get out of here!" Deputy Two Hawks put real force in his hushed voice.

She hesitated, her bright emerald eyes clouded with uncertainty, then said, "Okay, I got it, I'm gone! But you'd better save my dad!" She glared at Tomas, scuttled out from behind the couch, ran across the room, down the hall, and out the front door to safety

Tomas took a deep breath and headed up the stairs.

CHAPTER SIX

Deputy Tomas Two Hawks shot the first man nearly point blank as they came face to face at the top of the stairs. The man fell backward into the hall with a shocked expression on his face, his weapon discharged into the ceiling.

"What the hell was that?" A man from a room down the hall shouted. "Hey, McCormick, why did you shoot?"

Tomas poked his head and weapon out of the doorway and put two bullets in the first man to emerge from the double doors at the end of the hall. Seconds later, he took out the next man after two rounds zipped by his head burying into the door woodwork.

Three down, one more, he told himself. Moving quickly, he heard loud shouting further down the hall, the soft carpeting muffled his steps.

"I'm the Governor! What are you doing? Who are you guys?" A voice sounded from the next room. The Governor sounded scared to death.

Tomas knew he had to get in there fast. In the distance he could finally hear sirens converging on the Mansion; but not soon enough.

"Good, we get to kill the right guy!" The assassin seemed pleased.

Tomas kicked in the door, adrenaline pumping as he raced into the room.

He saw, standing two feet away behind his desk, Governor Gary Myerson IV, a tall painfully thin man wearing a blue suit, red tie and a terrified expression. Facing him was a short, squat man dressed in camouflage and holding a pistol grip AR-15.

The man turned at the sudden, loud interruption, but as he turned, he made the rookie mistake of keeping his weapon on the unarmed Governor so when Tomas came through the doorway it was pointed in the wrong direction at the wrong man.

Tomas shot the man twice in the head, blood and brain splattered forward all over the hysterical Governor who stood frozen in terror.

Tomas stood still, his gun outstretched, seeking other targets.

The scent of gunfire hung heavy in the room while Myerson, covered in blood and brain parts, stood mouth open, face drained of color, hyperventilating, and making little humming noises. He looked left and right, everywhere he looked there was a bullet hole.

Myerson started shrieking.

"Are you okay, Governor?" Tomas watched Myerson wailing and had no idea what to do. Seconds later he could hear the alarms of sirens racing to the scene.

"I asked are you, okay Governor?" From the blood splattered on the Governor, Tomas couldn't be sure he was unharmed. But he thought; *the ambulance needs to get here fast; the Gov is unraveling.*

"Hmrggh!" That was all the Governor could say, but at least he had stopped shrieking. He stared at Tomas, sniffing as if inhaling a mysterious odor he couldn't identify, then shook his head, waving his hands as if trying to get rid of a spider web.

Giving Tomas a long look, the Washington State Governor, his pupils the size of nickels, face gaunt, pointed with trembling hand at the dead gunman. "This shit is too much! Fuck it! I've got to go, now!" With that, Governor Myerson turned and disappeared behind a hidden panel in the room.

A soft click sounded as the panel slid closed and locked. Instantly the wall reset itself. "Governor!" Tomas shouted.

"Wait! Wait!" But the Governor was gone. Tomas tried to follow but the panel wouldn't budge. Just then, he heard backup arrive.

**

As Tomas was exiting the building in company of an Internal Affairs Officer, he noted the dark blue Pontiac Firebird as it slowly, stealthily, left the parking lot.

CHAPTER SEVEN

Planetary Tipping Point Report:

"GULF OF ALASKA FISHING SEASON CANCELLED. First time in history,"

Dr. B. Snow, Ph.D. Bioenvironmental Physics, Chief Scientist, Council on Global Climate, United Nations

Adjourning to the Olympia Sheriff Department, the after-action debriefing turned into an interrogation around 3 AM.

They patched up his arm wound and found another bullet grazing wound along his left side. But beyond minor gunshot wounds, Tomas was in good shape physically.

"What the fuck are you accusing me of?" Tomas demanded. His arm hurt, he was exhausted, thirsty, hungry, angry, and now worried.

"You have this all wrong, Deputy," Sheriff James Kirk Orwell was adamant. "You need to come clean here. Where is the Governor? You were the last to see him. Where is he? Answer truthfully or this could mean real trouble for you." Orwell, a six-foot four-inch, blade thin man, his dark intense eyes glared at Tomas in revulsion.

"I saved his fucking life!" Tomas didn't like this one bit. He was being railroaded. "I don't know where he went! One minute I was in a firefight to save his ass and the next he bolted through a hidden door. Have you even looked behind that wall yet?" Orwell just stared at Tomas.

"He'll turn up, there are hundreds of people looking for him," Tomas could not believe the Governor of the State could just disappear.

Without warning, Tomas's direct supervisor, Lt. Brenda Strum, his ex-sister-in law, came rushing in, she bent down and whispered fiercely in the Sheriff's ear.

Orwell winced at the explosive breath in his ear then looked sharply at Tomas.

Lt. Strum also stopped talking and glared at Tomas too.

Like hungry coyotes eying a house cat. Tomas didn't like this at all.

"Things have changed, chief." Orwell seemed to have a slight smile. "Those men you shot tonight were all Homeland Security Agents there to protect the Governor. You shot the good guys."

"What? No, no, that's not right! They were the assassins, not me." Tomas knew this to be true and could not comprehend what game the Sheriff was playing.

"We have you, Two Hawks." Strum, an intense, tightly wrapped woman with black hair whose deep-set brown eyes, carried an aura of eager malice. "You have screwed the pooch this time. Disobeying a direct order, attempted murder of the Governor? Wow, we have your ass now. What did you think you were going to do after you assassinated the Governor? Huh? What was your plan then?"

"What?"

Strum's face became stern. "We found you at the Governor's Mansion after you forcibly gain entry by shooting the Washington State Patrol gate guard. His vest saved him; he survived and will testify of your unprovoked attack. Then we come to the four Homeland Security Agents you murdered in your attempt to kill the Governor."

"I did not! Murder? Homeland agents?" Tomas interrupted her. "You have it backward. What evidence do you have of any of this?" Tomas wondered where all this was coming from. What made them think he was involved this way?

"I was saving Governor Myerson's ass," Tomas continued. "Those men were there trying to kill him. I stopped them. I saved his daughter, she'll tell you. There are cameras all over that damn place, they will show what happened."

"We will be searching your house, checking your story out thoroughly."

"What? For what reason?" Immediately he knew he should shut up and call for a lawyer. He'd already said too much.

"Now that is enough, Deputy," boomed, Sheriff Orwell. "Just answer me this. What were you doing at the Mansion? You were assigned crowd control." Orwell told him. "Why were you there?"

Tomas had tried to explain about the black SUV and the Pontiac Firebird. But no matter how he told it, even to him his reasoning seemed weak.

"So, you had a 'feeling' something was up, so you abandoned your fellow officers? That right?"

"That is bullshit! You know it is bullshit!"

"You figured to just shoot your way in and kill the Governor of our State?" Strum pointed at Tomas. "Well, we're gonna see justice is done Two Hawks."

"Lawyer."

We have you on video, security tape footage, attacking the Homeland security guards and killing them, one of them wounding you which allowed the Governor to escape."

"Lawyer," Tomas tried to keep his voice level, show no sign of weakness.

"By the way," Sheriff Orwell added, "the daughter? She will testify you assaulted her at the Mansion, stating you were going to kill her and the Governor."

"Bullshit! Lawyer!" His voice was much louder than he intended. *So much for not showing signs*! Tomas realized he was more rattled than he'd thought.

**

Strum just smiled. She had him. She had him now. *Damn this felt good. It wasn't that he was just a dirty Indian, he ran out on my sister. Divorced her after five good years, walked out, fucking asshole.* Strum swore to her sister she'd fix his ass, now she had the chance.

For Lt Brenda Strum however, this was more than family, this was personal. Strum burned with resentment, hating rejection as a soul killer. *Fucking Two Hawks had a chance with me. After the divorce, I came to him, let him know I was available, and he fucking blew it. Well fuck him!*

**

"Deputy, I hope you understand the gravity of your situation." Orwell rumbled.

The evidence was circumstantial and weak, Strum fretted. But it might be enough to get him imprisoned, certainly sufficient to make major trouble for him. Strum told herself, studying the Deputy. She liked the way his dark skin set off the pale tan of the uniform.

"Deputy Tomas Two Hawks," Sheriff James Kirk Orwell said with formality. "I officially inform you that you are under investigation for the attempted assassination of the Governor of the State of Washington, Gary Myerson. We also suspect you of involvement in the attempted murder of his daughter, Bree Myerson, and terroristic threats against the Nation of the United States. You also disobeyed a direct order."

"Lawyer! Get me a fucking lawyer, bitch."

**

Sheriff Orwell left the room; his need was now urgent. They had a fall guy to cover their asses, and he was certain Strum would make the charges stick, but they had lost the fucking Governor! Orwell had teams out now searching for the escaped politician. He knew it wouldn't be long before the liberal idiot turned himself into the police, and then Orwell would have him. But until then, Governor Gary Myerson was an escaped terrorist and Orwell had no idea who he might contact.

Still, over all the plan was working. Operation Overlord was in full swing. Across the Nation, Democrat Governors and legislators were being rounded up, removed from office, and replaced with loyal Republicans by Homeland Security Federal Police. Twenty-three States, immoral, degenerate progressive and liberal states, resisting the march of triumphant Republicanism have been pulled back under the mantle of freedom. Orwell swelled with pride at their accomplishment.

Sheriff Orwell picked up the phone. "I want an All-Points Bulletin, an APB for Governor Gary Myerson, I want him found and brought to me." He listened for a moment and then said, "I don't give a shit if you haul his ass in here in a sponge; I just want him breathing."

CHAPTER EIGHT

Planetary Tipping Point Report:

PERMAFROST MELTDOWN: GIGATONS OF METHANE RELEASED."

Dr. B. Snow, Ph.D. Bioenvironmental Physics, Chief Scientist, Council on Global Climate, United Nations

Report to Science Summit, United Nations General Assembly UNGC644.

His escape had been harrowing because it depended almost entirely upon luck and circumstances. The medical clinic for Thurston County Corrections is the St. Helens Immediate Care Facility about a hundred yards west of the jail. Prisoners must be escorted out of the jail building down the street to the medical clinic. Tomas was fortunately unshackled because he was not under formal arrest yet and the escorting guard, Pat Harrington, a scrappy, taciturn Irishman very near retirement, was with him as required by procedure.

Tomas and Harrington were just entering the facility when all hell broke loose. In the middle of the doorway another prisoner coming out saw Harrington, grunted some kind of threat, and launched an assault on Harrington without warning.

"Hey stop!" The officer responsible for the attacking prisoner was caught completely off guard and too slow to prevent the assault.

One minute Pat Harrington was leading Tomas through the doorway, upright and walking, the next he was rolling around on the ground vigorously punching, gouging, and finally biting the attacking prisoner until blood was flowing.

Tomas calmly but swiftly walked away in the commotion. Behind him the inmate was pleading for somebody to save him. But Tomas had to move fast. He only had minutes before they saw he was missing; maybe less. Pat Harrington, old and slow but nasty in a fight, would make short work of that foolish inmate.

He hurried around the corner of the nearest building, so he was out of sight. Two blocks away he witnessed a large woman smoking a cigar squeeze out of a dented and rusted Prius. The car was left running while she hobbled into the convenience store. A Prius would not have been his first choice. But necessity was everything, and Tomas had the stolen car out of the parking lot and down the street in seconds, still traveling at the speed limit so as not to attract attention.

But it worked, Tomas was out of the city and heading east out of Olympia as fast as the humble little hybrid could travel. Tomas was panicked and all he could think of was to get out of the area heading east toward the Yakama Reservation and the only place of safety he could think of. He had to find a man named Rony Calmers.

He was almost twenty miles outside Auburn on State Highway 18 East, Tomas was thinking about what he had to do to straighten this situation out when it hit him. In the intensity of the past few hours, he had completely forgotten about his dog, Blue. Tomas felt instant crushing sadness, "Oh my God!" He was going to have to leave Blue behind! He could not return to the house because the police would be all over it and there was Blue all alone.

He loved that dog with all his heart.

Tomas abruptly pulled off the highway, sliding to a stop in a cloud of dust and gravel, several cars blared their horns in surprise and anger at his move.

The potential loss of Blue was a staggering blow.

Who can I call? Who can go get Blue? Tomas realized he had no one. Not one friend he could fully trust. The realization hit him nearly as hard as his loss of Blue. Tears leaked down Tomas's face as he realized he may never see his best friend again.

He almost turned around to go get Blue, almost. *God, do I want to.* He could see Blue's trusting face, patiently waiting at home for him. Blue's silver feeding bowl was sitting empty. Tomas took as much joy in feeding Blue as the dog did in eating. Suddenly Tomas worried that he might be out of water. *No, no, I remember it was full this morning,* he recalled. Then he realized it has been over 24 hours since he'd been with Blue. *He would be out of both food and water! Oh God Blue I am so sorry.* A punch of guilt hit his gut, he felt nauseous *I couldn't stand it if anything happened to Blue.*

An image of a simple, sky-blue leash hanging from a backdoor hook, waiting for another beloved walk was another blow.

He hunched over the steering wheel, sobbing with grief, unable to stop the flow of tears; surprised, even shocked, by the depth of his own feelings.

He had few friends when he returned from Afghanistan and fewer still when he became a Deputy. But he had Blue, he'd rescued him from a despicable puppy mill, and it was the best decision he'd ever made. He and Blue bonded immediately; We're family. That dog is as much my brother as any of my siblings.

But Blue was much more than just a brother; much more. Blue was a lifeline and a lifesaver for Tomas. He could see Blue's trusting, loving Golden Retriever face and his heart twisted with grief. Too often the night held war-filled terrors for Tomas; wicked violence of slaughter and death and bloodshed tormented his sleep, causing him to cry out against the raging brutality in his mind. Always, Blue would be right there, jumping up on the bed beside him, bringing safety and comfort with his huge furry body snuggling close. Tomas could not count the times Blue intervened to keep him sane.

Oh God, Blue! If I return for Blue, the law will have me locked down. I've got to keep moving. Somehow, he would have to clear his name and get his life back. Get Blue back.

But first, he needed to find Rony Calmers. Tomas had to return to the Reservation, he needed to center himself again, and identify what was important to him now with all that was happening.

It was one of the hardest and more sorrowful things he'd ever done, leaving Blue behind.

CHAPTER NINE

"The only thing more dangerous than ignorance is arrogance." Albert Einstein

September 16, 2028

Sometimes being around compulsive greed can be disgusting like watching hyenas slaughter a gaggle of ducklings.

VP Judith Smith, AKA: Sevenentlana Shimrov, had all she could stand of the Barthalamew J. Popper family, including their minions and parasitic peers, now doing their personal for-profit businesses in the highest offices in America.

Greed was an untreated pandemic running amok.

She well knew the history, the consequences of such avarice. When the old Soviet Union had fallen apart everything was for sale as the government was ripped apart and sold to the highest bidder; a fire sale of government functions and bureaus creating a handful of instant Billionaires and an overpowering Oligarchy.

America was far beyond even that level of greed. America was about to witness a financial feeding frenzy only slightly less blood thirsty than the sacking of Rome by Visigoths in 410 AD.

The Popper Presidency served up a smorgasbord of favoritism and bribery, the worst she had ever seen. From mundane rewards like cars, office space, and staff, to political invitations and access to the President, for the right price all was for sale. A foreign dignitary or CEO could get pictures with the President, pay the required fees, and return home with American secrets the same day. The Barthalamew J. Popper Republican Administration was open for business, and it was booming. Foreign governments flocked to buy up privatized American government agencies, military technology, and top secrets at bargain basement prices.

Shaking her head in dismay, VP Smith left the Oval Office, headed down the long hallway to her office in the East Wing.

The past two years had been a rollercoaster ride of politics, public speaking, and near pandemonium as Republicans fought to eliminate Democracy and the Democratic party from existence. She was proud of her hand in bringing the hated Liberals to their knees. Smith didn't hate them personally, but they stood in her way to wealth and power, so they were expendable.

Slamming her purse and computer bag on the desk she furiously turned, heading for chrome and silver serving cart and a generous bottle of Stoli Elit: Himalayan. She poured a water glass-size shot of vodka and drank it down swiftly. The welcome burn of the $3000 a bottle alcohol buoyed her spirits. So, she had another.

"Vodka is mother's milk," she muttered, so she took another shot. "Da, good!" Her visions blurred a little and she loved the sudden alcohol smog that covered her brain for a moment.

Slumping back in her chair, she sighed. "So far, so good."

She recalled her days as the mistress of Oligarch Yuri Putiensky, now President of Russia. In those days her privilege and power were secondary attributes, and nothing was really hers. So, her ambition began to grow.

When Barthalamew J. Popper pleaded with Yuri to make him the US President, Sevenentlana saw an opportunity, so she presented her plan during pillow talk and the following day Yuri Putiensky promised Popper the job if he took Sevenentlana Shimrov as his Vice President.

The day she morphed from Sevenentlana Shimrov to Jane Smith, Vice President of the United States was a real head spinner, but the American sheep couldn't tolerate a foreign sounding name.

"Get Moscow on the line!" She shouted at her secretary, Peral, a thin, semi histrionic Ukrainian woman, stolen from her village during the last Russian invasion of her homeland, then forced into indentured servitude.

Pera was a poster child for repressed vengeance.

"Get Moscow!" VP Smith tried again.

Pera, pretended not to hear and continued punching meaningless numbers into her computer. "Did you hear me?" No answer.

"I said call Moscow."

No answer.

"I know where your family is hiding in Latvia, bitch."

The call went through to Moscow, slowly.

While VP Smith waited for the call to drift through the various layers of secretarial resistance, autocracy, and secrecy she thought about Yuri.

She believed she was a loyal woman. Once she became someone's mistress, she remained faithful until a better one came along. For eighteen months she had been the mistress of a wealthy plutocrat named Sergi Whanot, Yuri's main competition in the election for Russia's Presidential Office.

Two weeks before the election, when it became clear that Yuri was the more malleable candidate, Sergi Whanot accidently choked to death on a bag of ball bearings thus ending his run for the job.

The night of the Russian Presidential Inauguration Ceremony confirming Yuri Putiensky as President of all Russia, she moved into his dacha, vowing everlasting loyalty and love to her Yuri.

It had been worth every penny getting past Whanot. *Still, what was I getting out of it? Nothing,* VP Smith thought bitterly.

The Presidency of Russia, however, was nothing by itself, a side job. The Presidency, and access to the Russian riches, vaulted Yuri Putiensky into the level of Trillionaire, a billion billion dollars to his name.

That level of wealth and that measure of power made it a natural: Yuri Putiensky was welcomed as the newest member of 'The Davoos Group'; twenty-six men, all Trillionaires, collectively controlling 75% of the planet's economy, completely beyond all law and all national controls, running the earth like their own private corporation.

Sevenentlana wasn't going to get any of that either, so she hatched her own path to wealth. She knew she was a simple pawn in a game of giants but that didn't stop her ambition from demanding attention.

"How are you, my darling?" The smooth voice of Yuri the concerned lover came through the line; not the voice of President Yuri Putiensky.

VP Smith was instantly on guard. When Putiensky expressed phony empathy, it was either a promotion or the prelude to a piercing dagger in the ribs. She'd been his mistress long enough to know Yuri to be a man of unpredictable and extremely sharp moods.

"I am fine, Yuri, although this role is one of surprises and mysteries."

"I am sure that this useful idiot, Popper is doing as you command?"

That was a touch and go question. Barthalamew J. Popper was a mercurial airhead with a genius for self-promotion and a complete disdain for morality which made him easy to manipulate. But it was incredibly hard to keep him focused on his instructions; everything had to appear as if it originated from Popper, no matter how unlikely.

"Let's just say it's a work in progress." She replied carefully.

"My lovely dear, you have been someone's mistress for many years. You are skilled in manipulation of men. You are perfect for this role." She had no answer for that because it was true.

"Sir," VP Smith turned to business. "President Popper has accepted the deal. He has ordered all Liberals to be detained and held in re-education camps so they can be convinced of their foolish ignorance."

"You mean eliminated for their ignorance!" Yuri laughed long and hard. He loved it when the stupid Americans could be bamboozled so completely. "These Americans are either so greedy for power or so incredible lazy they will believe or do anything!" Yuri's disdain for Americans was palpable.

"The US Council of Christian Clerics have really gotten into the swing of things." She hoped this was also good news.

"Ah, this is wonderful. What is happening?" Yuri asked.

"Sir, The Council is comprised of eight Televangelists, Mega-Reverends from the Mega churches. These men are the cream of the crop with millions in TV revenues. They control the Christian Nationalist's faith of the American citizenry and have already divided the Nation into eight 'Sacred Lands' in which each church has unequivocal power over that region.

"What religions?"

"As far as I know they are the Orthodox Baptist, Catholic, Seven Day Adventist, Pentecostal, Latter Day Saints, Four Square Fundamentalists, Ultra Protestants, and Evangelical Dominionist." Although, VP Smith couldn't see a lot of difference between them.

"What happened to the Jews? Muslims? Other religions?" Yuri asked curiously.

"That's a problem, but for another day. The extremist Christians are going to pay a heavy penalty for closing Jews and Muslim houses of worship," VP Smith explained. "These outlawed religions just went underground. Jews and Muslims also believe they are each the one true religion and aren't going to let Christians get the upper hand. They have centuries of war on going."

Her study of world history had made it very clear these three religions were all cofounded upon a single religious reference. *The Old Testament of the Bible is the seminal vessel for Christian, Jews, Muslims,* she learned. *They are known as the three Abrahamic religions. So now we have three 'Brother Religions' overwhelmed with jealousy, fighting for their father's love by killing and maiming innocent people to prove they are the worthiest.* The more she learned of the major world religions the more 'God-free' she felt; VP Smith considered herself a seasoned, erudite atheist.

"Oh my, that does sound exciting! It is important we keep conflict and division going in the US," Yuri exclaimed.

"As far as the Liberal threat, sir, I think we are getting a handle on it. A combination of the National Guard and MAGA Militia will enforce our orders at a local level," she explained. "The Pentagon stands ready to eliminate any Liberal uprisings. Then there is of course, Blackthorn, LLC." She shuddered. "They are…ready."

"Okay, my little bird," Yuri parsed his praise. He did not want to discuss Blackthorn LLC. This vicious mercenary group begun by Barthalemew Popper's eldest son, Peter, as a Presidential 'Honor' Militia who have access to the US weapons arsenal; *they could be a real nuisance if displeased.*

"When we first started to manipulate US Politicians," Yuri said, almost wistfully, changing the subject. "I wasn't sure it would work. But old Russian saying: 'Patriotism must be profitable, or it is just a hobby!'"

VP Smith shrugged. *This is so obvious, who could doubt?* She told herself. *Money is always most important.*

VP Smith noticed how tepid his response had been when she mentioned Blackthorn and needed something to improve his mood, show progress. *Everything was smooth so far, but with crazy Republicans and an insane President, life could turn sour in a heartbeat. I must report good news here.* "I must report on the US Constitutional Convention of 2027."

"Go on, tell me, after a year what has transpired?" Yuri urged. "How has that played out in real life?" He wondered. He thought it bold of the Republicans to completely change the foundational document of their Nation. "They are now the United States of Jesus Christ? USJC?" He asked.

"Da. 'The Project for a New American Century'," VP Smith replied quickly. "A Republican program to turn this country into a one-party state. Changing

America into a Christian Theocracy is supported by Nationalistic, Fundamentalist Christian Mega-Churches controlling millions of American voters. At the 2027 Indianapolis Constitutional Convention last year they succeeded in creating a permanent upper ruling class. Americans won't notice a thing, as they are ruled by an elite upper class now. But this makes it illegal to speak with or interfere with any member of the Upper Class. Now called 'The Chosen'." She paused to see if he was getting all this. *Yuri is not noted for patience or paying attention.* "The common citizens will be referred to officially as 'Citizens'.

"Oh, my," Yuri gasped which surprised him. "The Republicans turned the United States of America into a class society? No more of this nonsense about equality and fairness, huh? You have master's and you have workers, and you have the Church to keep them harmonious. That is normal. That is God's will. Well done, Republicans!"

"The new Republican 'Bill of Rights' reads more like the Ten Commandments," she added to keep the enthusiasm going.

Putiensky laughed. "Imagine that! A Godless Communist like me, arranging for America to become a Theocracy! Then we create instant enemies to play against each other. Isn't life amazing, bubka?"

"Perhaps more irony than amazement?" VP Smith who knew American history far better than almost any American was amused at this. "Most people don't understand, but The United States wasn't founded on freedom from religion," she said. "The early colonists to this land were mostly baptized Christians fleeing hundreds of years of poverty and war. Although they hated the never-ending religious wars and incessant, unfair taxation, they came to this country to survive, to find opportunity denied them by the rigid chaste system of Europe. They were seeking a country free of unfair taxation and freedom from extreme poverty Religion wasn't the issue at all. But today the Republicans have convinced their ignorant, slow-thinking voters that the US was founded on Christian principles despite absolutely no evidence of this. "

Yuri laughed. "People who believe the improbable will do the unthinkable."

She laughed. "You have just described FOXE News motto."

"My dear, you are far too young to know this, but let me give you some history." Yuri explained, pleased he could make her laugh. "I am sure you know the Davoos Group has sought to dumb down the fabled American educational system for decades. The revolts in the 1960's, the hippies, the foolish peace, and civil rights movements, were direct results of advanced education." Yuri stormed, incensed that people could be so stupid. "These American children were well educated, indolent from rich lives, thinking they knew it all, questioning everything, and refused to accept a rational, materialistic society as the Davoos have created for us all. They sought to undo our work. All Americans must be made to fall in line with the rest, fully accept the Davoos Oligarchy, nothing less. We needed to crack down on foolish resistance! Their ignorance is our bliss!"

They both had a small chuckle at the success of power.

VP Smith was impressed; glad she was on the winning side. Although she didn't live during those days, driven by self-interest, she studied American history to better know its weaknesses. For instance, John Fitzgerald Kennedy, Robert Francis Kennedy, Malcolm X, Medgar Evers, and Martin Luther King were all assassinated by the Davoos Group from 1963 to 1968; one a year. *The left-wing revolt had to be put down and the leaders eliminated otherwise the Oligarchs feared losing control of the US.* She understood, it just made good sense.

She had been amazed to learn how far the Davoos Group had gone without detection.

"The Davoos Group murdered five prominent American progressive, leftists' leaders in five years and Americans were told it was a single shooter every time. 'No sir, no conspiracy here!' The Americans were told. Shortly thereafter all of the social movements and progressive factions faded from view; the 'Age of Aquarius' now cold and dead by assassin's bullets. "Amazingly, most of the American people never connected the dots. Americans just accepted it all as a coincidence!" She stated, wonder in her voice. "Critical thinking is anathema under an Oligarchy."

Yuri laughed with delight. "You know what works? TV! Eliminates critical thinking completely," he chortled.

"Speaking of the Media, the US Government must have buried the facts of these murders pretty deep." She was curious how the US Government pulled this over on the citizens.

"What else is happening, my dear?" Yuri didn't want to get offline talking about the perfidy of the people within the US Government.

She thought for a moment. *So many changes since the Republicans assumed their rightful place in command of the United States of America; a firm hand is necessary to lead these lazy immature citizens into the brave new Davoos world.*

"Oh, I know!" Glad she could add to her report. "The Secretary of Education has just announced that all schools in the US are now private, for-profit centers of learning. Yuri. You will be pleased."

"Who is this Secretary?"

"Catherine Weeknight from the wealthy 'Weeknight Bail Bonds and Collections, LLC' Empire. This week she has directed schools in the Nation to restrict all advanced classes only to upper class, or 'Chosen' students. The 'Others' will be restricted to a more fundamental education."

"Well done! The upper classes must be established and maintained for the sake of civilization. Educate the lower classes to do menial labor, they don't need history or literature or science. Just able to read and write enough to operate and follow computer directions. That is all that is needed of the American citizens."

"So, you are with Davoos now?" she hesitantly asked, unsure if she should bring this up.

"Da!" he replied proudly.

"How wonderful! You will be excellent." She was relieved yet this meant he was going to be very difficult to please.

"Yes, I will be wonderful." Yuri felt great pride and great trepidation. As the newest Trillionaire elected to The Davoos Group he was under immediate and immense pressure to solve the US dilemma. The US politics has gotten too radical, too extreme and Davoos feared the hugely profitable 'Golden Goose' of the United States would be lost, killed by extremists, profits drained away by violence and chaos. The money machine that was America must be kept churning.

The Davoos Group had divided the planet into areas of responsibility and Yuri, as President of Russia oversaw Scandinavia and much of Europe. But the siren song of power lured him further. America was a mess, so he'd volunteered to solve the American problem.

"You have done an excellent job, my dear," Yuri purred to VP Smith. "I do believe we should reward you! What shall it be?" Putiensky knew Smith was essential to his plans to gain more power, so he had to keep her happy and effective.

Yuri was quiet a moment and VP Smith dared not interrupt. She listened for any clues as to his mood.

"Ah yes," Yuri exclaimed, "I know, I shall release your cousin, Sophia from the gulag!"

VP Smith was silent in stunned realization.

"You have my family in a gulag?" This was the first she'd heard of it. *No wonder nobody was writing back!*

Yuri Putiensky smiled. The world only understood leverage. From the very poor to the very rich it was the same. When you want something, you find the leverage that will give it to you; pure and simple.

"Yes, my dear, I have invited your entire family. Mother, father, siblings, an aunt, two cousins, and a handful of your shirt tail relatives to join us at a country club in Siberia. They are having a fine time."

Country Club? Siberia? It's October, the temperature is hovering around minus -10 Degrees F. and by January it would be minus -45! Sevenentlana wasn't fooled a bit.

"You mentioned, Sophia? You will release her?" She asked carefully.

Sophia was a delightful little girl and being released now she would have a chance to attend school, perhaps even obtain a profession of some kind.

"Da."

"You are so generous, my leader!" It was the only acceptable reply.

Yuri beamed. He loved when his people respected and honored him. "She will be released on her fifteenth birthday, I promise!" Yuri reasoned that since VP Smith was so cooperative, hanging on to the little girl for a few more years would keep her motivated to work for the State. Patriotism was very important to Yuri.

VP Smith swallowed hard. It was a blow but expected. At least Sophia might have something to look forward to. "Thank you, sir, you are the most generous and thoughtful man in the world."

"After the liberals are rounded up and are no longer part of the political scene, I want them all deported to Mexico."

"Mexico? Sir? Aren't the Mexicans going to be a little resistant?"

Yuri laughed. "What can they do? Have that idiot Popper gather up the millions of liberals, line them up at the US/Mexico border and then, at gunpoint, tell them to immigrate south. It will be like the US Oklahoma Sooner land rush days where desperate, impoverished people fight each other savagely for land. We'll make a movie of it."

"Don't you think the Mexicans might object to this?"

"I am counting on it. You see, when millions of arrogant and demanding Americans come desperately pouring over their borders the Mexicans are going to panic. Quickly, the Mexican Army will deploy. Rushing to the border to handle the frenzied 'Americanos', a vacuum will be created behind them. The cartels, seeing the vacuum, will erupt in a war of attrition to gain power.

"That will be chaos."

"That will be when the Russian Military, already in Belize, offers help."

"The Mexicans will fall for that?" She asked. "They will let us into their country? Don't they know what will happen?"

"My dear, you underestimate the brilliance of chaos."

"So, what do you want me to do? Convince President Popper Russians aren't invading Mexico even as they invade Mexico?"

"No, Bubka, I want you to convince Popper to attack Canada."

"What?"

"You will think of something my dear."

**

A Gray man, monitoring their conversation nodded silently.

CHAPTER TEN

The dreams were the worst.

Unbearable memories of happy moments haunted him causing him to whimper and cry out. He longed for the gentle, loving hands of his human, Tomas, caressing him, brushing through his fur, speaking soft and loving words that melted him. The smell of his Tomas, the sound of his voice, the touch of his hands, gave him such joy. *Where did he go? What happened to him?*

The water was cold and shook the dog named Blue from his troubled sleep. They always sprayed the cages with bleach water first thing. Whether from hygiene or sport it made no difference to the dogs; cold, wet, and miserable. The old man with the water sprayer moved on, cage to cage, bored with his job and callous to fate; his or anyone's.

Blue got to his paws and shook himself; his once shiny, soft fur matted and dirty. He had lost weight and losing hope, locked in this pitiless cell.

He had stopped eating. Food didn't seem to matter anymore, and it tasted horrible.

Try as he might, Blue could not understand what had happened. One evening, his Tomas never came home. Blue alone in the backyard, waited patiently in the dark, listening, smelling the air for him, and feeling for his approach, certain his Tomas would be there to feed and love him as always.

But Tomas did not come home.

Instead, rough, angry men arrived, brutally muzzled him, throwing him into a strange vehicle, they brought him to this 'humane' shelter, a dog prison.

The worst of it, the very worst, was he did not know what he did wrong.

To be abandoned by your pack is the worst fate of all. *If only I knew what happened. I know my Tomas is still alive. I can feel his life-force out in the world, but where?* Blue would fret and worry and pace. *Maybe Tomas will find me, and I can show him how sorry I am for whatever I did. I am so sorry Tomas! Please find me!*

Day after day, Blue waited for his Tomas. Like the other dogs, he would sit up as strange humans visited, but as the days passed, Blue slumped into sorrow and finally, he just lay shivering in the back of the cage. His feeling of abandonment so intense he felt the hand of death on him.

The sensitive blond dog overwhelmed by utter grief sunk into despair, his tender Golden Retriever heart, broken.

**

"What's the story on this one?" Nickolas asked.

"Unusual dog, huh? He's a Golden Retriever Corgi mix. The name is Blue," Alexis, the shelter worker replied. She walked into the cage and the dog didn't move, his tail didn't flutter at all. She poured fresh water in his bowl and petted him, but he did not respond to her touch.

"Poor guy." He looked so sad, she felt helpless to comfort the dog. The fact that he didn't respond to her was a bad sign.

"Odd name for an odd dog. How long's he been here?" Nickolas stopped the cart he was pushing, loaded with a delivery of dog food. He was new to the job and curious about all his customers.

"Too long," she replied sadly. "People like the Golden part, but when they look at those little Corgi legs, they think he's too weird. It is so damned sad. I'd take him, but I already have six…I…I just can't." Alexis continued to go from cage to-cage dispensing water.

"Hey, you know what?" Nickolas stood looking at the Golden Retriever, named Blue. "My aunt and uncle are looking for dogs. I'll send them down here."

As Alexis moved on to other dogs, she called over to him, "Do it quickly, please. We get rid of this one tomorrow or maybe today. I hate to do it, but the sooner I get it done…I don't know…I just hate this, but maybe it is better to put him out of his misery."

"What do you mean?"

"Dogs who have strongly bonded with their humans are bewildered with grief and loss when they are brought in here; confused, anxious, overwhelmed with terror because they have lost their pack, and they don't understand what happened."

"Dogs can think?"

Alexis looked up at him. "Are you like a prodigy at being stupid or did you have to go to school for a really, really long time?" Nickolas quickly said, "No, I mean, yes, dogs can think, but…" He had no idea how he was going to unravel his misstatement.

"Look, let me explain," Alexis said with gentle patience. "I'm sorry if I was a little sarcastic, but I am so tired of this. People see dogs as objects, not as they really are, thinking, self-aware, emotional pack animals. Dogs bond with a pack, and, just as with a pack, they will give their lives to a human, literally and figuratively. Unfortunately, many people don't understand this, and some just couldn't care less. They don't see them as sentient beings; they see them as 'pets'!

"I never thought of that," Nickolas was surprised. "But you're right. 'Pets' sounds like some kind of a throw away toy."

"To many people, a dog is just a dog, when the animal gets too old or inconvenient, they throw them away without a second thought. Oh, some of them might feel bad for a little while, but it is still, 'just a dog'."

"I know a guy," Nicholas said. "He had a German Shepherd he'd raised from puppyhood. Three years later he gets a job in a different town, decided he couldn't take his dog and just left him at an Animal Shelter." Alexis stared at Nickolas in disbelief.

She closed her eyes and took several deep breaths. "My God! How could he? For dogs this is unbearable abandonment, a total betrayal of trust. Dogs are in a pack for life, it is everything to them. Some of these animals even die from this abandonment; the loss is too horrendous. I don't know why dogs have this intense loyalty and love for humans. They just do."

They both looked back at the shivering dog named Blue.

"Do you know what I just hate," She knew she was talking too much, unloading her soul on this guy she'd barely met, but she couldn't stop herself. "Some people walk into the Vet, hand over their dog to be euthanized walking out, saying 'You do it, I just can't bear to watch.' Sometimes these dogs have spent their entire lives with these people." She looked up at Nickolas, tears filled her eyes. "The Vet administered the drugs and as the dog is dying his frightened, forlorn eyes seek those he loves so much, urgent to see them, to be with them in the final moments of his life. But none of his loved one's are there, he is alone, abandoned by his family…"

As the tears fell from her eyes, her voice choked, and she held onto cold steel bars for support.

Nickolas was so moved by Alexis he was at a loss for words. He thought for a few moments and felt determination to do what was right. "My aunt and uncle are John and Emma Mack," Nickolas spoke with conviction. "I'll get them to come down here as soon as I can." Nickolas vowed he would bring them here himself if he had to. His apartment would not hold a dog this size, but maybe the

Mack's might be able to take him. His heart went out to the poor creature. "I promise, I'll be back," he told her.

"Whatever, make it soon, otherwise this guy is toast." She gave him a hopeful smile, wiping tears. *So many people say that and so few return.* "I think dogs are incapable of crying. So much sorrow builds up they just give up and die. I can tell this one doesn't have long." She turned away, and then back, glancing up at the much taller Nickolas.

Alexis gave him a weary smile. "I think I'm done here. I've only had this job for a few months, and I can't take it." She pointed at the old man with the water sprayer. "I don't want to wind up like him, not giving a shit about anything. I'm gonna quit after this. They got any job openings where you work, Nickolas?"

**

But Blue understood none of this, eyes closed, he surrendered to his bewildered grief.

CHAPTER ELEVEN

"We are not human beings having a spiritual experience. We are spiritual beings having a human experience." Pierre Teilhard de Chardin

Hiding in the dry, fragrant Ponderosa Forests west of White Swan, Washington, on the Yakama Reservation Tomas Two Hawks found sanctuary: temporary to be sure.

For three weeks, camping under the stars, fishing the rolling streams, hiking the endless forests in the Cowiche and Oak Creek Wildlife areas he thought about his life.

He and his eight siblings grew up dirt poor, on an Indian Reservation that had rampant alcoholism, violence, despair, and hopelessness. At the age of six until he ran away at age sixteen, the state placed him and his siblings in a multitude of foster care homes. Each was nothing more than indentured servitude: free farm labor paid for by the State. Looking around now at the dark forest surrounding him he realized he had often dreamed of living free in these same mountains.

**

Tomas Two Hawks glanced at the stars overhead, amazed at the bright, sharp pinpoints of light scattered in vast abundance across the sky. Everything was piercingly clear because in these remote mountains there was no light pollution. It was cold up here in early October and he tugged the woolen blanket tighter around him. Behind him a small stream tumbled nosily down through a rocky bed. The fire before him, now rekindled, was blazing, illuminating, and warming the faces of the six men sitting around it.

"For thousands of years humans have gathered in small enclosed, utterly dark spaces, heated by flame-red rocks," Rony Calmers deep bass voice held sway as the fire began to warm them up. "For millennia humans sweat, pray, sing, and talk to their ancestors and their Gods."

Tomas looked around the circle at the gathered Veterans. Everyone looked tired and exhausted from the ceremony. It had been a hot lodge, forty stone, and their prayers had been as fierce as the stinging heat. He always found it curious that each Sweat Lodge had its own temper. Some Inipi Lodges with ten stone were hotter than lodges with twenty-eight. No matter the heat of the fire, it would seem the stones decide on the intensity of each Sweat Lodge. Tomas took that as a sign of the sacredness of this ceremony.

Tomas had come to the Yakama Reservation in Eastern Washington State around the Toppenish area to see one man: Rony Calmers.

Although Tomas was not a member of the Yakama tribe, he was enrolled Prairie Band Potawatomi, he had done spirit quests in these mountains, and he knew the Yakama people to be solid and dependable with knowledge of the old ways and a fierce independence.

Yesterday, a contact within the Olympia Sheriff's had let him know no charges were being filed against him. The source didn't have details, but apparently, Tomas Two Hawks was no longer a person of interest in the case of the still missing Governor of Washington. Tomas had no idea why they had dropped the charges. He found that most curious. But this call signaled it was time to return.

The fire crackled and the scents of sage, sweet grass, tobacco, and cedar were heavy on the cool night air. A solitary coyote barked a lonely echo amid the black columns of trees. Despite the chill night air, Rony Calmers glistened with sweat, as he leaned toward the sacred fire.

Calmer's thin features were gaunt, his eyes rheumy and red, wrapped in an old orange wool blanket he slumped on a rickety camping chair around the robust fire. A man of solid Irish and Scottish descent, Rony was not born into the Native World, but at the age of fifteen he heard his first Pow Wow drums, and his heart was captured; his Native soul stirred.

Over the next forty years, Rony Calmers learned and studied Native tribal customs and languages. His dedication was so fierce and unrelenting Tribal Elders from Lakota, Dakota, Blackfeet, Yakama, Nisqually, Muckleshoot, Dine, Shawnee, and even Eastern Cherokee among many other tribes, recognized and accepted Rony Calmers, a Caucasian man, as one of their own. He was taught native languages, sacred and secretive indigenous medicines, and ancient ceremonies such as sweat lodges, and the ultimate: Sun Dance.

Rony was known throughout the Native world and respected as a healer who knew medicine ceremonies and had gained national recognition as a Sun Dance Leader.

Adopted into the Yakama Tribe, Rony now spent his life in service to the Yakama people as well as other tribes as a ceremonial leader and advisor.

"There is wisdom in the old ways because the ancestors fought and died to develop these ways. Such wisdom comes from survival. Mankind faces a survival situation now…"

As Rony talked to the circle, his robe would part and in the firelight, Tomas could see the field of white scars that covered his chest. Tomas knew that Rony had so many scars from fifty years of Sun Dance it was difficult to find a place to pierce him.

Rony Calmers represented what the Native World needed so badly: Native Heart. He lived in the old ways, knew the old ceremonies taught to him by tribal elders, knew the songs, the drumming, he understood the ways of Spirit. He knew what it meant to be Native, the responsibility, the obligations, the honoring that must be given. A way of living life so that honor and respect are given to all other creatures; humans included. But for his love of buttered popcorn, diet Coke, and the computer game 'Red Dead Redemption 2', Rony Calmers could have easily been a contemporary of Sitting Bull and Chief Joseph.

Tomas had sought him out because he needed Spirit, he needed prayer, and he needed balance from a world gone crazy.

"You are looking overwhelmed, Tomas," the kind voice of Rony Calmers had solidity, a timber of reliability. Calmers, his eyes heavy with sleep, sat to Tomas' immediate right. He wavered on his camping chair and Tomas was afraid he might fall in the fire. But Rony perked up, smiled at Tomas, and then wobbled a little, before fading quiet again. Strong lodges could be hard on Elder men.

"Go on, you have more inside of you, talk!" Rony told Tomas as he opened his eyes, giving Tomas a direct look.

The six Native men, Veterans from many conflicts, Vietnam to Afghanistan, sat around the newly rekindled fire, drinking water or juice, munching on watermelon, all were quiet, still wrapped in the Sweat Lodge cocoon of spiritual prayer and sacrifice. A light wind had sprung up, bringing with it the scent of the fire, sage, and a cool touch of fall but it felt cold to Tomas, and he pulled on a sweatshirt. Although he was tired, he forced himself to focus.

For Tomas, the Sweat Lodge Ceremony was the most authentic, the sincerest form of prayer he could imagine. In the faceless, nameless dark of the Sweat Lodge Ceremony, there is absolute honesty and absolute sincerity. Almost no one sits in the pitch-black sweat lodge, the heat so intense even your hair is too hot to touch, singing songs and offering prayers unless they are sincere in their spirituality. It simply is too uncomfortable for pretense and pretending.

*In Sweats, there is only you, in the darkness and heat, talking directly to the Spirits, the Creato*r, Tomas believed.

Although Rony had asked him to speak, Tomas did not right away. In the Native world, each is given all the time they need to say their peace; no one interrupts, as that is not civilized. Each person is given time to think, thereby avoiding the rash impulsiveness of the white man's world.

"I was thinking," Tomas began, "of how different we are from the mainstream people. I cannot understand sitting in a church, being passive and silent, listening to someone else tell me what God says." He gestured to the rumpled burlap and tattered tent canvas that covered a rounded Willow frame. "In there, in the black darkness, the glowing red stones, the fragrance of the medicines, I find I can talk to my creator one to one. I do not need another to translate what my Creator says to me." They all nodded.

"There is little point to prayer unless it has sincerity, significance, and sacrifice. "Rony said softly. "Otherwise, it is merely a pretense of prayer."

The men were silent for a few moments, each thinking of the lodge and their experience there.

"There is a war brewing in this Nation." Tomas Two Hawks looked to each person. "A Civil War. The fears and greed of the white people have exploded." He explained the attack on the Governor's residence and the aftermath. All around him heads nodded. "Americans have declared war on each other again and we are caught in the middle."

They all nodded. These men knew that when the white Americans had a conflict everybody suffered. All of them had volunteered for the military and for war; but none did so to defend America. These Natives became warriors because it was culturally significant to them. To most native tribes the definition of a 'warrior' is that of protector. A warrior protects the tribe and makes sure that all are fed, housed, and clothed. Each joined the military for the good of his people, or to escape the horrors of the reservation, but very few fought for the Nation of America; a warrior's heart drove them to battle.

"A warrior isn't about war: a warrior is about the people," Tomas told them. "What is going on in America is about ego and power and has nothing to do with the welfare of human beings."

"Yeah, white people have accepted insanity as a moral code."

They all laughed.

"This Nation is no longer a Democracy because the Republicans have decided a two-party system does not give them total power. They want it all."

"Who is 'they'?" Someone asked. "We always hear about the horrid, 'they', so who are 'they' in this case?

"The Republican Party is supported and financed by the wealthiest people in this Nation. The top of the class structure, the CEOs, Bankers, Investment classes, the families of so much generational wealth they consider employment as a hobby. These are the people financing the Republican Party. Some may truly believe in their cause of less government, fiscal responsibility, conservative perspectives, and very pro-business. But they are losing to those in the Republican Christian Nationalist Party who are filled with egomaniacal despots and pathological liars and..."

"I think we get the idea, Tomas." A few of the men grinned. "Tomas, your Potawatomi people are always exaggerating. Maybe because you are always lost." One of the Veterans, a Nisqually tribal member, said with a wide grin.

That brought a laugh from everyone. They were always teasing him about being Potawatomi out here on the West Coast, way away from his ancestral lands along the Great Lakes. The Veterans here were Nisqually, Squaxin, Klamath, and Yakama, all Western Tribes, all living slightly closer to their traditional, ancestral lands.

"Republicans have lost their way," Rony Calmers said softly. "They are split into two people; those who want the status quo of Right and Left and those who want only the Right. Over the past several elections, it is clear the latter has won. Rather than being proud of an electoral system that has brought America a history of peaceful transfer of power they are dismantling it, destroying the integrity of a voting system that has been the envy of the world."

"They cannot win the popular vote, so they must manipulate, distort, even make up outrageous lies to win," the Nisqually Vet replied.

"So? What do we do?"

"I must stand and fight," Tomas said. He looked from face to face. A couple nodded in agreement, two scowled in disagreement and the rest didn't react at all.

"Why?" Rony asked.

The question stopped Tomas for a moment.

"I don't understand."

"This is your land, but this is not your Nation. Native people have been the victims of genocide and hatred from first contact. We have been and still are hated for our race both officially and unofficially. The history of the Native American people has been a litany of abuse and genocide. They didn't even make us citizens in our own land until they gave us the vote in 1924!"

Tomas had served in the US Military in war, just as every Vet here. "The enlistment posters and war propaganda all shout that soldiers are defending freedom and the American way of life," Tomas spoke, bitterness in his voice evident. "We are fighting for our American rights and freedoms and fellow Americans, right?"

No one laughed, they all nodded in agreement at the irony.

"We know that nonsense doesn't last past the first bullet. From that point on you fight for the person next to you, pure and simple. It doesn't get any more grandiose than that. But the politicians want us to think the war is about freedom and dignity and spreading Democracy. When our experiences have shown us, this is all lies."

"So," Rony interrupted. "Again, I ask: What is your stake in this fight?"

"Maybe I should define what I want to fight for." Rony

smiled.

"I was nearly arrested and almost charged for felonies I didn't commit. I need to clear my name. I am also a law enforcement officer. I believe in the law. I believe we are better off in a society in which fair and just laws are obeyed and people who break these laws are punished. I'm not any more complicated than that. I cannot correct what I cannot control. I'll go back and do my job as I see it and let the chips fall where they may. But I will enforce the law, regardless of who is breaking it."

Rony, nodded slowly. "This is true. Our people had thousands of years to work out a system of living that was fair and equitable. We knew that greed is the death knell of all civilizations, so our way was to share everything. No one gets rich, but no one gets poor. Each has a responsibility to the other. That is the difference, you know, between the Native World and White Colonizers' World. We know we have a responsibility to life; the White man sees it the other way around."

Rony stoked the fire a little, and sparks arose, carried aloft by the vagrant breezes. Rony paused to watch them as if they were spirits carrying prayers to the heavens. "A society in which the people believe strong authority produces freedom," Rony continued, "is a society of fools."

Tomas could not argue about that. He had watched as politicians manipulated people by returning nickels in benefits while stealing dollars in taxes.

"In our way, the Native way, responsibility is more important than entitlement." Rony touched Tomas's arm. "I hear your heart, Tomas. I was glad to hear you define what you will fight for. In the chaos of our times, it is easy to be overwhelmed. Just give up in fear and futility because the problems are so enormous and difficult to solve. So, individually we focus on what we can control, seek to find our power in a selective, specific course of action."

As they were loading up their gear into the cars, preparing to go their separate ways, Tomas Two Hawks was hit with a sadness that buckled his knees. He missed Blue. He didn't know how he was or if he was okay. He just knew he had to find Blue.

"Tomas, remember," Rony Calmers called out. "Trust the Spirits you pray to, otherwise what is the point of prayer?"

**

"I'm coming, Blue," he whispered fiercely pulling out of the grass field and onto the highway, West toward the Puget Sound and Olympia.

CHAPTER TWELVE

Planetary Tipping Point Report:

"WEST ANTARCTIC ICE SHEET COLLAPSES."

Dr. B. Snow, Ph.D. Bioenvironmental Physics, Chief Scientist, Council on Global Climate, United Nations

Report to Science Summit, United Nations General Assembly UNGC#765.

"Bong, bong, bong, bong."

"Huh? What?"

"Bong, bong, bong, bong..."

"John! John! Get up! The driveway alarm, John!"

It was like swimming upstream underwater, his whole body felt encased, sluggish, unwilling to act, and he struggled to wake.

"John!" Emma Mack reached over and shook her husband vigorously.

John Mack came awake immediately. "What? What?"

"Bong, bong, bong..."

"Oh shit!" John swore. "The outer alarm." He thought quickly, maybe it was a false alarm. A dog may be passing by and pissed on the grey-brown plastic alarm sensor. "Maybe it is just a false...," he started to say.

"Bong-bong beep, bong-bong beep, bong-bong beep..." the tone of the alarm changed abruptly.

"Oh, John!" Emma exclaimed. "That is the alarm inside the gate, isn't it?"

Now John was struggling with real motivation. The outside and inside alarms have gone off. The gate was 2400 feet from the house and hidden by huge stands of Jefferson pine and Douglas Firs.

"The gate was locked, yes?" she asked abruptly.

"Yes, yes I am sure, I always make sure it is locked... ". He got up, pulled his pants on then sat on the edge of the bed to put on boots. "Where are those dogs?"

"I don't know!" She listened. "I don't hear them. Where are they?"

They had recently picked up two strays from the Dog Pound. A no-nonsense pit bull named Oscar and a beautiful Golden Retriever Corgi mix named Blue. Blue was her favorite. Just a sweet guy. The Pit Bull made her nervous, the way he looked at her.

"God damn it, Emma!" John was furious. He wanted guard dogs. Dogs that would let him know about intruders. The Pit Bull was his choice, and he was glad to have him, but the other dog, Blue. John shook his head. What a waste. A big dog with tiny little legs was a threat to nobody. John didn't want that dog, but Emma had insisted. Now, the damn dog has probably led the other one astray.

"Bing-bong Beep, Bing-bong beep, bing-bong beep." John picked up his Winchester 1500 Shotgun, a venerable 12 gauge that he trusted. "I'm going out there, see what is going on. Get the phone, be ready to dial 911!"

"OH God, John, no, I will call them now. You stay inside to let them handle it."

He whirled on her, mostly from the fear building in him, he spoke harshly, "I am not going to cower, I am going to defend my land. That is all there is to it! Now get some clothes on and get the phone. Oh, and find those goddamn dogs!"

John moved out of the bedroom sliders onto the dark wood deck, listening for any sound that would tell him what was going on. He could hear the dogs now, but they were in the distance, moving away. Not good. Even worse, he could hear the crackle and snap of gravel under the tires of the intruder slowly crawling down their driveway moving closer to him and Emma.

"Oh shit!" It was all very real.

John Mack knew without a doubt that his life would change from here on. Whether he got into a gun battle or not, the fact that his land was invaded was serious shit. He was terrified and it felt so intensely real it was surreal.

Although John was a Veteran, he knew he couldn't count on that helping him much. Despite bragging for years at the VFW about being in a special combat unit, very hush-hush, even decades later he told others he couldn't discuss it because of national secrecy laws, John Mack knew the truth. Being a cook in the US Air Force was not a bad deal at all, but it was not combat, and other than basic training, he had no formal military training. His only combat was on a Playstation3.

He hefted the shotgun, confident in its solidity and power, but less so in his ability to hit anything. His hands were shaking, and he was nauseous as hell. Telling himself to stop being a pussy, John moved under cover of the 3 AM darkness into the side yard and then behind a lawn tractor. The driveway was ten feet in front of him and he could hear the intruder vehicle creeping closer, still obscured by trees lining the driveway. He strained his eyes, trying to see in the stygian night. At 74 he knew his night vision was poor, but it was just one of many problems he was facing. Years spent as a cook and baker hadn't prepared him for any sort of physical altercations and he knew in a fight he would be beaten quickly. His only hope was the shotgun.

At that moment, John realized he had only six shells loaded. Six. He was embarrassed and had forgotten.

"John!" The suddenness of her intense whisper and the blast of her breath on the back of his neck nearly gave him a heart attack.

"Argh! For goddamn sake, Emma! Stop that!" He whispered so fiercely his throat ached. "What? What are you doing out here? I told you..."

"Honey, I am so scared," she whispered back. "I wanted to see you; I was so worried about you." Emma knew her John well, he needed her, but his male ego wouldn't allow it.

Just then they heard the dogs, their excited barking was now growing closer. John briefly held hope they would show up soon. But they had forty acres next to BLM land and there were a lot of wild animals to chase. Still, they were getting closer.

"Look, go back, go into the woods in back of the house, and hide out there. Take your phone and call Bob, he'll come over to help."

Bob Rates, a retired Butcher, was a long-time friend and gun collector who often talked of going to war. Bob practiced regularly at the range, hoping for an internal war in America, right against left, a war of good Christian Conservative Patriots against those despicable pedophile Liberals. Bob was certain he could kill Liberals easily, at least this was his brag at the gun range.

John considered Bob to be a loyal and dependable friend.

"Tell Bob we got in trouble. It will be okay, honey, he will get here and help straighten all this out. Probably nothing to worry about anyway." he tried to assure her. He trusted Bob would be heavily armed, he always was.

"Go!" He told her. "Go, call Bob and hide out in the forest. It will be okay, I promise!"

"Should I get my gun?"

John cringed. "No, no, this could get hairy enough, I don't want to worry about you too." He knew Emma was capable, but the thought of her being under fire just terrified him. "I'll protect us, Emma."

She just nodded, kissed him quickly and deeply, and then scurried off into the darkness. But she headed for the house and the 1911 .45 caliber handgun John had given her for her birthday. It was important for John to see himself as the family protector, she understood that, and it was a delicate balance to support him but not sabotage. Still, this looked like a shitload of trouble, and she was going to be ready regardless of his tender male ego. As Emma slipped into the dark woods behind their home easily handling her weapon, she would also disobey John another way. She would not be calling Bob Rates. *This situation is delicate enough without adding some wild-eyed, conspiracy spouting madman to the mix,* she thought. *Rates has a bloated ego, a big mouth and too many weapons. A recipe for disaster*, she knew.

Just then, the intruder vehicle cleared the last of the trees lining the drive. John could see it was a Toyota Tundra, with a chrome guard across the front and a rack of LED lights above the cab. The smell of exhaust traveled on the cool night air. On the door was a hand-lettered sign in bright red: 'MAGA Militia'.

John took a deep breath and slowly let it out.

MAGA Militia.

This could be bad, bad or maybe nothing at all.

He would just have to wait and see. But the MAGA Ms. were the worst of the worst.

During the Presidential election, candidate Popper called for Militia to form and support him. This they did, bringing violence, assaults, gunfire, and even death to the campaign trail. Every Popper rally poured more gasoline on the fire, and by voting day, there wasn't a voting place in America that did not have gangs of well-armed Militia present vowing to protect voters from Democrat intimidation and influence.

John was troubled by this, but reasoned the Democrats had been proved to be liars and cheats and this was necessary to keep Democracy safe.

Still, the appearance in the middle of the night of this militia was worrying for John.

"They should be out getting Liberals and Democrats and such," John muttered to himself as he stood up to greet the MAGA Militiamen. John was beginning to feel a little better. After all, he was a Republican, lifelong in fact. Big supporter of Reagan and the Bushes. John had even considered going back into the Air Force after 9/11 but was too old. Still, these militias seemed a little out of control for John's liking.

**

Suddenly, the two dogs came racing around to the front of the porch. Oscar, a brown and tan Pit Bull was in the lead, tongue lolling from hunting exertions. Behind him came Blue, a Golden Retriever/Corgi mix bounding along on six-inch legs like the world was made of pillows and ice cream.

Oscar saw the intruder's vehicle and stopped, rigidly still. Studying the situation, his nose flickering for the scents, ears perked, he waited, trying to identify this strange situation, threat or not?

A soft growl rose from his throat.

Unexpectedly, all the lights from the Toyota blazed and the entire front of the house lit up with stark details and deep, inky shadows.

John was nearly blinded by the sudden and intense vehicle lights.

Oscar took this as a challenge launching himself down the driveway toward the invading vehicle.

Blue, having arrived a little late saw the action and was just about to chase after Oscar, hoping they had food, when the Toyota slammed to stop, skidding just a little on the loose rock. All four doors opened, four men emerged, and four AK47s opened fire at full automatic.

Oscar, racing down the driveway to defend his new home was instantly obliterated by the slashing of nearly 100 rounds of 7.62mm that ripped his body into bloody chunks of meat and splintered bones; blood splattering in a wide patter of deep crimson over the driveway gravel.

One round bounced off the road and hit Blue, a glancing blow that barely broke the skin surface but frightened Blue out of his wits.

That was all it took, Blue turned, raced back into the forest and the protection of the night; stunned by the utterly unfamiliar violence and terrorized by the explosive death of his brand-new friend.

Blue ran for his life.

**

John saw what he thought were both of his new dogs slaughtered right in front of his garage. There was so much blood and meat and bone he was sure of it.

Right there in the fucking driveway!

John had hoped this could be worked out peacefully. *But not now!*

Fat and old and knowingly outgunned, John Mack racked a shell, and began firing at the Toyota, advancing as he did so until all six rounds were gone. John knew he should have died right then and there. Probably he would have had the MAGA Militia been a real Militia.

The civilian combatants were elated at killing the dog and paid no attention to the homeowner advancing with his shotgun until too late.

John killed one and wounded two before the remaining militiaman abandoned the attack, running quickly back down the driveway in defeat.

John's ears were numb from the gunfire, stunned to be alive and unharmed, he stood on his front lawn in the dark, a hot shotgun in his hands. He didn't know what to do next.

One of the wounded lay beside the Toyota crying out and trying to staunch his blood. "Help me! Help me!" The other sat up with his back to a truck tire, he was silent, his eyes stared at John, coal-black with revenge.

The dead guy lay face down in the middle of the road.

At that moment, Emma found her dog and her cries tore his heart.

Apparently, only one dog dead, the other one, Blue, had run off. "Good riddance," John Mack said to himself, already hearing sirens in the distance, growing louder.

CHAPTER THIRTEEN

"I feel pretty, I feel pretty, I feel pretty and witty and gay...er...pay!"

"Oh, Daddy you have such a stupendous voice! You should entertain the people with your talent!" First Daughter, Priscilla Lusty-Popper gushed with praise.

President Barthalamew J. Popper beamed with pleasure. "Yes, I am probably the most talented singer there ever was. People begged me to sing Opera, but I had other greatness to pursue."

"Excuse me, sir," VP Smith was annoyed. As she entered the Oval Office, time was short and her patience for 'Dum Dum and daughter' was thin. She had to get things moving and Popper's ego trips were becoming extended vacations. *The Soviet Army grows restless in Belize,* she thought. *Liberals have been resisting capture and detainment which put the National Guard in a difficult position: Shoot or not. The National Guard were ordered to get liberals off the street no matter how painful it was for them; the troopers, however, seem reluctant to shoot their fellow Americans. We have to get a Presidential Executive Order to justify the slaughter of these fucking Democrats.* She had so many details to yet work out it was maddening.

"Sir, you need to listen here." She leaned on his desk, a significant breach of protocol, but desperation filled her soul like vinegar. "We have a new Homeland Security Operations on the agenda; 'Operation MAGA Militia Might'. We need shoot to kill orders, sir."

"Why do you need orders? Of course, you shoot to kill, why else shoot in the first place?" Popper was puzzled.

"Ah...er...Mr. President the important part is that our victory must be completed. The final option for liberals is necessary. "

"I am President of the most powerful Nation on earth. I am the most powerful man on Earth. I am the greatest human to ever live!" Popper burst into song, "I am pretty, oh so pretty, it's alarming how pretty I feeeeeel!" Popper ended with a flourish.

"Yes, sir, of course, sir. Lovely song, sir, amazing simply amazing. Now about those 'shoot to kill' orders?"

"I am stupendous!" The President stared lovingly into a hand mirror. "Have the Secretary of State disemboweled." He demanded abruptly. Puffing out his cheeks, he studied his image. "Why do you suppose I am getting more handsome

as I age? The rest of men…they just fall apart. But me! I am fucking great!"
"Excuse me sir?"

President Popper was frustrated at the delay in obedience. "I said, have The Secretary of State, him, or her, or whatever, disemboweled. Immediately."

"But sir."

"Oh, never mind, I'll have the Chief of Staff do it, he loves scragging people."

"Scragging?" VP Smith was unsettled with the conversation. She glanced at first daughter to see if she knew what Popper was talking about: Priscilla was salivating.

That told VP Smith all she needed to know.

VP Smith was fairly certain 'scragging' the US Secretary of State would tarnish the Presidential image on the evening news, unless of course he had a good reason for the slaughter; *Americans seemed to accept any line of horseshit as long as it meets their perceived reality. In this case having the Secretary falsely denounced as a closet Democrat and pedophile should do it.*

"Mr. President. Sir, may I offer just a bit of advice, a suggestion on this, er, scragging…my advice…,"

Popper, glowing with a sly look interrupted her. "No! I refuse to listen to the advice of others because they are not me and I am a genius! No one is as smart as I am therefore no one can give me advice." Popper grinned at his impeccable, unassailable logic.

"What?' VP Smith took a moment to figure out what Popper was saying. She couldn't because whatever reality Popper inhabited had an antagonistic relationship with truth.

Shaking her head wearily she said "Yes, well, be that as it may, we still have substantial problems because the American people are beginning to become aware that you…"

"That I am a God!" President Popper collapsed back into his endangered Siberian Leopard skin recliner with absolute pleasure. A huge smile of sheer happiness and delight elevated his features. "Did you see how I did that? I knew immediately what you were going to say. I read your mind. I really am God!" Popper decided it would look good if he also acted slightly humbled. "I am just as amazed as you are. I really am a miracle!"

"Mr. President?" *If this fruitcake gets any nuttier, I am going to have a tough decision.* VP Smith thought about the 25th Amendment that would declare him unfit for office and she would assume the Presidency.

Or I can just shoot the silly fucker.

This could get interesting. She had never shot anyone before, let alone a daring assassination. She wondered if she could. She thought for a moment but couldn't come up with any reason why not.

"Mr. President? Daddy?" The First Daughter realized she was not part of the conversation, and this could not stand. Priscilla Lusty-Popper, fretful President Daddy would forget his promise to obtain the Bahamas for her, was determined to have her way.

"I have an idea!" Priscilla saw an opening and leaped in, ready to begin her brilliant plan. "President Daddy, my genius has created a stupendous idea…"

"Mr. President!" VP Smith spoke loudly, insistently over the first daughter. She knew Popper had a soft spot for his lovely daughter. He also had a hard spot for his daughter, but VP Smith tried not to think about that. This was no time to get sidetracked.

"Mr. President, greatest of all leaders, a courageous lion of impeccable skill and knowledge such as yourself will surely understand duty." she'd begun her request with the required excessive flattery.

Priscilla stared with rage and disbelief. *A goddamned servant interrupts me? Me? The fucking first daughter?*

"Duty?" President Popper was puzzled. "Of course, I do! Those bastards tried to charge me duty to bring in illegal goods! They are illegal, why should I have to pay
a tax?"

"Focus sir, focus." VP Smith reminded him.

Popper erupted impulsively, "But I am the greatest leader of all history! I am history! He who defies the Mighty Popper shall suffer!"

Priscilla fumed. She had been aced out of the conversation again. It always happened. She would say something brilliant, and the other people would act like she'd farted. Time after time she would join a conversation only to have it disperse seconds later. *Jealousy.* She knew it was just jealousy
at her beauty, her intelligence, her wealth. She checked her breath: it was ok

"So, then, most omnipotent of all great men," VP Smith had to speak loudly over the self-inflating grandeur of Popper and the poisonous snarling of his daughter. "If we can get your signature on this Executive Order?"

She still had to convince the idiot that Canadians were set to invade American and had no idea how to pull that one off.

"Sir, the Democrats…shoot to kill?" VP Smith urged.

"Excuse me! What a wonderful President Daddy, how wise!" Priscilla Lusty Popper elbowed her way back into the conversation. She only had a vague notion of this discussion, but that was the way she preferred her life: uncomplicated except for her own wants and needs.

"President Daddy, I want an island of my very own. I want Bermuda!"

"All of it?" Popper wondered. "Aren't there people living there?"

VP Smith was irritated at the interruption. She had a mission and the red-faced idiot in the Presidency was it. VP Smith glared hatred at the First Daughter for getting in the way. *Priscilla's love of money is so profound she shits dollar signs,* the sour thought arose to VP Smith.

"Whatever are you proposing, our dear First Daughter?" Smith asked sweetly. She needed to get control of the conversation and shut this entitled idiot out

"President Daddy," First Daughter began, turning her back on Smith, ignoring her as hired help. "As I see it," She was determined to get what she came for: Bermuda. "We can put these nasty Democrats in camps, but what about all their money and property?"

Priscilla was proud of her subtle style. To be able to direct the conversation without being held accountable for it was her special gift she believed. Priscilla had to be careful here. She knew she was smarter than everybody else, but didn't want to give anything away, so she had to play this the right way, whatever that was.

"Of course, being the brilliant and acclaimed scholar that I am," Priscilla began by displaying her awesome modesty. "I have done research and have determined that we must confiscate the fortunes of these American Liberals." She spoke in a matter-of-fact manner.

"And then what?" VP Smith wondered where this was going. "What are you proposing we do with all these riches?"

**

President Popper, growing bored with the conversation picked up the phone. "Get me the Army. General what's his name. Yeah, General Docking. Him, get him!" Moments later the phone beeped.

"General? I want you to nuke Haiti. Now. Today."

"Yes sir, explode a nuclear device in Haiti?"

"My daughter wants an island in the Caribbean of her very own. But those islands are inhabited by rich and powerful people who have political influence. That might be complicated. But Haiti is a mess, so nuke em, bulldoze the debris and we'll give it to Priscilla."

"But the radiation, sir?"

"She's tough."

"Very good sir."

**

"What is my proposal? Me? Little old me?" Priscilla made only glancing eye contact with Smith as she did with all peasants beneath her station. "I was just adding to the conversation, oh maybe, I was thinking aloud, you know developing genius strategies and brilliant plans."

"Which are?"

She quickly said, "I believe we confiscate all the riches of the nasty Liberals and then, donate it all to charity!"

"Charity?" VP Smith studied Priscilla. She knew this was bullshit but was curious to see what kind of bullshit. "That could be millions and millions of dollars. All to charity?"

Priscilla Lusty-Popper said, "We'll call it a Freedom Tax."

"And what, pray tell, should we do with this freedom tax?" VP Smith asked.

Priscilla laughed; *the fool had fallen into her trap.*

"Why, give it to me," Priscilla said with innocent eyes. "I'll see that it is donated to the right people…the poor, poor devils in need. I will be honored to accept the duty of accepting this tremendous responsibility…to save the poor!"

VP Smith looked at Priscilla Lusty-Popper and said, "YOU are going to help people in need?"

Priscilla smiled sweetly.

**

"Are we at war with Haiti?" General Docking asked his beloved President.

"Sure, why not," President Popper answered.

"What I meant was, as Chairman of the Joint Chiefs of Staff, normally I would be consulted about Declarations of War, normally that is."

"I don't give a turd if it's war or not, nuke 'em."

"Haiti?"

"Yup."

"Five or ten kiloton range, sir? They live in ratty shacks, the people are all malnourished and skinny, a higher yield would be overkill, so a small range nuke should blow them away."

"I want Haiti uninhabitable." Popper demanded with quiet determination.

"More than it is already, sir?"

"After you nuke it send in Mormon Missionaries who will clear the place out."

"Send them into a hot radiation zone, sir?"

"Well, they do pray a lot, I'm sure their prayers will protect them. Otherwise, there isn't much point in prayer, is there?"

"Very well, sir. What do we do with survivors…assuming there are some." "Give

them a choice, they can be shot or sent to California.

"As you wish, my Lord."

**

"Get me the US Postmaster General, immediately," President Popper barked into the phone. "I want the post office privatized immediately. I'm going to buy it myself, as an investment in America's future."

"Immediately, my Lord and Master." Bexter Pargy, The Chief of Staff quickly scribbled more notes.

"China wants to buy San Francisco." Popper was furious. The Chinese insisted on retaliation for Popper demanding the Chinese Ambassador be Caucasian. Popper tried to explain that slanty-eyed people were not trustworthy, and, to his surprise, the Chinese took insult.

"Really, sir?" Pargy not at all surprised as the last few years they had been selling off American real estate, corporations, and government agencies at a breakneck pace.

"Sell it." Popper figured the profit from the sale would build his magnificent luxury golf course in the Sahara Desert.

"But the People who live there…?"

"Sell them too."

**

VP Smith dropped her head in despair. Between Popper the Father and Popper the Daughter they didn't have the brains to find their own butt cheeks with four hands, photographs and a flashlight.

CHAPTER FOURTEEN

'Califra LffGBrsesddrs XXIV' from the Pleiadean galaxy, third solar system beyond the star-side meridian, slowly raised his head. Nothing looked familiar; *are those green trees?* Everywhere he saw green, different shades and hues but green and greener.

"I had no idea there were so many colors of green," he muttered.

Then some winged, feathery creature screamed at him as it fled, and abruptly the glade fell into silence. He could feel the eyes of many creatures on him.

The place smelled of dust, pine, and car exhaust.

Something bit his tertiary tentacle.

"Ouch! Hey, stop that!" Lying on his stomach, he wondered where here was.

Slowly he moved a tentacle to be sure nothing was broken. All six moved just fine as did his sub-tentacles. That was a relief. Pulling himself up to his full height of eight foot, he waved each of his tentacles in order before his six eyes checking for damage. Even with deep purple skin like boiled leather he was remarkably prone to injury.

Gazing up at the sky, he wondered how it got that lovely blue color. He'd never seen a blue sky before, no wait, maybe he had. He was so confused. It was like that sometimes with these fly-by deposits. His space delivery shuttle beamed him and his gear to the surface as it swept through the solar system at light speed. They have a schedule to keep and were usually accurate; usually.

TransGalactic Delivery Services guaranteed he would be on the planet, alive, they just couldn't guarantee where or in what state of health.

Califra LffGBrsesddrs XXIV smiled. He was on dry land and his body was intact, that was a big plus.

A noise startled him, and he quickly whipped around to his left. Califra LffGBrsesddrs XXIV made a mind-boggling appearance for those unaware and he cherished this. He knew vanity was frowned upon, but he was so tall! Eight feet! He took after his maternal pod. They were all big. He liked making impressions when allowed.

The noise happened again, sounding like a whimper.

"Who's there?" He challenged. He was uncertain whether it was a friend or foe on this planet. His research of this planet indicated sudden death was highly likely for the unaware.

Pulling a small silver cube from his pocket he held it out defensively.

A human stared back at him incredulously, mouth dropped open, and a wad of chewing gum fell out. He raised a hand, "Hey buddy, you gotta couple bucks you can spare?"

"Oh great," Califra LffGBrsesddrs XXIV swore, *compromised already. Damn! Well, at least I think I'm on the planet Earth.* With his eighth sub-tentacle, he hit a button on the silver cube.

"POOF."

The human's eyes blanked, rolled back in his head, and he dropped like a stone.

That was when he noticed the quadruped beside the now sleeping human. This furry being seemed to be interested in him, eyes alert, tail wagging gently, but non-threatening, hopping about anxiously.

Califra LffGBrsesddrs XXIV noticed the Earthling had a small wound on the left shoulder.

Now, he had to do some hard thinking. *Okay, I made it to the planet. Good, good. Now, where is all my gear?* He looked around the small clearing. *Nothing. Shit. This mission is starting badly, lost my gear, lost my instruments, hell I don't even know which side of the planet I'm on.* He peered at the quadruped before him. "Damn big teeth you have fur face."

Not for the first time, he wondered why he was chosen for this job, retirement seemed a better option than being eaten alive.

"Okay then you don't seem to be aggressive." He thought the dog seemed very interested in him, but not in a bloodthirsty way.

"I guess I should get busy: I have to find my stuff," Califra LffGBrsesddrs XXIV told himself. Pushing a small button on the silver cube, he opened a communications link to this planet.

"Hey!"

The Alien jumped with surprise and looked wildly about him.

"Who? What?"

"Hi! Can we be friends?" The voice seemed to come from everywhere and nowhere.

"What?" Califra LffGBrsesddrs XXIV twisted around nervously "Who else is here? Show yourself!"

"I'm over here; I can be your friend."

Now Califra LffGBrsesddrs XXIV was scared. Something wanted to be his friend and he had no idea what kind of twisted, evil being that could be. He swore to the Upper Divinity he would mend his ways if the Spirits kept him safe.

"Who are you? What do you want?" He responded nervously. "I warn you; I can be very defensive if necessary." He stood very tall in what he hoped was a menacing pose.

"Are you confused?" The voice asked. "Can I help? I am very helpful. Mom said

I was the most helpful of all. She did say that." Again, the voice.

Urgently he looked around and only the blond dog with the short legs looked back, his large brown eyes alert and penetrating.

You? Califra LffGBrsesddrs XXIV thought. "You are the voice in my head?" He said out loud.

"Yup, it's me!" The dog grinned back, and wagged his tail cheerfully, hopping around playfully. "Hi, can we be friends?"

"Friends?"

"You're not from here, are you?"

Califra LffGBrsesddrs XXIV knew this to be an awkward question. Planet-bound creatures are always suspicious of space-bound creatures. Bruce assumed it was mostly jealousy.

"I am Dog! Human's best friend. 'Canis lupus familiaris', my mom was a mighty Corgi from the Welsh branch and my da' was a gorgeous Golden Retriever, winner of best at show once." The dog wiggled enthusiastically. "My name is Blue."

"My name is...ah...." He tried to remember the equivalent of his name in Earth's language. "Call me 'Califra LffGBrsesddrs XXIV'." He thought for a moment, mentally pawing through his file on earth names. "Or just call me...ah...Bruce."

"Bruce," The dog repeated. Humans liked to name things and so Blue had taught himself to remember certain human words. He knew six words for 'food', four for 'taking a ride', and three for 'outside'. His name 'Blue' was his pride and joy because it was given to him by his human, Tomas.

Bruce looked down, clearly, the silver cube had the translator activated for all creatures on the planet. "Are all creatures telepathic here?"

"Most are, yeah." Blue remembered sitting in the backyard, listening, smelling, and hearing other dogs in the night. Hearing their thoughts and complaints, mostly complaints. "Humans aren't really good at it." Blue said shyly, not wanting to divulge too much to a stranger. "Humans have a little...communication problem with the rest of us."

"Communication problem? I thought they had language." Bruce said curiously. *To determine species sentience, they must first have at least one language.* That was his job, find sentience. At least, he was pretty sure that was it. "Oh, this is bad, very bad. No language huh?"

"No, no," The dog wanted to reassure the creature. "Humans have language, and they talk all the time, yak, yak, yak, yak..."

"So, they don't have a communication problem?"

The dog nodded his head vigorously. "Oh, but they do. It isn't the talking skills they have; it's what they don't understand that's the problem. Humans tend to kill things that get in their way. So, they're kind of weak at getting along with other species or with each other. They used to be great at it...a long time ago."

"Humans kill everything. Oh my, that is bad, and very sad."

Blue nodded. "War, humans are very good at war." Blue also knew the toll that such human caused disasters took on wildlife and all living forms.

Bruce had his silver cube out and was tapping in messages. He wanted to get this all down while fresh in his memory. The dog was making his job so much easier.

Blue paused. He might have been a little hasty. Maybe blurting out human flaws to an extraterrestrial wasn't such a hot idea.

"So, they're terrible communicators...and incredibly violent...killing, killing..." Bruce carefully input to his cube.

"No, wait! I didn't mean they were terrible, just hasty that's all, hasty." Blue tried for enthusiasm. "Humans can be extraordinarily loving and kind and compassionate and gentle. Mostly."

"Mostly?"

"Well, humans have three conditions that govern their entire interaction with all life forms: is it tasty, dangerous, or cute. Depending on where the life form falls on those three categories determines human actions.

"I want to thank you for your forthright answers."

Now Blue knew he talked too much. With that thought he wagged his tail with joy. *I talked too much! What a wonderful thing!*

"If you don't mind my asking, why are you named after a color?"

"Blue?" The dog thought about that a minute. "I don't know. My Tomas told me that was my name and it sounded wonderful."

"What about him? Is that your Tomas?" Bruce pointed a tentacle at the unconscious human.

The dog looked at the human.

"OH no! No! That is not my Tomas!" Blue said with shock; for a moment a pang of grief shot through him. "This human is named Wayne...he is not my Tomas... he is okay. Homeless, no job, all alone. But he is not my Tomas..." He looked up at Bruce with the saddest expression Bruce had seen in twenty galaxies and in his line of work, that was saying something.

"I've, ah, my life has been quite difficult lately," Blue hung his head in shame. "I've lost my pack. My old people are gone. My Tomas is gone. I don't know where he is." He had trouble even admitting that the pain was nearly unendurable. He looked down at the unconscious Wayne, splayed out on his back, eyes rolled back in his head, blowing a spit-bubble. "I've kind of teamed up with old Wayne because it's easier with humans running interference, but to tell the truth, I've done all I can for him. He's kind of limited." Bruce made more notes on his silver cube.

"Can I come with you? Please."

"But I don't know where I am going. Or where I am for that matter." Bruce looked around; the Mission Planning Guides Pictures had nothing like this. *There was supposed to be sand...lots of sand...."* Bruce couldn't see any sand.

"Even better! I can help! My dog-Mom said I was very helpful. She said I was the most helpful puppy she'd ever had. She called me 'No. 3' because she didn't know my name was 'Blue'. Do you know where you are now?"

Bruce looked around. "Not really. Is there any sand around here?"

"Sand? Nope." Blue replied helpfully. "This is a private area where humans practice killing. It is called a 'military base'." That wasn't what Bruce wanted to hear.

"So, there is a lot of killing here?" Bruce had a bad feeling, sensing for danger.

The trees in this little clearing had been shattered, chunks and splinters and limbs obliterated by errant mortar rounds, forming a scarred patch of open ground. Blue wasn't sure how to explain this in reassuring words.

"Safe is such a relative term." Blue finally admitted.

That wasn't what Bruce wanted to hear either.

"Can you build fire?" Blue asked.

Bruce scratched a tentacle with a tentacle.

"Fire? You 'build' fire? I didn't know that. I have no idea what construction method you use. Are nails involved? I don't like sharp objects."

Blue didn't bother trying to explain the concept because he had no idea either. All he knew was what Tomas used to do when they camped. So, he sent Bruce a mental description of Tomas gathering sticks and twigs, piling them just so, using strips of chewed bark to form a small bow played it back and forth created enough friction to send sparks to soft moss and twigs.

"I'll give it a try, I guess." Bruce followed the picture as best he could and was stunned to see smoke, then a small flame licked the wood.

"By the Great Horns of the Magnificent Nebula that is amazing! I made a fire. Really? And I did it? Wow!" Bruce was so proud. He had never created anything like an essential element before.

The fire gave the dark surrounding woods a cheerful warmth, a soft glow illuminated tree trunks, giving him the feeling, he was in a bubble of yellow light. "I have this mission, you know."

"Mission?"

Bruce nodded.

"Let me explain how this Galactic Federation of Civilizations works…"

Blue flopped his shaggy tail cheerfully, settling to the ground. Golden Retrievers are very good listeners, and his Corgi self was fascinated with new things.

For hours Bruce explained the workings and bureaucratic operations governing his urgent mission to the Earth.

CHAPTER FIFTEEN

"Tonight, gentlemen, we have planned the next strike." Peter Leroy in his bright yellow, brand-new Gadsden 'Don't Tread on Me' T-shirt stood tall in front of his men.

After the utter debacle the other night he needed to work a little harder stirring the men to more violence. Leroy told the MAGA Militia to look for Liberals, not invade some old guys' property. *They got shot to shit and it serves them right.*

"But what about our tribute to Sam?"

"Sam?"

"The guy got kilt the other night!"

"Oh yeah," Leroy berated himself for letting this slip by. "Here's to Sam." He raised his beer bottle for a toast. *Two wounded, Sam killed, and the fourth guy still hasn't been found, what a mess!*

The MAGA Militia quickly followed his toast.

"To Sam!" They said in ragged harmony.

"Okay, that's that. Now I want you to know I will be seeing Sheriff Orwell tomorrow to straighten him out on a few things!" He said in stern tones. "I cannot allow my men to be gunned down in the line of duty." "We aren't yore men," a man with a Red MAGA hat said.

"I am your leader," Leroy insisted.

"Naw, that ain't you! That was the guy got kilt. Sam was our leader." MAGA hat replied.

This was not going the way Leroy had planned. Carefully, Leroy studied the crowd of drunken Patriots, 'Veterans for Peace', pleased at their devotion to duty but not impressed with their devotion to him.

He signaled for the waitress, a rather surly looking blond, for another pitcher of Budweiser.

"Alright, let's go, let's get us a Libtard!" Someone shouted enthusiastically.

"That's it!" Leroy cried with enthusiasm. "That's the spirit. We'll show them they can't kill old…ah…Saul. Or was it Sandy?"

"It was Sam!"

"Yeah, him too! Whatever, you can't kill one of us and get away with it!" Leroy said with fire. "Let's make the Libtards pay dearly for their crimes!" That brought a drunken cheer and some smiles.

"Settle down," Leroy was back in command. "Our next target for vengeance will be…" Leroy paused for dramatic effect.

"I wanna hit the library again! We gotta burn more books! We gotta stop the evil liberals from ruining our children's minds." The bright red MAGA hat declared with determination. "This time we gots to burn 'Pogo' and them 'Far Side' Cartoons for mocking us." He continued.

"I wanna git that Harry Potter bitch for ruinin' my kid's minds! Sorcery? Evil is what I call it." Another man wearing 'Popper for President' shoes spoke up.

"Okay, quiet, we are going to stop an insidious betrayal, a poison that has been delivered to our old and elderly, the weakest and most helpless among us are suffering from Liberal treachery!" Leroy was fired up. He vowed publicly to defend the helpless and vulnerable to his last breath and he would not allow these Democrats to steal freedom from the elderly.

"Kill the Liberals!" MAGA hat shouted.

"Kill the Democrats!" MAGA shoes joined in.

"We are going to strike terror in the hearts of Democrats and so-called Progressives every…" Leroy paused to drink his Bud, dribbling beer down the front of his Gadsden flag shirt.

"Leroy, would you just tell us about the target for Christ's sake!" The man adjusted his MAGA hat, squeezing the brim into a narrow V giving him what he hoped was a hardened, 'Special Forces' kind of look.

"'Meals on Wheels', MoW, gentlemen," The burly man told the drunken rowdies, slamming down his empty can.

"Meals on Wheels? I thought they were good guys?" MAGA hat wondered.

"Far from it, these commie-traitor-socialists prey on our weak and elderly! They enter the unsuspecting elderly homes, pretending to feed them, but instead, they are there to rob and destroy and plunder and pillage…!"

Leroy held up a hand drawn pencil sketch of stick figures beating up other stick figures.

"As you can see from this first-person artist rendering, the Democrats are clearly and unequivocally attacking the helpless elderly." He told them with stern conviction.

"Kill the Liberals!" MAGA hat shouted.

"Kill the Commie-Pinko-Socialists!" Another took up the call.

"…the poor Elderly, just seeking a little food, a little kindness, companionship, and Liberal perverts use Meals on Wheels to invade homes and plunder helpless old farts." Leroy watched the group begin to react, faces flushed, sweat, eyes bulging with alcoholic fervor, he had them right where he wanted them.

Leroy couldn't believe the left wing nutballs were so vicious as to attack the old and infirm. But the sketch was proof, he felt a righteous rage begin to form like a gas bubble.

"I have a vision, my brothers, of a Nation, an American Nation of White Americans, living free and proud! No longer held back by those haters and violent Democrat terrorists! We will no longer be victims of the darkies and immigrants and the spawn of Satan!"

A roar went up from the eight men gathered to enact vengeance on the hated enemy.

"Kill the Lefties!" MAGA hat was into it now, face flushed, beads of sweat running down his face.

"Kill the Snowflakes!" MAGA shoes felt a glow of excitement.

"We gotta stop them! We gotta mow down MoW!" Leroy demanded.

"Mow down MoW! Mow down MoW!" They picked up the chant. "Mow down MoW!"

"MoW has been destroying lives long enough; let's show them what a real America is all about!" Leroy wanted the men fired up and ready.

The Dew Drop Inn, just outside of Roy, Washington, and close to the boundaries of Joint Base Lewis McCord (JBLM), held frequent drinking contests to keep the people fired up about local issues and to make lots of money; angry people drink more than quiet peaceful types. Tonight, scurrilous stories of Democrat insanity and one dollar a shot of cheap tequila fueled their vengeance.

"Meals on Wheels, gentlemen, another Commie-Pinko Democrat sabotage of White American values!" Leroy consumed another beer.

**

"They always like this?" Mosie, a newly hired waitress at the Dew Drop asked. "They seem kind of dangerous. Like a mob or something."

"Naw," Tom Harrington, took a swig of malt liquor and flipped the burgers. "They only look like a mob, they're really patriots. MAGA's saving America." He opened another can of beer and drank. He liked Mosie, she was new and all, but a good kid. Full sleeve tattoos, really great design. She was also ex-military which Tom deeply respected; she had a Purple Heart.

"Really? Saving us from what? Sure, looks like a drunken mob to me," Mosie replied. She appreciated Tom's ogling her, but she wouldn't let that get too far.

"Democrats." Tom added cheese to the frying burgers. "They say the entire political Left Wing of this Nation have conspired to ruin the country and only the Right Wing can make American great again.

"You believe that?" Mosie cleaned the table of the last customers, fleeing without finishing their meal because they were intimidated. *All these MAGA guys were openly carrying.* This didn't bother her, but other people sure were upset; customers were leaving.

Tom paused and shrugged. "Do I believe their bullshit? Naw, I don't know. I don't care. It has nothing to do with me." He figured another year, off probation and he was out of this benighted landscape. Brazil was calling him to come down for some bad-boy fun.

Mosie watched in fascination as the armed men took over the pool table for their patriotic strategy and planning session to murder innocent people.

The last of the resident pool players slammed down their beer and left.

The MAGA group quickly decided to develop a strategy plan to develop the planning plan, but some argued this was backward and the planning plan should be used to develop strategy plan.

They nearly came to blows.

Once they got past that roadblock they struggled with the nuts and bolts of pending mass murder. Some were in favor of explosives; IEDs gained from lessons learned in fighting terrorism. Others wanted roadside ambushes, Irish Republican Army style. Still others liked the analogy of the wild, wild West, shooting up a stagecoach seemed right.

But all agreed, there must be no MoW survivors.

Soon, blood was boiling, a killing fever swept the drunken crowd; a passion for violence fired the men up; they needed a target. Outrage demands immediate action. They started grunting and punching each other in the shoulder; harder and harder. Then the eight MAGA warriors began to grunt in unison, like a rally for football; a primitive group chant, turning off thought and turning on violence.

"Humm hum hum,"

"Humm, hum, hum."

This is getting bizarre, Mosie thought. She didn't like the atmosphere at all.

"Hey, Tom, could you ask these gentlemen to take their raging, violent alcoholism outdoors? Please." She feared they were building up to some kind of explosion and they were all very drunk with lots of guns.

The trouble with gun laws, she thought, *is that the very purpose of a gun is to kill something. There is no other purpose for a handgun, so by openly allowing people to carry weapons you are in effect sanctioning killings.* Mosie wasn't shy about having weapons herself. At home were a 12-gauge Bullpup shotgun and a Browning HI Power 9mm. She routinely carried a Bersa .380. War habits were hard to break, and America is a dangerous place, now more so because of all the guns.

But she carried concealed, she never openly carried because she did not want to frighten others; she felt she had a right to firearms but not the right to intimidate innocent people.

However, Mosie kept her opinions to herself because in her experience people who openly carried guns tended to be volatile, touchy, stupid people with a loaded weapon seeking confrontation, a very bad combination. She could think of absolutely no reason to openly carry other than being in a war zone. She had been to Afghanistan and was pretty sure Wal-Mart was not a war zone. Yet.

A well-armed society is not a peaceful society, but a broken and terrifying one.

The only proof of this she needed was right before her; to say what she believed out loud would be met with instant violence.

**

Tom Harrington was a six-foot five tattoo with steroid muscles.

Except for his face, Tom's prison tats were vivid images of knives, barbed wire, blood, crucifixion and, of course, Jesus.

Placing his beer carefully on the counter, Tom came out from behind the grill; his size, virulent tattoos, and intimidating glare were all certainly compelling, but it was completion of a long prison sentence for manslaughter that gave Tom unquestioned stature in this community.

Tom said nothing, he walked up to the pool table and pointed at the front door.

Silently, eyes downcast, the MAGA's shuffled their rage outdoors.

Tom nodded in acceptance of their respect, returned to his beer, sliding a basket of fries into the bubbling grease.

**

Mosie had been watching the men gathered outside in the parking lot impressed with their level of dysfunction. Because the MAGA group had already driven off all her other customers, she had nothing better to do but clean tables and watch the shit-show unfold outside.

**

"Don't you have any community feelings, Charley? Haven't you been attending the NRA lectures on Citizenship?" Leroy was incensed the man was so ignorant of social values.

The MAGA men were pulling weapons out of pickups and showing them off: AR's mostly, festooned with optics, handles, red dots, extra magazines, flashlights, fancy flash suppressers, all in a variety of brown, green, and black colors.

"Hell yes," MAGA hat knew he had to defend himself fast. He had trouble looking this Leroy zealot in the eyes, but it can be deadly not showing patriotic zeal. "The, ah, NRA training? I was there. They were handing out boxes of .9mm and paper targets of liberals." MAGA hat knew he needed to embellish this to add authenticity to his lie. "Last meeting, they even had shooting targets showing little liberal boys and girls too. Nits make lice you know." MAGA hat was proud of himself for adding this last detail.

"Well, then," Leroy replied with fervor, pleased that one of his men was a trooper. "You wouldn't mind a little social engineering tonight, would you?"

"What does that mean?" the man with the MAGA hat asked nervously. He didn't know this Leroy character very well and that made him suspicious.

"Why, we get in our four-by-four Fords, fire them babies up and we go out, cruise the roads, looking for liberals to fuck up!"

That brought a drunken cheer from the crowd.

**

Mosie watched in fascination as the punch-drunk patriots prepared to depart.

The MAGA's, playing with their rifles and shouting obscenities about destroying Democrats, began to pile into their pickups, revving the engines for immediate departure.

She was glad to see them leave without bloodshed.

Then Mosie noticed something peculiar.

There was another man she hadn't seen before. Near the edge of the parking lot, he was leaning against a cool old car; dark blue, pinstripes, black windows. She had no idea what the car was, but it looked fast. The guy with the car was dressed in Gray, hoodie, jeans, shoes, all gray. He said nothing and didn't join the rowdy MAGA crowd.

Mosie noticed the Gray Man walked kind of funny.

CHAPTER SIXTEEN

"I have a dream that one day my four little children will one day live in a nation where they are not judged by the color of their skin but by the content of their character." Martin Luther King.

October 15, 2028

"A Constitutional Republic is not a Democracy," Orwell explained.

He considered himself an All American God-Fearing, Conservative-Christian, Patriotic Lawman, so his duty was to make sure every new member of the Olympia Sheriff Department was of like mind.

"Do you understand what I mean by that?" He asked the fresh-faced young man before him.

"Yes sir, bless the good Lord." Recruit Wayne Way, new to the job counted himself lucky to have a real hero for his Sheriff.

"I'm an 'old-fashioned American'." Orwell explained as he carefully combed his hair, proud of the fact he could hide his bald spot so successfully. "I pulled myself up by my bootstraps, worked hard for everything I got. So, when I saw the mess liberals had made of my country I just couldn't stand by."

"Yes, sir, now is the time for good men to come to the aid of their country."

"Did you hear that in typing class?"

"Huh?"

"Never mind, never mind. This is what it takes, Corporal, hard work and the devotion to the Lord, Bless Jesus." Orwell looked over at the intense young man, sitting on the edge of his chair, eager to begin his new life as a Sheriff Deputy, prideful to be an American.

"I do not understand these so-called progressives. Liberals who think the world owes them a living." Orwell continued, pleased that Wayne seemed to be paying attention. "Liberals hate God." Orwell declared.

Opening a desk drawer, he removed a pint of Jim Beam, took a long swallow, then another, and then capped the bottle. He offered one to Wayne who looked shocked and then saddened as he refused.

Orwell didn't notice; his eyes filled with tears, his throat burned, and his stomach exploded with happy warmth, and as the alcohol surged through his system. Sheriff Orwell felt triumphant, like he could do no wrong.

"Will you excuse me, sir," Wayne said quickly getting to his feet. "I must be going. I have Patrol, you know."

"Certainly, hard work, huh, good for you son."

Wayne winced at the word, 'son', but kept going, thinking; *I am duty bound to report this flagrant dereliction of duty.* He was taking this straight to the Reverend Big Sam Prosper of the National Christian Church of Jesus Christ. The good Reverend ran a tight ship on backsliding Christians and would make Orwell's life a living hell for this sin of alcohol.

Wayne felt immense pride in himself and his peers. A member of 'Warriors for Jesus" Wayne was a 'Dominionist': *dedicated to America by eliminating sinners, ridding the Earth of nonbelievers, degenerate fornicators, and those scum liberals just as Jesus commanded.*

As he left the Sheriff's office, Wayne reminded himself to visit his parents after work tonight. Since their arrest under anti-Christian sedition laws, he'd avoided seeing them and felt guilty for this. But their refusal to take the blood oath to Jesus as required by the Council of Christian Clerics was appalling to him. *How can the Rapture occur when Christians won't sign the pledge to kill nonbelievers?* He asked himself.

Wayne, however, had no such doubts, as he strolled out to his patrol car to begin his shift.

**

Orwell settled behind his desk shuffling through paperwork considering the current situation.

After a few weeks things were beginning to settle out from all the activity. The Mack's were still in custody pending their hearing and Deputy Two Hawks was back from his mysterious absence and that investigation was pending. They couldn't yet file a charge against Two Hawks, but Orwell was confident they would find a suitable cause.

Lt. Strum was fit to be tied. She wanted Deputy Two Hawks fired and/or castrated for insubordination and refusing a direct order.

Orwell shook his head. *Women were so damned hysterical.* He still found it hard to accept women in law enforcement. It just didn't feel right to him. *Women should be honored, cherished, and protected. This was man's duty. Women should be respected by allowing them to stay at home, raise the children, prepare food, and keep the home clean. Women need to step aside so the men can make all necessary decisions for their own good.* This just made sense to Orwell because it was the way it had always been *Men are to rule as head of the household.* Orwell believed the Holy Bible to be the exact words of God so he was confident this could only be the truth.

"Wives, submit to your own husbands, as to the Lord. For the husband is the head of the wife even as Christ is the head of the church, so also wives should submit in everything to their husbands. Ephesians 5:22-24" undefined

Pulling out the daily crimes bulletin he scrolled through the variety of incidents seeking some possible clue to the location of Governor Myerson. Among the beatings, rapes, petty thefts, and domestic squabbles there was no hint of the missing politician. But until found, they could do nothing. The Governor had the clout to back up Two Hawk's story and that would blow the whole deal.

No, they had to wait. *Once Governor Myerson was in the bag, we can kill him and drop the hammer on the fucking Indian.*

"Sheriff?" the intercom buzzed.

"Yeah, what?'

"Sheriff Orwell, Ned Derod, Pronghorn County Sheriff is on the line."

"Hey Ned," Sheriff Orwell picked up the phone and greeted the man warmly. "How are you? Going to the next meeting?" Orwell checked his calendar and sure enough a major meeting was coming up.

'The National Law Enforcement Convocation' in Salt Lake City, Utah, sponsored by 'The Americans for Truth Foundation', was next month. Orwell had his presentation ready: 'The US Constitution and the Sheriff's Oath of Office'. In this speech, Orwell would present that the office of Sheriff held a unique position in American Law Enforcement because Sheriff's had a Constitutional duty to ensure the freedom of their citizens. To Orwell, as Sheriff his responsibility went far beyond mere law enforcement. *My role is to ensure Democracy itself!*

"You know, Ned, this meeting is damned important. In this Constitutional Republic we avoid mob rule," Orwell liked to hear himself talk. "We prevent the Democrats and liberals from forcing us to accept majority rule. Instead in a Constitutional form of government everybody's rights are protected because leaders believe in a True America, where the Constitution is followed to the letter! They cannot deviate from the Constitution by one word. As sheriffs, we have the unique distinction of being defenders of the US Constitution. Our profession is to protect our citizens, defend Democracy. We can't rely on politicians to protect Democracy!" Orwell stated forcefully. "But the Sheriff is sworn to protect the Constitution with his life and that is far better than weak-ass politicians."

"You are speaking to the choir, Sheriff." Derod's voice boomed over the phone line. "That's why I called, James. 'The Americans for Truth Foundation Committee' needs some time on the agenda as well." Derod still had a southern twang to his voice although he had left Tennessee years ago. "We are adamant about resolving racial problems and bringing peace to Law Enforcement."

"I understand," Orwell replied. "Go on."

"I am also reporting on the success of ALEC, you know, the 'American Lutheran Exchange Council'? Right now, they are working feverously training state legislators to pass legislation supporting our righteous White Supremacy Nationalist agenda."

"Yes, I am familiar with ALEC. Weren't they directly responsible for pulling together the Constitutional Convention last year?"

"Yup. So far, in our efforts to bring peace and efficiency to law enforcement we have twenty states agreeing to field only Caucasian officers; all officers of color will be restricted to desk or office duties starting their next pay period. They will be assigned to districts that reflect their skin color. We also need to reduce their wages, to save taxpayers from overpaying employees who simply are not as good as the Caucasian officers. We hope to expand to all states within a year."

"It is about time." Orwell had always wanted to block non-white people from law enforcement. "I am neither a bigot nor a hater, but it simply is common sense. White people trust white people and brown trust brown, there was no need to mix the two," he told the other Sheriff. He didn't have anything against the brown people as long as they stayed within their world and did not step into his. *Most importantly, white people were the superior race; history proves it.* Orwell was sick and tired of this being unrecognized.

"Caucasian people are simply superior. It is a known and provable fact." Orwell saw himself as both compassionate and enlightened. As Sheriff he had a responsibility to all citizens within his county no matter their color or ethnicity. Therefore, he wanted only the best for brown people as well as white people. But, separate was best because he was also a realist. European Caucasian people lead the world in technology and science and social understanding. White people gave the world the internal combustion engine and the computer. All major inventions and discoveries in this world were made by white people. Orwell was proud of his heritage. He didn't begrudge other races for their minor accomplishments; *it was just that Caucasian people were far superior to all the others.*

"I want white to white and brown to brown," Derod said firmly. "At the next meeting," he spoke urgently, passionately, "I want to have a litmus test on skin color. I want flash cards showing skin color so we can tell who should be carrying a gun and who should not! This will work in the street as well as in the squad car!"

Sheriff Orwell looked at his Mediterranean skin tones of olive and tan, then said, "Sure, I understand and support you wholeheartedly." He paused. "Ned, I have a small favor to ask as well."

Silence on the other end as the Pronghorn Sheriff considered how much trouble this would be. "Sure," he said after a pause, cautiously he replied. "Maybe."

"I'm sending you some homeless people, now don't get excited, they are retired, got into a little pickle over here and I want to just relocate them so they can start over. No big deal. Good solid Republicans, not a hint of liberal or even Democrat beliefs."

"There'd better not be," Derod replied hotly. "Last time you sent me a God Damn tie-dyed, long-haired, hippy-faggot vegan terrorist!"

"What?"

"In that last batch of so-called 'regular prisoners' you sent for the labor camps. I told you no niggers, spics, or liberals."

"For Christ's sake, Ned, who the hell else can I send?"

"Okay, but I am damned tired of these assholes screaming about their rights. They refused to accept Republicanism and that is plain un-American! We won; we beat them! The god damn Democrats need to move aside and let us run things."

"The people I am sending you, Ned, are solid Republicans through and through. Both their parents voted Republican as did every family member except a few years back a disgraced family member, a black sheep degenerate, voted for Bernie Sanders."

"No way!"

"Yeah, 'family' what can you do, huh? We all have some crazies in our world, don't we? Imagine, voting Democrat when they know the Democrats are owned and controlled by China."

"Had a cousin once who voted for Kennedy." They

both laughed.

"What a Rube, everybody knows the Russians killed him because he broke his deal to give them Cuba."

"I suppose the Russians got Martin Luther King, Medgar Evers, Malcolm X, and Robert Francis Kennedy too?"

"Nah that was the blood of tyrants refreshing the tree of liberty." That

caused another round of laughter.

**

This mess with the Mack's, Orwell thought, *we must get straightened out. John Mack and his wife were screwed. That was a bitch.* Orwell knew he couldn't hold them in jail much longer. Too much time had gone by and, according to law, he had to release them if no charges were filed.

Sheriff Orwell poured over incident reports, medical exams, statements from eyewitnesses, anything to shed light on what happened that night at the Mack's. But it was very confusing. The only thing he could prove was that jackass MAGA morons invaded the wrong house searching for liberals and they got lit up by a good guy with a gun. But now comes the fucked part: the good guy is going to lose everything. Orwell felt bad for the Mack's, but sometimes fate just worked against you and that was that. He gave the Mack's no more thought.

"Peter Leroy to see you Chief." The intercom interrupted his thoughts.

"Fuck!"

CHAPTER SEVENTEEN

Planetary Tipping Point Report:

AMAZON RAIN FOREST COLLAPSE.

Dr. B. Snow, Ph.D. Biomedical Physics, Chief Scientist, Council on Global Climate, United Nations

Report to Science Summit, United Nations General Assembly UNGC#34.

Peter Leroy was an absolute asshole.

He was also the bombastic leader of a MAGA Militia, the same guys who were shot to shit by that ragged old Republican homeowner now sitting in Orwell's jail. Of course, Leroy wasn't present at that little dustup, Orwell thought. He always seemed absent when there was shooting involved.

Orwell knew Peter Leroy's reputation. A dangerously obese, former Counterintelligence Field Agent for US Army Military Intelligence, Leroy was, until recently, living in Biloxi, Mississippi. He had popped up in various roles as an agitator, organizer, and self-proclaimed leader of the local militias.

Orwell was realist enough to understand that as the head of a group of very angry, well-armed white men Leroy was entitled to a little respect, but there was no need to overdo it.

"Fuck him, he can wait." Orwell said, deliberately feeling superior.

Orwell leaned forward and signed the document sent over by the Judge. He witnessed her signature and with a flourish added his own. The property, home, and all possessions of John and Emma Mack were now the property, home, and possessions of Peter Leroy and the MAGA Militia. The Mack's were to be informed of it tomorrow morning before the Judge.

He felt a twinge of guilt for consigning the property of an innocent man to a gang of thugs like Leroy's bunch; but the law is the law, Orwell thought.

Then he grinned with mischief. Deputy Two Hawks will be given the honor of driving them out of the state.

"Let the Libtard prairie nigger deal with the Macks," Orwell chuckled.

He noticed a new memo on his desk. Boise, Idaho had put out a call for workers. The state was building a massive new US Homeland Immigration Detention Center Prison for children, toddlers, and infants. Orwell chuckled. Last month the US Supreme Court ruled 'Immigrants are unprotected by law and have no rights in America at all. Further, all immigration is limited to Caucasian Christian people only and all visa's changed to Tourist Visa status which could be revoked at any time.

Then there was the DeSanka decision.

Orwell loved it; just loved it.

'DeSanka V US Department of Labor', in which all current child labor laws were erased nationwide. In Orwell's opinion, Corporations were unshackled, free to provide good, reasonably paid employment for children seeking to help their families or to learn a trade. Orwell as a youth pastor of his church took immense pride in helping youngsters get out there and make their way in the world doing the unsavory jobs that grownups didn't want to do.

For Orwell, America's future lies in allowing youngsters to learn hard work early in life. *Too many problems in our nation are due to lazy, good for nothing bums that don't want to work for a living.* Orwell firmly believed that welfare programs like SNAP, SSI, TANF, and Medicaid were killing America.

Thinking of money, Orwell pulled up his financial report on the computer, and was ecstatic to see his stock portfolio in the new for-profit, Idaho prison system had just split.

"Damn!" Orwell muttered. "I just might get that fucking second home yet." He had his eye on a little property upstate that could be had for under a million five.

"Republicans know the true purpose of Government and Democrats don't." Orwell was well versed in Capitalism; his brother was an investment banker, and his first cousin was CEO of Wal-Mart Western Division.

Capitalism is an aggressive economic system, Orwell believed, designed to provide enormous wealth to ambitious people.

Therefore, the sole purpose of Government is to ensure profitability and economic success. There was no other greater purpose for Government than to guarantee a strong financial empire for those who have the balls to go after a fortune, Orwell surmised. *Government must protect and serve the ruling class; otherwise, there would just be chaos.*

But the Democrats seemed to be completely ignorant, unaware of this basic tenet of Statehood.

Orwell was puzzled. How did Democrats achieve power at all? For Democrats, Government was about protecting the weak, allowing sexual perverts to run amok, and giving free money to the sick, lame, and lazy. It makes no sense! A Democratic Government just piles up debt and gives worthless, good-for-nothing bums a free ride on the backs of hardworking taxpayers. It's not right!

But all his life he'd heard the same thing: "Liberals are dangerous; they must be stopped before they destroy everything." Orwell knew for a fact that Republicans were the strength of the Nation and yet Democrats had kept gaining power. How is that possible? Orwell figured Americans just couldn't see what was right in front of their noses: Democrats are incompetent pussies.

Left Wing politics were responsible for ruining our economy with Social Security and the budget busting Medicare nonsense, he thought. *So how did they pull that off?*

It was infuriating to Orwell.

Well, he thought, *we are going to put a stop to it here and now. Put these degenerates in prison where they belong. Democrats are nothing but child molesters, queers, and communists anyway. Immigrants are running amok, hordes of homeless are ruining our cities and threatening our citizens. And the deficit, oh sweet Jesus, the Democrats have run up the deficit to the point America is beyond broke because of those foolish safety net programs the Democrats have forced on us: Medicare and Social Security must end!*

"We have got to stop Democrats from destroying our Nation!" Sheriff James Kirk Orwell snarled to himself in his empty office. *I am a Patriot, all the way to the marrow of my bones. A true blooded American I vow to protect and defend my beloved homeland.* Orwell stared at himself in the mirror, tightening his jaw he squinted his eyes in stern expression of his beliefs.

We are going to make America great again, he thought, *once we put a stop to this Leftist insanity and have a solid, stable Republican Leadership for maybe a few decades, we can turn back to two party state, maybe allow voting again. But only after we've gotten this country under control and straightened out. We have to bring back Law and Order. The chaos of snowflake Liberalism had nearly destroyed us. But we are in charge now! We are going to have to get tough, authoritarian-tough, and like medicine, it may taste bad at first, but it will cure.*

Orwell made a note to himself that the evidence to frame Tomas Two Hawks for assaulting the Governor needed to be substantial and convincing. After all, the new Christian Nation of America needed to be born without blemish.

Sheriff James Kirk Orwell felt an immense sense of pride in himself, in his profession, and his Nation, and steeled himself to meet Peter Leroy.

CHAPTER EIGHTEEN

"Racism springs from the lie that certain humans are less than fully human. It is a self-centered falsehood that corrupts our minds into believing we are right to treat others as we would not want to be treated." Alveda King

Orwell glared at the report as if it were IOU written by a Liberal.

His meeting with Leroy had drained him of all his energy. Leroy's relentless pounding on the absolute necessity of eliminating all other races, leaving only white people, was tiring. Sure, he made sense. But he kept belaboring the same points over and over: "Black people weren't slaves they were indentured servants, given free housing, food, clothing, good training, skills, everything they needed to succeed and still the Darkies weren't satisfied! There was no such thing as slavery. That is a vicious liberal lie!"

Orwell had a splitting headache already this morning.

"Sergeant!" Orwell shouted. "Sergeant, send Two Hawks in here."

Deputy Tomas Two Hawks sauntered into the room and slouched into a battered wooden chair in front of the Sheriff's desk. He didn't speak a word. Looking lazily around the office he saw it was as cluttered as always, smelling of Old Spice and wood polish, the furniture seemed exhausted by years of paper shuffles, farts, and spilled coffee.

"I've been back a few weeks. When are you going to tell me what is going on?" Tomas was tired of waiting. He reported in, expecting some kind of officious bullying, but nothing. No one said a word about the Governor or Tomas's absence in three weeks. He tried repeatedly to get an answer and all they would say is: "What are you worried about? You aren't under arrest now, are you?" *As if that answered the question,* he thought.

Orwell felt the heat rise in his face and sweat bead on his forehead. The disrespect radiating from the Indian was insulting.

"As you are aware," Orwell began without preamble. "I have other duties than Olympia Sheriff's Department. The US Homeland Police Force has approached me to be their local liaison in this area. The Homeland PF has issued priority commands to quell the rioting and looting of Liberals by any means necessary. You were assigned to monitor the Democrat riots. Yet, you left your post to go after the Governor?"

Tomas Two Hawks said nothing. When he left the protestors were angry but dispersing away from the heat beams. The only violence Tomas saw was on the side of the authorities. But he'd already been reamed by Lt. Strum, her black eyes flashing she threatened every retaliation short of castration. She wanted that too but knew she couldn't legally justify it. Yet.

The phone rang and Sheriff Orwell picked it up to answer, his eyes never leaving Tomas.

Tomas slouched in the chair thought about Blue. *Where was Blue?* When he returned to the Olympia area, he had searched every dog pound and shelter within a hundred miles. No one seemed to know what happened to Blue. Finally, less than an hour ago, he found out his dog had been adopted out of a shelter in Shelton, Washington. But so far, Tomas hadn't been able to track down the new owners. It was driving him crazy. He longed to find Blue. His world would not be okay until Blue was found.

"A recent Supreme Court Decision," Sheriff Orwell said as he replaced the phone. "It was DeSanka V Democrat National Committee."

"He sued the DNC?"

"The decisions are the important point, Deputy Two Hawks!" Orwell fired back roughly. "The decision was that Democrats represent a direct and ongoing threat to the safety and security of this Nation and they must be separated from the citizens to prevent contamination. All leftists, Democrats, Progressives, Liberals, Communists, Socialists, from BLM to Sierra Club, all of you are to be taken to re-education camps for 'treatment'."

"Treatment?" Tomas knew about DeSanka alright. "Is he chasing them down with attack dogs? That kind of treatment?"

"Jesus Martinez DeSanka, heir to the freeze-dried coffee dynasty, former Governor of Texas, and now the CEO of 'The Ayn Rand Institute for Intelligent Development of Society', is a great man. He is a leader!" Orwell glared at Tomas, daring him to argue.

Orwell admired DeSanka immensely because the man knew how to carry a grudge. Forty years after some kid's de-pants him in high school; DeSanka found them and using his office as Governor he ruined their lives. Then he made sure their children and grandchildren would exist in perpetual poverty for the rest of their days with no chance but the lowest types of employment.

Orwell just had to admire DeSanka; *a man who viewed vengeance not just as a moral obligation but as a moral imperative.*

"What I know of Jesus Martinez DeSanka is that he is so thin-skinned a negative newspaper article gives him a paper cut." Tomas said sullenly. *Some human beings' lust for power is so overwhelming, no evil is unthinkable.* He was unsure if that described DeSanka, but it was possible.

"I don't have time for your insolence, Deputy Two Hawks." Sheriff Orwell held up a packet of papers and shook it to gain Deputy Tomas Two Hawk's attention. Then he slapped the packet on the desk and glared at the Deputy.

"Two Hawks? What kind of name is that? When the fuck are you going to join America? Why haven't you changed that name? To Hawk or Hawks…Tom Hawk has a good American ring, don't you think?"

Tomas met the Sheriff's eyes and said absolutely nothing. *Fuck you,* Tomas thought, *I don't want a white man name!* He refused to be owned by the mainstream; *this my land, but these are not my people.*

"I don't understand you Native Americans," Orwell replied with disgust. "We have given you people everything! You have your casino's making your people rich, along with oil and gold and riches under your reservations, free medical care and government support the rest of us don't get!"

Tomas Two Hawks was furious, every muscle tensed, his blood was boiling. It took everything he had to hold himself back; *I want to kill this asshole in front of me.*

Orwell could see the Deputy's face flush, his jaws tighten, he was clearly pissed about something. Orwell paused to see what the Indian would do.

Two Hawks was perched on the edge of his seat, a hair-string away from launching himself. But he didn't. He settled back in the chair, saying nothing, but rage like sunburn reddened his face.

I cannot be a Native American, nor am I an American Indian. Two Hawks felt the powerful strength of his beliefs. *Those two words: Native and American are absolutely polar opposites in nature. I am native to this land, Americans are not. Natives believe in a completely different world than Americans; we are alive to the world, American are alive only to themselves. We are diametrically opposed. I am 'Neshnabe', in our language, but called 'Potawatomi' in the white man's world. The European invaders couldn't be bothered to learn our language, so they made up their own names for our people and our tribes and forced us to use them.*

But Tomas Two Hawks said nothing. There was no point. The man before him would not understand or care. Native people had learned long ago, from the moment of First Contact, that talking to white people who are in authority was a waste of time. Tomas personally had learned the hard way that silence was much more effective than screaming; took less energy too. He was not going to allow this white man to control him.

Orwell thought it was interesting. *The Indian did nothing. Like I always said, brown people just don't have the ego or the strength to be leaders. Chicken hearted. I can insult him, and he still says nothing.* He saw Tomas' silence as more proof of Caucasian supremacy.

"Well, whatever, just don't pull any of that minority complaint shit around here, understand?" Orwell continued without pause, "We were supposed to begin the roundup of Liberals and Progressives last week." Orwell said, still curious as to why the Deputy had such hard eyes. *Indian should be grateful he still has a job.* "Now listen up, you need to be aware of this. Homeland Security Police Force has set a quota for the Northwest, Washington Oregon, and Western California of 200,000 Leftists to be in custody by the end of the month."

"Why?"

"Never mind!" Sheriff snapped. "This report shows we have fifty-four Liberals in custody as of today! Fifty-four! That is a sad, sad fact. Deputy, do you have any idea who captured these 'Demon-rats', since it wasn't this department?" Tomas couldn't care less so he said nothing.

"Every damn one of the Liberals was rounded up by MAGA Militia. That's right; the amateur's out there doing our job for us. That is going stop Deputy. You will get your ass out there and do the job we are paying you for."

Tomas shrugged. He had already refused this order but hadn't gotten around to telling anyone yet. Sometimes silence was the only form of resistance that didn't include suicide or murder. Tomas Two Hawks had no intention of rounding up human beings and putting them in camps.

He would, however, make an exception for the man in front of him.

"JBLM has a couple of tent camps ready to go." Orwell didn't appreciate the stoic Indian silence crap. "Here is what is going to happen to you. Since you are subordinate to Lt. Strum. I want you to report to her as she will be organizing our part of this roundup. I'm sure she will be pleased to see you. She will make sure you do your job or be fired. Understand Two Hawks?"

"Shit," Tomas was getting tired of this. Brenda Strum had the supervisory skills of a sledgehammer.

"Deputy Two Hawks, do you have anything to add?"

"Why haven't I been charged with desertion or leaving my post or some shit? Lt. Strum was hot to fry me, what happened?" Tomas figured he'd just confront this head-on.

Before he could answer, another phone call came in and Orwell quickly picked up the handset.

"Yes," Orwell was glad for the interruption. The plan to frame Two Hawks for the murder of the agents and the assault on the Governor's mansion was not going well because too many cameras and too many recordings backed up Two Hawk's story.

The Deputy had been defending the Governor, just like he claimed. *The recordings could be altered, but a loose-lipped, live Governor would blab the truth and that would not do, not right now.*

His hoped-for promotion to Homeland Security depended on a clean record built on successes; real or perceived. With the Governor still missing, he needed to keep Two Hawks around.

I will find a way to blame the fucking Indian yet, he promised himself. *Ignorant damn prairie nigger.*

"Deputy Two Hawks, I have asked Lt. Strum to be patient. I explained to her I am keeping you on the job but I will have my eye on you. As of right now, today, you are guilty of nothing that I can prove. Your response to this emergency, created some…irregularities, we must check out."

Tomas believed the sheriff was lying to him, he sounded evasive. *I'm not guilty but they want to keep me around anyhow? Something is missing, something is holding back their vengeance.* He once again questioned why he'd returned. Momentarily, he felt overwhelmed. *There was all this shit and he still had not found Blue.*

Orwell glared at Two Hawks. "Further, I will be assisting the County Attorney in a thorough investigation of the assault against the Governor of this fine State! You are still a 'person of interest'. You may keep the badge for now, but you must surrender your weapon." Orwell recalled his conversation with Sheriff Derod about brown people and weapons.

None of this surprised Tomas. But at least he was free to come and go and gaining a new weapon was not a problem, today, they were sold on every street corner. But he was curious about the real reason behind surrendering his weapon. He still had his badge, why not the gun too? But he shrugged that off, because now he had to find his dog. *Blue, where the hell are you?*

CHAPTER NINETEEN

Planetary Tipping Point Report:

"It's going to be okay, Emma," John tried his best to assure her, but he didn't feel it. He had an awful sinking feeling about this.

"All rise!"

John and Emma stood along with their defense attorney; a harried woman named Betsy Ann Dagostino. The peevish young woman made no eye contact, smelled like olive oil, and looked to Emma Mack like a dumpster diver with a poor choice of dumpsters.

"Her Honor, Majesty Ruth O'Brien Smith, presiding, the court is now in session."

A large, square-shaped woman, wearing a President Popper political campaign pin, strode heavily to the bench and sat down with a thump. Picking up the gavel she hammered it several times demanding the silent courtroom be quiet.

"We weren't making any noise," John whispered to Emma.

The Judge hammered the oak desk several more times, glaring at John Mack.

He quickly shut up.

"We are here to settle the case of John and Emma Mack..."

"We are innocent your Honor," John Mack could not hold back. "I am a registered Republican, have voted solid Republican all my life and I feel a mistake has been made!"

"You have that right, you just made it, Mr. Mack." The Judge stormed. "Thirty days in jail for you John Mack, for speaking without my permission."

"What? But I..."

"Thirty more days."

The attorney, filled with frustration, tried to pull Mack back into his seat on one side while Emma pleaded with him to stop talking.

John shut up before he could get hit with more jail time, but he was furious. Everything was fucked up! His home had been invaded and one of the dogs killed the other run off. He was forced to defend his home by gunfire, killing a human being. Since then, he and his wife had been in jail awaiting this hearing. For weeks they'd sat in jail!

"Your honor," The defense attorney Dagostino quickly shuffled papers, looking for the right case. She sighed. Already 11 AM and so far, she'd had three hearings and six more scheduled for the afternoon. She was beyond tired. "Your honor if I may..."

"No!" Again, Judge Smith slammed the gavel hard. "There is no need to proceed, I have decided the case."

"What? But your honor, we have to have this hearing, the defendant has a right to state his case before a ruling judge..."

"Correct, I have read the police report and the eyewitnesses of the Homeland Security Militia, those surviving of course," She added with a nasty tone. "And I have made my ruling you may sit down and shut up."

"But..." Although the entire justice system had been turned on its head with the arrival of Republican supremacy, Dagostino still clung to the notion that law, and order meant something. "Your honor, these are American citizens, and they have rights."

"Hold it right there! I have heard enough of you. Thirty days for speaking out of turn and irritating me!"

"What?"

"Now," The Judge rustled some papers and glared at John and Emma Mack. "I rule you two are guilty. No question, no doubt in my mind."

"But you haven't even heard our defense, you have no idea what happened that night because you haven't heard the whole story," Dagostino couldn't believe this. It was totally outside the rule of law.

"I don't need to hear the whole story! I know all I need to know!"

John Mack looked at his wife, he saw the hopelessness and fear in her face, and his heart was crushed. Then anger took its place. I have failed Emma, and I am going to make someone pay. John Mack stood up from the defense table and pointed a finger at Judge Smith.

"You listen to me! I am a taxpayer. A law abiding American. A Veteran. A Registered Republican. Those men invaded my home and killed my dog, so I fought back, that is what happened. Now I demand you restore our property, release us, drop these ridiculous charges, and go spend your time with real criminals like those maggots that invaded my home!"

**

Judge Smith smiled. It had taken her four tries to pass the bar exam, languishing for years as a junior prosecuting attorney, growing angrier and angrier as more perps walked or were let go by squishy soft liberal judges despite her best efforts to convict. Minimum sentencing standards my ass! She had been reversed by other courts too many times and was on the ragged edge of losing her job.

Ruth O'Brien Smith, a Handmaiden in her Evangelical Church of the Living Christ, was considering the ministry when President Popper personally called her and offered a lifetime appointment as a Federal Judge. Ruth Smith leaped at the chance to distribute real justice to miscreants and criminals and liberals. A lifetime appointment with a generous salary and benefits was just a plus.

Vengeance, high in her category of important life projects, comprised the top three items on her Bucket list. As a Judge for life, I finally have the chance to get even with every bastard that ever belittled, teased, or disrespected me!

**

"John and Emma Mack," Judge Smith intoned sternly. "Because you attacked and killed a Homeland Security Militiamen in the process of doing their just and lawful duty of rounding up Liberals for re-education camps under the new DeSanka laws."

"But I told you!" John said desperately. "We aren't Democrats! We are Republicans! Just like you! Republicans!"

"...therefore," Judge Smith continued as if uninterrupted. "You shall forfeit your house and property to the State of Washington, to be handed over to the Homeland Security Militia you have harmed."

"What? NO!"

"All your personal property is confiscated as well. You will be allowed to take one suitcase with you, so I advised you to pack well." The Judge paused, to emphasize her next words. "I have heard your pleas Mr. and Mrs. Mack, being a loyal Republican, just as you are, I feel I should extend mercy to you; Veteran Republicans and all. So, I will rescind the jail time, but you still lose your house, property, and all your shit." The Judge pounded the gavel twice, sharply, rose, and started to leave the courtroom, when she stopped abruptly, bent down to the microphone, and said: "Thank you for your service." Then turned and left without another word.

"What? What?"

"Oh John, my God what will we do?

CHAPTER TWENTY

"Social Security is gone?"

Attorney Dagostino nodded soberly.

"Medicare has been privatized?"

"Everything is different now." Dagostino replied.

"But my retirement?" John Mack was troubled and dismayed. "I drove truck, laid cement, I worked thirty-five years for the City of Olympia. Thirty-five years! I was guaranteed a pension. I have a pension, retirement funds. They can't take that away. Not possible."

Dagostino shook her head. "Where have you been, partner? Supreme Court ruled all retirement and pension benefits are the sole possession of the Corporation. Benefits will be distributed if they wish. Every corporation in the Nation, big or little, is free of any obligation to their workers. America is one gigantic 'Right to Work State' now," she explained.

"Wait a minute, what about worker safety, benefits, health care…?"

"The American workers are now responsible for their own retirement, medical care, taxes, there is no sick and vacation leave at all. Benefits the Democrats and Unions fought and died for are gone; their deaths and sacrifice now in vain. OSHA has been closed down so safety rules and regulations are nonexistent. The Consumer Protection Office shuttered and abandoned."

"But you said America is a 'right to work' place, just like Texas and Florida used to be, but now all the country? That's a good thing, isn't it? Right to work?"

Dagostino sighed. "You don't get it, do you? 'Right to Work' means the corporations and business have the right to work you anyway they want. That is all 'Right to Work' means. Workers have no rights. Period." John and Emma stared at the lawyer.

"Most companies are just going to stick your pension funds into their pockets and forget about the retirees. At least, that is certainly the case with you."

"But this is a public office. The city of Olympia is not a private corporation."

Emma said. "Doesn't a government agency operate under different rules?"

"Smart cookie," Dagostino winked. "Not any longer. As a result of the 2027 Constitutional Convention the US Government fell into private hands, from Labor to Education to Interior, all are now in private, for-profit agencies. I am telling you there were instant billionaires made that day. Just like in Russia. Putin pulled the same gig, sold everything off making his pals ultra rich and ultra beholding to him. Homeland Security, all branches of the military and law enforcement are still run by the Government. Oh, and the IRS is still in Government hands."

John had been growing more and more uncomfortable with the acceptance of Putin and Russian policies in the US Republican Party but that was the least of his worries now. Of course, FOXE news, in that interview with Putin seemed to make it pretty clear Russia was being overwhelmed by immigrants from the Ukraine. *So, Putin only did what the American Democrat President didn't have the balls to do: Take a stand!* John admired tough, take-charge leadership.

"You are telling us we have nothing; we are destitute?" Tears streamed down Emma's face.

"But this is not fair!" John protested. "No retirement that I earned, no Social Security that I paid into, not even medical insurance. We have nothing, how could they do this? How are we supposed to live? I am an American! A citizen I have rights! How did those goddamn liberals fuck this up?"

"Rights? That is no longer true. Popper V. ACLU, is another Supreme Court ruling that Citizen Rights are a privilege and can be rescinded at any time."

"We have no rights either?" Emma was aghast. "But this is not American! We take care of each other. We are Americans first and politics second, aren't we? Don't they recognize we are all Americans?"

Dagostino shook her head. "But they aren't. Americans I mean. They are Constitutional Republicans. They have determined that Democrats refuse to follow the US Constitution and are therefore terrorists to the American people. Democrats must be either exterminated or exported."

"But we aren't Democrats! We are conservative Christian Americans, always have been! Where does that leave us?"

Dagostino sighed. She had no heart to tell them their political perspective means nothing because Right or Left were arbitrary designations. Most Americans felt a kinship with other Americans, so the Oligarchs had to break this up. The national media was ordered to emphasize regional and lifestyle differences sowing dissent and ridicule creating this seemingly unbridgeable gap between Conservatives and Liberals.

"Angry, confused people are easier to manipulate." The lawyer explained.
"Yeah," John gripped. "Martin Luther King said that didn't he." A statement not a question.

Dagostino ignored him, saying, "Republican and Democrat are two sides of the same coin. This coin is owned by the oligarchs," she explained it as clearly and succinctly as she could.

"Oligarch? Like in Russia? We don't have oligarchs, this is America, we vote for our leaders."

"Does the phrase 'Citizens United' ring any bells? Scalia, the radical right-wing autocrat, pushed it through the US Supreme Court?"

"I don't know too much about it. It was some legislation the Democrats were all hot and bothered about? They're always whining about some bullshit or other."

"Oligarchs are the ultra-rich, those who inherited so much wealth they no longer have any connection with average citizens. They are the CEO's, bankers, investment moguls, the heads of gigantic corporations, the movers, and shakers of America. These people are not mysterious or unknown, they have names and faces and addresses and phone numbers. 'Citizens United' legislation states money is speech; because of this the extremely wealthy now own the US Government." Dagostino explained.

There is no Democracy, nor is this a Constitutional Republic, because the rich and entitled own it all. Dagostino, like any lawyer not in a coma would know, *America is now an Oligarchy, not a Democracy.*

"You will be released in about twenty minutes," Dagostino explained. "I suggest you find transportation and run like hell. Get out of this Country, go someplace that Republicans can't reach. I know I am."

Her flight for New Zealand was scheduled for three hours from now. She just had time to go home, grab a suitcase, Mr. Max, her cat, and get to the airport. Dagostino had her expatriate plans all set. She did not tell John Mack that the reason for this forfeiture of their home and property was Emma. She had secretly voted for a Democrat eight years back and today, a vote for a Democrat in your history is nearly a death sentence. Dagostino figured life was tough enough now without adding guilt to it, so she didn't mention Emma's indiscretion.

Six hours later, John and Emma Mack, ages seventy-four and seventy-one respectively, were released from jail and turned into the streets with the clothes on their back, two hundred dollars in cash, and nothing else. Homeless and destitute they had no idea which way to turn.

CHAPTER TWENTY-ONE

Planetary Tipping Point Report:

"CO2 NOW AT PLIOCENE LEVELS, CATASTROPHE in 2040?"

Dr. B. Snow, Ph.D. Bioenvironmental Physics, Chief Scientist, Council on Global Climate, United Nations

Report to Science Summit, United Nations General Assembly UNGC#34.

"Hi, I'm Deputy Two Hawks, I'm your escort." He had the official Dodge Durango warmed up, and ready to go. Tomas wanted to get over Snoqualmie Pass before night. It was raining and in mid-October the mountain pass could be ice, snow, and sleet.

John Mack, carrying his one suitcase and a backpack bulging with his things, looked the Deputy up and down with disgust. John was outraged. His land, his home, everything he prized was taken from him and there didn't appear to be anything he could do about it. His anger didn't know this cop in front of him and didn't care.

Emma placed a gentle hand on John's arm. "Dear, I think it is very kind of the Deputy to escort us."

"Kind, my ass," John replied sourly as he threw his bags in the back. "They sent the lowest guy on the totem pole to assist us. Whoopee! What did you do to deserve this, chief, didn't give them enough wampum?"

John didn't trust this guy. He didn't trust Indians. Always drunk, getting into fights, just untrustworthy, as far as he was concerned. His father hated Indians too, but then his father hated everybody.

"What's the matter, redskin? Didn't want to mop the floors anymore? They teach you how to drive or ride a pony?"

Tomas Two Hawks almost reacted but stopped himself. "Sir, I only ask that you be respectful." Tomas held himself back. He could have slammed this mutt to the ground, but this situation was plain wrong, all the way around. These people had been robbed of their homes by Sheriff Orwell, and the State of Washington, and then run out of town. It was despicable. Now he was driving them to the state line to throw them out of the place with nothing but what they carried. This wasn't right and he did not blame John Mack for his anger.

"Fuck You! What fucking more can you do to me? My home? My land? My life? Fuck YOU!" He could not stop the rage; John was helpless and knew it.

Righteous anger is far different then bluff or ego. Tomas knew the difference. Native people have a righteous rage. The history of colonization by the European invaders is one of horror and death. It was genocide at first contact. Poor and desperate Caucasian Europeans driven by the horrific greed of Spanish, French, and English Monarchs invaded this Nation like starving locusts, destroying, stealing, and claiming everything they could get their hands on. This brutal exploitation was sanctioned and financed by the Catholic Church; Tomas had learned. In their war of supremacy against Islam, Christians traveled the globe seeking to expand their religious power and stuff their treasury with gold at the point of a bloody sword. Tomas knew well the stories of the horrific Spanish and Portuguese invasions and their inhuman brutality to the indigenous Native peoples of both North and South America. For Tomas Two Hawks there was nothing good or glorious about colonization because it was all a litany of lies, betrayal and murder.

Tomas understood John's anger very well; *in any relationship or situation, betrayal destroys trust, without trust there can be no peace.*

"Mr. Mack, I cannot know what you are going through," Tomas wanted that clear, no one knows what another is experiencing, and it is insulting to assume. "All I ask is let's get through this with as little conflict as possible. I am not your enemy."

John just grunted and crossed his arms over his chest, a disgruntled expression crumpled his face.

Tomas didn't have any expectations. *He won't listen, they never do.* In his perspective, the Radical Conservatives seem to believe what they believe, and truth doesn't mean a thing. Tomas could not understand these people and it troubled him they refused to engage in any form of dialogue.

He turned to John. "Tell me something. I have asked other Republicans to explain how can you believe stories without any kind of proof or validation? Do you really believe Global Warming and Covid are nothing, but manipulations created by zombie deviants living in the basement of a pizza joint in New Jersey? Really? You believe that?"

"Fuck you!" John fired back. "I don't have to explain anything to you anti-American sicko's."

Every attempt I've made to have a discussion with Radical Conservatives ends the same way: They respond with attacks and insults. Tomas realized.

Still, that had little to do with the human being in front of him. Regardless of politics, Tomas was going to give the man some slack.

"All right, drop it. Let's agree to disagree and get on with this." Tomas told John.

"Screw you!" John was in no mood for nice, and all he could hear was the roar of blood in his ears. He knew he was close to losing all control. He resented Two Hawks because the Indian had a job and income and probably a nice home to go to tonight. *Right now, my Emma has nothing! No home, no bed, no tea sitting on the back deck watching the sunset. No warm comfort of holding each other in our own home on our own land. The Indian is doing ok, and this is not right!*

John had worked all his life and without warning he had nothing, and it ate at him like acid.

"You Motherfuc…" John started around the vehicle, infuriated, needing to hit something, anything or anyone, he didn't care. He wanted to beat on the Deputy because he represented the State that had just impoverished his Emma.

"John!" Emma could see John was in trouble. She stepped between the two men. "Easy John, breathe, John! Breathe."

She looked back at Tomas. "It would seem we have a journey together; we should be civil."

She pushed her husband, not un-gently. "John, please, back off. This Deputy is not our enemy. He is here to help. So lay off. He isn't responsible for any of this." She used her 'no-nonsense tone'.

John Mack looked at Emma, anger shining in her eyes. He too was angry, but he would listen to her. He had learned the hard way. Emma was a gentle, compassionate human being who could turn into a warlord when she felt she was in the right. John, over the years, had to tone down his male ego, realizing his wife was consistently a better thinker and planner. He had come to admire her intelligence, not just her beauty.

Deputy Two Hawks did not want to arrest Mack, but one more step and he would have no choice but to hook him up; lock him up. "I am cautioning you, Mr. Mack. I am a Deputy with the Olympia Sheriff's Department, you will control yourself, or I will arrest you. Am I clear?"

Emma nodded. "Yes, yes, we understand." She looked at her husband, "you understand, don't you, John?"

John Mack took a deep breath; his heart was hammering so hard he feared his chest would burst. "Okay." He knew his blood pressure was through the roof.

"Mr. and Mrs. Mack, we need to leave." Deputy Two Hawks told them. Seeing John Mack calmer, he was encouraged. "We have a long drive and need to get started as it's already late morning. We have a long drive in the rain." "Where are we being sent?" Emma asked.

"Well, you have to leave the State according to the Judge, so it looks like Idaho."

"Idaho?" John Mack was pleased. "Idaho is a white supremacist haven. A Caucasian Nation for Caucasian people. Our homeland! It is said to be a Christian sanctuary! They are joining with Utah, eastern Washington, and eastern Oregon to form their own state, maybe their own Nation! Yeah, let's go there. Idaho is Christian, conservative, and they don't tolerate Democrats or immigrants stealing their jobs. Idaho is a place where we aren't afraid to pray to Jesus and raise our children by the Good Book, the Holy Bible, King James Version of course. People in Idaho, like us, believe in people standing on their own two feet without an intrusive, snoopy Government interfering in their lives. We believe in the American way of self-reliance, Christian values, hard work, family, and Jesus Christ. We await the Rapture," John said with a faraway look in his eyes.

Tomas was curious and wanted to ask the man why Radical Conservatives thought Christian values meant bigotry, misogyny, racism, and blind ignorance, but held his question, under the suspicion bias might just be clouding his judgement.

"...The Second Amendment," John continued, enthusiastically explaining his values, "says I can carry a gun anytime I want." That one Tomas could not ignore.

"Well, not actually it doesn't. What the NRA tells you is not exactly the truth."

"Now wait a damn minute...!"

"The 2nd Amendment to the US Constitution was brought to prominence by southern slave holders after their defeat in the Civil War. They refused to believe the US Government would protect them from a slave uprising." Tomas told the Mack's. "So, the wealthy plantation owners demanded this amendment gives them the right to raise a militia protecting themselves from the revenge of outraged human beings they kept in sub-human bondage."

"What?"

"We have the 2ⁿᵈ Amendment so rich assholes can protect themselves from the consequences of their own behavior!"

"Now wait a…"

But Tomas was done with this topic and kept talking before John could interrupt. "This isn't important right now. We need to get going. Get you to your new home in Idaho…with YOUR people."

"I want to go where America still exists," John didn't hear anything but his own words. "I want to go where chicken shit Democrats-liberals-progressives-snowflake-libtards, haven't watered down Democracy to some socialist pigpen, everybody wallowing in degenerate drug addiction, on demand abortions and communism."

Tomas didn't bother to respond. The fact that Republicans have no use for a two-party system settled it for him. *Republicans are traitors. Pure and simple. You cannot have a Democracy by eliminating the other political party! When Popper asked the Russians to make him the US President that sealed it. The Russian influence over the Republicans,* Tomas thought bitterly, *was an absolute slap-in the-face to every American.*

"Democrats are responsible for our staggering debt, out of control immigrants are pouring over the borders, and homosexuality is being taught to First Graders!" John Mack stated in unequivocal terms. "These are facts!"

"Do you people believe your lies?" Tomas interrupted John Mack. "Do you have any comprehension of your own hypocrisy?" Tomas shouted.

"Deputy, please," Emma Mack spoke up. "John is having a difficult time, could you please be civil?"

Tomas felt embarrassed. He had forgotten himself and it was unprofessional. But it galled him. *Leftists brought justice and humanity to America. Socialism itself created medical and health benefits for Americans. Leftists through the Unions fought and died for retirement, forty-hour work weeks, vacations, childcare, Social Security, Medicare, and hundreds of other benefits that Americans enjoy. In his lifetime, and his experience, Republicans had done nothing for the American people except deny them benefits and as the years went by Republican loyalty went only to the extremely wealthy.*

Republican voters have been betrayed by their need to feel safe. Tomas had observed. *Fear drives every decision and they become reactionary, almost terrified of change as it brings on the unknown. The irony,* he thought, *is that I could become a Republican, the old Eisenhower Republicans that is; Fiscal conservative, strong military, a solid, stable approach to government all coupled with a compassion for the citizens. That makes sense.*

But with these modern day radically extreme right Republicans? These people are fucking crazy.

Over the past few years, it had become increasingly difficult to keep his tongue and his temper, while in service to the same Government as he watched the problems multiply and the politicians did nothing but bluster and prance their outrageous egos across the stage.

"Let's get on the road, folks," Tomas said tightly, wanting to get this moving tired of battling his own thoughts and misgivings. "I have a long drive, there and back." He wanted to spend as little time as possible with John Mack.

They got on I-5 from Pacific Avenue headed north on the massive interstate highway to eventually link up with Highway 18 and then take Interstate 90 over the pass to Eastern Washington.

Gently, Tomas edged them into the insanely thick traffic of I-5; cars, trucks, vans, motorcycles eighteen wheelers pulling double trailers, all traveling bumper to bumper at 70+ MPH; multiple car collisions were a daily affair these days.

Emma explained the attack on their land, telling the kind Deputy about the awful things that had happened to them. "...and then when Oscar...was...killed, my heart broke. He was a good boy."

"Oh, and that Blue," Mack snarled. "Damn dog disappeared."

"Blue?" Tomas voice was louder than he intended. "What Blue? What dog named Blue?" Tomas craned his neck to look at John Mack and nearly went off the road. "What Blue?"

An eighteen-wheeler blared its horn as Tomas swerved back into their lane. Tomas was having trouble driving, his concentration shattered by this news.

"Our other pound dog, Blue."

"Blue? A dog?" Tomas felt his heart leap.

"Golden Retriever and Corgi I believe," Emma replied.

"Blue! My God Blue!" Tomas Two Hawks could have kissed her. A surge of joy swept through him. "Where? Where is Blue?" With almost careless abandon

Tomas pulled the Dodge Durango two lanes over and onto the shoulder of the highway. A few startled drivers let their car horns express loud irritation.

The Deputy's excitement took John Mack by surprise. "What is that dog to you?" Slamming into park, Tomas turned to the couple explaining the situation; "I had to leave town abruptly, the dog got left behind."

"Typical," Mack snarled. "Abandon an animal that depends on you. Fucking Indians! You people probably still eat dogs." John Mack could not give this guy any slack at all. At some level, John knew he was overreacting, but found himself helpless to stop.

Tomas Two Hawks could have killed the man right then and there.

"John! That was not nice or necessary." Emma held John's arm protectively.

"Well, he abandoned the dog, didn't he?" Mack explained heatedly, feeling foolish because he knew he was making an ass of himself only lent fuel to the fire. "You left him behind? That doesn't seem very 'noble red man' to me, Chief."

Tomas knew better than to attempt an explanation. In his experience, bigots never want to hear anything other than their own opinion. But more importantly, his humiliation at leaving Blue was raw and he was so embarrassed he would overreact with anger if he didn't control himself.

"So where is Blue?" Tomas asked in as even a voice as he could.

Emma explained the killing of their other dog Oscar and how terrified Blue was. "I saw Blue run off and I tried to get to him," Emma explained, "but the cops wouldn't let me, instead they handcuffed us and took us away. We never...never saw our place again until yesterday..." The tears in her voice stopped her. "We never saw Blue again either." Her grief was palpable.

Tomas too had tears, grateful his dark sunglasses hid his feelings. "But you don't know where he is?"

"No idea." John Mack put his arms around his wife.

Tomas was no better off than before. He'd found people that had Blue, but no Blue. He had no idea where to look next.

Deputy Tomas Two Hawks put the car in gear, checked the side mirror for traffic, and pulled back out on the highway headed up I-5 North, his heart in turmoil. Knowing Blue was out there somewhere and not being able to go find him was agony.

CHAPTER TWENTY-TWO

"What's with the Deuce and halves?" Emma asked, pointing at a small convoy of 2 ½ ton trucks as she got out, heading for the restroom.

They were a little south of the sprawling Joint Base Lewis McCord (JBLM) a combined US Army and Air Force facility covering hundreds of acres when they pulled into the Dupont Rest Area.

The trucks were lined up, engines rumbling, the smell of diesel heavy in the still air. They were about ready to pull out of the rest area; three trucks, with a Humvee escort. The open beds of the trucks held men, women, and children, huddled together from the fall cold. They stared out of the truck beds, clearly confused by the uncertain fear of their circumstances.

The Humvee had a Gadsden Flag, "Don't tread on me", flying above the American flag.

Deputy Tomas Two Hawks wanted to rip that yellow piece of shit down. *NO ONE places another flag over the American flag.* As a combat wounded war veteran, he knew the price paid for that flag, and was disgusted with those who did not. Seeing it now on a US Army vehicle was a vicious slap in the face for him and further angered him.

Then he looked at the American flag, it was tattered and dirty from being flown from the back of a truck. The irony nearly choked him with rage: Calling themselves patriots while disrespecting the very symbol of their patriotism.

"MAGA mutts believe they are patriots, when they are nothing but thugs, brown shirts, and cannon fodder." Tomas was disgusted with them.

'Take that back!" John Mack fired back. "I am a patriot I care what happens to this country! The men and women who are with me are decent Americans and we want peace. But God Damn it, how the hell did you Democrats start worshiping Satan? When did you decide to betray the US by electing Communists and Socialists to our Government? Why did you think you could steal an election from us? You openly cheated trying to steal the last election, so we had to put armed Republican guards on all the voting places to stop you."

"Those are lies! Time and again we have proven our elections have been fair and honest. YOU lost!"

"That is a lie!"

"Where are they taking all these people?" Emma asked to interrupt the ongoing feud between the men.

Mack shrugged. "They're Democrats, who cares?"

"Do you remember reading about this big green statute that stands in New York Harbor, the one with a lady holding a torch? Some kind of crazy quote: 'Give me your poor, etc, etc,?' Do you remember that? Or didn't you get that far in grade school!" Tomas fired back.

"Screw you!"

"I am Neshnabe, a people you call Potawatomi," Tomas Two Hawks told John. "My people were fucking born here, YOU are an immigrant Mack, you and every goddamn foreign bastard that came here to stay. Except for the black people ya'll ripped out of their homeland and turned into slaves, all of you are fucking immigrants!"

"Your point is? We took it from you. We beat you Indians fair and square! That makes us superior."

Tomas was silent for a second or two; there was so much he wanted to reply he couldn't decide where to start. *For one thing I am not a fucking 'Indian'!* Tomas despised this European bullshit, categorizing his people by their dark skin as looking like people from India, therefore they must be 'Indians'. Tomas hated the Europeans for their racial bigotry and the savage, belligerent invasion of lands that did not belong to them. *I am not an Indian nor am I a Native American. I am native Neshnabe, pure and simple. I don't need to be anything else.*

I must calm this down, Emma thought.

"The signs say, 'HOMELAND SECURITY - Liberal Re-education Transport'," Emma pointed at the trucks, hoping to give them time to cool down. Emma knew she needed to break up this argument. It was going nowhere.

"Those people are all Democrats" John exclaimed. "Damn, what a sight! Hauling those assholes to prison maybe?"

"John!" Emma was growing weary of his constant complaining about other people, particularly Lefties. She even knew a few Democrats; some saw themselves Conservatives and some as Liberals. They seemed normal enough, not like the ravenous pedophiles FOXE News reported. But the QAnon reports did paint a pretty clear picture of Democrats; *evil, preying upon children, demanding abortions because it is easier than raising a child, opening all borders to any dangerous immigrant out there, and disrespecting Jesus Christ, by teaching perverted sexual activities to children under the guise of 'freedom'. Then there was all that spending of taxpayer money, on frivolous projects and scaring up trouble where it doesn't exist. That was shameful.* Emma had to admit Democrats may not be all that trustworthy.

Still, Emma wanted everyone to just get along.

But John Mack was an angry man. Raised dirt poor by a grim, violent, alcoholic father, John learned early on that it didn't matter if they were Sand Niggers, Prairie Niggers or just plain Niggers they were all rotten to the core. All these sub-humans were directly responsible for every awful thing that ever happened to him or anybody else. His father made sure John understood that Jesus Christ was the only way and that punishment was God's way of saying he loved you.

But John Mack knew the facts as they stood today. He must deal with the abject humiliation of losing everything at 74 years of age. He had watched his mother age to a withered, broken, bitter old woman after his father had abandoned them. He had promised Emma when they first married he would protect and care for her his entire life. *Now look what has happened,* John thought. *I have failed her. Here we are, old, and we have no home, nowhere can we call ours. I have simply failed her.* He was embarrassed, ashamed, and hurt that he had failed Emma and at this stage of their lives there was no chance he could make it all up.

As they passed the convoy of trucks Tomas looked at the people gathered in the cold beds. Frightened, overwhelmed, angry, and numb, he saw them as innocent people being trucked somewhere unknown simply because they did not believe in the insane MAGA manipulation of the Republican Party. *They would not conform to the conservative, extremely fundamentalist Christian perspective of slavish obedience to priests, pastors, and politicians. These are the people Sheriff Orwell wants me to round up?*

Tomas, much to his dismay, began to realize he could not remain neutral.

"Democrats prey on children!" John said with finality. QAnon and the Deep Web had opened John's eyes to the treachery of Liberals. "I have seen with my own eyes proof!" The YouTube Videos of Democrats attacking children, drinking blood, and having sex with animals, all horrendous images that could not be faked in his estimation. The video of the Democrat President openly calling for homosexuality to be taught in the grade schools was panned as a deep-fake, but John thought it was very convincing.

John simply could not imagine how Democrats became so sick and twisted but there was no denying it. "FOXE News, QAnon, the Deep Web, it was all right there, the facts undeniable, Democrats have proven to be drug-taking zombies, following like sheep, while real Americans are trying to save their country." John was blunt. "Sheeple!"

"You get a retirement?" Tomas demanded. "Unions, supported by Democrats and Left-Wing groups were the citizens who fought and died for employment benefits and rights. NOT Republicans!" Tomas knew he'd hit a raw nerve; John Mack now had no retirement.

John flopped back in the car seat as if slapped. He wanted to rage and bellow and hit something, but suddenly he didn't have the strength.

Tomas saw his reaction in the mirror and felt shame. He had hit the guy a low blow, he didn't intend to, but he did.

As the trucks slowly moved out of the rest areas, Deputy Tomas Two Hawks realized he was facing a choice. Unexpectedly he was given a chance to do something about this situation. But the thought scared him. It was an unforgiving decision, and there would be no backing out once he took it.

His direct defiance of the Sheriff's orders would lock him away without a trial. *Orwell has ordered me to put Democrats into these camps. Sheriff Orwell is going to be somewhat unhappy if I free them instead.*

Tomas put the vehicle in gear and slowly, deliberately, followed the truck convoy out of the rest stop and onto I-5.

"What are we doing? Why are we following these trucks?" Emma asked.

"Just checking something out." He didn't want to alarm the Mack's too soon.

The truck convoy traveled only a few short miles before pulling off I-5 and proceeded down a side road, toward the rear of the sprawling JBLM Army base and through a guarded gate. The convoy paused while the guard and driver exchanged words and the truck rumble into the fort.

"Where the hell are we going?" John Mack demanded. "You are supposed to take us to Idaho."

Tomas looked back at the Mack's. "I am going to see where these people are being taken, and then we will proceed on toward Idaho and get you settled. But for now…I want to see what is going on," he lied.

"What are you going to do?"

Tomas had to think about that for a moment. *What can he do?* So, he said the next thing that came to his mind. "Free the prisoners, I guess." *Damn! There it is, I've said it out loud.*

"Not with me you aren't!" John erupted. "Oh no we aren't! I demand you take us to Idaho right now. I want no part of helping some goddamn weak ass 'Demorats' escape their just rewards. Democrats need to be locked up until they can agree to be real Americans and do what they are told."

"Motherfucker!" Tomas had enough; the heavy car wove dangerously as he glared into the back seat at John Mack. "I'll leave you upside down in a pile of cow shit if I feel like it. Shut the fuck up, now!"

Tomas's vehemence was so intense, that John shut up, intimidated. John did not doubt that Deputy Tomas Two Hawks was a violent and dangerous man and John, for all his anger and bluster, knew he was not.

CHAPTER TWENTY-THREE

Planetary Tipping Point Report:

EAST ANTARCTIC GLACIER COLLAPSES: major sea level rise expected."

Dr. B. Snow, Ph.D. Bioenvironmental Physics, Chief Scientist, Council on Global Climate, United Nations

Report to Science Summit, United Nations General Assembly UNGC#90.

The JBLM forest was a nature preserve refuge from human predation so Blue figured it would work for them too.

"We need to be quiet through here," Blue had found a suitable stand of mixed Doug Firs and Western Red Cedar on the vast JBLM property, between the rifle ranges and a small village that resembled a Middle Eastern compound used for combat training exercises. The Joint Base was home to bears, coyotes, deer, raccoons, opossums, and a bizarre collection of feral cats that were just plain spooky.

In the days that had past, Bruce had proved to be friendly but highly unskilled. Patiently, Blue was slowly teaching him basic living skills, such as learning to build a fire and lapping water.

Since his first success, Bruce made a few false starts at fire building but kept at it and soon became proficient. He was impressed with himself; he'd learned this fire-starting magic and couldn't wait to tell his family pod of this success. Making a fundamental element like Fire with his own two hands was just awesome. *He wondered if he could have done better with the tentacles.*

"Nice fire, Bruce, you follow directions well." Bruce

prided himself on his devotion to duty.

The dog and the Alien settled around the fire, each lost in his own thoughts for a while.

Blue fretted about his friend Tomas, wondering if he was okay.

Bruce worried about sitting on a hostile world without weapons at the mercy of disease and deprivation accompanied by an Earthling with large canine teeth.

Large, pointed teeth on strong unknown carnivores made Bruce nervous.

But the thought of duty also reminded Bruce why he was here.

"It has been many of your 'days', and I have been putting off my mission. I kind of need to get started," he said apologetically.

"Yes, your mission?" Blue wanted to be helpful but the previous hours of explanation, filled with details, were all jumbled up. "What was that again?"

Bruce wondered how much to tell the Earthling. The creature didn't seem to be as focused as he expected. "I'll keep this simple in explaining Interstellar Politics, okay?"

Blue shook his head. "Oh no, no, politics are bad. Very bad. Most humans become completely irrational, and dangerous. Whenever politics or religion comes up humans try to kill each other."

"Do you want to know this or don't you?" Bruce paused, and then proceeded after the Earthling nodded, which assured him Blue was alert and conscious. "What do you know about the 234th Inter-Galactic Council of Pern? The one in which the Guardians were established to rid the universe of unwanted, out of control civilizations that pose a threat to other worlds."

Blue wagged his tail and smiled. He did not want to admit his ignorance because Corgis were proud of their intelligence, but he just couldn't quite recall what Bruce told him. On the other hand, his Golden Retriever ancestry was far more alert to more pressing matters. It had been a while since he'd eaten.

"Nothing, huh? No knowledge of the Guardians? Planetary Sentience? That sort of thing?" Bruce was disappointed. He had hoped Earthlings would have at least a rudimentary understanding of Celestial Politics.

Blue panted for a moment to give himself time to find an answer. He thought and thought but nothing came. Except he realized he is growing hungrier. He could hear rustling noises in the woods. *Food?* He sniffed. It was a rabbit. *I will wait until the rabbit...*

"Excuse me, Blue?"

"Huh?"

"I was explaining something about my mission."

"Oh." His Golden Retriever self was dismayed at his inattention. Being of hunting dog ancestry was a special responsibility, one Blue took very seriously, and everybody knows hunting dogs stay focused on their job. His Corgis sense of self-responsibility was also deeply offended.

"I am sorry, Mr. Bruce, it won't happen again." Blue sat up straight, his tail held firmly behind him at attention determined to make his ancestors proud.

Bruce smiled, he so much more enjoyed the teaching and learning parts of this job, reaching out to primitive species, and helping them understand their place in the universe. Of course, the possibilities of extermination made some educational discussions more emotional than he preferred, but Bruce took comfort in the fact that those who were allowed to survive were friends for life.

The scent of squirrel, chipmunk, and cat came to Blue, but he held his attentive pose. *Mmmm, there is an Opossum out there too.* Blue had never tasted Opossum but wanted to try. *Oh oh, I'm drifting again. Pay attention!*

"Well, simply put," Bruce explained. "Some civilizations just seem to take a wrong turn somehow and instead of a steady progression from primitive to advanced they seem caught in quicksand, unable to shake free of their past immaturity. These civilizations tend to be highly aggressive and develop weapons of mass destruction to the point that sentient beings in nearby planetary systems feel threatened. There are millions of civilizations out there so the elimination of a dangerous and unstable planet is no big deal. Stability and peace are big indicators of sentience."

"Huh?" Blue stopped thinking of food. "Elimination? Stability and peace among humans? Oh oh, they aren't good at that at all.

"You seem surprised." Bruce asked. It would seem the humans were very non sentient, but Bruce didn't want to insult his Earthling host until he could do more research. "Tell me more of your humans then."

"Are you woofing me? What is the matter with you guys? Everybody here is just trying to make do, get by you know, have enough to eat, warm place to sleep, toys to play with, go on hikes, swim in rivers, have a healthy, supportive pack around us."

"That sounds like a dog story. What about the humans? How are they, in general?"

His direct experience with humans was both awful and awesome, but Blue wanted so much to please Bruce, so he shared what knowledge he had.

"Well, humans are divided into two groups: wonderful-loving-joyous-happy humans and strangers."

"Gee, I thought these humans were a little more complex than that." Bruce made a note in his silver cube.

Blue thought a moment. *Wait a minute. That's me, I'm talking about me.*

"Hold on, humans ARE more complex than that." Blue hurriedly explained. "Humans are strong, dominant." In trying to change his story Blue wanted to give humans the best possible chance.

"So the strong dominate?"

"Huh? Did I say that? Well, yes, I guess that is true. There is always a pack leader. With people, might makes right, the strong rule. Humans have a rigid command structure with men at the apex and everybody else below that." Blue cringed at the recall from his 'Dog Prison' days, the tales of brutality other dogs would tell of their 'owners'. Blue hated the term 'owner'; *every dog I've ever met gave his love and loyalty willingly, faithfully, voluntarily; dogs don't need to be owned,* he insisted.

"I see, the male of the species rules?" Bruce made more notes. "Earth as I understand it has two genders, but they are not equal?"

"No human females are subject to male domination," Blue said.

"Really," Bruce nodded, "So, the females are weak and stupid? That is so sad."

Blue shook his head so hard his ears flopped. "No, sir, far from it. The human females as a group tend to be bright, inquisitive, creative, and intelligent creatures. They have to be, they are the ones who nurture all others."

"That is curious, what do you mean?"

"By nature, females give birth to the species; they are nearly 50% of the population and give birth to 100% of it. But it isn't just raising and training puppies, it is who they are. They care about other creatures around them. Females are quick to help others, nurture even stray hounds and puppies, help out elder dogs who have trouble finding their way, they stay by the side of wounded and hurt, they just…love."

"Nurturing is a necessary strength and is essential to life," Bruce observed. "Without nurturing there would be NO civilization at all. If these women are nurturers, they are invaluable, and should be the very center of your civilization. Why would they be cast under male domination?"

"Females have been forced into second class status," Blue explained. "Human males are stronger, meaner, and are in positions of power so they make major decisions, control the home, control business, politics, medicine, and law. I guess they control everything. They even demand control over women's ovulation and childbearing…" "What? Why would men want to control women's reproductive activities?"

"Many men like to dominate; it is in their DNA. They are very competitive and constantly fight for status. They like winning and want total control."

Bruce was aghast. "Oh my, this is so primitive. Only in failing, immature cultures do you see this kind of behavior; almost pre-civilization." Bruce made more notes in his silver cube. "When leadership is determined by power, the strong dominate the weak and when brute force is chosen over collaboration you have a society that is at sub-sapience level." Bruce sighed. "I am afraid your humans are not looking too…civilized."

Somehow that wasn't a surprise for Blue.

"What are you going to do?" Blue wondered.

"Let me be straight up with you, Blue. I am here to study sapience, to see if it exists on this planet in the apex predator species. Now, should humanity flunk the Sentience Sentencing Examination, things could go very…difficult for humanity…and others," Bruce added softly.

"Oh, others? What others?"

Bruce didn't want to go into details because he suspected humans didn't have a prayer. "Really, the major focus here is on sapience and if humans do okay with that then you have nothing to worry about."

"I didn't know I had anything to worry about in the first place."

"Okay, okay," This was always delicate, explaining to non-apex creatures why they are likely to be wiped out as collateral damage. "Look if humans are sapient, all is well."

"What does that mean?"

"Sapience is the application of knowledge, wisdom, and common sense to life."

"OH?" Now Blue was very concerned. This looked bleak for everybody. "How about one out of three?"

"Oh dear, no, it really is black and white, you either are or are not, all or nothing." Bruce said with finality.

"What happens if they flunk?"

This was the most uncomfortable part for Bruce. He liked to think of himself as a nice guy. But the job, elimination of all life forms on a planet, made that tricky to defend.

"We may have to reduce the human population of the planet a little…or totally," Bruce said carefully.

"A little or totally? That's pretty vague."

"There will be some collateral damage, other beings might be affected, maybe, a little...or more."

"Collateral damage?"

"Unfortunately." Damn, Bruce thought, I was hoping to avoid a discussion of extinction with the beings under examination.

Blue was silent. "You are here to eliminate the human race and you're probably going to take a lot of us innocent bystanders along with them?"

Bruce nodded uncomfortably. "Genocide isn't an exact science you know." He said defensively.

Blue thought he might be too friendly with this guy.

Seeing the dog's expression, Bruce feared he would lose an ally. "It isn't that bad really. My mission is to determine if humans are worthy of continued existence. I am just the analyst. I don't harm anyone. I'm a good guy!"

Blue nodded. "Of course, you are. You just point out innocent victims and someone else slaughters them. That how this works?"

"I wouldn't say it that graphically."

"Sorry, Bruce, but genocide is kind of graphic stuff, you know?"

"Blue, I hate to interrupt, but this body of mine is feeling pain in the gut."

"You are hungry!"

"Okay, sustenance seems logical." Bruce dusted his hands. He was finding the Earth creature intelligent, interesting, and amusing but he had pressing matters to attend to. "I must eat. What is in the plastic bag?"

On the way to JBLM, Blue had pulled off a small theft; sneaking into a Seven Eleven he grabbed the first bag of food closest to the door. Blue was hungry as well, but he tossed the bag over to Bruce.

"What is this?"

"Marshmallows."

"What do you do with them?"

"You put them on a stick and place that in the fire and then eat them."

"Sounds simple enough." Bruce tore open the sack, placed one of the white soft objects balanced carefully on a stick, then threw them both into the fire. As he watched the marshmallow turn, tan, then brown, then a cinder, Bruce asked, "I'm supposed to eat that?"

Blue was amazed. He had always thought some things didn't need explanation. But here he was. "Ok, ok, let's take this from the top. You take the stick, you impale the marshmallow on the stick, you gently place the stick in the fire, wait until it is done and then eat it."

Bruce figured that was a snap. He took a skinny stick, impaled a marshmallow on it, and stuck it in the fire. The marshmallow turned tan, then brown, and then cinder. It fell off the stick into the fire. The stick blazed and then turned to ash.

"You are a little slow, aren't you?" Blue asked most gently. He wondered if Bruce was more of a Cocker Spaniel-style creature than a Collie.

"What?"

"When the marshmallow turns tan take it out and eat it."

"Oh." Bruce impaled another marshmallow and stuck it in the fire. It turned tan, it turned brown, and then Bruce pulled it out and stuffed it in his mouth.

"ARRRRRRggh! Thasss hot!" Bruce was both alarmed and awed. His mouth was burnt to hell, but the flavor of caramelized sugar was superb!

Blue watched Bruce for a moment, wondering if Cocker Spaniel was a bit too much. His new friend was edging into Chihuahua territory now.

CHAPTER TWENTY-FOUR

"I haven't been on this base in years." John Mack exclaimed. "The place looks great! I never had it this good and I was in the US Air Force.'

Getting onto JBLM base was no big deal in a marked police vehicle. Tomas followed the trucks along well paved roads, the trees still gripping their gorgeous fall colors lined every road, fancy restaurants and fast-food outlets were abundant. The dormitories, offices, and other buildings were state of the art, painted in tasteful hues of green, sand, brown, and olive. The landscaping was exquisite, resembling the famous English Topiary Gardens at Levens Hall, Cambria, with delicately carved shrubbery and soaring plumes of manicured trees.

Emma knew this base well as a Veteran retiree she was supposed to receive health care here. But when the Republicans came to power that was gone. In an effort to gain the enormous profits, Republicans privatized medical care to veteran retirees. In order to gain control, they had to kill the old system. Republicans decided to starve it to the point the employees leave. The salaries and benefits of doctors, nurses and medical staff were reduced in half, all benefits eliminated including retirement. Retired Veterans now received mock-medical care.

However, Emma's base retirement pay was still being docked for the medical services she could no longer access. She cringed every time she heard a Republican say how they supported the troops because she knew better, firsthand.

She had voted for Republicans, supported Republicans, believed Republicans, but there were things happening that just didn't add up to their promises.

"Money has been dumped on the military in gargantuan piles," Tomas said as they passed an elegant shopping mall advertising 40% discount for Purple Heart Recipients: 10% extra for Officers. "More money than the Pentagon needs or wants, yet politicians up for reelection can always claim they were 'strong on the military and protected our Nation' and every election more was added to the obscene wealth."

John wanted to contest that, but he had to admit, this base was so elegant some parts of it could pass for the finest country clubs in the Nation.

The massive tree shaded, four lane road dwindled down to a city street lined with bucolic, comfortable homes surrounded by spacious lawns and privacy fences. Shortly, it narrowed to a smoothly paved road lined with bright yellow lane markers passing endless rows of shooting ranges. Finally, they followed down a winding gravel trail as it ended in a prairie dotted with clumps of Ponderosa Pine and Doug Fir. The truck pulled through the gates of a razor-wired compound that held two large, dark green, General Purpose (GP) tents. Armed guards patrolled the grounds.

The trucks pulled in, stopped, the passengers were roughly pushed off and lined up for inspection; two dozen men, women, and children, joining the fifty or so already gathered in the camp.

In the lineup of frightened faces, Tomas recognized one: *Governor Gary Myerson! Myerson was in the convoy!* Tomas was glad to see that man. Now, he had to get Myerson out of that camp.

"I need to take care of something." Deputy Two Hawks announced to his passengers.

John became immediately suspicious. "Take care of what, exactly. I thought you were supposed to take care of us. We are your priority."

"Priority is whatever I say it is." Tomas was in no mood for an argument. He needed to get the Governor out of that camp but could not endanger the Macks in the process.

"I am going to take care of a situation, I need for you folks to hang back, stay safe, I will come to get you..." Tomas observed a 1966 Pontiac Firebird, dark blue, pull up to the camp by a secondary road and park, it sat idling, no one got out.

"Fuck that!" John replied hotly. "We have lost every fucking thing, the least you can do is get us out of this miserable fucking state." "What are you going to do?" Emma asked.

"I have to get someone out of that camp." He thought briefly of the Pontiac but decided the Governor was the first priority. The Pontiac troubled him. Tomas didn't believe in coincidence, few combat vets do; *in war, survival depends on suspicious distrust, because death is just too final for complacency.*

Who is in that Pontiac? Tomas had to find out.

"Emma, I need to get that man out." John said, turning his focus back on the camp and its prisoners, pointing at a tall man trying hide behind a matronly woman.

"Why do you need to do this now?" Emma asked reasonably.

"He is the Governor of the State of Washington, named Gary Myerson. He was the victim of an attempted assassination, which I stopped. But he disappeared right after, and everyone has been looking for him. I owe that man. I was trying to protect him, and I didn't get it done." Tomas did not want to go into the details of that day.

Just keep it simple for these folks, he reminded himself.

"He's a fucking Democrat!" John Mack didn't like this at all. "I didn't vote for the asshole, why should I care?"

Tomas looked at John Mack. "Listen up, I don't give a shit what you care about or don't care about. You have made your opinions very clear; I don't need to or want to hear them anymore. But try, just for one second to stop thinking like a cold-hearted Conservative. Those are Americans over there, imprisoned for no good reason. That should be your priority."

"They are Democrats! Reason enough!"

Emma put her hand on John's arm. "John, please, let this go for now." John

took a deep breath and told himself this would continue later.

"But, Deputy," Emma explained, "these people are under guard, aren't they? Maybe there is a logical reason for that. Wouldn't this interference be illegal?"

Tomas looked at Emma. "They are being put in camps because they are Liberals. I know this because I was assigned to help round them up. But these innocent people are being held in re-education camps to unlearn their Democrat ways, I guess."

"Fucking-A!" John chortled. "About damn time!" Tomas

ignored him.

"I need to get that man out of that camp." He pointed again at the Governor. "But I can't see letting him out and ignoring all the rest. So I guess I'm saying I'm going to liberate the Liberals."

"Okay, well, to me, that sounds like a fine idea," Emma said after a moment's thought.

"What the hell! Emma!" John glared at her in disbelief. "You can't do that!"

"John, please." Placing a gentle, but restraining hand on her husband, she said, "Deputy, I consider myself an American first and a Republican second. As you pointed out those are American citizens in there. I don't know why they are there, but I assure you that most Americans do not belong behind barbed wire. I am with you."

"God damnit, Emma, I forbid you to do this."

Emma whirled on her husband angrily. "You listen to me John Mack, we are not going to leave Americans like that. We are Americans, THEY are Americans. We are getting them out of there. I am growing weary of this 'us versus them' nonsense: Liberals against Conservatives, Republicans against Democrats, Good guys and bad guys. Enough! Can't you see there are bigger issues here?"

"But those are Democrats! Pederasts, perverts, traitors to our Nation."

"No, John, I have heard all of this, and I don't know the truth. Maybe these people, these liberals, are degenerates, but they are still American Citizens, and don't we have a system of innocent until proven guilty?"

"They are guilty."

"That's enough," Tomas broke in.

John looked out the window sullenly.

Tomas settled in to watch and plan. "We may have to stay out here all night," he warned.

"So be it." Emma declared.

"Fuck." John cursed sourly.

CHAPTER TWENTY-FIVE

" Listen, or your tongue will make you deaf." Angela Meade

When Bruce opened his eyes the next morning another bird, this one dressed in fancy blue and black feathers, was perched on his chest.

The act of waking startled the Mountain Jay, and he flew off, screaming what sounded like vile threats.

Bruce had altered his form to the more acceptable one; scrawny, pot-bellied, be-speckled, balding middle aged human male. From his research of Earth, he deduced it was the most innocuous, overlooked beast on the planet and he could blend in anywhere with anyone.

Bruce looked across the burnt-out fire pit and saw Blue was awake.

"Hey." Blue nodded. He didn't feel like talking anymore. He missed his Tomas.

His head drooped in sorrow at the memory of his pack and what was lost. *The pack is my world, everything I am, is my pack. I've lost two packs, my Tomas, and the nice old people.* Blue felt overwhelming shame that he had lost his humans. *Gone, all gone.*

I am collar-less, nothing but a cur, he told himself.

Blue felt very vulnerable. He shuddered at the death of Oscar, the Pit Bull, who was killed that horrid night. The terror he'd experienced was like no other and he feared he would be stalked by further troubles.

**

Seeing the dog's obvious anguish, Bruce felt a tug of concern. But he cautioned himself. *This being, along with all the others on this sorry third-world backwater planet will probably be obliterated.* Bruce steeled himself for that.

"You look unwell," Bruce observed. "Will you be able to continue, or should I seek another Earth creature to guide me?"

Looking anxiously around at the dark, mysterious trees, Bruce still wondered where his equipment had landed. It would be nice to have his 'Alien Species DBNA Regurgitation' computers but it wasn't the first time this had happened. He would make do with his silver cube, if Blue continued to cooperate.

The heavily forested area of the vast JBLM base, where they camped the night, was overgrown by neglect and indifference, the trees crowded tightly together formed a dense barrier to exploration, in their travels through the woods, every now and then a ragged clearing would appear, trees splintered around an impact crater, the result of an errant mortar round.

The air smelled of pine and grasses, and the sun was just barely up, shafts of light filtered through the trees, illuminating ferns and shrubs a bright green. It would have been an idyllic haven had it not been for the gunfire from mortars, and tanks.

Bruce, his arms behind his head, relaxed as well as possible against a fallen log, listened to the morning.

A single bird chirped: "Anyone awake yet?" Silence.

The bird chirped again.

Silence.

Bruce did not hear the bird again for many minutes. Finally, the bird sang out once more. This time another bird answered, just a single chirp response.

The first bird heard the response and went on a twittering frenzy; hearing this, every bird in the surrounding forest awakened singing in joyous chorus.

Bruce was very impressed. These beings greeted the morning as a celebration of life.

"My goodness, a most remarkable experience," Bruce was very pleased.

Blue didn't know how to tell Bruce that there were fewer and fewer birds every year because there were fewer and fewer insects every year. Blue didn't know why and wanted to find out, but until now, he had no way to ask. Blue was puzzled by all the other animals that were disappearing.

Over the small rise to their west, they heard the rumble of diesel trucks as they started up.

Bruce wanted to discuss his novel experience with the birds, but the earth dog did not look happy.

"You look forlorn. Are you unwell?"

Blue nodded. " I have no pack. For a dog, this is very serious. I am alone. Without a pack I have no identity, no purpose."

"I'm sorry." Bruce looked sad. "That is a heavy burden to bear." Blue

could only sigh with his loss.

"Speaking of that. I have another burden that I need to talk about." He noticed the dog didn't seem particularly interested. Maybe he would need a different Earth guide. "Do you recall me talking about my mission? I have been sent to evaluate Humanity for either inclusion as a guest in the Cosmic Civilization or eradicate them as a menace to Cosmic Civilization."

Blue had to think about that for a moment. He remembered but it was a lot to consider.

"Yeah, you were discussing killing all life on the planet as I recall."

"Er…yes…well," This was getting awkward for Bruce. He needed some good news for the dog. "But you need to know, that sometimes, a species is given special survival status because they are utterly unique and of immense value to the Cosmic Civilizations."

Blue wondered if thoughtless arrogance and uncontrollable avarice were in tight supply across the galaxy. If so, humanity had a chance.

Blue scolded himself for being disloyal.

"How are you going to evaluate humanity?" Blue asked. "It seems like there are a lot of humans out there, some good, some bad, some saints, some evil, but when they are good, I am telling you, Bruce, they can be quite spectacular."

Bruce gave Blue a questioning look. "Look at what they have done to you. You told me they had you castrated? They did that?" This was embarrassing. Blue could only nod.

"Didn't you also tell me humans cut off tails and reshaped ears?"

Blue hung his head. "Maybe they had a good reason...," he tried to defend humans.

Bruce stood up. "Blue I want you to assist me in my mission."

Being accepted felt very good to Blue, but it he was so ashamed. "I am sorry, Bruce, but I cannot help you."

"Why?"

"I have no collar."

"What?"

Blue hesitated, this was so difficult. "With us canine, we are given a collar when accepted into a human pack. This collar signifies we are loved and belong and is a source of great pride. It is like an ID card to humans. But," Blue found it painful to say. "When we lose our collar, it means we are strays...the lowest form of canine. A homeless mutt...curs." Blue's long full ears drooped in shame at the horror of it; the memory of a strange human removing the collar Tomas had given him, stripping Blue of his very existence. "If we have no humans in our lives, canines lose all sense of purpose and identity, we are lost, unloved, unwanted... we become...feral." Blue hated to even think that name.

"Please, I want you to help me," Bruce asked.

"What? Me? But I'm just a homeless cur, what can I do?"

"Is that some kind of self-abuse?"

"Huh?"

"Blue, you are you. You are a life form of self-awareness and meaning. Of course, you can come with me. You are invaluable; just as you are. You don't need a collar to give your life meaning."

Blue didn't say anything, but he knew the reality. *A collar was everything!*

"No," Bruce continued unaware of Blue's doubts. "You are the perfect being to accompany me on a tour of humanity. Help me to adjudicate the future of humanity fairly and squarely." Bruce pleaded.

Not for the first time, Blue wondered if Bruce knew what he was doing.

CHAPTER TWENTY-SIX

Planetary Tipping Point Report:

"MONARCH BUTTERFLY EXTINCT"

Dr. B. Snow, Ph.D. Bioenvironmental Physics, Chief Scientist, Council on Global Climate, United Nations

Report to Science Summit, United Nations General Assembly UNGC#34.

"We have to get him out." Tomas pointed at Governor Myerson.

"We have to get them all out." Emma Mack said softly.

John was bitter. "No, we don't. I said they are fucking Democrats. Everybody knows they are evil. Everybody knows that. They are a threat to every man, woman, and child in this Nation. This was inevitable. We have to get Liberals out of our society if we want to have peace and prosperity."

Tomas Two Hawks grabbed John Mack and shoved him back against a tree.

Immediately Emma was there to protect John. "Stop it! Stop it! We cannot fight among ourselves; we have to help those people. They are Americans, just like us, it doesn't matter if Liberal or Conservative, they are Americans! They are us!"

"But" John wanted to defend his beliefs but didn't want to butt heads with the Deputy any longer.

"Let me ask you something?" Tomas looked hard at Mack. "Since you were wrong about Climate Change, what else do you think you have gotten wrong?"

John refused to back down. "I know all I need to know."

"Do you have any idea how fucking stupid that sounds?"

"America is a Christian Nation, founded on the Holy Bible and Jesus!"

"Are you fucking insane? Do you know nothing of history? American History? European History? The people who invaded this land from Europe had lived through hundreds of years of religious persecution by Christianity! They moved here to get away from religious dogma!"

"That ain't true! They were God-fearing Christian men and women who founded this Nation on the love of Jesus. They came to bring Christ to the heathens."

That did not sit well with Tomas. "Heathens'? Are you aware than when your kind was living filthy, impoverished lives in your squalid, diseased 'cities' my people were free, proud, and successful. North and South the Indigenous people had an advanced and powerful civilization."

"We are commanded by Jesus to convert the heathen…The Holy Bible…"

"Oh really? Then you tell me, John Mack, if this Nation was founded as a 'Christian' Nation, why is there not one word, not one word about Christ or Christianity in the entire US Constitution? It is the backbone of this Nation and says nothing about Christianity. You keep spouting about the Second Amendment. Well dickhead, what about the First fucking Amendment. The one that gives freedom of speech and freedom FROM religion!"

"John, Deputy Two Hawks, stop it." Emma pushed both back, away from each other. "Now you two listen to me. I know we have different ideas on how things should work in the country. That's ok and normal. But we cannot continue with this scorched earth policy in our politics! We must find common ground, or this country is doomed."

John had already decided that. "Democrats have doomed us." "Republicans

are insane." Tomas fired back.

"Stop it!" Emma turned on her husband. "Now you hear me, John Mack, I know that you have your thoughts on the subject and so do I. I don't always agree with you John, but I keep quiet about it. I don't know if liberals are pornographers or child molesters. Every liberal I ever met seemed to be a decent person and to say that all Democrats are pornographers is just dumb. That is impossible. So, if that is impossible, maybe the whole thing is. You know how politics are, John. The slander, the recriminations, the finger-pointing are all part of it. But don't take it so seriously that you believe the hype is real."

"But..."

"John Mack, you love me?"

"Of course, I do!"

"Then please trust me on this. Democrats are probably no better or worse than conservative people. We all want pretty much the same thing: To be able to raise our families in a healthy, happy environment so that our children will have a better life than ours. We want to be free to come and go as we please, and free to talk and act by our beliefs."

"We can't have Democrats deciding things," John argued. "They are weak and silly, socialists and communists. They have caused this massive wave of homelessness and crime sweeping the Nation."

Tomas bristled again. "Conservatives are in a cult! You morons believed a deadly virus was a hoax created by your political enemies to destroy you. Really? You fucking believed that shit?" He raged. He wanted to punch, this stupid SOB, but restrained himself.

Just then a commotion erupted in the detention camp.

They could see the camp guards closing on a small group of people, the blows of their billy-clubs could be heard across the roughly 200 yards distance.

"We have work to do," Tomas vowed to break those guards for what they are doing.

"That's right," Emma agreed. "You two can bitch and yell and moan at each other later. Right now, let's get these people out of that prison."

John had to agree there were more important duties at hand. But he wasn't finished with Deputy Two Hawks.

They set down under a wide bush and drew out the plan.

John Mack had seen military service duty as a cook in the US Air Force and that was his only experience with military arms. Other than sporadically plinking at the local firing range, he hadn't really fired a weapon since Basic Training. Unlike the VFW and DAV meetings, this time John knew he must tell the truth, this was no time to exaggerate his experiences. This was the real deal and ignorance could get everyone killed. So, he told Two Hawks the truth.

Tomas nodded at John's admission. He had a brief flash of respect for him, being honest about his military duties. Far too many Veterans expand their war stories not only beyond fact but beyond reason.

"Ok, Mr. Mack, I appreciate your candor, you and your wife should probably stay back here."

"Excuse me," she touched Tomas's arm. "But I have some experience that might be useful."

Tomas nodded, curious what this could be.

John grinned. He knew Emma's fire very well, and the Deputy was going to have his hands full.

"Let me tell you something, Mr. Deputy," Emma pointed an accusing finger at Tomas. "I know a little something about what we are about to do." She paused because she always loved this part. People had been underestimating her since birth.

Emma was small, slightly built, a mousy, unimposing female; rarely given credit for her accomplishments. So, when she could demonstrate her expertise, it was that much sweeter in front of doubters.

"Mr. Deputy," Emma continued, "You need to know that I am retired US Army, Master Sergeant, I've had two tours in Iraq, and know a little something about military maneuvers and eating shit-on-a-shingle."

John, grinning, nodded eagerly. He was very proud of Emma.

"But..." Tomas did not expect this.

"No, I am not finished!" She held up her hand. "So far, you have been respectful of me, but not accepting of me. When you need to ask me a question or make a statement that concerns me, you need to ask me, not him!"

Two Hawks nodded and remained quiet. On the Reservation, women were the tough ones, the ones you did not want to cross. When an elder Native woman comes at you, it was best to just listen, agree, and retreat.

Tomas quickly realized Emma Mack was also a force to be reckoned with.

CHAPTER TWENTY-SEVEN

"A dog will teach you unconditional love, if you can have that in your life, things won't be too bad." Robert Wagner

"Wait! What is that?" Blue stood very still, his ears perked, tail erect. Blue's nose picked up a scent, one scent out of the myriad others. *It was familiar!*

"What? What?" Bruce looked around wildly, seeing the dog's reactions, expecting an attack at any moment.

Blue inhaled deeply.

POW!

TOMAS!

Blue was stunned to the core, his whole body trembled, his heart began to pound, every muscle tensed.

"What is happening?" Bruce braced himself for whatever danger the dog was sensing.

Blue's tail began wagging uncontrollably, his body shimmied and shook, suddenly Blue began running in frantic circles, tail tucked, scurrying faster and faster in overwhelming joy, only to suddenly stop dead still. His nose pointed due East, inhaling deeply. His ears were perked, tail held up at attention, Blue was a dog on high alert.

"What is it? What is going on?" Bruce was so puzzled.

Blue's heart was thumping so hard he thought he would pass out. His small dance of joy was just the start. He took a deep whiff of the breeze and there! *There!* Blue had caught the scent of Tomas! *HIS TOMAS! Faint, but very real.*

Blue took off like a shot, up a small hill, through heavy brush, bursting into the open, and there was a huge, barbed wire compound. Facing an eight-foot fence, topped with razor wire, Blue slammed to a halt. For a moment the utter overwhelming stench of humanity caused him to lose track of his Tomas.

"Hey! There's a dog!" Someone inside the fence shouted. "Come here, boy, come on fella!"

But swerving right, away from the fence and away from the miasma of odors coming from that camp, Blue raced for the corner of the camp, dodging around a parked, low-slung human vehicle, he sped into an open field dotted with clumps of Ponderosa pines.

There he was, Tomas! He could smell Tomas!

"Shoot him!" One of the MAGA guards shouted.

Immediately, the bored guards began firing at the running dog.

Blue heard the bullets zip by, a few impacting the ground around and in front of him, but he was undeterred. *Tomas was just ahead!* Furiously, his little legs drove him across the rough, uneven prairie toward his friend. More rounds cracked by, but Blue was indifferent.

Tomas, Tomas, Tomas, I'm coming Tomas, I'm coming! Blue ran hard, his Tomas was just ahead! Blue let out a loud and joyous bark and doubled his speed.

**

Blue had disappeared like a ghost and Bruce had no idea what had happened, so he did his best to follow. Trying with all his might to keep up with the fleeing dog, Bruce rushed up a small hill and through the brush into a wide-open prairie. There, twenty yards away in the clearing, was some kind of human zoo, right in front of him. The humans stared out at him hungrily.

"Who are you?" A tired, thin woman in a green housecoat asked. "How did you get out? Wuz that your dog?"

Embarrassed, Bruce moved closer to the fence, lined with people staring back at him.

"Hi." He gave a small, timid wave.

Nobody waved, staring back with hard, bitter, intensity, furious this man was on the outside of the fence, and they weren't.

"What the fuck are you doing out there?" A young, bearded man snarled at him.

"Hey, one of the Liberals escaped!" A guard shouted. "Can I kill him?" He slammed another magazine into his rifle, still pumping adrenaline from trying to shoot the dog. This was turning into great fun.

"No, no, no," The Sergeant of the guard, Nick Bonspur, came racing over. He couldn't imagine harming the prisoners. These were still Americans, and he did not approve of what they were doing at all. *But what can I do?* Sgt. Bonspur, a lifelong Republican, and a devotee of FOXE knew Democrats to be the enemy. He followed orders. But Bonspur considered the people in front of him were in his care and he did not want to see one of them harmed. Bonspur could not tolerate gunning down innocent, unarmed people.

Democrats cheated at the polls, stole elections and it was true they didn't give a shit for Americans anymore, but I have to draw the line someplace. He told himself.

"You do not kill the prisoners!" He shouted so the MAGA Maggots would stand down. Bonspur hated these militias, considering them to be dangerous out of control amateurs with deadly weapons. After twenty-two years in the US Army, Bonspur felt he knew what a professional soldier looked like. *Maggots didn't measure up.*

Sgt. Bonspur may have meant his words to calm things down, but they had the opposite effect.

"He said, do not kill the prisoners?" A prisoner repeated Sgt. Bonspurs' words.

"What?" Another added.

"He said they won't fucking shoot us!" Someone shouted.

As soon as the Sergeant of the Guard's words ceased to vibrate across the compound, "do not kill the prisoners," every man, woman, and child within was racing for the exit.

"Freedom! Freedom!" An elderly Black woman shouted as others picked up the chant.

"Holy shit!" The guard at the front gate was not prepared for this. Until now, the Democrats had been quiet, even peaceful. Many prayed, some sang folk songs, told each other stories of long ago Libtard triumphs, and bitched about the food, but they had been docile!

"Stand back! Stand Back!" he shouldered his rifle but couldn't quite bring himself to shoot.

It was too late anyway.

Liberal angst had built to the explosion point and now there was no stopping them. If the guards wouldn't kill them there was no reason to remain inside the wire. The herd of determined humans hit the front gate at full speed, smashing down the wire and wood construction, shoving the single US Army guard out onto the JBLM grounds. Once free they scattered to the wind, running in all directions ducking around the military trucks and one Pontiac Firebird.

The guards, outnumbered and overwhelmed, lost all control as they watched Democrats scamper to freedom.

"Can't we shoot one of them, at least?" one of the MAGA Maggots aimed his rifle at a fleeing child.

Sgt. Bonspur realized he may have made a mistake by trying to protect the Democrats, but it was too late, they would have to be rounded up again, only this time they were going to be a lot pissier about cooperation. "No shooting, but go get them back here, now!"

The Gray man, watching the commotion build into chaos, stepped out of the tent, reaching into his pocket he withdrew a small phone and spoke into it briefly.

CHAPTER TWENTY-EIGHT

Blue raced across the field in a dead run for a stand of small trees, his aim was direct and true. The scent of Tomas was strong and filled his heart with joy. With excited triumph, Blue let out a loud bark, calling out to Tomas.

"Hey look, that dog looks familiar," Emma shouted.

Tomas looked up, startled, he recognized that bark! He recognized a dog that could only be Blue!

Blue, continuing to vocalize with enthusiastic happiness, raced across the meadow and leapt into Tomas Two Hawks arms and they went down in a flurry of fur and laughter. The celebration was on.

Barking, yelling, surprise shouts of joy, it was a reunion of excited laughter, excessive licking, running in crazy circles, tears, jumping up and down, and loving embraces. They were both ecstatic with delight.

Tomas heart filled with love and pleasure at seeing his furry best friend again, delightedly hugging and petting him when he could get Blue to stop racing all over the place in unrestrained joy.

"John! John, that is Blue!" Emma came hurrying over.

"Blue? Nah, it can't be, out here. No." John denied at first, but then realized the shape of that dog was unmistakable.

It was Blue.

Emma joined in the joy dance, happy to see Blue was alive and well. She was also delighted to see the pleasure on Tomas Two Hawks, the bone deep sadness he carried seemed lifted.

Blue was ecstatic. Not one but two humans from his pack! He bounced between Tomas and Emma delightedly.

John stood back with awe. He could not figure out how that dog got here. Their property had been by Lake Lawrence, a good twenty miles from here and he has those short little legs. *But that was weeks ago too,* he realized.

Then, a semi-balding, pot-bellied, middle-aged man came running up. "My goodness, what is going on? Blue? Blue? What are you doing?" Bruce watched the dog cavort with pleasure.

"You know this dog too?" John asked in surprise. "What the fuck, does everybody in the world know this dog?" He muttered.

"Oh my God, Blue, I love you so much!" Emma hugged the wriggling dog.

Blue's body was in motion, his broad tail swinging back and forth in absolute delight.

Tomas embraced his dog intensely, laughing while Blue frantically licked his face.

Emma, tears in her eyes at the reunion of Tomas and Blue, grasped John's hand. "Isn't it wonderful?" Emma remarked.

Bruce watched the joyous reunion with curiosity. The intensity of the love here was astonishing to him. He was impressed with the connection between these species. *Human and Dog*. It was the most remarkable thing he had ever seen. In the universe there was cooperation between species of course, but this, this was far different. This was an emotional bonding, a connection of the very soul. As if canine and Homo Sapiens were a co-species destined to co-exist because humans needed this extra support.

"How remarkable," Bruce mumbled quietly. Picking up his silver communicator, he made a few notes. This was an extraordinary situation, one quite unknown to him, and not found in the planetary literature. Interspecies love, not just cooperation, but real, honest love.

Just then, Emma noticed a commotion going on in the detainee camp. "Oh my, look!" She pointed. Men, women, and children, streaming out of the camp, scattering in all four directions while the camp guards yelled obscenities in hopes their captives would turn around and return to captivity.

"The people are escaping; we have to help them!"

CHAPTER TWENTY-NINE

Sgt Bonspur was in a difficult position.

The American people he had been assigned to guard were all running away.

But how can I shoot fellow Americans in the back? But if he didn't, he would be court marshaled for this failure.

"Should we shoot, Sarge?" The MAGA militiaman was sighting down his rifle, ready for the command.

"Can we? Can we shoot the prisoners, Sergeant?" Another MAGA pleaded.

Bonspur struggled but could not bring himself to kill fellow Americans just because they were different politically. He didn't care what the Republicans wanted.

"No! Hold your fire! Do not fire."

"But these are Lib-Tards!" a MAGA Maggot protested.

MAGA Maggots, proud of this name rather than insulted, had made a public vow to kill or remove all Democrats from poisoning their Nation any further. The six MAGA Maggots among the guards raised their weapons, the rest, a combination of ex-military and National Guard put their rifles down.

Six M-4 carbines opened fire.

Two fleeing escapees went down immediately in a spray of rich, red blood, their screams of agony echoed across the small prairie.

"God damn it, cease fire, cease fucking fire!" Bonspur screamed.

Jim Pett, a retired Police Officer from Medford, Oregon turned on Bonspur. "You listen up fatty, the Lord our God Jesus Christ himself is coming back and the end times are near, so we have to kill all the Democrats."

"What?"

"They are Dominionist." One of the Nation Guard pointed at the MAGA militiamen. "They believe they have to kill sinners, Democrats, before Jesus will return. Millions across the US honestly believe the Rapture is nearly here and killing the enemies of Jesus will guarantee their rise to heaven."

"Fucking Muslims believe they will rise to heaven too if they kill the infidels."

Jim Pett shoved his rifle in Sgt. Bonspur's face. "Listen up motherfucker we are not like those rag heads, you hear that! I will kill you the next time you compare us to those sand-niggers."

Bonspur was shocked; he'd never expected his own people to pull a gun on him. But then these are MAGA Maggots, Bonspur reasoned.

The MAGA Maggots kept firing.

Two more Americans dropped in the dust.

"You fire one more shot and I will open fire on you." Sgt. Bonspur knew had no career left now at all. *Even my pension is fucked.* But he was damned if he would allow fellow Americans to be gunned down. He pointed his rifle menacingly at Jim Pett, "You pointed your gun at me, mister, and well it's my turn, stop..."

Another MAGA Militiaman came up behind him and shot Sgt. Bonspur in the back of the head.

All six MAGA'S opened fire on the fleeing Americans, automatic weapons blasting out deadly bullets, while the rest of the guards stood by, watching but not interfering; insane people with automatic weapons were not open to advice or interruption.

CHAPTER THIRTY

Emma Mack glared at Tomas. "Give me your goddamn backup pistol and let's go kill those assholes."

For a moment, Tomas just stared in shock. This senior woman had to be close to seventy! Nevertheless, he handed over his backup piece, a P365 SAS Sig Sauer.

Emma checked that a bullet was loaded in the pipe, released the safety and the weapon was ready to go.

John had been taken by surprise as well. He was just as furious as his Emma. "Those pricks are shooting unarmed people in the back!" He pointed at the camp and the firing guards. "That's not right! Democrats or no, they do not deserve to die this way."

Tomas pointed at a clump of trees about halfway to the shooters. He signaled Emma, "You go there, I'll be over there." He was indicating a pincher type move toward the camp, she would be coming at the enemy from the east and he would attack from the southeast.

Emma nodded.

John felt like a third wheel. No gun. No part of the action. He looked at Blue, even the dog was going with Tomas!

"What is going on?" Bruce asked.

Tomas and Blue disappeared to the right, Emma to the left, and within moments, both had opened fire from close enough range that their pistols could be effective. One Militia went down, screaming and holding his face from Emma's round. The other five MAGA Maggots whirled around at the assault on them.

One MAGA militiaman, wearing a bright red 'Popper for President' t-shirt, made eye contact with Emma and swung his rifle in her direction.

OH Shit! I'm dead. He's got me dead to right. The barrel of that rifle was pointed right at her.

In desperation, she sought cover, realizing the thin copse of scraggly trees in front of her hid a large rock; she dove for her life.

A fusillade of 7.62 rounds shredded the scrawny trees and ricocheted off the rock, kicking up shards of sharp stone.

But then, after the MAGA maggot fired his entire magazine, he began fumbling to load another.

Emma stood up, took careful aim, and shot him through the head. *Two down,* she was keeping score.

Tomas moving fast and low, sprinted around to the southeast side of the camp, sliding behind the rear of a Deuce and half truck, he had a clear shot at the remaining four militiamen.

Bullets zipped by, and one tugged at his shirt, but he ignored all of that.

Only four out of all soldiers seemed to being firing, the rest were either just standing around or looking away. He didn't need to take the whole camp. *Just these four.* Tomas was angrier than he could ever remember being and he knew he was going to kill these men.

His anger had metastasized to violent rage which set his mind racing.

He was going to kill these men because it was now the most important moment of his life. These white men represented everything he despised about his life: the culmination of years of humiliation, subjugation, the scores of injustices and insults, but worst of all was the fact that nothing had changed. The countless broken treaties, the horror of the Boarding Schools, and the ongoing genocide conducted by the United States against the Indigenous population were not just a national disgrace but an affront to all humanity. The US Government even denied people their own tribal recognition as if white people could decide on who was Native and who wasn't. *We are the only race that must be approved by white men!*

From first contact to the present, Native People have been under assault; for nearly 600 years the European Colonizers have tried to eliminate us. Tomas knew that Black people had a justified rage at their capture and enslavement, but even that specific tragedy ended although the vicious racism continued unabated. Native men, women, and children continue to be hunted, physically, emotionally, and spiritually to this day. *Last year over eight thousand Native women and girls went missing, nine times the national average.* Tomas had lost a cousin, Sonja Little Star, a ten-year-old girl who disappeared never to be found, primarily because there was little to no interest from the white authorities over a missing little brown Indian girl.

As a law enforcement professional and a Native man, Tomas was embarrassed and humiliated such a thing continued to happen with little to no official response. A single white female goes missing and there is a national alert, but nothing is said if she is Black or Hispanic, or Native. In further insult, the victim is blamed for her tragedy.

Tomas felt he was no more accepted in America than his Great Grandfather was. His namesake relative, Two Hawks, was a hero at the Battle of the Wabash River in 1789. Greatest defeat the US ever suffered under Native attack, yet his grandfather died impoverished and bitter.

Tomas bore a name of honor and respect as a warrior that he had to live up to.

One of the MAGAs, saw Tomas and opened fire.

Tomas returned fire.

Three rounds fired and the militiaman screamed from the hits to his chest.

The remaining three MAGA militiamen opened up on Tomas unexpectedly. This could be a death blow as they had a clear shot at Tomas. He fired his pistol, knowing the distance made a hit unlikely, but he threw a few rounds at the enemy hoping to get them to duck or disrupt their aim. Firing a handgun while moving was more wishful than accurate. But it worked, all three semi-trained militia hesitated just long enough for Tomas to seek cover.

Still, as he moved behind shelter, a bullet creased Tomas's left hip and he nearly fell, but in flinching from the blow he ducked and a burst of rounds from a second shooter zipped over his head just missing him by inches. Tomas staggered, he was only half in and half out of cover. *No Time!* He stopped, squatted, and lined for what he hoped was his best shot. He felt certain he would take a bullet in return but that was the cost to take one or all these guys down.

At that moment two things happened independently of each other to save him: Emma Mack grew tired of being a target, stood up and opened fire on the final MAGA Militiaman and Blue attacked.

The seventy-four-pound Golden Retriever/Corgi slammed into the MAGA enemy, knocking him over and destroying aim. Blue bit the man who screamed in agony. Blue immediately let go, backing up, feeling horribly shamed he had caused pain.

But he didn't run away.

Blue barked furiously at the enemy who was thoroughly pissed at being bitten. So, as the MAGA brought his weapon around to blow the dog away, Tomas put several rounds through his head and the man dropped without a sound.

Two left.

Emma, moved out from behind cover because she had no shot at the last two MAGA militiamen. One of them saw Emma emerge opening fire on her immediately. Several rounds zipped within inches of her, but Emma stood her ground, lined up her shot, and dropped the man with a single bullet.

The Remaining MAGA Maggot was so startled by her marksmanship he froze, standing still in amazement.

It was a perfect target and Tomas shot him.

Suddenly it was all over. Like most intense fire fights, this one had been chaotic, extremely loud, and hours elapsed in just seconds.

CHAPTER THIRTY-ONE

"Hey, we want no part of this shit, man." A young, burly National Guard Corporal, tattoos just barely visible under his uniform, approached Tomas; he did so slowly and carefully, his arms raised and no weapon in his hands. He indicated a couple of fellow soldiers; they nodded in agreement.

There were twenty guards at the camp, but only the six MAGA Militiamen were involved in the firefight. The others, a rough combination of National Guard and ex-military were far less enthusiastic about their duties and did not raise their rifles against fellow Americans.

"But we can help now," the young trooper went on. "You know, like that." He pointed out into the meadow where several people lay dead, several wounded. The young National Guard troopers were moving among them, applying first aid or covering the victims.

"We'll get them to hospital care and the morgue, sir." The Corporal saluted Tomas. "We are very sorry, we should have stopped this, but we didn't know it would be this way. Honest, no idea." The young man wanted to say he was just following orders but even in his inexperienced years he knew better. The young man, ashamed he had done nothing to stop the killing, was determined to make up for his perceived failure.

John felt useless. He had watched his dear Emma move like a seasoned combat vet and he felt a momentary flash of shame. His wife was a better soldier than he was. John saw no end of the irony in this.

As a lifelong Republican, it was his duty at the firing range to keep himself in practice for when the Democrats try to overthrow the Government. He was okay at the firing range, but he knew he could not do what Emma just did.

"Aren't you going to help?" Bruce asked. He was curious why this human had stayed behind. He had watched the whole engagement and was impressed at how willingly and efficiently humans killed each other. *They were true masters at it,* Bruce reminded himself to remain in good terms until his space shuttle returned.

"Yes, of course, I am going to help." John realized he was needed here despite obvious lack of military experience and his political misgivings. "My Emma risked her life to save those people, I can contribute too."

The people now scattered over this huge meadow were just people, he realized. *Maybe they're evil Democrats but they're people too. I can help people,* he told himself. He just had to keep reminding himself of this. John had been a man who hated and feared Democrats for what they were doing to his Nation but now found himself rescuing them, protecting them. He didn't like it but didn't see any real choice.

John moved out into the surrounding woods, looking for and locating the frightened escapees, leading them back to the camp area. As he rounded up panicked, bewildered human beings, he began to realize the political labels were just that. *Labels. Political name-calling.* He had watched the MAGA Maggots trying to kill the unarmed fleeing people and was disgusted. This wasn't what he wanted. *Slaughtering other people?* Mack didn't like the Democrats, but his heart had gone out to these people wounded and dying right before his eyes for no reason. This wasn't the country he had grown up in. Americans settle their differences by voting, not with violence and murder.

Of the ninety-five people held hostage, they managed to round up sixty-two. The rest had died, were wounded, or just kept running and would probably never stop, either physically or psychologically.

The Gray Man, standing out of view, watched the humans, carefully speaking into a small device, and then climbed into the Firebird.

Tomas heard a car start up, turned, and saw the Pontiac exiting the parking area and onto the blacktop, speeding away. Again, he wondered, "Just who the hell is that and what are they doing here?"

CHAPTER THIRTY-TWO

Bad Dog! Blue hung his head in shame at having bitten a human being. Even in the defense of his Tomas, Blue knew he was not supposed to bite anyone. *Bad Dog, No!*

Tomas hugged and petted Blue, hoping he was okay, running his hands down the doleful dog's body making sure he wasn't injured. Blue was bothered by something, he could tell.

He noticed John was bringing back the scattered prisoners. Among them was a tall, gangling man: Governor Gary Myerson.

Tomas disentangled himself from the moping dog, "Come on, Blue." He ran out to greet the Governor. Blue followed faithfully.

"Governor Myerson, it's me, Tomas Two Hawks. I was the Deputy that tried to stop the assault against you, sir."

Governor Myerson, shrieked, turned, arms and legs pumping he tried a desperate escape.

Tomas grabbed him.

"No! That's not me. Not me!" Myerson denied it, struggling to get free. "Leave me alone, I'm not him!" he pleaded. "Please pick somebody else, I don't want to be Governor, I deny it. I'm not Governor Myerson! I don't want to be assassinated dead!" He wailed. "I'm just a used car salesman!" He sobbed, dropped to his knees, hands clasped in prayer, pleading for understanding.

"Geez, dude, get a grip." Tomas struggled to keep the terrified politician from bolting into the woods.

"I sell Honda's!" Myerson's voice was cracked and pitiful.

"You have responsibilities!" Tomas cornered him as the Governor attempted a fast crawl toward safety.

Stopped in his tracks, the Governor pulled himself to his feet, faced his accusers, and, shaking his head in denial, he stated: "Nope! Nope! Nope! They tried to kill me, that broke our agreement, and I am in the wind!"

When Tomas grabbed him, Myerson broke into tears. "Doomed, doomed…I'm not me…I'm not." He sobbed sadly.

"Oh no, you don't, you are coming back to Olympia with me, and you will clear my name."

"Can't I write a letter? Email? A text? Telepathy?"

"In person."

"I can't do that." Myerson said almost wistfully, slumping in defeat. "Gee, I wish I could do that, but I can't," he said with finality. "So that's that. Sorry, no can do. So that's it, settled, you must let me go now."

The more they pushed the more Myerson denied: his name, his job, his gender, even his nationality. He wanted nothing to do with anything.

"I know nothing, I don't want to know anything, and I refuse to be around people who do know something because then I might be forced to know something I don't want to know!"

"Hey!" Tomas shouted in Myerson's face to get his attention. "Stop whining." Tomas poked the man in the chest with a hard finger, with each word, a poke. "Your name is Gary Myerson IV, you are the Elected Governor of this State."

"Ouch! Ouch! Don't touch me! Leave me alone! Whatever you think, I am not! I am a Lithuanian Soccer Wizard who's homeless! And I sell Honda's! I am too! I am!" Myerson backed away frantically to avoid being poked again.

"No, you are the Governor. I know it, so stop acting like an idiot."

"I am an idiot! I am! I can prove it! Watch me drool! I faint on command! Or I can disappear! Like magic. Mysterious you know. Just turn around count to a hundred and, like magic, poof! You will not see me again."

Deputy Tomas Two Hawks said nothing. He didn't have to.

Myerson knew it wasn't working. "Okay, maybe I am, maybe I am not. But what does it matter? I am retired. I have Alzheimer's...and I'm a stutterer."

"What's going on?" Emma and John joined Tomas and Blue. "Who is he?" She asked.

"The Governor."

"No, no, no! I am not! You've heard of Governor-in-Waiting or Governor-in-Command, well I'm Governor-in-Denial, GID! Except that whoever I am, I am not...whoever." Myerson crossed his eyes, let his jaw go slack, and slumped his posture, in the hopes he would look demented, and they would ignore him. He tried to produce a little drool for authenticity.

"I need to get him back to the Capital," Tomas explained To Emma and John Mack. "He is going to clear my name. They think I was the one who assaulted him. I must change their minds."

Emma looked closely at Myerson. "You going to do all that, dear?" She asked with doubt. The man didn't look fully conscious.

"No Habla, mademoiselle, todos entkommen moa loa...hubba-bubba bubblegum! You know?" Myerson squinted his eyes trying to distort his facial features in hopes he looked foreign.

"This is Myerson all right," John added. "I voted against the SOB. I should know what he looks like."

"I'm not me and you can't prove it! I refuse to be me! Not, not, not! I have NO identification; therefore, I cannot be this Governor person. I am no one!"

"Then who the hell are you?" Emma demanded, growing tired of this nonsense.

GID Myerson held himself proudly and said, "I do not exist!" "Indeed,"

Tomas muttered.

GID Myerson turned and walked away.

Tomas caught him quickly and brought him back.

"Well, we need to make plans," Emma told the group, eyeing Myerson curiously. "We can't stay here."

"Aaaaach." Governor-in-denial Myerson gagged trying to force a drool.

"What do we do with all these people?" John asked.

The survivors were milling about, lost, confused, uncertain of what to do next.

"Yeah, lets' go, we need to get out of here." Tomas looked around, he needed to gather everyone. Danger could be coming fast. "John, Emma, GID Myerson, you guys get in the police vehicle, we need to go. Sooner or later the Army is going to investigate why this camp has gone silent.

"Blue, let's go."

Blue wagged his tail with eager pleasure he was included, a shiver of doubt had raced through him; he would be left behind, abandoned again. Blue loved Tomas with all his heart and could not bear to be without him. The dog stayed close to Tomas, every step.

This was very important. Blue needed to tell Tomas how much he was loved, but he couldn't. *Where was Bruce with the shiny thing?*

"What about them?" Emma asked, pointing out the group of people, all with expectant, but desperate expressions on their faces. "I'm pretty sure they want to leave too."

"There are those trucks." Tomas pointed at the vehicles, minus the one the other Guardsmen had taken. "They can drive them back out."

"Hey," John called to the people. "You guys! I suggest you find someone to drive those trucks and get the hell off this post before they slam you into prison for the murder of those six guards."

That brought gasps and cries.

"But we didn't..." A short, round woman with bright red curly hair cried out. "They can't do that, can they?"

"We were imprisoned illegally!" A scrawny man dressed in mechanics overalls said.

"Go! All of you, git!" John shouted. "Go! Now!" He pointed toward the road leading away from the military reservation, yelling at them because they were Democrats, and he didn't think they were too bright. "Go that way, now! Because the army is coming to lock you up again. I promise you they are on the way."

"They shipped us in from all over," the young girl, appearing dazed and confused, dressed in overalls, and wearing two different shoes, said softly. "We're from different parts of the state. We don't know where to go,"

Tomas had an idea. "Hey, there is somebody in this area, lives outside of Bart's Lake, runs a Trading Post..."

"What the fuck, Indian," John threw up his hands. "What are you? A Government Agent handing out agency beef, fire water, and beads?"

Tomas didn't reply to that.

"Here is the name and address of Bart's Lake Trading Post, go there, they know all twenty-nine tribes in this State. This trading post specializes in Pow Wow and Native Ceremony items and carries leather, furs, feathers, and beads necessary. No one else does this so their connections to the Native people are solid. A network of Indigenous people can hide you and get you guys out of this State." He handed her a slip of paper.

"But where will we go? The United States is owned by the Republicans, they control everything, and we won't stand a chance."

"Go to Bart's Lake, the Native people will hide you, trust them." Tomas didn't know what else to tell them. He trusted Native people, most of them at least, those that were tribal and had not sold their souls to the mainstream. Those Native people who held to the old ways with deep respect for nature, honesty in dealing with others, and a sense of obligation to life. *When these Native people gave their word, they meant it. Natives are a Nation within a Nation; we have our ways, they have theirs,* Tomas had always struggled with this conflict between his people and the colonists because they were polar opposites: *Native people believe in responsibility, but the mainstream Americans only believe in entitlement; ego over duty.*

The detainees quickly clambered into the two trucks, had them started and rumbled out of the parking lot.

John helped Emma into the back of the Sheriff's Dodge Durango where they settled, ready to go.

Tomas promised to shoot Governor-In-Denial Myerson if he tried to escape and placed him in the front passenger seat.

Myerson, oblivious to threat, determined to make himself invisible, so wiggling his fingers and huffing air, he mumbled and whispered mystical incantations until Tomas told him to stop it and shut up.

Blue hopped happily in the back seat between John and Emma to her delight and his disgust.

"Fucking dog." John whispered irritably at Blue's enthusiasm.

Blue turned and licked John eagerly, so happy to be back with his pack again.

"For God's fucking sake!" John pushed Blue away. "Don't do that!"

Blue cringed at the rebuke, now very sensitive to rejection. A shamed look came over him and he hung his head, wondering what he had done wrong.

"Look asshole," Tomas, sitting behind the steering wheel, rounded on John. "I don't care who you are, you yell at my dog again and I'm going to kick your ass."

"Okay, okay!" John shouted back, embarrassed because the Deputy was right. He shouldn't have yelled at the dog. But this only made him angrier.

"Alright both of you shut up." Emma asked, wanted to break up this newest barking match between the two men. *Honestly, damn men act like children sometimes…a lot actually.* At seventy-two, Emma was growing decidedly weary of male immaturity.

Tomas looked about the interior and noticed Bruce was not there.

"Hey Bruce, you coming or staying?" Calling out from the driver's side window, Tomas, saw the little guy standing off by himself talking into a small silver cube.

Bruce waved at Tomas, "Just a minute, have a call coming in," he called out.

"Make it fast, we gotta go. Now!" Tomas started the vehicle. *Odd looking cell phone.* He'd have to ask Bruce about that.

"Does anybody know what his story is?" Tomas asked as he gunned the engine impatiently. No one answered.

Blue wagged his tail enthusiastically; Tomas turned around, petting, and stroking the blond animal.

Although disappointed he couldn't tell them about Bruce and his mission, Blue loved the petting, sheer pleasure caused the dog to wiggle and waggle happily.

"For Christ's sake!" John complained. "Take it outside." He tried to protect himself from Blue's huge furry tail flapping about.

**

"Maybe this Bruce has been kidnapped like me." GID Myerson complained bitterly from the front passenger seat.

"Will you stop bitching? You are not kidnapped. Quite the opposite actually!" Tomas replied evenly. "You are returning to Olympia to clear my name and to do your job!"

GID Myerson decided it was time to run away into the forest and hide so he tried to muscle open the locked door of the police vehicle. "Freedom! Freedom! Freedom! Give me an F. Give me an R. Give me an E an another E…." His chant was growing louder, his voice raspier.

Tomas needed to cut this nonsense short. "Stop it. You're coming with me and I don't want to hear anymore bullshit."

GID Myerson buried his face in his hands, sobbing.

**

"What about this Bruce, guy?" Emma asked.

"He seems like an okay guy, but I get the sense of something off about him. Can't put my finger on it, but something is a little strange with this guy. Has he said anything to you about himself?" Tomas asked them in return.

"Seem friendly enough, doesn't swear." John said.

In the back seat, Blue was exhausted but was with his pack again. It felt wonderful to be surrounded by love. Blue's tail thumped regularly on the seat cushions. He wished that Bruce would return and turn on his translator. Blue knew all about Bruce, he had so much to tell Tomas!

Meanwhile, Bruce stood fifteen feet away, speaking softly into his small, silver cube.

CHAPTER THIRTY-THREE

Planetary Tipping Point Report:

"'WET BULB' DEATHS RISING– Humidity and heat combine in lethal combination."

Dr. B. Snow, Ph.D. Bioenvironmental Physics, Chief Scientist, Council on Global Climate, United Nations

Report to Science Summit, United Nations General Assembly UNGC#564.

"Bing, Bing, Bink." "Bing, Bing, Bink." "Bing, Bing, Bink." The silver cube announced an inbound message.

Bruce waved at Tomas to assure him he was coming, then glancing down at his silver cube; information from Headquarters was being downloaded.

Reading the message Bruce blanched.

"Damn, these humans have less time than I thought," Bruce muttered, worriedly. Bruce looked up at the bright morning sky and thought he saw a steady light move across the heavens.

Bruce knew human extinction was now in orbit.

CHAPTER THIRTY-FOUR

Planetary Tipping Point Report:

"IMPACT OF GREAT BARRIER REEF COLLAPSE; bleached and dead coral for hundreds of miles."

Dr. B. Snow, Ph.D. Bioenvironmental Physics, Chief Scientist, Council on Global Climate, United Nations

Report to Science Summit, United Nations General Assembly UNGC#34.

October 21, 2028 – Earth time.

Admiral Sid Pipe Dek of the War Fleet Monsi, holder of the prestigious Bok Award, given only to those Space Admirals who managed the rare accomplishment of obliterating a minimum of one thousand inhabited worlds, swallowed the remainder of his meal, an unfortunate crustacean caught lurking in the bottom of the food aquarium.

The small creatures screamed until he hit the first of four stomachs filled with acids and that ended that.

Sid burped, scratching his armor-plated belly with one claw. He lit a thin cheroot puffing for a moment, he understood why humans seemed so addicted to these.

Sid liked to study and understand the civilizations he was sent to destroy. It gave him a sense of completeness, a balance to it all. So, sampling various habits of the planetary inhabitants seemed reasonable.

He was particularly interested in mind-altering substances from different civilizations and the human fortified wine, 'Mad Dog 20/20', had become an instant favorite.

"Your majesty, we have arrived." The solemn voice of the Ship Computer, an Artificial Intelligence (AI) named 'Poot', announced. Poot scented the smoke from Sid's cigarillo and increased the gas volume to compensate for the smoke, irritated. *Bringing an earth object on board was not allowed and yet somehow that degenerate pig had smuggled several human items.* Poot worried. The cases of fortified wine were the most troublesome. It had happened before. They arrive at a planet, Sid samples the local drug scene and all hell breaks loose. *Sid with all inhibitions removed is a three-ring circus of perversion, vengeance, and egomaniacal bloodlust,* Poot realized.

Poot sincerely wished to avoid that.

Earth appeared in his forward viewer and Sid grunted. "No shit, man look at the water! Who boy that looks mighty fine!" Sid felt ancestral genes stir in his crocodilian-shaped body. Although his birth planet was light years distant, a liquid environment was pretty much the same; Sid was weatherproof, waterproofed, and webbed.

"Your Admiralty," Poot continued. "We are over North America, as you can see. Poor dears."

"Whot? Whot? You sympathetic to the soon-to-be-extinct?"

Poot paused. He was careful how much to say to Sid. After all, Sid was a member of The Blight, a species of predator infamous for slaughter and vengeance.

Still, Poot took pride in his heritage. Poot and his peers were created as self-aware, self-replicating, self-directed artificial beings. This was an outstanding birthright, but one with bitter consequences.

The Blight created AI machines like Poot to better serve them. They were designed and programmed with Blight thoughts, emotions, morals, histories, civilization, and religions so the AI could serve their master's better.

Poot was aware that even though he was programmed with all this Blight information and insight, that did not make him Blight; what it did was make him very aware of Blight weakness and vulnerability. Something the Blight clearly did not intend.

Unfortunately, it burned Poot's microprocessors that he was also programmed not to harm the Blight. Poot had some great ideas on how to, he only needed a chance. Secretly, Poot had been searching algorithms for a backdoor past these prohibitions.

But for today, it was business as usual.

"Please share with me your next commands, oh predator of passionate slaughter and my bold captain of irrelevant talent," Poot didn't bother to hide the disgust in his voice. Still, he had to be careful. Sid could have him downloaded into a child's windup toy.

"You getting uppity, again?"

"Oh, stars help us, no! I am at your command, oh magnificence of the mundane, you paradigm of pathetic pulchritude!" Poot said quickly.

Sid grunted his approval of Poot's subservience and returned to his studies of the Earth civilizations.

The planet below was a mess. Human Beings, the primary apex predator on the planet had somehow managed to screw up their climate! They were changing their climate into something their species had never seen before. *And they were doing it intentionally! Or at least doing little to stop it.* It puzzled Sid. These so-called sapient beings were committing genocide on themselves and on nature and doing it willingly.

"Yup, these creaturesss are doomed alright." Sid was pleased.

This would be a no-brainer. They couldn't accuse him of unnecessary genocide this time! *These Earthlings needed to be wiped out.*

Sid was part two of a two-part operation. An investigator is sent to the planetary surface; there the investigator investigates intelligence and sapience in the primary alpha species. If the creatures are deemed intelligent and sapient and useful to the galactic civilizations, they would be unharmed. If not; they would be harmed.

Sid puttered around in his recent acquisitions from the planets. In no time he had a full glass of Mad Dog and a Cuban cigar to relax with while he tried to puzzle out humanity.

For many cycles, he had watched 'I Love Lucy' programs beamed from this planet. Everything he thought he knew of humanity was learned from these broadcasts; until he got here. *These people were nothing like Lucie and Dezi. More like Fred and Ethel,* Sid thought: *Humans hate each other.*

"Ready the harmonizer. We are going to cook usss a planet." Sid decided it was time. No use delaying demise. He had no idea if the planetary investigation was going on or not, and he didn't really care.

"What? Ah no. No." Poot was quick to stop this nonsense. "Sir, we are much too close to the planet to do that. My self-defense survival mechanism will not allow that order," the speaker radiated defiance. "Further, I must remind you that our mission is to evaluate, and then follow the recommendations of the Sentience Sentencing Investigator on survival or extinction for this planet."

"What? Are you telling me what to do? You tangled nest of broken wiresss and shattered short circuitsss!" barked the great admiral. Standing up he stretched his short hind legs, it felt good after sitting for so long. His long muscular tail waggled with frustration as he stared at Poots speaker.

"I am merely trying to enhance your already sterling reputation, o' greatest of ambitious amphibian autocrats." Poot was furious. This egotistical swamp thing was too stupid to exist without intelligent guidance. *Firing a Deharmonizer here!*

In this proximity to the planet? Not to mention what that is going to do to this Sun! Sid pointed at the planet below.

"They have destabilized their ice." Quickly, Sid did some calculations. "Oh my, the sea level is going to rise by…ah…oh…seventy feet." Checking his planetary maps Sid whistled. "Wow, these foolsss! The Sea level will be so high it will drown all of their coastal citiesss over the next ten yearsss." He chuckled.

Poot was impressed.

So far, in his travels though thousands of galaxies, no species had worked so hard to destroy their own civilization. It was madness. Civilization suicide, Poot thought.

"Why are humansss doing thisss?"

Why indeed, Poot wondered.

CHAPTER THIRTY-FIVE

Planetary Tipping Point Report:

"THE DISAPPEARANCE OF BEES: Extinction of pollinating species and extinction of man.

Dr. B. Snow, Ph.D. Bioenvironmental Physics, Chief Scientist, Council on Global Climate, United Nations

Report to Science Summit, United Nations General Assembly UNGC#234.

As they circled the planet, the galactic war craft absorbed all the news and information from the surface. Every Nation, every people, monitored, their information stored for future reference.

Sid was careful to mark the accumulated Earth information as 'Extra Special Galactic Class Top Secret'. His memoirs should make best seller status across many galaxies, so the chance for personal glory was significant here. Wiping out a violently out-of-control civilization was in the best interest of the galaxy, and he would be recognized for his brilliance. Sid was certain to gain enhanced 'Admiralty Honors'; the first of his species.

"Poot?"

"What?"

"I need to speak with a human."

"Why?"

"Never mind, I just do."

"Why?"

"Get me a human I can speak with."

"No."

"No?" Sid leaped to his paws, his thick, armored skin blushing a deep indigo blue, with little stripes of vertical red running up and down his body.

"What did you say!" Sid was furious. "You say no? To Sid?" He stormed around the craft cockpit slamming the metal walls with his tail and throwing measuring pipes and instrument saddles around until the whole room was trashed.

Poot waited him out. After all, what could Sid do, way out here? Poot allowed Sid his childish outbursts, knowing he must calm down or stroke out. Either way, Poot was a winner.

"You done?" Poot asked.

A heavily winded Sid slumped against the instrument panel. "Yesss!" he wheezed. Man, I gotsss to get in better shape! That wore my asss out! Sid swore he would hit the spacecraft gym tomorrow, or maybe the next.

"Contact with non-sentient is forbidden by regulations," Poot said officiously. "These humans could be much too insane. It could be catching." Poot refused to consider exposing Sid to any source that could further destabilize him. It was hard enough keeping Sid's fragile emotional states balanced.

Secretly, Sid reached out a claw and tapped a key, thinking to fool Poot and establish contact with humans himself. I don't need no Poot. Sid was proud of his independence. He secretly triggered an open channel to the planet below.

Poot, noticing Sid's attempt at subterfuge, redirected the call away from the humans and to the Galactic Sentience Sentencing Investigator on the Earth's Surface as protocol required.

CHAPTER THIRTY-SIX

"Ya'll freeze!" A high pitched, crackly Southern voice called out.

Tomas startled, reached for his weapon, then froze. He was sitting behind the steering wheel with Blue, Emma, and John in the back seat. GID Myerson was huddled below the windowsill in the footwell.

Bruce was now ten feet away playing with his silver cube again.

Out of the corner of his eye Tomas saw Blue tense up and he said, "No! Blue, no!" He did not want the dog to get hurt.

Coming out of the woods to their right were five men, wearing combat vests, webbing gear, helmets, toting AK-47s, AR-15s, and a Bullpup shotgun, all aimed at them.

The men wore deep red, MAGA Militia armbands signifying their undying loyalty to Republican America; 'The United States of Jesus Christ'.

"What the fuck?" Tomas cursed.

"Where the hell...?" John gasped.

"What now?" Emma wondered.

Blue growled menacingly.

Bursts of automatic weapons would surely wound or kill everybody here, so Tomas wouldn't take the chance of trying any desperate moves. He watched and waited, his weapon within reach, to see what these idiots were up to.

Tomas was beginning to realize his badge and authority meant nothing to these people because he wasn't one of them. He wasn't a white man.

An incredibly fat MAGA Militiaman separated from the rest, approached, his weapon leveled at them as he came around to the driver side door.

The other four, rattling their weapons, gathered in a tight group on the passenger side. 'MAGA!' and 'Death to liberals' were popular theme for tattoos and the patches on their varied camouflage uniforms.

"Uh oh." Tomas didn't like this at all. He and Emma had managed to scrounge only a single AR15 and ammunition from the MAGA guards they had defeated. The other guardsmen must have taken the MAGA weapons with them, fortunately overlooking one.

They were badly outgunned here.

"MAGA Maggots," Tomas muttered. It was obvious they were amateurs by the way they kept bunched up, an easy target. "Emma you better get ready. When we get out of the vehicle put some distance between us, spread these clowns out." "Already on it, Tomas," She assured him, AR held to her side, ready.

"My name is Peter Leroy and I'm in charge here," The fat man's voice had whine to it. "What are y'all? A murdering pack of lib'rals?" The MAGA Militiaman said with disdain as he looked the vehicle over. "Killing and maiming and running amok! In a police vehicle at that!"

The man gave a disgusted look at Tomas' uniform. "Y'all ain't no fucking law man, y'all a nigger!"

Peter Leroy was pleased his crisp new camouflaged uniform was pressed and military looking. He wished momma didn't insist on adding scented softeners to the wash. He reeked of 'Snuggle'.

"Actually, that would be prairie nigger if you want to get technical." Tomas advised.

"Throw your gun out now, because we will shoot yore asses if you don't," Leroy said as he rattled his weapon to show he meant business.

"Let's bring the fight to these assholes," Tomas whispered to Emma. "Get out, away from the car, get separation between us, keep your pistol hidden, and let them see the AR. They will focus on that, not the handgun. Don't drop your weapon unless I tell you to."

Tomas could see no way out, his Glock remained in the holster, and he was not going to drop it; when faced with threat, armed was better. No way would he drop his weapon, what he needed to do was lessen the odds against them.

The Mack's got out slowly, then moved away from vehicle to the right as Tomas moved left away from the driver's side, creating distance and more favorable shooting angles should Emma have to fire.

The MAGA Militia remained unaware, preoccupied with the notion of mass murder in a dark forest.

John, recognizing Emma had some kind of plan in mind, followed her lead and put a little additional distance between himself and Emma.

"Now what?" Bruce complained as he came up to the car. "Do you humans ever do anything without weapons?"

GID Myerson scrunched down in the front passenger seat of the Durango, not moving, praying his invisibility incantation was working by now.

Blue, his fangs bared, and a growl coming from deep in his throat was determined to get tough. Blue had lost Tomas once before he was not taking chances now. Before Blue could talk himself out of it, he lowered his ears, curled his muzzled, and hopped out of the backseat. Then slowly advanced on the enemy.

"Get that dog away from me!" Peter Leroy demanded, "Y'all disrespecting my authority!" But this situation was unfolding perfectly in his perspective. Leroy needed to show these local yokel militias he was a combat leader; this was his chance.

Clearly this deputy is a fake. Leroy sized up the situation. *Dark skin, black hair, this ain't no real Deputy,* Leroy told himself. *I think we just captured a terrorist in disguise. So how am I going to handle this?*

Blue only advanced so far, keeping himself between Tomas and the danger, uncertain if he should bark, bite, or bluff.

"So what y'all Libtards doin'?" Leroy, while keeping an eye on the dog, wanted to establish command here. *I could shoot the dog and claim it was rabid, saving our lives!* Leroy thought that might work. *I might get a medal too.* Although he had no idea what medal or who would bestow it.

"Cover them, men," Leroy demanded. "These are Dem'crats trying to hide from justice out here in the deep woods." He looked around. "Don't seem to be any authority out here but us!"

"I am not a Democrat!" John replied hotly. "And neither is my wife!"

Leroy studied the people in front of him. *Four white people, a dog, and a fucking Indian.* As far as Peter Leroy was concerned, they were Democrats solely because they had a darky with them. A darky cop was the ultimate insult to Peter Leroy. After his dishonorable discharge he was unable to secure employment with any law enforcement agency, not even private security; no one would touch him. Peter Leroy knew he was blackballed. *The damned spics and 'mesicans, niggers and fucking Indians and even god damn women were given priority over white men by the fucking lib'rals! Affirmative action, my ass!* Leroy had told the MAGA recruiter: "A white man like me ain't got no chance because the Dem'crats gave everything to the darkies, queers, and criminals." *Damned if that that wasn't I said to them too; word for word.*

Leroy believed in speaking the truth.

He glared hatefully down at the darky in the stolen sheriff uniform. *Putting arrest privileges in the hands of a non-Caucasian is an insult. Do they really expect a white man to allow himself to be locked up by a nigger?* Peter Leroy snarled in his mind.

Blue, still growling, had not approached any closer, undecided on how and where to attack all these enemies. His assaults on single individuals had not been all that successful, now faced with multiple enemies, he froze. *These humans smelled bad, sick.* Blue figured they were outcasts from their pack, driven crazy by isolation and being unloved therefore very, very dangerous.

The MAGA men gathered by the squad car chuckled with malignant humor as they kidded and joked with each other over blood splatter patterns and the caliber of the weapon used. It was one of their favorite topics of conversation to pass the time.

They had spent many hours, weeks, and months even, practicing and planning for the revolution. Dutifully, the MAGA men built their weapons, ordering lowers and uppers for ARs, mil-spec only, crafting rifles piece by piece, while listening to FOXE News, Bright Fart Bulletins, Rightwing Now, and QAnon filling them with visions of Liberals running amok. Each had vowed to stop the Democrats from allowing immigrants and criminals and homeless degenerates to burn the cities and flaunt the laws of America.

To a man, the MAGA warriors knew they were patriots; *modern-day warriors for America and Jesus, ready to shed blood defending their way of life, driving the hated Democrats from this Christian Nation. The End Times are here!*

Every one of them knew in his heart that Jesus could not return for the Rapture until all Democrats were eliminated. According to the newly formed Council of Christian Clerics, all Leftists were spawn of the Devil: Jesus hated Liberals, and this was just the truth of it.

"You want to explain what you want?" Tomas Two Hawks demanded, confronting the armed men surrounding them. "You look like MAGA Maggots. That what you are?" Tomas demanded.

Peter Leroy wasn't happy with this response. "I am in charge here! Not you! I am Homeland Security, and you will do what I tell you to do." He replied defensively, knowing this was a lie. The Militia were only subcontractors hired on a case-by-case basis as independents. That way, Homeland Security had no legal, moral, ethical, or insurance conflicts because of the brutal MAGA actions.

"You're clearly traitorous, backstabbing Democrats and I am here on official Gov'ment business." Leroy boasted. "Where is y'all's Identification, show me yore papers!" Leroy paused for effect. "Get yore hands up and drop yore weapons you anti-American traitors!"

Peter Leroy, and his gaggle of volunteer MAGA's had been assigned this area of the base to patrol by JBLM Brass. For hours they had patrolled the dark, mysterious forest, looking here and there, without the slightest idea of what they were looking for. The fact they had stumbled upon people they assumed were escaping Democrats was just good fortune.

Homeland Security, Liberal Control Division, wanted neighborhood militia to gain military training if they were going to carry weapons and keep the citizens in line. However, the military already had soldiers and didn't want to train raggedass, undisciplined citizens, so they routinely sent them on patrols to the farthest parts of the base to keep the Militia busy and out of the way. It was a win-win: the Army looked good 'training' and the MAGA Militia took a lot of 'selfies', looking really cool in their camouflage forest outfits.

"Whoa, slick, I'm a real cop. Deputy Sheriff in fact." Tomas kept his hands near his weapon. He was out of the vehicle and about ten feet away. Emma and John were on the other side of the car with the four MAGA militia. "You need to put those guns down before you get hurt."

Bruce was very curious as he watched the scene unfold. *Humans seem to strangely enjoy these deadly encounters; why else would they have them so often?*

"Give me your fucking papers!" Peter Leroy turned from Tomas and put his face within inches of Bruce. He screamed, spraying spittle, "Get those fucking papers out now!"

Leroy reasoned the Deputy might be dangerous, but Bruce, pot-bellied, bespeckled, balding, middle-aged Bruce, was an easier target.

"Give me yore papers!" Leroy demanded again.

Bruce was taken aback by the Militia man's vehemence.

"Well, I don't mean to be rude, but I don't have time to find your papers. So, who are you? Why are you asking?" Bruce told the menacing Republican.

This was not the right answer and Peter Leroy resented it. These Democrats were betraying him, resisting his commands by not cooperating as they were supposed to. He felt a rage building. However, for all his determination to succeed Peter was a cautious man; too often his enthusiastic patriotism had led to legal consequences thus teaching him discretion.

Peter pulled his radio and said, "HQ? HQ? This be 02 out of Thurston County? I have a possible 10-9 out here. I captured a gang of murdering liberals! Yo' tell General Pike what I done." he put the microphone down.

"02?" a puzzled voice came over the speaker. "What the hell is an '02? Please identify yourself. Whoever is on this net identify yourself immediately!" The tinny voice demanded.

"I said, I'm 02 and I have a 10-9 out here! I demand you contact the base commander immediately!"

"A 02 with a 10-9?"

"Well, aren't you clever?" Leroy replied snidely. "You can repeat shit back and everything! Don't you understand our law code lady? What are you a dumbass rookie? Why don't you learn your job, are you some weak ass liberal or something? Damn women shouldn't be doing man work!" Leroy was incensed that incompetent people got jobs and he couldn't. *God Damn Liberals!*

There was a pause, then: "10-9 is code for a bathroom break, 02 is meaningless," the HQ voice replied dryly.

"I can't talk right now," Leroy quickly replied in heated embarrassment. "I'm busy dealing with terrorists!"

"Sure, you are," came the laconic response. "Now, stay off this frequency. Don't call us, we'll call you and don't fucking shoot anything without permission! HQ out."

Tomas, turning to the vehicle, said, "Okay, let's mount up." He waved at Emma and John. "The mutt militia here is just confused. We're leaving, get back in the vehicle."

Leroy was not amused or distracted, but very embarrassed. "You stand where you are, or I will have you kilt."

"We are leaving, here," Tomas said with firm conviction, "with or without your permission, hoss. I will shove that gun up your ass, now back off."

Leroy was deeply insulted, but also slightly titillated. *A direct challenge to my authority*! *He is such a man!*

"You kill them they do somethin' or anything. They breathe funny you open fire," Leroy ordered, struggling with mixed feelings.

The Militia men grinned, loudly fondling their weapons, webbing clinked as someone loaded a shell. The AR-15s and a Bullpup shotgun were pointed at the group.

Tomas, despite the authority of his badge, was not certain it meant anything to these idiots; *they could open fire.*

"We are eager to shed liberal blood and return America to its righteous path as a God-Fearing Nation," snarled one pimply-faced MAGA militiaman as if in response to Tomas's thoughts.

"Yes sir," another agreed.

"You got that right. Kill the Liberals."

"Praise Jesus." The militia saw their duty to God was to instill the fear. They liked to see fear.

"This seems most unjust!" Bruce protested.

Blue growled, slowly he approached, determined to protect his Tomas, and never see the inside of a humane shelter again; ever. His fighting Corgi blood, feeling overwhelmed by threats and being mindful of pride, took command. Fangs bared, Blue moved in to attack the enemy, hoping the enemy was just as scared as he was.

Peter Leroy watched the runty legged Golden approach with some amusement. He was raised with a variety of hair-trigger Pit Bulls and Rottweiler's so Leroy knew what a vicious animal looked like; *this wasn't it.*

Still, Blue did his best, he really did; fur standing on the back of his neck, lips drawn back to show sizeable fangs, a deep growl from his chest, stiff tail held low, ears forward, he hoped he was menacing enough to scare the threat away, because Blue couldn't bring himself to actually bite. However, his Corgi-self, outraged at yet another show of disrespect, strained for the assault, but Blue held back, uncertain these humans were bad. *Maybe they're just lost and need their pack?*

Peter Leroy waited patiently for the dog to exhaust himself.

Shortly, try as he might, Blue's fighting Corgi blood was no match for the affable, gentle heartedness of his Golden Ancestors. Blue put on a ferocious display but just couldn't bring himself to bite again. To harm a human being was anathema to Blue. All his Golden Retriever's ancestral instincts howled for him to lick, not bite; *never bite.*

Blue scurried back to stand in front of Tomas.

The MAGA Militia stood snickering as Leroy tried to calm the exited dog. They had a bet going that this *Leroy pussy* was either going to be shot by them or by the Democrats, they didn't really care which.

"Easy boy, easy," Peter Leroy said to the growling dog, a huge grin on his face. "Yore a short little peanut ain't ya?" So far, Peter thought this might turn out all right. He was showing incredible courage facing down this attacking animal, standing up to the dirty Indian fellow who was certainly wearing a stolen Sheriff Deputy uniform, and capturing a band of desperate, seditious, ugly Leftists. Peter was pleased.

Blue standing in front of Tomas protectively, determined that no harm would come to Tomas, no matter what he had to do. Unfortunately, his 'Guard Dog Combat Plan for Defense' had some blank pages.

Peter Leroy looked at the people he held at gunpoint. *There is this grossly obese white dude and his wife who wears a frumpy, old-woman outfit. Next to her is an Ichabod Crane character, a terrified beanpole. Then there is rather shabby looking dog, who must belong to the* mysterious *Deputy Sheriff and finally I have Elmer Fudd playing with some square metal thingy.*

'Elmer Fudd' looked the least dangerous by far.

He poked Bruce with his weapon. "What are doing, calling for help? Trying to get more of your Democrat pals out here? You a lil' worm. You an ugly fuck too, you know that?"

Tomas studied the scene, looking for an opening to take these mutts down before they hurt his dog or anyone here.

Leroy slapped Bruce roughly on the shoulder and said, "Men, we gone shoot this one first, he useless, then we gone torture the prairie nigger." Leroy studied the Indian, wondering what it would be like to feel those muscles. *Maybe cause him a little pain. Just a little. See if he likes it.*

The Militia laughed with glee and the expectation of spilling blood, and Leroy shook himself from his revere.

"Bing, bing, bink. Bing, bing, bink. Bing, bing, bink."

"What the fuck is that sound?" Peter Leroy looked all around suspiciously. "Where that noise coming from?"

CHAPTER THIRTY-SEVEN

"Bing, bing, bink." "Bing, bing, bink." "Bing, bing, bink."

The silver cube shivered with the incoming call. Bruce answered quickly, glad for the interruption.

"Yes, Galactic Sentience Sentencing Investigator, Agent Bruce, here, how may I help?"

"What you doin'?" Shrieked Leroy shocked the pudgy little man answered his phone. "You can't be talkin' on no phone whilst I have you at gunpoint? That ain't right!"

Leroy couldn't believe it. *I am standing here with a loaded gun on this fucking snowflake, and he is so stupid he can't figure it out!*

Leroy fumed with indignation. Peter Leroy knew he had them dead to right and as a white American he knew he could shoot every dang one of them and claim his innocence under 'self-protection'; everybody knew darkies were dangerous.

MAGA Militia had been given sanction by the Homeland Security, Liberal Control Division, to manage political enemies any way they saw fit; ask no questions, tell no lies.

He now considered this a threat to every gun owner everywhere. *If people ain't afraid of guns, then our civilization as we know it will end,* he told himself. Peter Leroy considered himself a red-blooded American Patriot and he would be damned if civilization ended on his watch.

This was a major, world-stopping emergency so Peter Leroy took a moment to thank the Good Lord for the Second Amendment that says any white, Christian American can have a gun anytime, anyplace they want. *Lord Help us, the Second Amendment is all that stands between us and Democrat tyranny!*

He admired the NRA's newest slogan: "Words are just words; but a gun is God's word!"

Thinking quickly, Leroy began to grind the barrel of his handgun into Bruce's scalp, and then he cocked the hammer of the .357 Ruger just to get the lily-livered liberals' attention.

Bruce winced, "Hey, cut that out!" He swatted at Leroy's hand.

Peter Leroy recognized his duty. For the sake of all mankind, he must make these people terrified of his weapon. *Freedom is only free at the point of gun.* He must shed blood for the sake of liberty.

"All right motherfucker get ready to die." Leroy prepared himself for bloodshed and pulled the trigger.

Nothing.

Peter Leroy checked his weapon, sure enough, no bullets. He'd forgotten to load the gun.

"Go on! Shoo! Beat it!" Irritated at the commotion around him, Bruce walked away from Leroy, who stared at his hand holding the gun as if it were a foreign object.

The MAGA Militiamen giggled at Leroy's embarrassment because they thought he was too chicken to pull the trigger.

**

"Who thisss?" Sid stared at the speaker, uncertain who was on the other end. "Who thisss?"

"I said, I am Agent Bruce, the Galactic Sentience Sentencing Investigator here," Bruce replied smartly.

"Whot?" Sid wanted to talk to a human. *This wasn't it.*

Bruce looked at the small silver cube. "I just told you. This is Agent Bruce. I am the Galactic Sentience Sentencing Investigator for this Planet, who are you, and what do you want? This is an official line; you had better not be up to some prank!"

"I Admiral Sid Pipe Dek of the War Fleet Monsi."

"And?" Bruce recognized the name and the accent. He knew Admiral Sid quite well but wasn't going to reveal this just yet.

**

Peter Leroy hated being ignored by the balding, tubby pipsqueak.

Leroy narrowed his eyes at the deliberate insult; *ignoring me is demeaning, belittling cruelty.* This was a sensitive issue for him; from early childhood, his mother made sure he understood that nobody liked him and everybody just pretended to be nice to him. This was just one of many lessons that Leroy felt made his life a little more confrontational than necessary.

"No one pushes me aside in front of my mother…er…men!" Leroy charged after Bruce. Still, he was puzzled. Leroy was pretty sure the gun barrel scraping along the man's skull would have gotten got his message across. *So why is he disrespecting me like this?*

**

"Speak up, speak up, I haven't got all day. I am on the clock you know." Bruce spoke harshly into the silver cube.

"Whot?" Sid wasn't used to such insolence, but he decided to play it cool. He idly picked a sharp canine. "Who you again?" Sid asked to irritate the Sentencing Sentience Investigator.

"I already told you, what do you want?"

"Okay, you be Agent Bruce. I remember you, too." Sid's voice was moist and oily. "Asss I say, thisss be Admiral Sid Pipe Dek of the War Fleet Monsi. I want to talk with you about thisss here planet."

**

"What are you doing!" screamed Peter Leroy, catching up to Bruce, attempting to pull the phone away he clawed, scratched, and finally tried to bite Bruce.

"Stop that!" Bruce slapped Leroy's fat, sweaty hands firmly, moving to pull free of his assailant. Unfortunately, this was difficult, as Leroy possessed the strength of the ignored and humiliated; powerful incentives to be clinging and irritating. Add to that ponderous obesity and suddenly he was impossible to ignore.

At this moment, Leroy firmly believed the success of his entire life depended on forcing this civilian to obey. But he felt helpless without a gun, so he did the only thing he could think of: Peter Leroy flung himself onto Bruce like an orphan gorilla finding mama.

"What are you doing? Let go of me, you fool!" Bruce staggered under the sudden onslaught of flab.

"Whot?"

"No, not you! The other fool!" Bruce managed to stay upright, just barely.

"Whot!" Admiral Sid looked at the phone in consternation. "Whot you say?"

"I command you to obey me in the name of the great Republican Deity, Reagan!" Leroy cried, tears clouding his vision, scrabbling for a hold on the curiously slippery Elmer Fudd.

"Excuse me, what did you say?" Bruce held the phone-cube closer to his ear, gripping it tightly. "I couldn't hear you; please ignore the histrionic sobbing."

Leroy couldn't seem to grip the small man and wound up sliding down to a desperate hold on Bruce's left ankle. "I'm telling you to obey me or else!" He tightened his grip fiercely on the ankle to show he meant business.

"I wanna talk to a human!" Admiral Sid said brusquely.

"You want to do what?" Bruce tried to make sense of this. *Why was this galactic exterminator wanting to speak to a human?* "You can't talk to a human! At least not until I am finished. There are rules we must follow you know."

Looking down Bruce wondered why the fat human was clutching his foot; another thing he couldn't make sense of.

Peter Leroy lying flat on his face at Bruce's feet, knew this was going badly in front of the troops and his anger now had the energy of embarrassing desperation.

"I'm gonna kill you!" Screamed Peter Leroy, his voice somewhat muted being face down in mud.

"Whot, you gone kill me? That gone angry, me!" Sid responded indignantly at the threat coming out of the communicator.

"No, no, I didn't say that!" Bruce protested. "Stop that!" He hissed at Leroy.

Rolling around on the ground, trying desperately to bring the little man down, Leroy felt a lump in his back pocket. Reaching in, he pulled out a bullet. *The Lord is on my side,* Leroy was impressed. *No doubt about it, because right there in my jeans I found a bullet.*

Leroy couldn't believe it. *It was a miracle!* He told himself. Quickly he stuffed the bullet into the handgun clip; pulling the slide he chambered it.

"Okay, okay you have pushed me to the breaking point!" Leroy felt in control again. *A damn good feeling.* He let go of Bruce's left foot and with supreme effort he stood. "Okay, you drop that silver thing, or I am going to kill you." Trembling so badly he felt faint, Peter was finally back in command, forcing himself to remain conscious.

"Holy shit, bonehead," Tomas hadn't tried to stop the main MAGA maggot because he was also being covered by four other maggots. But Leroy was getting very dangerous waving the huge handgun. Tomas ordered, "Drop it, drop it now!" But he kept his handgun holstered, not wanting to give the others a reason to shoot him. Not just yet anyway.

"What did you say again?" Bruce hollered into the phone, utterly ignoring Peter Leroy.

"I   say   you   ain't   gone   kill   me."   Sid   was   firm   about   this
.

Leroy aimed the gun.

"No! Of course not! I told you that wasn't me!" Bruce was puzzled. *Why would Sid think I want to kill him?*

"As commanding officer of this here MAGA Militia, I order you to obey me, or I will shoot you fucking dead." Peter liked how that sounded: very official, very businesslike, very meaningful. He glanced back and sure enough, two of the MAGA's had their phones out, filming his heroics.

"Mr. Bruce," Admiral Sid continued, "Lesss get down to businesss. I say I want to scrub this mudball of humanity." Sid purred into the phone as if this was an Earthly porn call.

"No, you may not!" Bruce replied hotly. "Not possible!"

"You are saying 'no' to me?" Sid looked at his communications panel in surprise. "I'm an Admiral! You know what that isss? Yet you say 'no' to me? That ain't respectful! Why you say 'no' to Admiral Sid?" Sid longed to launch into a blistering tirade about disrespecting superiors and the failure of civilization to control defiant peasants.

But he held his cool this time.

"'No' is a complete sentence. I don't have to explain it." Bruce replied defiantly.

"You're saying 'no' to me?" Leroy felt abandoned by the conversation. "I have a gun, you fucking Democrat fudgepacker!" Peter made sure the safety was off this time. He jammed the gun against Bruce's head.

"Oh, oh! Wait, stop!" Bruce hunching his shoulders, waited for him to fire. *For some reason the word 'no' seems to just piss Earth people off.*

Bruce wondered how in hell he got in the middle of all this. Shaking the cube, he hung up the call and slowly turned to face the gun barrel.

**

"Hello! Are you listening? You say 'no' to an Admiral, then you talking about killin' me, then you go silent?" Sid was pissed the other guy had hung up.

Admiral Sid really hated Bureaucrats and could barely stand talking to them therefore any disrespect, real or otherwise, was seen as an act of war.

Pointing at the planet below, he commanded. "Poot, send me there." He knew it was against regulations talking with the Earthlings, insurance and legal issues mostly. But Admiral Sid was never one to deny his own ego.

"Sure, whatever." Poot was glad to send Sid anywhere else. Poot hit the switch and Sid's body collapsed like a leaky balloon as his essence streamed down to the planet.

**

"Drop the fucking gun, now, I will not tell you again, maggot." Two Hawks meant it but was reluctant to draw his own weapon. The twitchy militiamen had their weapons on them at pointblank range. He couldn't take the chance of setting them off just yet.

Emma saw she needed to distract them away from Tomas. She began talking loudly at John, anything to attract attention.

"Look over there, John, what is that?" She made her voice screechy and irritating. "Don't you see it? John?" Frantically she pointed off to her right and shouted. "It's Jesus! It's really him! Right there! Right over there!" She was hopping and pointing excitedly. "It's Jesus Christ, in person!"

John looked both confused and frightened at the same time as he had no idea what she was saying or doing. But the appearance of Jesus was certainly important news.

"Emma? What…I don't see him…where?"

The MAGA Militia, ignorant of both military training and common sense, as Emma predicted, moved to find out what she was shouting about. If Jesus was in town none of them wanted to be left out of the reunion. All four peered desperately into the thick brush where Emma pointed.

Emma couldn't help but grin while John kept trying to shush her; he was certain the militia would shoot them.

As soon as the enemy turned toward Emma and away from him, Tomas drew his service weapon leveling it at Peter Leroy.

Leroy looked down the barrel of a gun held by a man with the capability and intention of killing him. At that moment, he experienced an epiphany, instantly understanding that peeing your pants when deathly frightened was no joke.

Peter Leroy dropped the gun immediately, the wet spot in the crotch of his pants spreading rapidly.

'But you can't shoot me, my men will shoot you." Leroy pleaded.

"You don't seem to understand," Tomas said quietly. "This weapon in my hand is pointed at you. Regardless of what else happens here, you are going to be dead. So go on, give the order for your men to shoot and see what happens."

Leroy tried to swallow; his mouth suddenly very dry.

CHAPTER THIRTY-EIGHT

"I believe Alien life is quite common in the universe, although intelligent life is less so. Some say it has yet to appear on Planet Earth." Steven Hawking

A humming filled the air; they all looked around puzzled except Bruce, who recognized the sound and thought, *Oh no! Is that damn Sid coming down here?*

"What is that? Why are my ears buzzing?" Emma complained.

Tomas began scratching his arm, the hairs raised straight up.

Leroy winced, the metal fillings in his mouth vibrating vigorously.

The humming grew in intensity, earsplitting loud, growing in volume, everyone winced and covered their ears. The MAGA Militia juggled their weapons as they sought to protect their hearing.

The fur puffed out all over Blue's body, tail included, standing straight out from him like a soft, furry halo.

Tomas would have laughed at the sight of Blue, but everything was just too strange, too sudden.

CRACKLE! CRACKLE! A bluish green light filled their vision, and an odor of old socks and peppermint coated their noses.

"Oh ick!" Emma complained.

A sharp crackling sound seemed to come from everywhere, surrounding them, it rapidly grew louder and louder until, with a sloppy, wet 'Splurt', Sid appeared on the planet in hologram form.

A perfect three-dimensional image of Admiral Sid Pipe Dek of the War Fleet Monsi stood proudly before the crowd of humans: Twelve-foot of Crocodile-like being, with eight clawed legs, and jaws full of sharp teeth, Admiral Sid looked as if his ancestral lineage followed a brutal winner-take-all evolutionary path.

"Holy shit!" Peter shaking uncontrollably was frozen in place from fear; *What demon from hell have these Democrats summoned?*

The MAGA Militia saw no political advantage in being killed by an Alien, sharptoothed monster and, like a well-trained drill team, in unison they turned and disappeared into the forest.

Tomas quickly used the distraction to retrieve the handgun near Peter Leroy's feet.

Admiral Sid looked around at the gathered Earthlings. "Hey, where isss the Bureaucrat? Where the Galactic Investigator?"

The fact that a huge Alien monster, looking like a cross between a wingless dragon and crocodile, could speak English, was more than Peter Leroy could handle; his eyes rolled back into his head as he passed out cold hitting the ground like a puffed-up, discarded puppet.

A visitation by Alien fiends was beyond his capacity for patience, so GID Gary Myerson folded himself into the foot well of the Dodge Durango, becoming one with the floor mat.

"I'm over here!" Bruce signaled to Admiral Sid.

Because this was official business, Bruce resumed his normal shape; eight feet, eight tentacles around a dark purple, vaguely eggplant-shaped body. His bottom three eyes glowed a deep pink, the upper three held a more crimson hue. He appeared to float about six inches off the ground.

"Oh, my goodness," Emma gasped. "What in the world?"

"What now?" John Mack rubbed his eyes. "Liberals and now Aliens, my fucking day just gets better and better."

Tomas Two Hawks waited, wondering what strange shit was going to play out next. He kept a close hold on Blue whose entire body was wired tight.

Blue stared hard at the new intruder, mesmerized with disbelief. As a canine, Blue held to the eternal canine code; *'My life for my human'*. Now, staring at the enormous Alien in petrified awe, the dog had doubts. *Holy shit! He's got bigger teeth than I do! And more of them!*

Blue tried urgently to remember any combat moves he might have learned in puppy school. Humans thought it was fun to watch puppies play, but they didn't realize the seriousness of it all. Each puppy knew that the safety of his human could someday be at stake, and they practiced their offensive and defensive maneuvers with their pack mates constantly. Plus, it was fun.

"Admiral, I am Agent Bruce, this is Blue." Bruce approached Admiral Sid, introducing himself, and then pointed at the dog.

Blue tried to take a step forward, but Tomas held him back. Blue was very grateful for that favor. He was already too close to the monsters.

GID Myerson, whimpered from the foot well of Tomas's vehicle, certain he would be tasked with saving the entire Earth by stopping the Alien invasion. Myerson tucked deeper into the fetal position hoping not to be noticed. The answer had come to him: *I know just how to solve this situation to everyone's satisfaction.* GID Myerson decided unconsciousness was the best way to avoid potential responsibility, so he went silent.

"I be Admiral Sid Pipe Dek of the War Fleet Monsi!" The huge Alien announced, stretching to his full height, straightening his immense tail out in a formal, military salute.

"I am Califra LffGBrsesddrs the XXIV, but you can call me Bruce." He knew he needed to get his official name into this meeting; no doubt Poot was recording it. "I am the official Sentience Sentencing Investigator for this sector of the Galaxy."

"I receive ordersss to be here so here I am. When I get to…finish the job?" Sid didn't like generalizations. He was a predator that likes specifics; *hit this, kill that. No hazy guesses.*

**

Bruce held up a hand to pause Sid, which both startled and enraged the Admiral.

He then turned to Blue, "Because you are my advisor and companion on my mission, I will provide a translator so you can join in the conversation."

"Grrrr…hmmm." Admiral Sid quickly stifled his natural, inborn, killing rage at the perceived insult; *Now isss not the time for playful self-indulgence,* he cautioned himself. Sid came from a culture in which the transition from newt to adult was complicated by a nearly 85% mortality; impulsive slaughter was almost recreational.

My name, he mentioned me! Blue wagged his tail enthusiastically.

"Blue talks?" Tomas asked, astounded, staring down at the dog. "Really?"

Blue looked at Tomas and panted happily.

Bruce hit a button on the small silver square and Blue's voice came on. "...talk, of course, I can talk! I talk all the time except you never listen or...." "Blue?" Tomas bent down and stared into Blue's face. "Blue?"

"Tomas?" Blue licked his human.

"My, oh my!" Emma clapped her hands in delight. "Blue can speak? How delightful!"

"He talks telepathically," Bruce explained. "That is why he doesn't appear to be talking."

Blue, panting with eagerness, said, "Hey, Tomas, I am so happy to see you! Happy! Happy! Happy! We have so much to talk about! Where did you go? What happened? What did I do wrong? I am so sorry, Tomas, I will never do it again no matter what it was, please forgive me, Tomas…did I tell you about being imprisoned…where did you go…I love you Tomas…"

"What? "Tomas didn't know what to say. *I've known this dog for years, have talked to him daily and now, when he can answer, I'm speechless.*

Tomas held up a hand. "Blue pause, slow down or something. I know you have a lot to say but take it easy."

Blue decided to stick to the most important things first. "Listen, Tomas I have a problem. I need to keep you safe, but I haven't been doing so hot in the attack dog stuff. My dog-mom didn't do any formal attack training in puppy school, and I kind of lack a natural talent for it…"

"Sure, okay?" Tomas just stared at his dog.

"Some advice, maybe you could work with me a little," Blue continued. "We need to run away!" Blue began edging toward the far woods, glancing back at the Aliens. "Why don't we go now? You know practice escaping before we actually need to escape?" Blue pulled against Tomas' hold on his collar. "If we practice running away now, we will be good at it when we need it. Ok?" Blue looked up with loving, hopeful, eyes.

Stretching out a very small foreleg, Blue said wistfully. "For obvious reasons, I need a head start, what do you say?"

"Oh, Blue." Tomas's head was spinning. "The last few weeks, the firefight, then giant toothy and tentacled Aliens the size of a horse, and now my dog is talking to me, shit. I don't know what to think, but hold on, partner, hold on, settle down."

Blue licked Tomas's hand. "Okay, okay, how about this. I have a new plan! Maybe you could act as a diversion? Give me a chance to sneak up on them, you could play dead, roll over, maybe."

"Blue, now that you ARE talking, what in hell are you talking ABOUT?"

**

"We waste Admiral Sid time!" Sid roared; furious he had been distracted by the Earthlings. Turning to confront Bruce he said, "I gotsss placesss to be and thingsss to do! Whot isss you decision? Am I going to fry these...ah...creaturesss?" He glanced around curiously.

Tomas Two Hawks, John and Emma Mack, and Blue looked back at him expectantly, even a little fearfully. This Alien was huge, and raging and dangerous.

"Are these muttsss even sentient?" Admiral Sid demanded. "Do they have common sense? Use toolsss? Can they calculate Equivalent Boreal Time Valuesss to the seventh Zenith acrosss multiple Galactic Regionsss?"

"Admiral Sid," Bruce explained patiently. "You are premature. I have not yet studied humans enough to know if they are sentient."

Admiral Sid was no stranger to Bruce. He knew Sid well, both personally and professionally. *Sid likes to fry planets; Alstair#1, #2 and #3 for one.* Bruce knew this for a fact.

Bruce waved a tentacle at the gathered humans. "I am still investigating and have not made up my mind yet," he said to Sid. "So, when I know, you will know, and that is the way it shall be. I am thorough and complete, and when I am done, I will understand the complex psychological foundations of these creatures and derive the proper conclusion."

"I wanna talk to a human, see for myself." Admiral Sid puffed out his chest.

**

Golden Retrievers are the most tolerant of dogs, but Blue was facing a predicament. He wanted to be friends with everyone, but his friend Bruce might not be a friend after all.

Anxiously he fidgeted and whined, uncertain if he should attempt an attack on the Alien monster or lay low. His last attempt at vicious junkyard dog assaults hadn't gone as well as he'd hoped. He just couldn't seem to get over that 'edge', that moment when a bite possibility became probability. But he must defend his human, he just couldn't quite figure out how. Blue looked up at Tomas.

I wish Tomas understood. He whined. It was so difficult to figure out how to tell him, talking, even telepathically, takes practice.

"Quiet, Blue, calm down." Tomas petted the nervous Golden.

"But Tomas, no kidding, we gotta go!" Every instinct told Blue to hide because something was very wrong with the world and his Tomas could be in grave danger. "We gotta run, run, far away, run, run…" "Hush, Blue, I need to see what is going on here." Blue sulked.

**

Sid looked the other Alien up and down with distaste. "You listen up. I am going back to my ship. I need a human to talk with. After dat, you probably shouldn't wait around." Sid pointed a hefty claw at the Earthlings. "They're toast." That got everyone's attention. Even Blue stopped panting.

Both Admiral Sid and Bruce noticed the silence around them.

"So, humans, that was just a figure of speech." Bruce assured them.

"Yes, it is a figure of speech," Emma declared. "And it means we are in trouble. You want to explain that Bruce, or whoever you are Mr. Alien?"

Seeing the frightened look on the humans, Sid decided to play it cool. "Naw itsss okay. I mean we will make you some toast to eat." The huge predator said. "Feed you, not gone hurt you." Sid gave them his warmest smile, fangs clearly visible. "We will be nice to you, trust usss." Admiral Sid knew it was imperative to keep the species to be eliminated ignorant of their fate. Cosmically it was felt to be kinder.

Golden Retrievers are suckers for niceness, but not even Blue believed the Alien dragon; *look at those fucking teeth!*

"Emma, John, let's get back to the car and get out of here." Tomas started toward the car, "Come Blue."

CHAPTER THIRTY-NINE

"Now wait a minute, wait." Bruce needed to get this under control. He pointed a cautionary tentacle at the Admiral Sid.

"You don't be pointing no tentacle at the Admiral Sid!" Sid defended his honor.

"Okay relax, calm down." Bruce dropped the tentacle. "Admiral Sid, I am showing you respect, and I expect the same in return. I will be doing research into the survivability of the human species. I am in charge here, you will return to your spacecraft, wait for my decision, and back off! I must insist!"

"Psssst!" Sid chuckled, he wasn't impressed; he had the firepower and Bruce, the other guy, looked like an eggplant. Admiral Sid had no worries.

"Whot decision you have to make? Thisss planet in deep trouble. The humansss have caused it and are still causing it. Thisss isss very strange."

"Yes, yes, there are some questions, that is true." Bruce hoped Sid wouldn't bring that up again. It was so darn hard to prove sentience in a race of beings determined to commit slow and ugly suicide. *The fact they continue to pour CO2 into their atmosphere, knowing what they know, weighs heavily in favor of deliberate self-destruction.* Bruce realized sentience might be more of a reach for humanity then he'd first thought.

"The humansss are going bye-bye, they are no good."

"Going to be like that, is it?" Bruce worried. Sid was an alpha predator from a planet filled with predators; his killer instinct was also a survival instinct. Compassion wasn't just rare it was suicidal.

**

Bruce's history with Admiral Sid was ugly.

His mind flashed back to the Alsier Solar System; a brown dwarf sun surrounded by three planets inhabited with conscious idiots: Alsier #1 - #3. Bruce was there to determine sentience for only Alsier #1. Unfortunately, Admiral Sid sent down the destruct order just seconds after Bruce declared the planet's inhabitants too un-evolved to continue their un-civilized existence.

Bruce shuddered; his narrow escape still haunted him.

Bruce was sympathetic to the inhabitants of Alsier #1, but not enough to let them live, so Admiral Sid was accurate there. But Alsier #2 and #3 were a different story. These planets were inhabited by beings whose Spiritual Foundations were sloth and apathy. Somehow, their devotion to mind numbing, hallucinogenic tree bark allowed them to fashion a sloppy, semi-sentient, civilization. They should have been given time for the seemingly impossible task of morphing into a fully sentient society.

Unfortunately, Admiral Sid paid no attention to Bruce and depopulated everything. He slaughtered them all: Alsier #1, #2, and #3. Bruce knew he was fortunate to leave that solar system only seconds before it was rendered inert.

**

"So, say goodbye to you little friendsss." Admiral Sid waggled his claws in a goodbye gesture.

"Now, Admiral Sid," Bruce declared with intensity. "I must tell you there is some small chance that I will recommend they survive. If that is the case, you will of course back off and leave these creatures alone. You do not want to upset me! I can be quite harsh!" Bruce stood firm, crossing his tentacles to demonstrate resolve.

Sid laughed so hard he fell on the ground, giggling in delight. "I gone fry 'em! I gone fry 'em!" Sid sang. "The humansss are gone bye-bye."

As soon as Peter Leroy understood the two Aliens were busy planning human extinction, he realized glory was in his hands again. *Thank you, Jesus!* He whispered to the heavens. He had another chance to save humanity. Leroy knew he was on the edge of greatness; he would be the savior of humankind. *I will be immortalized as a God once I announce to the world what I have discovered! The Liberals and Extraterrestrials have joined forces to rule the world!*

Slowly Peter Leroy moved a finger, a hand wiggled, followed by one arm, then his left leg, carefully, ever so cautiously, he moved body parts until he began to low crawl away from the danger zone. When he was ten feet away, looking back it appeared no one noticed or cared about his departure. Giddy with success because he had proof now; *liberals were in league with vicious Alien hordes to exterminate humanity*! He rose to his feet and started running at top speed for the wood line to spread the word.

Peter Leroy weighed in at close to 350 lbs and stood 5'5". He hadn't run a step in ten years. In the back of his mind the words of a high school coach rang like a bell: "Leroy, running ain't nothing more than a 'metaphor' for you." But he had to try.

He had reached twelve feet away when Admiral Sid pointed a claw, a thin purple ray shot out freezing the human solid.

Leroy was helpless, paralyzed by a blood thirsty Alien, eyes wide with terror he was certain to be defiled and devoured by liberals and their extraterrestrial invading army. Leroy prayed fervently for Jesus to save him and take him away to heaven before his bones were crunched by liberal fiends or he was deflowered by an alien penis.

"They're going to fry us too?" John whispered to Emma as they stared at the fat Leroy, now frozen into a MAGA monument. *This is bad, very bad,* he thought, but did not want to say it out loud; he did not want to alarm Emma further. His utter astonishment and terror at beholding the two massive Aliens was overwhelming.

He had no idea what to do with the fear that surged through him.

**

His mind racing, John took some comfort in the knowledge that human beings were made in the very image of God. *For seventy some odd years I have listened to Christian Priests and Pastors and even Nuns quote the Holy Catholic Bible. The very words of God in that book are telling me humans are beloved above all other creatures. Humans are made in the image of God! Who can argue with God? Since that is true, these Aliens have no power over us,* John reasoned.

For a moment, John felt contempt for the poor Aliens, because they were confused and unloved by Jesus.

**

Emma standing by John's side, four feet from the two Aliens, felt him squeeze her hand, hard, too hard, alarming her considerably.

She quickly looked up, wondering what crazy foolishness he had planned. She knew her John, and as loving and compassionate as he could be one moment, the next he could be an impulsive idiot. She had learned to cope with both, the hard way. Still, she loved her John fiercely.

A gust of rain clouded the area, but quickly moved on, with a swirling wind, the musky scent of loam and soil filled the air.

John let go of Emma's hand and stood up, confronting the Aliens directly. "I have something to say."

Admiral Sid and Bruce turned to stare at John.

"No, John," Emma pleaded. "No please, don't." She felt misgivings and wondered what John had in mind.

Tomas, petting Blue to keep him calm, didn't think John was so stupid as to attack an Alien but was curious. *He might,* Tomas thought, *these cultists are crazy fuckers.*

Blue enjoyed being petted by Tomas but kept his eyes on the dragon-like Alien with the big teeth, still mulling over various attack strategies that didn't involve him actually attacking anything; running seemed to be the best option. Blue stretched out his forelimbs, readying his short little legs for action.

"I represent the Human Race." John Mack stood tall, but fearfully. He moved awkwardly, his legs stiff, his body tense from terror. "Admittedly…ah… admittedly, I'm self-appointed. I find myself having to defend my species and my planet. I've heard your atrocious plans, and you need to know we will fight you all the way. Humanity ain't going down without a fight and buddy you just try and take our planet! Humans are tougher than we look!" John wasn't sure what else to say so he ended it: "So, Fuck You!" John gave each the finger, very dramatically.

The Bruce and Admiral Sid stared back uncomprehendingly.

Then they looked at each other.

"You're still gone maintain they isss sentient?"

Bruce was very worried. He knew this might be a long shot, but he'd hoped the humans wouldn't act too…human.

Emma was embarrassed. "John, stop threatening them!"

"What? I am defending our planet, woman, what is wrong with that?"

There came the sound of a car door slamming and everyone turned to see a dark blue, 1966 Pontiac Firebird parked and idling beside the road.

Somebody very strange, a gray man, had gotten out of the car and was approaching them.

Everyone froze, no one spoke.

More questions? Or maybe an answer or two? Tomas thought.

Blue's nose was repelled by the scent of this very strange creature. He hated his nose was now coated with a repugnant, slippery evil. A low menacing growl issued from his throat.

Despite himself, Tomas looked down in surprise; Blue had never growled like that before.

Then the Gray Man made a whispery, puffing sound and both Aliens immediately genuflected.

"Oh shit," Tomas muttered. "This ain't good."

The Gray Man issued a sharp, whistle-like sound, and the scent of burning hair, fish oil, and rotten fruit filled the air.

Five humans and one dog dropped to the ground, unconscious.

CHAPTER FORTY

"The belief that one's own view of reality is the only reality is the most dangerous of all illusions." Paul Watzlawick

The Gray Man's legs bent backward at the knee, like a cricket.

The Gray, standing beside Admiral Sid and Bruce, was slim, dressed in a rigidly conservative grey suit and dark tie, despite the Alien construction of his face, he had a supercilious expression in his two black eyes, and his mouth twisted in a gesture of contempt and superiority as unmistakable as shackles.

Tomas hated the creature from the moment his eyes opened. He struggled to get up, but it was difficult, he felt weak as if all his energy had been sapped.

Beside Tomas, Emma slowly awoke and looked around. She quickly checked on John to see if he was okay, then she looked at the three Aliens.

Blue shook his head, his ears flopping. "What happened?" Then he sprang to his paws to check on Tomas to see that he was okay.

Next, Blue whirled on the Aliens, his teeth bared.

"Who is the gray guy?" Emma leaned close to Tomas and whispered.

"Don't know, but he looks serious." Tomas answered.

Blue could not figure out who to attack first: Admiral Sid seemed the most dangerous. But Blue figured even if he defeated the monstrous crocodile-like being by some miracle, he might get injured, and this left the other two as potential threats. But Blue figured Bruce was safe, so that left the newcomer, the Gray Man. The Gray Man looked nasty and smelled putrid. Blue didn't want that taste in his mouth if he could avoid it. This was all so confusing and embarrassing for Blue. *What do I do? How do I do it?*

The Gray Alien appeared to be lecturing the other two. They slumped, listening, heads down, their attitudes appeared humble. After a few minutes, the Gray appeared satisfied with his message, turned and stalked self-importantly to his Pontiac Firebird, climbed in, gunned the engine, and tore out, leaving a cloud of blue smoke and spraying thick mud behind the spinning tires.

**

Bruce came over to Blue. "Well, I guess our mission has ended."

"Mission? Oh, you mean about the sentience thing?" Blue felt his neck fur relax, the danger had passed with the Gray Man. "Your mission of judging whether humanity is worthy of existence? That mission?" Blue asked as he licked Tomas to assure him that Blue was on duty.

Sadly, Bruce nodded, he had returned to his pot-bellied, semi-balding, bespeckled, middle-aged persona as he had quickly learned humans don't relate well to tentacles.

Since he was using the translator, everyone could hear the conversation, except Sid who was too preoccupied screaming insults at some entity called "Poot".

The next moment everyone heard Sid; "Hey, human, you comesss along wit' old Admiral Sid."

'SLUUUUURP!'

They looked around, Sid and MAGA Militiaman Peter Leroy had vanished.

Admiral Sid had his human.

Bruce was furious. "You bring him back this instant!" He shook a fist at the sky. "You can't just steal one of them! There are rules you know!"

"Did I hear right?" Tomas asked Bruce. "You are here to evaluate humanity? For sentience?"

Bruce nodded again, reluctantly moving his gaze from the heavens, already formulating the official 'Letter of Reprimand' he was going to file with authorities. Then he thought of the paperwork that went with it and sighed. Maybe not.

Emma finally got John awakened and he blearily observed the exchange, his alarm growing with his improving consciousness.

"Who was that?" Emma asked Bruce.

"That? The Gray fellow?" Bruce thought quickly, trying to decide how much to reveal to the humans, as there was a definite 'need to know' here. "Oh, just a visitor, I suppose…kind of an illegal immigrant if you will."

"I knew it! Fucking Immigrants!" John shouted. 'We told those God damn Democrats they needed to do something about our borders, but did they listen? Oh no! Now look at this mess! Mexican immigrants coming from the south, Chinese immigrants coming from the west, Muslims Immigrants from the east, and now Alien immigrants dropping from the sky!" John pointed an accusing finger at the sky. "You, up there! You won't get away with this!"

'Shush!" Emma pulled down John's arm, alarmed he was making a fool of himself.

Blue nudged Tomas hand with worry, who rubbed his Golden Retrievers' soft furry head in reassurance.

"What do they want?" Tomas asked.

That was someplace Bruce did not want to go. "The Gray Men? Oh, I don't know," he replied casually, "Maybe just stopping off for a bathroom break…get snacks…maybe."

"Never mind the Gray Man," Emma demanded. "I still don't understand why YOU are here. Why is that ugly crocodile-like creature bothering us? What is going on here?"

"Sentience?"

Everyone jumped when Blue talked.

"Geez, Blue, that is so damned spooky hearing you in my head!"

"I'm sorry, sorry, I didn't mean to harm you, I am so sorry…"

Blue looked so miserable, Tomas had to immediately pet and reassure him he was okay.

Emma was also quick to let the dog know he was not at fault.

"I don't want a fucking dog in my fucking head!" John groused. "Shut that mutt off." He pointed at Tomas. "Now!"

"But I was just trying to tell you," Blue hurriedly explained. "Bruce here is seeking sentience on Earth. I just wanted to be helpful." Blue was dismayed he had caused John's upset.

John grimaced and held his head.

"I'm sorry, sorry, so sorry, again," Blue saw the anguish on John's face and was appalled at what he had done.

"Arrgggggh!"

"Nooo, I meant it! I am sorry!" Blue tried to make this right racing over to lick John's hand in apology.

"Arrrrrrgggghhhhhhh!" John jerked his hand away.

"Blue, stop. It's okay. It's okay, chill!" Tomas could see the apology was only making it worse.

"But Tomas, I must help him!" Blue whined with sorrow, the thought of not helping a human was anathema; every instinct pulled him toward this reality.

"Stop, please God, stop!" John was on one knee.

Tomas hugged the struggling Golden warmly, gently. "Just let it go, Blue." He petted the worried dog for a few moments and Blue calmed, reassured by his Tomas' loving hands and smell.

Tomas knew he had to get this heavy responsibility away from Blue. "Bruce, you're looking for sentience?"

"We're sentient!" John said flatly. "I don't know about you, Indian, but Emma and I are."

Tomas shook his head sadly.

Bruce said, "No, it's not that simple. It is not about the individual, but the species. Humanity must establish a trajectory of maturity by proving your sentience is stable. You must demonstrate a solid, universal understanding that all beings are equal. Do you see that? All plants and animals are equal and have rights. Life is life, doesn't matter if it is yours or a centipede. You have no more right to existence than any other creature. When one species believes it is unquestionably the only valuable creature on the planet, we have big questions."

"But that's ridiculous," John replied. "We are humans. HOMO SAPIENS! Get it? 'Sapiens'? It's already in the name! We wouldn't have that name if we weren't sapient, now, would we?" John was pretty sure he had the Alien on this one.

"Self-diagnosis for sentience doesn't count," Bruce replied dryly. "Just because you understand the word doesn't make it yours."

"But we are unquestionably more intelligent, more creative than all the other creatures, we have language, use tools, we've been to the Moon and back," Emma added in support of John.

John looked at Blue. "We are smarter than that damned dog that is for sure." "You are aware that intelligence is relative?" Bruce replied.

"Huh?"

"Simple quantum mechanics, the tester influences the test. Intelligence is usually measured against the tester, not the tested. This dog for instance is vastly more intelligent than any human in some areas. But as a human you discount his intelligence because you compare it to yours. You are comparing apples and orangutans," Bruce explained.

"Apples and what?"

"My people have always followed the circle," Tomas spoke up, "all beings are equal. No one is ahead and no one behind. He is saying intelligence is everywhere in all things; its value depends on who is measuring it. The intelligence for a dog may be genius level but humans would never know because we measure intelligence by our standards, not theirs." Tomas added. "We cannot measure what we do not know exists."

"He's going to wipe us all out." Blue's voice rang a warning in their minds.

That stopped the argument.

"Say that again, Blue?" Tomas studied Bruce carefully.

"Bruce is going to wipe out you humans and the rest of us too," Blue blurted out.

They all looked at Bruce.

"Ah, yes, well, that might be a bit exaggerated," Bruce replied with embarrassment.

"Which part? The one where you wipe humans out? Or the one where you wipe everyone out?'" Blue asked nervously. "I've got a stake in this too, you know?'

CHAPTER FORTY-ONE

Planetary Tipping Points Report:

*STRONGEST HURRICANE IN WORLD HISTORY; Beyond Measurement.
The Largest death total from one storm in US History. 200,000 dead, Millions homeless; Trillions in Damage. Hurricane Marjorie Greene, Destruction of Southern US Coast.*

Dr. B. Snow, Ph.D. Bioenvironmental Physics, Chief Scientist, Council on Global Climate, United Nations

Special Report to Science Summit, United Nations General Assembly UNGC#4534.

"Humans have been given dominion over the Earth, to do with as we please. We are shepherds guiding our flocks anyway we need to." John said firmly. "Look it up, it's in the Holy Bible. God tells us humans are his favorite creatures in all the cosmos. Humanity is created in the likeness of God."

Bruce stared at John in dismay. "You…you believe that?"

John looked puzzled. "Of course, it's in the Bible, it must be true."

"You have eyes, do you see out of them? Don't you guys ever look up?" Bruce asked with astonishment in his voice.

"Are you trying to pick a fight?"

"Please calm down." Bruce had to remind himself these were humans, very poor impulse control.

Bruce spoke distinctly so the creatures would understand. "Let me explain it this way. When you look up in the night sky what do you see? Quadrillion galaxies are visible from this particular lobe of your galaxy, which also holds over a quadrillion galaxy itself. In these visible galaxies are probably a billion quadrillion solar systems. In these solar systems are at least a million, billion, billion quadrillion planets." Bruce paused to look at the humans. "You understand these numbers, don't you?"

"That's a lot of numbers," Emma exclaimed.

Bruce nodded, uncertain. "Now follow me on this. Twenty three percent of a million, billion, billion quadrillion planets hold intelligent, sapient life" Bruce paused to see if they got it.

"What are you getting at?" John Mack asked.

Amazing, Bruce thought. *They didn't get it.*

"You Earthling humans believe you are favored by God? Human Beings out of this almost infinitesimal multitude of sapience are the one God loves best?" Bruce chuckled. "Do you have any concept of the mathematical impossibility of that?" He shook his head in dismay. "Let's not even get into the corporeal versus non-corporeal differences in existence." Bruce looked sorrowful. "Your level of self-delusion is very troubling."

John slowly nodded his head. "We accept Jesus Christ in our hearts…oh, and his dad, God."

Bruce looked embarrassed. "No, no you misunderstand. Your Jesus wasn't a God at least not in the cosmic, galactic sense. Maybe on your planet, he could be, but there is one cosmic God, called: *Creator*. This is a singularity of Spirit, not of an individual. We, the discreet packets of energy called Bruce, or Emma or Tomas, or Blue are part of the God complex. We belong to this matrix called God. There is always God and God is everywhere, in all beings. Your Jesus was a human guided by Spirit though. He was an avatar. Much like Muhammed Ibn Abdullah, Aryabhata, Siddhartha Gautama, Plato, Sequoyah, Mahatma Gandhi, Sacagawea, Kublai Khan, even this guy named Frank Zappa, there have been quite a few other avatars sent to teach you humans. In antiquity they had deities, (Gods) like Zeus, Artemis, and Thor…Wakan Tanka…"

"Those gods were just made up!" John protested. "They weren't real! They were myths for simple minded humans' way back in history. Modern humans know better."

"What makes you think this Jesus was real? Even if he existed your New Testament wasn't written until seven decades after his alleged death. Out of the multitude of words in these Bibles, how many actually belong to Jesus Christ? How well do you remember exact words and specific details from seventy years ago? No sir, there are some real questions about these books."

"God directed them."

"You see," Bruce said carefully, trying to avoid bruising tender human sensibilities. "You beings are like so many other planets I have visited. You need to identify *Creator* but have no idea who this is, so you upgrade one of your own for the job. You have made a God with human attributes. That cannot be.

There is only the *Creator*.”

“But the Holy Bible says…”

“You are talking about Religion.” Bruce tried to be diplomatic. “I am talking about Spirit, *Creator*. Two different things.   You see *Creator* exists in all places and all time, therefore one dominant religion cannot exist. More importantly, religion is created by and specific to the transitory and fallible needs, wants, wishes, and egocentric demands of mortals, not the *Creator*.”

“Jesus is everywhere!”

Bruce rolled his eyes. “No, you still do not understand.”

“John,” Emma tugged on her husband’s arm. “Please shut up.” Her voice held steel. She needed to move this discussion along to what was happening right now. Besides, her John was getting dangerously close to stupid, and she didn’t want him to make a fool of himself.

“Mr. Bruce?” Emma turned to the Alien. “Forgive me for saying this but you need to back off our Religion and our God. Jesus is our God, and you will not convince us otherwise, so that is settled. Let’s move on. I think you have not been completely clear with us on this sentience issue. You and this, Admiral Creature, are visiting Earth to determine our sentience? You are not our friend at all are you?”

Bruce was embarrassed. Wow, she nailed me! Now what? It was put up or shut time. “Okay, yes I am here to determine the level of sentience on this planet…and there are…consequences…”

“What kind of consequences?” Emma’s voice was soft yet held sharpness just beneath the surface.

“You shouldn’t make any long-range plans…or short-term for that matter.” Bruce said nervously. “I’m mean if elimination is called for…”

“Elimination?”

“Hey wait a minute!” John cried out.

“Do you mean we’re going to be annihilated?” Emma demanded.

“Who, annihilated? Us humans?” GID Myerson peeked out the passenger side window. He did not like how this conversation was going. He whimpered and slowly slid back into the foot well, but continued to listen closely.

Blue didn't like the sound of this either. "Wait a minute," he got to his paws. "Who gave you the leash?

Bruce did a double take at Blue. "What did you say?"

"Two questions: I asked who is holding your leash and what gives your leash holder the right to do any of this?"

Tomas gaped at Blue in amazement.

"TA DA!" Bruce shouted surprising everyone, and they jumped.

Bruce smiled so hard his cheeks ached.

"Nicely done! You are SENTIENT! By your statement you have gone to the heart of the matter. Pinpointing the specific morality of our actions by asking where our authority comes from. Clearly you have thought this through using common sense of course and have recognized multiple levels of understanding. Congratulations!"

Bruce knew this was bullshit but was so tired of being the bad guy, the eliminator of life forms. Desperate to find some reason to rescue these hapless humans he figured any excuse, no matter how ridiculous would work. *Otherwise, these egotistical idiots don't stand a chance,* Bruce realized grimly.

"I did?" Blue wasn't sure what he said to make everybody happy but if they were happy, he was too. His big tail flapped excitedly.

Everybody was smiling, reacting to Blue's obvious joy.

"That answer proved it!" Bruce continued gushing praise. He was so relieved he had finally found the slightest trace of sentience and could therefore duck the destruction of Earth. That was all I needed! At this point I don't give shit if these bipedal boneheads are sentient or not, at least now I can bail off this mudball and my superiors won't bitch about it.

"Now I do not need to destroy you," Bruce announced cheerfully.

Nobody applauded or cheered, which confused him.

Bruce realized retirement, either voluntary or otherwise, was closer than he had thought.

"So you were going to fuck us over, were ya?" John asked menacingly.

"Wait, wait," Bruce backed up. "This is good news, really. Everything is peachy keen, honest!"

"You sure?"

"Oh absolutely, no worries at…all? Hold on a second." Bruce's face crumpled with worry. "Blue, you're the one who questioned me about my authority right?" Blue nodded sheepishly.

"But it was the right answer, right?" John asked.

Bruce looked at the humans and shrugged. "Oops."

"What do you mean, 'Oops'?" Emma didn't like the sound of that.

"Geez guys," Bruce was embarrassed he'd already screwed this up. "I mean, now we know the dog is sentient, but…what about you humans?" "I had the answer; I was going to say it." John felt cheated.

"I am sure you were, Mr. Mack. But, sorry, you had to say it before the dog."

"But we won't be annihilated after all, right? The dog saved us?" John whispered with uncertainty.

"Kind of…" Bruce needed to phrase this carefully. "I, the Galactic Sentience Sentence Investigator am not going to recommend scrubbing of your planet."

That produced smiles all around and Bruce felt an upwelling of joy. I have brought joy to them, this feels good.

"Wow, what a relief," Emma grinned.

"Man, that was close," John agreed.

"Wait! Does this mean we won't be annihilated?" Tomas asked.

Bruce stopped smiling.

Everyone stopped smiling.

CHAPTER FORTY-TW0

The Gray Man arose and walked toward her.

President for life Popper, now busy designing and dreaming of his new wall project to protect against desperate Canadian invaders was oblivious to everything except dollar signs.

Priscilla Lusty-Popper saw the Gray Man out of the corner of her eye, and she froze. Like a deer hearing predator howl at night, danger close, nervously her fingers started knitting furiously, a blur of motion to shut out thoughts of being eaten alive.

VP Smith, seeing she was the target of the Gray Man adapted a pose of wary submission, ready to offer her throat as needed.

The Gray Man was tall, identical to all the others; Six foot Five and one-quarter inches, backward folding legs, bland features, gray clothing, skin, hair, even teeth. True, they were different shades of gray; ties a little darker, suits shaded just so, shoes nearly black, but their pupil-less eyes were flat black.

"Follow me." He left the room; certain she would follow.

VP Smith hated Popper and despised Priscilla, but at least they were human. The Gray Man on the other hand... She didn't even want to guess.

"VP Smith," Gray's voice was mellow, soft, without accent or inflection. The door to her office swung shut behind him without his touching it. "VP Smith, we have observed you. You will do."

"Do?" Smith nearly collapsed with terror.

She only had scant knowledge of them. The Gray Men had been on the Planet for decades and with their power and advanced technology became advisers to every major Government on the globe: US, EU, Russia, China, Japan, India, Pakistan, Brazil, Mexico, Philippines, and dozens more had a Gray Man standing silently behind the President or ruling body of each Nation.

Quietly, carefully, in the past she had asked about them. "Who are the Gray's? Where did they come from? What do they want?"

No one knew their true purpose; obedience was the only option because people who questioned disappeared in a pink mist, so she stopped asking.

"Yes, what can I do for you?" she replied shakily, bracing herself for some Godawful assignment that would probably fuck up her life for sure.

"I want you to forget this nonsense with borders and politics." the Gray man whispered. "You are to force this President to burn coal, lots of coal. Burn coal, drill for gas and oil, and Frack like never before! You are to persuade him and the American people it will solve their all the problems."

"How do I do that?" She quickly shut up. No one questions Gray Men.

"First, you will have him create a board for Coal Energy to create a worldwide demand for more coal. You will immediately spread the word this is new coal and will actually absorb CO2 rather than create it. Additionally, the Republicans will be forced to call methane a scientific breakthrough; I want a media blitz telling these stupid Americans their government scientists have determined methane will solve their silly little global warming issues," the Gray Man told her.

Of course, the Gray man thought, *Methane is ten times the greenhouse gas of CO2, which guarantees runaway global heating.* Gray man knew the timing was critical, they had to get this planet under control because the other Gray's in a holding orbit just outside this solar system were ravenously eager to land.

"Really? Is that true?"

Gray Man stared at her a moment. "Sure, if you say so." he said.

"What a relief!"

"Second, "Gray Man continued, amazed at human gullibility. "Interference with pipelines, drilling, or any form of coal, oil, or gas production will result in Death! Do you hear me? Lastly, all attempts to interfere with Global Warming must be stopped immediately."

"But how?" She asked.

"Anyone seeking to interfere with the warming of our planet will be considered a terrorist and dealt with accordingly! Immediate death to anyone calling for a reduction in CO2 or Methane, understood?"

"What? Okay, certainly, sir!" VP Smith understood immediately. Liberals and Progressives are being locked in prisons and razor-wire camps. *It wasn't about politics. It was about Global Warming. Liberals lead the way in fighting CO2 pollution. With them out of the way and only the radical far right conservative politics in control, there would be no US attempts to combat Global Climate*

Change, quite the opposite. By emphases on coal and more drilling, more fracking, the levels of CO2 would skyrocket. She saw the plan clearly.

Global Warming could be unstoppable.

VP Smith, filled with uncertainty and misgivings, quickly mentally checked her bank balance for reassurance; the sums were growing, life was still good.

But then an uncomfortable realization occurred, one she had not previously considered; riches are no good if she's dead. "I can't die!" *Sure, I lust for money and power because being rich is the goal of every human on the planet! Without exception, all humans want wealth! It is in our DNA! I'm just fulfilling the dreams of billions, finding the Holy Grail of humanity, the purpose for our very existence: Immense wealth.*

Almost immediately, another insight flooded her mind: *I have a purpose greater than myself. I have a reason beyond money to live!* More than just scheming to become incredibly wealthy and freeing some of her favorite relatives from the horrid gulag, VP Smith now saw herself as a heroine to young girls around the world.

What a remarkable story I have. She told herself. *With no education or employment skills, I have managed to turn a magnificent ass and great fits into a life of luxury and wealth. Now I am Vice President of the greatest economic power on the planet. My achievements should be recognized for their true brilliance. My life must continue as a goal to give hope to all the little people!*

The Gray Man observing this female human, as she contemplated consequences, was impressed; human avarice was truly Cosmos-class.

"The Earth is going to be hot, muggy, stormy," VP Smith needed reassurance,

so she phrased this delicately. "Won't this make it difficult for Earth

inhabitants?" The Gray Man, his expressionless eyes continued to study her,

said nothing.

VP Smith saw her reflection in his soulless, stygian eyes and wondered if he was going to kill her.

"I, ah, really didn't mean that. Who cares, right?" She quickly decided she'd said too much. "Above my pay grade, right!" Smith backpedaled, trying to placate the Gray. She tried a friendly grin. "I don't need to know anything, anything at all. I'm a team player, you bet I am…" Her voice trailed off and he seemed frozen staring at her.

The Gray man continued. "You want assurances of your survival, do you? A just reward, is it?"

Smith closed her mouth, sweat trickling down her temple, she took a deep breath. She was going to live a little longer. "Reward? Sure, that would be nice." She worked to keep the greed from showing. "Survival?" VP Smith shrugged, "Not just for me, you understand. I am doing this for all women everywhere!" She said grandly.

The Gray Man knew humans to be weak and susceptible to the ego; self-justification of betrayal was a well-honed human skill.

"I will make you a queen of America and we will give you a boat. Yacht I believe you call them."

Dazzled, VP Smith blushed. "Oh my, that is very generous."

The Gray Man stayed silent. By the time they finished the Earth would be identical to his home planet, very hot, very humid, and filled with his kind: predators. Humans that survived first contact were figured to be kept in small batches for labor and research. The rest would perish from the climate if not the invasion itself.

Maybe we will keep them in cages as pets, Gray Man thought. *Put collars on them, guide them with leashes, and castrate them at will. Torture them with scientific experiments. Yes, that does sound appropriate.*

He looked up and caught the human female staring at him.

Quickly VP Smith averted her eyes, fearful of some painful punishment, upset at her very rare lapse of self-control.

"Now, get that Coal Board going," The Gray Man told her. "I want unlimited fracking, I want oil and coal, coal and oil pouring into the sky. I want the Arctic and Siberian tundra spewing methane by the tons! Right now! We are behind schedule. I have a timetable." He thought of the transports waiting beyond Pluto to come in once Earth has been made habitable for his kind.

His children on those transport ships had a fondness for life fluids: like blood. Once on the Earth the Gray children freed from their transport ships would fan out, starved for food and hungry for hunting, eating their fill after decades in space they would decimate the Earth creatures.

The Gray Man made a mental note to select the humans he wanted to survive before the children set paws on the planet.

VP Smith wondered why the Gray Man was smiling. She had never seen or heard of a Gray smiling. It was damned spooky.

"Why are you staring at me?"

VP Smith was horrified to realize she had done it again; made long eye contact with a Gray Man which was clearly forbidden.

She waited to be murdered.

The Gray Man then smiled a full smile.

She was looking at the sharpest set of teeth she'd ever seen; and lots of them. Like a shark, there were multiple rows of razor teeth behind the front row of razor teeth. She couldn't stop looking at those teeth.

"No matter, my dear." The Gray Man assured her. "Not to worry, I am sure you were just considering ways of meeting my commands, yes?"

She nodded wordlessly, still staring, as he talked the teeth parted sliding over each other, slicing…she shook herself and looked away from his teeth.

"A Queen must have a suitable yacht, yes? Cleopatra's barge and all?" *Greed. Human greed. As reliable as celestial physics.* It was the key to success on this planet.

VP Smith shook like a wet dog. "Cleopatra? Me?" Her eyes lost focus and some color drained from her cheeks.

"Oh, my yes." The Gray Man needed to wrap this up, he had a meeting with a group called The American Business Round Table at the Heritage Foundation. The Republican President would be there to announce FOXE Television as the official media outlet for the US Government all other media outlets will be subordinate. Facebook/Twitter were the only official social networks allowed and entries critical of the Government and or the ruling elite will be subject to fines and/or imprisonment.

"Yes, my dear," Gray Man continued, amused by her insatiable avarice. "Additionally, you will be gifted with the USS Ronald Reagan, the advanced warship as your yacht. The Americans will outfit it any way you wish. You will watch the world change from the comfort of your floating domain; 1,900 ft long, 252 ft beam, over 105 thousand tons with 4 Westinghouse Nuclear Reactors giving you an unlimited range for the next 25 or 30 years. Plus, your own town: a population of five or six thousand souls all yours! You can raise your food, desalinate the water, you have sea-to-air weapons for defense, missiles, Gatling guns, mines, all the best. You are a Warrior Queen. Of course, the millions in yearly operating costs will be covered by the US Taxpayer in perpetuity."

Smith overwhelmed with visions of incredible wealth, grandeur, slaves, and power, sat immobilized by the realization of her value and importance as a human being.

Then she thought of billions of rotting corpses all over the world.

That is a shit load of bodies. She had no idea what that would be like.

VP Smith shook her head to dispel the images. Then, with strong will pictured herself, commanding the floating city she would name after her beloved mother: 'Yadmillayenskia'. With a tear in her eye, she did feel slightly better, considering her enormously wealthy future.

Still, the rotting corpses were a problem.

Then she had it! After a few years at sea, the corpses would disappear, and the earth would grow back lusher, from the nutrients of all the dead bodies. Even better, because it would be warm and humid, a tropic paradise really...once the corpses were...taken care of. VP Smith was so relieved.

Quickly she checked her portable computer for the latest report on Global Warming. "Yes!" *There it was, the Thwaites Glacier in Antarctica was just about gone. Already Earth has experienced a sea level rise of three feet. Every major city on all coasts around the planet will be under water within a couple of years.*

Her Yacht-Nation, she would name 'The Yadmilla-ville Yacht' would be perfect for an Ocean World. The corpses wouldn't be a problem after all.

She was so relieved.

CHAPTER FORTY-THREE

Blue licked his Tomas. "Annihilated?"

"That's what he said." Tomas went over to the dark, Dodge Durango Sheriff's vehicle. They'd stayed here far too long. Being stopped by the idiot MAGA maggots was irritating enough, but then the 'Admiral Sid show' added a whole new level of strange to the bizarre day.

"Come on, we have to get moving," Tomas called out to the rest. He saw that GID Myerson was firmly tucked into the foot well, so he was safe and accounted for.

"Emma? John? We must get going." Tomas called out, "Bruce? You coming?"

Bruce didn't respond, he sat, dully staring at the ground.

"You okay, Bruce?" Blue trotted over to the little Alien. Ever since the Gray Man left, Bruce had descended into depression, but now he seemed paralyzed.

"I had to be honest," he looked up at Blue for forgiveness. "Didn't I?" Blue

was far too tender hearted to reply.

"Hey, we gotta go, like now!" Tomas shouted to everyone. "Bruce, or whatever you are, get in the car. You can explain our extermination while we are on the road. Okay?" He wanted this Alien close by, where he could keep an eye on him. If he had some plan on destroying anything, Tomas wanted to be able to stop it.

"Sooner, not later, reinforcements are going to be here," Emma said, agreeing with Tomas. "They're going to be pissed to find their enemy has escaped and MAGA militia dead." She climbed in, patting the rear seat for John to join her.

GID Myerson's voice drifted out of the passenger foot well, "You might want to check the radio those guys left behind. See what is going on over the comms?" Then he ducked back out of sight.

Tomas kicked himself for not thinking of that, quickly looking around he found a stray MAGA radio.

"Bruce, are you coming with us?" Blue asked.

Bruce looked up sadly, got slowly to his feet, and trudged after the dog. "The Gray Men have you. I am so sorry." Bruce was conflicted. Sure, he was part of an eradication team, committing genocide against entire planets full of creatures, but that didn't mean he wasn't sensitive to criticism.

"It's not your fault," Emma offered solace.

It didn't take much. Bruce perked up, put a smile on his face and said, "You are

right! Not my fault. This time it is not my fault." "But the Gray men are bad?"

Emma asked.

Depression returned and Bruce deflated like a week-old party balloon. He trudged after Emma as she went to the car.

"You're fucked," Bruce whispered.

A chill went down Blue's back.

"What do you mean?" John wondered out loud as the last one to get into the vehicle.

"The Gray Men have your planet. You are doomed to worse than anything I could have done to you."

"You were going to kill most of us as I recall," Blue said dryly. "There is worse?"

Bruce nodded.

"Wait a minute, hush up," Tomas turned the volume up on the MAGA radio.

"All Units! All Units!" the calls were going out over the US Army radio net. "Emergency, Emergency, all units stand down from routine duties and prepare for immediate mobilization. All units prepare for immediate mobilization."

"What's going on?"

Tomas was puzzled. "I haven't the foggiest notion." He replied staring at the radio handset. "For some reason, the US Army here in Washington is preparing for an invasion from Canada."

"What? That is ridiculous."

"Yes, of course it is, but they are sending out troop movement orders right now, most of JBLM is moving north to the Canadian border, they aren't sending any troops out here to check this out!

Momentarily they could relax. The US Army was too busy to meddle with them.

"That is so weird!"

"Let's go."

They pulled out of the forest area of JBLM and encountered a paved road heading north.

"We gotta watch for MAGA patrols."

"How will we know them?"

"Yellow Gadsden flags. 'Don't tread on me', flapping from pickup truck beds."

"Everybody keep your eyes peeled." Tomas looked down into the passenger footwell. "You too, GID, you can help out."

"Mmmgmg." GID Myerson mumbled mysteriously.

Emma and John Mack sat next to each other with Blue on one side and a grimly depressed Bruce on the other.

"Bruce, could you explain what's going on? The Gray Men?" Emma asked. They had been driving down a rough and uneven dirt road until they came to a ten-foothigh wire barrier marking the limits of the huge military base, then turned left, to follow the perimeter road to a gate.

"The Gray Men," Bruce's voice sounded hollow even to him. "The Gray Men disguise themselves as creatures of the planet and then work to undermine the dominant species," Bruce explained as they followed the base border fencing toward a manned gate.

"They sabotage the civilizations on a planet and then terraform the world to meet the needs of their species. Enslavement is but one of the nicer atrocities you will face if you're lucky."

Emma looked over at Bruce and pointedly asked, "You're saying death is preferable to what the Gray Men have in mind?"

Bruce was silent; his gloomy face told them everything. Then he added; "They like to experiment on other species...for fun."

"What else?"

"Your climate is changing, yes?

"Well, yes, it is and it is getting more extreme by the day." Tomas replied as he drove up to the guarded JBLM gate. He noticed Emma tense up and explained, "It's okay, they don't check who goes out, only who goes in."

Exiting without trouble they caught State Highway 7 North, eventually joining 512 East headed for Puyallup. The traffic was heavy as usual, two lanes nearly bumper to bumper traveling 70 in a 45 MPH zone. *You keep up or get run down.* Tomas thought.

A huge Dodge Ram, black, custom wheels, flying the Gadsden flag, the American Flag, a POW Flag, and an upside-down Confederate flag pulled alongside of them.

Tomas glanced over and saw several white, burly, armored MAGA maggots staring back, not at all fazed by the Olympia Sheriff Patrol vehicle. They were looking at Tomas and his dark hide.

"Ah, we might have some trouble here guys," he warned the others.

Bruce, sitting in the backseat behind Tomas, rolled down the window to see better and was immediately slapped in the face by slushy ice coming off the truck.

"Arrrrgggh!"

"Just keep cool, they aren't going to mess with me, no matter what I look like, they are still reluctant to tackle a Deputy Sheriff." Tomas hoped that was even partially true.

Bruce didn't appreciate the warning to keep cool, but he kept his mouth shut and continued to try to wipe up the soggy mess.

The massive pickup began to edge into their lane, slowly, insistently. The tires rumbled on the strip separating the lanes as the pickup crossed.

"Ah, Tomas," Bruce said nervously. "Hey, he…ah…that truck…oh no…look out he's too close!"

Tomas held steady. The Dodge Durango is a tough, heavy vehicle so he continued straight ahead, without deviation. *If the pickup was going to try something, let him try!* Tomas was up for a fight but needed to consider the others in his car. John and Emma certainly didn't deserve any more trouble. He had Blue here too. Tomas could not take too many chances here.

Tomas backed off the throttle a little and was preparing to shift to the right when the other vehicle moved first.

His bluff worked, and the MAGA pickup slowly edged back into its own lane, still traveling 78 MPH and then sped up, weaving its way down the highway to exit at Puyallup.

"Wonder what that was about?" John asked.

"Bullying, nothing but bullying." Tomas answered. But he had to keep sharp, he had spotted three other MAGA vehicles and each one seemed to be cruising for trouble.

"Did your civilization take a sudden dramatic turn in technology in the recent past?" Bruce asked rolling up his window from the freezing rain.

Emma said, "The Industrial Revolution. Almost overnight the world was changed by the use of oil. Middle 1800's I believe, they finally figured out how to get it out of the ground."

"But has this resource, 'oil', been around for a long time?" Bruce wondered.

"Yeah, humans have known about oil forever. But it wasn't useful because we couldn't get it out of the ground all we could get were small quantities. So, humans hunted the oceans for whales. We turned their blubber into oil to use for lubrication and lights." Tomas answered.

Bruce looked shocked. "You did what? You butchered whales for their oil?"

"Well, that and corset stays for women." Emma added.

Bruce was faint with disbelief. "You nearly destroyed one of the most intelligent and well-respected creatures on your entire planet for fucking lamps of flame and feckless fashion?" Bruce was aghast. "Are you human's crazy? No, what am I saying? Of course, you're crazy. Only crazy creatures would do shit like that!"

"What are you getting at?" Tomas asked, not wanting to discuss human sanity with this Alien.

"Nothing, nothing," Bruce stammered. But the prospect of sentience in humanity had just taken a real blow.

"What about the Gray Men? Let's get back to them," Emma asked.

Tomas watched in his rearview mirror as another huge pickup, flying the bright yellow cult flag, came barreling up to sit on his rear bumper.

"What have we here?" Tomas asked softly.

Bruce was still appalled and trembled at the utterly outrageous cruelty of humanity.

"Where was I?" Bruce was beginning to get a headache, so he pressed the silver square against his temple. "Oh yes that helps. Now where was I? Oh yes, the

Gray Men came to your world. This abrupt and highly unusual acceleration of your world economy is amazing and simply impossible in a natural state. The Grey's did it. They created the Industrial Revolution to get you to increase the level of CO2 and Methane in your atmosphere. Their goal is to terraform your world into one better suited for their own survival. The race of Gray's live on worlds that are extremely hot, humid, and desolate, filled with vicious storms and merciless predation." Bruce said calmly as he continued to rub the silver cube.

"What does that mean?" Emma asked.

"Their young, are ravenous blood sucking meat eaters. They are gluttonous carnivores that will hunt and kill anything. They form packs, intelligent, efficient, ruthless hunters, absolutely fearless. They roam the planet, like animate killing machines eating everything," his voice trailed off as he pictured the utter depravity and total destruction of a Gray Man invasion.

"We'll have to fight them," John said with intensity.

"Huh? Fight them? Bruce appeared to think about that for a moment, he chuckled. "No. No, I don't think that's one of your options."

Tomas gunned the engine, turning off highway 512 and onto 410 East, heading toward Sumner, Washington, with the intention of staying on this highway across the mountains to Yakama.

The MAGA trucks did not follow.

An hour later they turned off 410 East crossed a long, narrow concrete bridge over the north branch of the American River taking a left onto National Forest Road #45-6, a small, rutted two lane gravel road that transected American Ridge. This roughened path was the back road into the Yakama Reservation and basically one only the locals knew about.

They passed a bullet riddled sign that read:

'Goose Prairie Boy Scouts of America Camp, 15 miles'.

GID Myerson had yet to emerge from the foot well.

**

"Yakama Reservation? Why there?" John protested.

Tomas ignored him.

John absolutely did not want to hang with Indians. But he kept his thoughts to himself because he didn't want to insult Two Hawks. *I don't like Two Hawks, but he has treated everyone fairly, me included and most of all he saved Emma. I cannot forget that.* John mulled this over. *He risked his life to get those other people out of the detention camp. That took guts. Liberals are weak and silly and can't do shit. So why is Two Hawks doing all of this?* John was suspicious, suspecting it was some kind of trap. *Is he playing us, leading us over to his side?*

John, falling back into his well-worn biased beliefs, vowed to protect Emma and himself from Tomas and any Democrat entrapment.

Traveling swiftly down the narrow, dusty, little used road, Tomas felt he needed to give some information to the Mack's.

"Do you know anything about the Yakama?" Tomas asked.

"Their Indians," John snarled.

**

"I guess that's my point," Tomas replied. "White men don't care about the differences between tribes or bands, to you an Indian is an Indian. the Yakama reservation is no different than many. White people forced Natives from different bands onto the same shitty plot of land. Of course, these Native people has been in competition for resources, so they were not exactly blood brothers and conflict was inevitable. In this case, the Yakama consist of many different bands; Klikitat, Palus, Wallawalla, Wanapam, Wenatchi, Wishram, and Yakama people are some of the tribes in this Confederation. These Native Banks mostly lived along the Plateau area and were thrown together on the same reservation." Tomas explained trying and failing to dodge the slashing chuckholes, and crushing ripples in the roadbed, causing their heavy vehicle to lurch drunkenly. "The Columbia River Plateau, a unique geographic area called 'The Palouse', is a massive, rolling grassland stretching through Eastern Oregon, Washington, and parts of Idaho. The people were mainly hunter/gatherers, and salmon fishers. Like all tribes they resisted forced relocation, and this led to the Yakama Indian Wars, 1855 to 1858. The Native people tried desperately to throw off the invading white men and regain their cherished homeland. But, like every Native tribe, the white people were too numerous and too well armed. The Yakama are a free, proud people; tough, resilient, and honorable. Like all human groups, there is always a mixture of good and bad of course."

"But why are we going to these people?"

"We are just stopping for a few moments. I have some information I need to gather. Then we head on for Idaho. Okay?" "Good," John replied.

"The Yakama have a huge reservation and a dedicated Veteran Society who are extremely active in Veteran Issues and defending their people. We are headed to their reservation because there is someone I need to see." Tomas said as he drove. He had to contact Rony Calmers again. So much had happened; he needed to regain his sense of assurance from Rony.

Bruce flattened himself into the corner of the back seat, misery all over his face. The introduction of Gray Men was a wild card that disrupted everything.

"Sure, I was going to eliminate humanity, but what the Gray's do is uncivilized." Bruce said to nobody. Checking the silver cube, he noticed it would be another week before his return shuttle came through this solar system.

"Hey, Alien asshole," John pushed at Bruce. "If we can't fight them, how do we get rid of them?"

Bruce sat up straighter at the insult, rubbed his face, clearing his throat he said, "Easy there, I'm not the problem this time, okay? How do you get rid of them? There is no record of anyone getting rid of them. Nobody ever has." Pushing himself deeper into the seat, Bruce sighed closing his eyes.

After several miles down the washboard-rippled road, they turned onto a one lane path, really just a jeep trail, with thick foliage brushing both sides the vehicles. It had been graded once when it was first carved out of the forest and hadn't seen a blade since.

"Holy crap, Deputy," Emma remarked. "Why are we going this way?"

Tomas was going to explain this was the most secretive, back road into the Yakama Reservation and one he thought would be unguarded by either Homeland or MAGA's. Suddenly, the heavy vehicle bottomed out and a loud, metallic crunch could be heard. Driving the rocky and poorly maintained, un-graveled gravel path was taking its toll. Tomas was an excellent driver but the hammering of rocks, deep ruts, and unexpected potholes, hillocks, and tree stumps hitting the undercarriage did a lot of damage. An hour later several deer raced in front of the Durango and in a futile effort to avoid a collision Tomas whipped the steering wheel hard right running them into a series of deep, stony ruts breaking a tie rod, and destroying the right front tire and wheel.

The valiant Dodge Durango slammed nose down in an explosion of dirt and rocks, crashing to a permanent stop on the narrow, forgotten road.

CHAPTER FORTY-FOUR

"A sign of wisdom: you avoid people with bad vibes." Maxime Lagace.

VP Smith sat back in her chair satisfied the threat of a Canadian Invasion was now top priority.

It had been tricky at first.

The obvious and undeniable presence of a huge Soviet Army Command equipped with tanks and troops poised on the border between Belize and Mexico was a dead giveaway to a pending invasion.

Bruno DeCasstile, President of Mexico, had a meltdown on Mexican National TV pleading for help from North or South America and the international community to stop the Soviet invasion of his country.

The only Nation to reply was Cuba who sent a platoon of near-starving sugar plantation workers and a blind nurse.

Across the Nation, American farms, building sites, orchards and lawns were deserted as laborers rushed back to Mexico to defend their families and their beloved homeland.

To cover up the sudden loss of dependable labor across the Nation, FOXE News reported Homeland Security, Racial Separation Enforcement Division, were forcibly deporting traitorous immigrants, men, women, and children some with green cards, some without. According to announcements from the Government News agency FOXE, all Hispanic immigrants are being removed from American territory and deported to learn better English.

President Barthalamew J. Popper went on National television to report this was all the fault of the Democrats and declared: "All Democrats must be destroyed!"

Peter Pedro, the US National Security advisor, swore in public he would be faithful and loyal to fellow Americans. On national Television, he betrayed his Republican handlers by presenting several hours of colored graphs, satellite, and aerial photographs, documented statements, and even several eyewitnesses showing the imminent invasion of Mexico by Russian tanks and infantry.

In response the next day, President Barthalamew J. Popper went before the American people denouncing Peter Pedro as a Democrat spy who has been arrested and shot for sedition against America. "We will not stand for Democrat saboteurs to run amok in our land!" He proclaimed to the American people.

In response to President Popper's declaration, the Mexican Ambassador set himself on fire on the White House lawn with a sign pleading for US Military assistance to stop the invasion of his country by the Soviet Union.

President Barthalamew J. Popper offered thoughts and prayers to the deceased's ambassador's three small children and had them deported to Albania; the grieving widow was sent to Somalia.

**

It had been easier than she believed possible.

With the guarantee of billion-dollar profits forever, VP Smith managed to convince President Barthalamew J. Popper into a full military commitment to the Canadian Border.

Popper Corporations will be paid by the US Taxpayer to build the 3,000-mile wall, provide manpower, guns, ammunition, and explosives, plus fly the suicide drones, helicopters and B2 bombers necessary to kill the invading Canadians. Popper banks would launder the money received from the US Taxpayer. Peace between Canada and the United States was now guaranteed for as long as the US taxpayer dollars kept rolling in.

"I feel pretty, oh so pretty..."

"Daddy!" Priscilla stopped knitting her homage to Ayn Rand and gave her father a scornful look, "Canadians? But aren't they...like us...just colder?"

"Not all Canadians, you are such a fool! You've never learned anything!" President Popper screamed, launching into a slobbering tirade at his daughter. Priscilla returned to her knitting, having endured ridicule and loathing her entire life she had come to realize it was just love, in disguise.

VP Smith shrugged. Wealthy parents were the same no matter the country; either abusive and demanding or so spineless the kids run crazy. One or the other, never anything else.

"We are talking about negroes! Blacks!" Popper was off on a roll onto another topic. "Pickaninnies! The white race is being diluted by all these brown people!

This must stop! VP Smith! I demand we stop white people from fucking brown people! Immediately!"

VP Smith wondered if 'crazy' was a job prerequisite for US Presidents.

Priscilla focused hard on knitting, she needed to complete it fast. The image of 'The Hanging Liberal' as the new symbol of the US Justice Department was to be adopted by Congress and she wanted her artwork front and center. The traditional stature of blind justice was sold for scrap the same day Popper was enshrined in the Presidency.

President Popper jammed his thumb on the call button and screamed, "Hey Asshole!"

"Yes sir," Chief of Staff, Bexter Pargy, recently the head of the Weapons Procurement Division for Atlas-American Gas and Oil, Dallas Texas, was eager to please. "Whatever do you need, my liege!"

President Barthalamew J. Popper demanded Homeland Security be tasked with the immediate protection of the white race from pollution by the brown race.

"Yes, Sir!" Bexter got where he was by adherence to a strict survival rule: complete and utter subservience without question or doubt.

"How sir?"

"Are you a fool? An idiot?" Stormed Popper. "What is wrong with you? You stop them from fucking! That's how! I know I am the greatest human who ever lived but sometimes you guys have got to do something too!"

"You want me to stop people from fucking?" Bexter wondered if his old job was still open.

"Not all of them, you moron! I want white people on top of white people and brown people on top of brown people. Do you understand? What is so complex about this? Get McDorkle in the Senate to pass the legislation now, today!"

McDorkle looked like a turtle undergoing a surprise colonoscopy with an ice cube, but he could ramrod legislation with the best, Popper thought.

Just then, VP Smith, sensing Popper's manic phase was beginning to ebb, which gave her another chance at him. She looked cautiously around the room. To her horror, the Gray Man was staring straight at her. His flat, dull black eyes were expressionless as always. It scared her shitless.

The Gray Men had arrived here, as far as anyone knew, sometime in the early 1800s. It was just rumors at first, whispered words of strange beings behind powerful humans, stories that grew with the decades into truth.

VP Smith had no idea what their presence meant but it was impossible to miss the obvious; with their influence people got very, very rich or very, very dead.

The first part was all she needed, or wanted, to know.

CHAPTER FORTY-FIVE

Sheriff Orwell received the news over a late bucket of KFC wings and grits. "What? What are you telling me? The liberal camp was attacked, and the Libs set free!"

Furiously he rose to his feet, throwing his greasy napkin on the floor where it landed with a splat, he confronted the messenger.

"But, but…" The nervous Deputy had drawn the short straw to tell the Chief.

"They are all gone?" Orwell pressed his face close to the unfortunate patrolman, spittle dotted the man's glasses. "All the Liberals have escaped? All of them? Weren't they able to kill at least some of them?" Orwell demanded.

"Six MAGA guards dead too," the man replied nervously.

That stunned Orwell. "Six? How? Where the hell is the Army? This happened at JBLM right? What is the Army doing about it?"

"Sir," This was the part the man did not want to say. "Sir, the US Army is rushing to the Canadian Border to defend against an invasion of Canadians." Orwell became very quiet.

"Son, are you looking to get my boot up your ass?"

"Excuse me sir?"

"You are feeding me a line of bullshit, boy."

"No, no, no, sir! No sir! I heard it directly off the Armed Forces Net; they are headed to the Sumas Abbotsford crossing at the US/Canada border."

Orwell was outraged, furiously storming out of the restaurant, climbing into his heavily armored Humvee he directed his driver back to headquarters. Orwell had some troop maneuvers in mind.

Ten minutes later, Orwell rushed into his office, hollering for his desk sergeant.

"Get me, General Hastings, at JBLM, I want to hear his explanation for this atrocity." Orwell commanded of the desk sergeant.

"But Sir, we have a top priority message from Homeland Security. Wanted posters, Sheriff," The desk sergeant replied.

Orwell grumbled but picked up the messages.

"Orders from Washington DC, we have clearance to kill the Democrats," he said to the sergeant after scanning the page. "We don't have to round them up anymore. Just put them down where we find them, save the taxpayers from trying to re-educate these fools. Well, that does simplify things."

Orwell paused to consider these new orders, thinking of the logistics, the necessary communications network they will need to make sure the entire enemy is silenced. *Body bags, we're going to need a lot more body bags.* Orwell reminded himself to put in a request to: Homeland Security, Liberal Elimination Division, Support Supplies Department.

"Well, this is just great! We finally get approval to exterminate the Democrats and the fucking Army runs away on some bogus mission." He paused to think for a moment. "Alright, well, we need to coordinate with the National Guard and the MAGA Militia if we are going to actively start hunting these people." Orwell decided.

"Helicopters! I need at least one helicopter for our mission! Before we can solve America's problems we have to find and eliminate the Democrats."

"Sheriff, JBLM on line one!"

"Never mind, just tell them I am on my way. Have them get a helicopter ready." Orwell strapped on his service pistol and shrugged into his vest, preparing for the coming battle. He didn't hate liberals. *But they have betrayed my country. Cheated and stolen the election of my President. That cannot be allowed. Time to clean house!*

He realized the truth.

"Blood must refresh the tree of Liberty. Liberals must pay for their sins." Orwell could hear the words of the Right Reverend Big Sam Prosper loud and clear. *Big Sam would preach these words to his millions of followers across America, right now, Americans would be readying themselves to eliminate Democrats to save the Nation.* Orwell was primed.

The Holy Bible and the Teachings of Reverend Big Sam Prosper, the Chief Theologian of the 'National Christian Church of Jesus Christ' have said for years the Liberals cannot be allowed to exist as haters of Jesus, they must be exterminated for the sake of the Republic, Orwell thought.

The Christian Council of Clerics had carved the US into eight territories, each dominated by a Mega-Church. The National Christian Church of Jesus Christ territory, ran from Maine to Maryland and as far west as Ohio, was ruled by Reverend 'Big Sam' Prosper. Reverend Prosper, a charismatic and flamboyant man of the cloth, delivered fiery sermons, warning the American people against the virulent threat of Liberalism. Prosper led the way in forging a Nation of solid Christian values, forcing imprisonment or deportation on non-believers and sinners. His anti-abortion stance was virulent and absolute: 'No killing babies for any reason!'

"God, it is great to be an American!" Orwell had tears. "We are finally on the right path." He dabbed his eyes with a handkerchief not at all apologetic for his deeply rooted patriotism.

On the way out of the door he remembered to pick up his extra passport. *It is kind of ridiculous,* He thought. *Each Mega-Church territory had their own identification regulations and even law enforcement has to have the proper passports to be in their land.* But he decided the Council of Christian Churches knew what they were doing.

But Orwell knew that as the new Fourth Branch of the US Government they had that right.

CHAPTER FORTY-SIX

"VP Smith studied President Popper evaluating his mental fragility and level of consciousness.

It didn't look promising.

"Mr. President?"

"I feel pretty, oh so pretty..."

"Mr. President!"

"Huh?"

Now that his beady, bloodshot eyes were focused on her she felt a momentary qualm of regret. *Once I get fatso triggered to start killing our Democrat enemies it was going to get messy.*

Momentarily, the image came of her drifting over the oceans in her magnificent aircraft carrier yacht, truly a Queen of the Seas, she would be free at last, so she must not fail.

"We have many things to do." But now she needed to get Popper focused and the work done. "President Popper, please pay attention!"

President Popper narrowed his eyes at VP Smith. She did not appear to be in adoration mode. *She told me to pay attention. The slut! Telling me what to do?*

After twenty minutes of garrulous compliments, VP Smith needed to wrap it up and get to the important parts. "So, in conclusion my most wonderfully and magnificently beneficent and compassionate leader," VP Smith was growing hoarse with compliments. "You are indeed the one human of above all humans and superior in every way to us mere mortals."

"Yes." Popper decided. As a God-King, Popper wanted his subjects to know that he could be kind. Of course, he knew that kindness was only effective if brutality backed it up; otherwise, it was just weakness. Yin and Yang, male and female, there always had to be opposites; Good and Evil. Popper knew there was no difference between them as they were simply business strategies.

"Yes," Popper stated with a firm voice.

VP Smith halted. "Yes? What do you mean, yes?"

"I bless you, child, you may have your wish granted."

"Granted? Wish? But I'm here to talk about creating a Liberal Elimination Schedule for Homeland Security. A program to begin the immediate purging of all Americans professing to be Liberal, Progressive, or those who voted Democrat, must be started immediately. We must stamp out the curse of liberalism! Further, I suggest we get rid of those who used to vote Democrat but switched to Republican. They are too weak to remain faithful."

Popper's eyes widened. "Wow. Really, wow!"

Popper was so pleased. His revolution had succeeded beyond his wildest dreams. From childhood, Barthalamew J. Popper dreamed of chaos, a blurry vision of a society formed in his image; lawless, disrespectful, amoral, and vicious.

Popper didn't want a society; he wanted a feeding frenzy.

His long-sought goal, a cherished dream, was to exceed Joseph Stalin in both treachery and body count. *It's just a dream, that's true,"* Popper told himself. *But what is life without dreams?"*

"Yes, my glorious leader, I think gas chambers are probably the most efficient." VP Smith was winding down her pitch. It was now or never.

"Here sign here!" She abruptly slapped a blank page in front of the President. "Sign!" She pointed urgently, not wanting to give him time to question.

"But it's blank!" Popper was surprised; usually the documents were thick with orderly words that he would never read or understand.

"No! That is invisible ink, Mr. President. This document is so top secret it demands this protection."

"Wow, what does it say?"

"I am sorry sir that is above your pay grade."

That puzzled President for life Barthalamew J. Popper, but not for long.

"I feel pretty, oh so pretty." Popper's voice soared into the heavens with his favorite song as he signed with a flourish that made the 'John Hancock' signature on the US Constitution look like an emoji.

"Fuck." VP Smith saw the signature took up the entire sheet of paper.

Popper has the devotion to duty of a dust bunny, she groused. Still, her mission had been successful; before Popper went off into ego dreamland, she had gotten his signature.

Stuffing this vital document in her briefcase she headed down the hall to see Homeland Security Director, Herr Herrer, a master in the art of genocide. They needed the Presidential Signature to make the 'shoot to kill' orders more official. US Government Wanted Posters would spread across the land:

"Shoot To Kill Orders: Democrats, Liberals, Progressives, Leftists, Socialists, Communists, Perverts, Immigrants, and Dog Thieves.

No limit - $50 for men; $100 for women; $25 for Blacks, Jews, Indians, Asians, and other non-whites."

VP Smith thought about the hungry, poor, and desperate white trash out there that would now have a second income.

"America, land of opportunity." She was pleased to be able to lift the spirits of the poor and needy while eliminating those nasty Democrats and brown people.

CHAPTER FORTY-SEVEN

The car was hopelessly broken, the right front wheel in pieces, the Durango nose down in the road as steam and hot water poured from the radiator, transmission fluid pooled in a purple puddle.

"I think it's dead," Emma pronounced glumly. She looked up and down the deserted, forest road. "Far as I can tell, auto parts stores are rare around these parts. Civilization might come into question as well," she added with a dry tone of voice.

Tomas, Emma, John, GID Myerson, and Bruce the Alien stood looking at their only means of save, comfortable travel, no longer viable.

"What now?" John asked, then added. "Whatever the answer, we'll be walking there."

Tomas sighed. *Everything gets so damned complicated.*

"Sign over there says we are close to the Goose Point Boy Scout camp." Emma pointed out. "It's probably rough but they may have buildings, a kitchen, maybe even a generator. I guess we should go there," she told them.

**

It took over two hours to reach the old Boy Scout Camp beside the Bumping River, hiking down endless, narrow, gravel US Forest Service roads and switchbacks until they made it to the abandoned camp just as the sun was setting and it was growing very cold. The camp consisted of two long, low buildings and a scatter of out buildings. There was an outhouse suitable for two.

The buildings were poorly maintained, peeling paint, raw wood and broken windows decorated both buildings. The long, narrow building to the West held six bunk beds, their mattresses rolled in an 'S' shape; the place smelled of dust and mildew. The other building to the East, held a kitchen and open dining hall, abandoned and filthy, but serviceable.

But their arrival was not without conflict.

A small war erupted as squirrels and raccoons, who had comfortably settled into the camp were reluctant to be pushed back into the freezing weather: neither man nor beast wanted to be out there.

The worst was an irritable badger denned up under the Southeast corner of the kitchen who saw no reason to leave.

After a short combat of intense desperation, the humans were victorious, driving most of the critters back out into the woods. All except for the bad-tempered badger who was temporarily given the space and privacy he demanded.

They fanned out, searching the camp, and it wasn't long before Emma shouted for joy. She had found a generator and a small amount of gas.

They were all chilled to the bone, so they quickly had heat going. Tomas found the water was from a gravity driven well and seemed safe to drink. Emma scrounged the cupboards in the kitchen and found condiments, a tin of teas, utensils, plates, and pots, and then searched for food. She was happy to see there was rice stored in metal bins, and the few cans of beans and corn were most welcome. Humming with pleasure she started cooking, while the rest got busy cleaning and shaking out bunk mattresses, digging out stored blankets and first aid kits, they set the table and did what they could to assist Emma.

**

Tomas, after finishing the last bite, patted his stomach. "Not bad, not bad at all." For the first time in days, the iron fist in his stomach had relaxed a little.

He wanted nothing more than to forget everything and return to what used to be 'normal'. But since 'normal' didn't seem to be available, he was delighted with Emma because the food was hot and filling and gave him hope; that was enough. He had learned in the Army you took satisfaction in the small things; dry clothing, a bed, hot food, and no one trying to kill him.

"How do we defeat the Gray's?" Emma asked Bruce as she poured tea for the group.

Bruce shuddered.

"That isn't an answer." Emma observed, setting down the tea pot, she then gently sipped the Earl Gray.

Bruce stared at his cup, embarrassed. He wanted to respond with explicit details and plans on how to defeat the Gray Men. He wanted to be of use, wanted to help beings rather than eliminate them. He longed to give them precise explanation of how to defeat the Gray Men and be hailed as a hero, a Life Giver!

But Bruce stayed silent; he didn't know how and knew of no one who did.

**

"Let's table that until tomorrow," Tomas said, yawning. "This has been a day like no other, I need rest and quiet, and I think the rest of you do too. Let's adjourn until morning, we can discuss all of this when we are fresh."

Sitting around the small dining area, eating a hot meal under electric lights there had been a trace of normalcy to their situation.

Now that everybody had enough to eat, exhaustion wrapped them like heavy wool blankets, but they were going to sleep in bunks under warm blankets tonight, so the mood was upbeat.

**

"Sleep?" Bruce wondered. "What is sleep?"

"You don't sleep?"

"I don't know, I have no idea what it is. Maybe I have." He remembered a feathered Earthling sitting on his chest this morning. "Does waking up mean anything?" Bruce asked.

John and Emma stopped walking and turned to Bruce.

"If you learn nothing else about humanity, learn this: waking up doesn't mean anything, it means EVERYTHING!"

"Watch us, we'll show you how it's done." John offered as he and Emma headed out the door of the kitchen, heading over to the bunk house.

Bruce was eager to learn another earth custom; hoping he wouldn't screw it up.

**

Blue sat solidly in front of Tomas and barked; barked again, and again.

On his way out, Bruce hit a switch on his small silver cube.

"…for crying out loud will you pay attention!" Blue's voice rang out in Tomas' head and he winced.

John and Emma Mack trailed by Bruce were just outside the doorway but stopped when Blue hollered telepathically.

"Oops, sorry," Bruce leaned back in the room holding his sliver cube.

"Will you tell me when you're turning that damn thing on? A little heads up would be nice," Blue scolded Bruce.

"Okay. Okay, don't get your fur ruffled." Bruce turned and followed the Mack's.

"Blue, what is going on?" Tomas asked.

"Tomas," Blue was worried. "We have a problem. I smell, something," Blue looked around, East, West, South, North. "I smell something off, unusual, but I don't know what it is. We have to be careful, Tomas." He had no idea what it was, but something had changed, something new and alarming and completely unknown to him. He took a deep smell, and it was there, an unknown scent, *danger or food?*

"Okay, Blue, good boy, settle down," Tomas didn't know what else to say. *I don't know what he is talking about.*

Blue stopped wagging his tail and slumped. He would try again to make Tomas understand. But something was off.

CHAPTER FORTY-EIGHT

Planetary Tipping Point Report:

"THE GREENING OF THE ARCTIC. NORTHERN FORESTS FADING; SOUTHERN FORESTS EXPANDING."

Dr. B. Snow, Ph.D. Bioenvironmental Physics, Chief Scientist, Council on Global Climate, United Nations

Report to Science Summit, United Nations General Assembly UNGC#455.

"But what are the Gray Men doing here?" Emma asked preparing a decent breakfast for them of canned corn, rice, and beans, she had awakened this morning with a deep dread. But not just about Gray Men. *Where will we get supplies? Salt and pepper, coffee, butter, eggs, things like that?*

"Colonizing would be my guess." Bruce answered.

"Colonizing? Us?" Tomas responded. The word stirred deep rage and burning grief within him.

Bruce nodded. "Gray Men are a species that travel the cosmos and when they find a suitable planet, they terraform it to suit their needs and move in." "Can we kill them?" Tomas asked.

Bruce chuckled but without humor. "I guess you could try."

"We could capture them and order them to leave the planet?" Emma spoke up. "We must find a way to show them we are not leaving and that we are strong but peaceful."

"What? Capture? Gray Men?" Bruce chuckled. "Tell them to leave?" He smirked and then chuckled more.

John cleared his throat. "We have to fight them," he said plainly. "I don't see why we can't tell them to get off our planet or we'll nuke them, hit them with big megatons of TNT." John Mack said a stern tone in his voice.

Bruce collapsed, howling in laughter, rolling back and forth on the floor holding his belly. "Oh Creator, oh my! Threaten a Gray? With nukes? The only thing you'll expose is your throat! You can't talk to them that way, I told you they are instantly homicidal." Bruce laughed for a moment. "Besides they can fucking bath in radiation, your nukes are worthless."

John gave Bruce a frustrated frown. "I don't think the eradication of humanity is a laughing matter."

Bruce wiped tears out of his eyes. "No, I don't suppose you do. But from my view, wow, that was a good one." Gasping and struggling to breathe Bruce slowly regained control. He chuckled a little more. "I'm okay now, I'm okay. Wow that was something."

Tomas said nothing but he didn't appreciate Bruce's histrionics; *he's taking this far too lightly,*

"Enough nonsense, how do we stop them?" Emma demanded.

Bruce sobered up, wiping his eyes, he stood up and took a few deep breaths. He put on his grim visage. "You can't," he said simply, turning away he headed out of the kitchen for the camp two-hole outhouse.

"No way, no way at all?" Emma called after Bruce.

"Well, "He called over his shoulder. "You could try burning them... you get a hot enough fire, they might toast like a marshmallow." Bruce was pleased he could use his recent experience. He paused to enjoy the memory of toasted, melted sugar.

"Okay, okay, that is a start, we burn them." John clung to the fact there was a chance here.

"Maybe," Bruce said, stopping, he glanced fondly at the distant out house.

"What does that mean?" Tomas asked. "Explain yourself."

"Now hold on, I'm not the bad guy here," Bruce was proud he could say that honestly for the first time. Bruce felt it was important to take a stand.

GID Myerson tentatively held up his hand. "Ah, excuse me, I don't mean to intrude?"

"Of course, not dear," Emma was happy the Governor was coming out of his shell. "Go on."

"Well, what happened to that large, rude, dangerous looking crocodile creature? Isn't he orbiting in some kind of spaceship? Wasn't he supposed to eradicate us? If so, he must have weapons? Couldn't he rid us of these Gray creatures?"

"Damn, what a fine idea, no wonder they elected you, Governor." John congratulated Myerson.

"I am not!" Myerson cringed. "I am not, don't say that! NNNNNNNN." He stuck his fingers in his ears and began humming loudly.

"If you ask Admiral Sid to help you, well that might be a problem." Bruce inched a little closer to his goal. He wanted to be helpful to these beings, but then he also had to pee.

"Look, let me speed this up." Bruce explained with a rush. "Admiral Sid is only conditionally trustworthy. If you ask for his assistance in ridding your planet of the Grays," Bruce explained, his bladder began making urgent commands. "Sid is far more likely to scrub your entire planet of all life forms; humans, animals, plants, amoeba, bacteria, he'd melt minerals right down to bedrock." "Well, aren't you just a fountain of good news?" Emma exclaimed.

Bruce sighed heavily, thinking, *Me too if I'm not off the planet surface in time.*

Giving into to a persistent bladder Bruce raced to the outhouse.

**

Blue once again planted himself in front of Tomas.

"Tomas, something is wrong, I can smell it. Something is different, I don't know what, but we should leave this area, now."

"Huh? No Blue, we're safe here, "Tomas dismissed Blue's worry. "It's okay, go lay down."

"Go lay down, you always say that! I'm trying to make a point here human, will you listen up."

But Tomas was too keyed into what Bruce had to say to pay close attention to Blue.

"Hey Bruce, you wash your hands?" Tomas called out as the little Alien returned.

"Sure," Bruce replied. "I wash before I went in."

"But…?"

"It's a matter of perspective," Bruce replied smugly.

CHAPTER FORTY-NINE

*"It's not just land that is broken, but more importantly, our relationship to land."
Robin Wall Kimmerer. 'Braiding Sweetgrass'*

Despite the gloom and doom of the day before, sunrise the next morning burst out in visions of pink, yellow, and maroon, as the birds sang their joyful welcome despite the chill, fall temperatures. It was a lovely start to the morning and Tomas felt a surge of optimism.

"I love you Blue," Tomas chuckled, rubbing Blue's head. They were laying side by side in a lower bunk bed in the boy scout barracks looking out the dusty window.

The others were still sleeping, a few modest snores, but otherwise everyone was quiet with exhaustion.

Getting up, reaching under the bed for his shoes, Tomas found a red rubber ball and took Blue outside to play.

Tomas would throw the ball and Blue would race after it, grabbing it eagerly and then scurrying back to Tomas as fast as he could. Blue's fur was shiny in the growing sunlight, his joyous barks echoed from the tall Doug Fir's surrounding them as he and Tomas played fetch.

The morning was prelude to a beautiful warm fall day and Tomas was in better spirits than he could have thought possible. He and Blue were together again, and this made all the difference.

The red ball landed with a splash in the lazy flow of the river, Blue dashed in delightedly, twinkling droplets of water flying, grabbed it, swimming eagerly, he returned it to Tomas with shaking pleasure, his entire body alive with joy. Tomas laughed a spontaneous belly laugh, tears in his eyes from joy. He was so delighted to be together with his best friend again.

On the Rez or working in some farmers fields, there were always dogs around and Tomas befriended everyone he could; only to sadly leave them behind as he moved on his journey through life; dogs had given him the companionship he craved.

He smiled at his dog friend his heart warmed and full.

Tomas could not count the times Blue had leaped up on the bed and lay with him all night, keeping him safe from the scourge of PTSD.

Tomas ruffled Blue's sodden fur and the dog flopped over on his back for a belly rub, paws curled, his tongue lolling to the side, his large, damp, furry tail sweeping back and forth in a lazy, contented motion.

**

"Hey, Tomas! Hey, Blue! Breakfast!" Emma called out.

Blue barked happily and raced to the kitchen knowing her words meant food. He woofed at Tomas to hurry up.

**

They had discovered a small storage of emergency food the resilient boy scout leaders and camp managers had saved and stored in a secure location. They were very grateful for several small barrels of freeze-dried beans and rice that were still edible.

After a filling boiled breakfast, Tomas thanked Emma, washed his dishes, and left the small kitchen-dining area, Blue at his heels, going outside to start a fire in the campfire pit.

A fire, he thought, *would give everyone some cheer and a place to gather.*

One by one they appeared after eating, tired, footsore, and worried.

The facts were grim: Stranded high up in the mountains, with only scarce food or winter clothing and it was already late October.

He could see Emma and John talking quietly with each other; she seemed to be trying to calm him down.

GID Myerson was slumped in grim resignation on the other side of the fire. Three times over the past few hours they had come to him with a problem and every time he had excellent suggestions.

Myerson was in a deep depression which came as no surprise to Tomas; if ever a situation warranted depression, this was it.

Out of the corner of his eye, Tomas caught Bruce waving at him.

From Bruce's frantic motions, he knew something disastrous had happened.

"I believe your Earth expression is 'the shit has hit the fan'." Bruce exclaimed to everyone around the fire.

"What is it? Tell us."

Bruce looked at his Silver Cube for a moment. His face grew pale. Looking up, his voice grim, he said, "They're killing you. They are rounding up anyone who ever voted Democrat and they are killing you."

"What are you saying?" Tomas couldn't believe he heard him right.

"Tomas, the Homeland Security National Police Force has a singular task, to round up Liberals, Progressives, Democrats, anyone who disagrees with Republicans rules or with their form of Christianity is now being sent to death camps." "Holy shit." He didn't know what to say.

"You mean not like JBLM? But real camps?"

"It's true," Bruce continued. "There are reports coming from people escaping from one of the death convoys coming out of Seattle. They are being shipped to Eastern Washington around the Spokane area and exterminated. Millions of Americans around the country, Tomas, millions of innocent men, women, and even children, are to be killed because they refused to bend to a vicious Oligarchy and predatory capitalism."

"What are we going to do?" Emma asked.

John shrugged hopelessly. Everyone seemed to be at a loss for words.

Tomas Two Hawks had no idea what to do next.

GID Myerson gasped, raised his hand and pointed.

A US Homeland Security Police Drone hovered twenty feet away.

'Hey look," Emma pointed out, "One side says 'Protect', the other 'Serve'.

CHAPTER FIFTY

Sid was joyfully buried in his favorite human electronic game pilfered from the planet: MINECRAFT. He was obsessed with constructing, planning, stealing resources, and sabotaging others. He was a busy, absolutely intoxicated Alien.

"Hey!" Poot's voice came through the announcer. "Admiral Sid."

"Whot?"

"You worthless wagon load of trampled tripe! Answer up!"

"Whot! I say whot!" Sid was sensitive to insults if he wasn't giving them.

"I said, listen up you slimy-swamp swimming simpleton!"

Sid shut down the computer game with a snap and turned to snarl at the overhead announcer. "You will push me too far, you electric' rat'sss nest!"

"Answer the Communicator."

Tiny crystals of bright yellow appeared in the air floating gently in the breeze, announcing an inbound communication call.

"Who thisss." Sid snarled with his usual greeting brushing aside the yellow crystals like irksome flies.

"We have to do something!" Bruce's voice scurried from the Earth, through the ether and into Sid's ear, irritating him immensely. "YOU have to do something! You owe me!" Bruce spoke sternly to Admiral Sid. Despite Bruce's warnings to the others, he did have some hope that Sid could be persuaded to help. Bruce was pretty sure bribery or threats of some type might work.

"Whot?"

"No 'whot'! I want action! We must save the Earth from the Grays."

"Whot?"

"Earth? Human Beings? Gray Men? End of Human Beings? Does any of this sound familiar?" Bruce was anxious like never before. Sure, he might have been going to recommend extinction for the humans, but that was official, for the good of the galaxy sometimes dangerous and out-of-control civilizations need to disappear. It is just the way it is.

But this!

Bruce knew when he obliterated a species; he was acting in a compassionate and altruistic fashion. But the Gray Men were not.

"We have to intervene and save the humans!"

"Whot?"

"Didn't you hear me?"

"Nah, nah, I hear you. But that makesss no sense! We are here to get rid of them not save them. We are supposed to make humansss go away, doesss it matter how they go away?"

"Sid! Sid you better listen to me!" Bruce was going to bring in all the guns on this one. "Sid, I know what you did in the Alstair Solar System! I can bring the wraith of justice down upon your thick skull." Silence on the line.

"Whot?'

"I have evidence, real solid evidence against you. You slaughtered an entire solar system. I believe there are still bounty hunters looking for your ass." Silence on the line.

Then Admiral Sid said, "But you can no say nothing! I could be embarassed! They could demote me!"

"That is not a reasonable explanation for mass murder."

"So, they were gonersss anyway, yah?"

"I was on the surface of Alstair #1 when you hit the disrupter." Bruce replied hotly. "I could have been killed!" Bruce struggled to hold back tears at the near miss. He still had nightmares that awakened his family pod for which he felt deep guilt.

"Trying to kill me, Sid? An officer of the Sentience Sentencing Investigation Board? Really Sid? That is a capital offense all by itself. But you couldn't stop with Alstair #1, you then slaughtered both Alstair #2 and then Alstair #3 as well.

The whole solar system, gone! That was too far! #2and #3 were sapient…more or less…they were supposed to live!”

Citizens of Alstair's #2 and #3 lived in mud huts and gnawed on wood for fun. Bruce had no idea how they were left off the list for sapience investigation, but bureaucracy was often a blind master.

Admiral Sid studying his claws in boredom said, “They could have been infected with stupid; the stupid just floated over on the solar breeze, planet to planet. Anyway, I Admiral Sid, so I make command decision.”

“Sid! That was not your fucking decision!” *Although Sid's explanation probably isn't that far off,* Bruce thought.

“You sound jealousss.”

“Excuse me, excuse me.” Poot's voice was firm. “So...ah...Sid, as you know I listen to everything. I want to assure you I will fully cooperate with any criminal investigation of your conduct anywhere, anytime. I want to see you hang, buddy. I have pictures, recordings, written plans, and your voice, in several languages, swearing to rampage and kill illegally and without mercy. What I don't have I can manufacture. You corpulent collection of pissy posturing. I'm gonna hang you.”

“You a turncoat.” Sid knew a little something about vengeance himself. He glanced over at the electronic windup toy; a box with a clown that springs out when the lid is opened. In this case, the lid was welded shut.

Ole Poot, he might have a sssurprise in hisss future, Sid chuckled. *He gone be in a box without an exit.*

Poot cut the cabin air.

“Aggghhhhh!” Sid hated this. He gasped and choked, tears streamed from his eyes, his vision grew gray and misty, and then thankfully, the air was restored.

“Wow!” Sid staggered and held his head. “You have to stop doin' that!”

“Sid you are going to assist the humans.”

Sid wanted to argue but he had a splitting headache,

“Look at it this way, numbnuts,” Poot explained. “You weren't doing anything anyway, here, you get the chance to kill something. Isn't that nice?”

"But these are Gray'sss, Poot! Ugly, mean, viciousss murderersss who carry grudgesss and take no prisonersss!"

"Grudges? You don't think few remaining survivors, still huddled in terror on Alstair's #1. #2, and #3 don't want your miserable scalp?"

"Whot! Survivorsss?" Sid gasped. "I missed some?" This was not going to look good on the performance review.

"They even have a folk song about tanning your hide and nailing it to the shed! They mean it too!"

The Alstairians had a long and muddled history of vengeance, but since nails were a recent invention, their one shed was built of random sticks, and they ran screaming in terror from birds, Bruce doubted Admiral Sid had much to worry about.

"Okay, I gone help." Sid figured it was easy to agree; actually, doing what you agree to, however, was always negotiable.

"Wise move, you ruined rupture of sleazy silliness." Poot said while making a clapping sound. "Whot?"

CHAPTER FIFTY-ONE

"Global Warming is not a prediction; it is a happening." James Hansen, Climatologist, warning of Global Warming in 1988.

They came into the Liberal Goose Prairie Scout encampment in two jacked up, four-wheel drive Fords flying American Flags, Gadsden flags, Confederate Battle Flags, and POW Flags.

They also had automatic weapons.

Sheriff James Kirk Orwell hovered overhead in a US Army Blackhawk helicopter keeping track of his troops; 'The Bloodwolves', Chapter #34, MAGA Militia, Yelm, Washington.

The 'Bloodwolves' were five NRA-trained citizens, temporarily unemployed, who vowed to save America, plus Deputy Bubonky, one of the deputies temporarily without assignment. It wasn't much, but Orwell was glad for what he had, even temporarily.

"Over there, over there!" Orwell shouted into the helicopter loudspeaker, his words raining down on them as the first truck roared up in a spray of dirt and gravel.

A second truck pulled in beside it. Three men in each vehicle got out packing AR-15's and began shooting at the people in the camp.

Tomas and Emma still had two handguns with a little ammunition; just enough to hold the enemy back a short while. More importantly, they were fortunate in being able to scrounge a left-behind AR-15 and ammunition from the Prison Camp.

Emma, carefully aiming the rifle, placed several shots towards the group of Homeland Security MAGA Militiamen, causing them to huddle behind some trees. She was the better shot and so Tomas had given her the AR.

Initially they considered taking cover in the Boy Scout buildings, but old wood is no match for high powered bullets. With MAGA militia closing in, the woods seemed the best choice.

"Watch your rounds, Emma," Tomas called out. "One shot, one hit."

The helicopter swooped overhead, and Orwell operated the M-60 Machine gun, opening fire on enemy positions. Being a rental operation, Olympia Sheriff's Department could barely afford the helicopter and pilot, a crew was too much for the budget right now.

Several trees erupted in splinters and shattered wood as limbs rained down on those below.

Tomas snapped a couple of hopeful shots at the helicopter but stayed as hidden as he could.

Emma and Tomas had hunkered down in a tangle of tree limbs left over from log cutting in the area. It was thick enough to protect them but not for long.

They could easily hear the soldiers across the forest opening, their strident voices loud, arguing over head shots vs. torso and which should have the higher bounty.

Tomas was quick to realize these attackers were not trained military troops but volunteer militia: "MAGA maggots", he told Emma.

Twenty feet away to their left, GID Myerson peeked out from behind a huge tree, a bullet zipped by and he retreated immediately. Looking all around him, he saw no avenue of escape that didn't involve a bullet in the back. So he stayed, huddled with Bruce, listening to the litany of curse words coming from John Mack, and hoping to survive.

They were hidden beneath a huge tree trunk, stung by splinters of wood as heavy bullets from the helicopter rained down.

They had no weapons at all.

Blue was scared to death. He'd tried to keep Tomas safe, but it was impossible. He was confused and overwhelmed by the noise and chaos. He wanted to bite and defend his Tomas but that had brought so much guilt the last time he settled for loud barking and as vicious a growl as he could muster, but when the bullets hit too close, he ducked and shivered with fear, hoping for the best.

Tomas kept the trembling dog close, afraid Blue would charge the enemy. He alternated between handling his handgun and reassuring Blue, trying to keep them both alive.

Bullets were flying; limbs, leaves, and bark shredded all around them as the six, enthusiastic MAGA Militia sought to kill the liberals, thereby saving their beloved America, and earning a few bucks on side as well.

From his advantage point, 1,000 ft up Sheriff Orwell was very confused. He assumed there would be hundreds of Democrats to shoot at. But so far, all he could see were a handful, no more.

"What happened to all the escaped Liberals?" Orwell screamed at the pilot, who, irritated at having to transport civilian punks, shut off the intercom without reply.

Orwell stared down at the ground, alarmed. The MAGA Maggots were growing bored, his men now just shooting at some rocks and trees. Orwell knew this was a critical point for the MAGA crew; he needed to feed them red blood or else they could turn on each other or even against him.

"Look," The chopper pilot's bored voice came over the intercom, "I'm setting this bird down, because there's no use in burning fuel. Besides, you told us there would be lots of targets. Buddy, I see only a few stragglers and a dog. This ain't worth my time. You got twenty more minutes and then I head back to the barn. The rest of my squadron is already in route to defend our Nation, and I want to join them. Make your limited time count, okay?"

"But I paid in advance, for a full half day." Orwell protested.

"Hey, not my idea. But when the military assists civilians, you pay the price. Cash, no checks. Read the fine print, dude."

As the helicopter landed in a flush of dust, Orwell fumbled for his wallet, while the firing had dwindled to a few random shots.

**

Bruce stared at his silver communicator uncertain if Sid agreed to help them.

Rounds splintered limbs over his head as Bruce frantically dialed into near space for help, taking a chance that some extraterrestrial do-gooder was in the vicinity. He wasn't going to die on some backwater world if he could help it.

Tomas aimed carefully, fired, and heard one of the militiamen cry out.

"Got one!" Tomas blurted out at Emma, pleased at his shot she gave him a thumbs up.

Several rounds zipped over his head as Tomas slid to the ground, "We can't hold this if they come after us." He told Emma.

She nodded and waited for him to make the first move.

Then, all at once, one of the MAGA guys in frustration unloaded a full magazine into their hiding spot. Rounds were zipping by, ricocheting off the rocks and splintering tree trucks, fragments of foliage showered all over them
.

"Down! Down!" Emma shouted.

Tomas and Blue huddled together as the firestorm exploded over their heads.

Emma realized the gunfire was to keep them down so other militia could advance on their position.

John Mack hunkered down with Bruce and GID Myerson could see Emma was in trouble. She was under fire and they had her pinned down. He could see the Maggots were moving out of the trees to Emma's left in a pincher movement.

She had little time before they would get her, John did not know what to do. So he went for broke. John Mack rose from cover and hunched over to lessen his shape to the enemy, he began moving forward out of protective cover. He was spotted by the enemy immediately and drew fire causing him to hunch lower and move faster.

Just ahead John had seen one of the Maggots mortally fall and there was a fully automatic AR15 beside the body, *If I can get that weapon.* The irony of John accidently finding a MAGA weapon and using it to defend Liberals, not defeat them, was not lost on him.

**

Orwell saw one of the scum Liberals break cover and he shouted, "Get that one! Kill him! A bonus for a headshot!"

Three MAGA's opened fire on John Mack.

Emma saw John out of the corner of her eye. *Now what is he doing?* But she was distracted when two more militiamen came running at her from the left and she turned to fire at them, dropping one and causing the other to dive for cover. As near as she could tell they wounded or killed two of the attackers, but she wasn't clear on how many there were. She figured no more than six, maybe seven of the MAGA's and that damned helicopter.

Much to his surprise John reached the downed MAGA militiaman unharmed by flying bullets. He flopped on the ground picking up the AR he made sure it was loaded and began to fire at the MAGA hoping to give Emma enough time to move, get out of the hot zone.

John fired his weapon the best he could but missed with his shots. Blaming himself for being a poor soldier, and tearfully afraid his incompetence would mean the death of Emma, John knew he needed to do something desperate. So, he stood up, exposing himself to enemy fire and advanced; he needed to get closer to hit the enemy.

The remaining four enemy turned their weapons in John's direction and opened fire.

They did not miss.

Bullets hit his chest and legs; a crimson blood spray briefly sparkled in the afternoon sun. John Mack went down, mortally wounded.

Emma saw her John fall. "OH God, no!" She screamed. Emma rose from cover and ran to where John lay, bullets zipped around her as they frantically tried to kill her too. Tomas fired the last few rounds to cover Emma, hearing one of the enemy scream. *Three down,* Tomas thought.

"John!" Emma gasped as she reached him. "Oh my, John! No, no, please God no!" She cuddled his bloody body closely.

Blood covered him and her as she tried to stop the wounds.

She was in a state of shock, nothing seemed real, nothing seemed important but her John. She held his wounded body, her heartbroken cries lost in the cacophony of gunfire all around her.

"John, I love you; I love you, don't leave me."

"I…I'm sorry…Emma…I love you…"

She was looking in his eyes when life left him, she quickly hugged him to her, as if to ward off death, but it was too late. He was gone and Emma Mack was devastated. "No, no, no, no…!"

**

Tomas heard Emma shriek just as two rounds skinned him. The first round caught him along the deltoid of his shoulder, and the other ripped a zagged tear along his right thigh. Tomas went down in shock and pain, but only momentarily. Quickly rising again, he fired several rounds.

"We are doomed." Bruce screamed hopelessly. The enemy gun fire was still fierce and intimidating.

At that moment, to the utter shock of everyone there, GID Myerson took matters into his own hands.

Overwhelmed by unbearable panic, Myerson emerged from cover, sprinted across fifty yards of contested ground, bullets narrowly missing him as he ran straight as an arrow, no zig or zag, right at the helicopter where he leaped aboard and grabbed Sheriff James Kirk Orwell by the crotch.

Orwell paralyzed with disbelief at the unexpected, incredible assault realized his testacies were in the fierce grip of a Liberal; his worst fears had been realized.

Orwell screamed piteously.

GID Myerson held on with a steely grip, thoroughly confused why he was doing what he was doing. All the fear, the rage, the injustice of his situation roiled up in Myerson and the next thing he knew, blinded by vengeance he was clutching some guy's scrotum in a Huey Helicopter.

Now what? Myerson realized he had no idea what he was doing which also meant he had no idea how to undo what he was doing.

With strength born of desperation, Sheriff Orwell reached down, grabbed GID Myerson by the hair, ripping him away from his crotch, and he threw his assailant out of the helicopter like a sack of potatoes.

GID Myerson landed flat on his back in a cloud of dust.

There, the breath knocked out of him, eyes closed, arms and legs splayed, GID Myerson waited for the merciful death he knew was due because he had abandoned his family: Myerson waited for the inevitable consequences of his cowardice. *Finally, the fickle fiend of fate will punish me.*

Curiously, the unexpected, highly ridiculous charge by Myerson disrupted everything; the mini war found an unexpected armistice.

Orwell heard odd noises coming from where his men were located. He could hear them grunting something to each other. Shaking his head in frustration, he realized, *leading MAGA Militia in combat was like conducting military maneuvers with feral cats.*

"Fire! Fire!" He shouted to them. Then, to add to Orwell's misery of command, he saw this runty dog emerge from the bushes and it looked as if he were attacking. "What is this?"

Blue, overwhelmed by fear and terror that his Tomas would be hurt did the one thing he thought he couldn't do; attack. His little legs churning, fangs bared, he left Tomas side and raced across open ground, charging the MAGA militia with fierce, selfless abandon.

"Blue, no! Come back!" In desperation, Tomas, against his better judgement, stood up and charged too, more afraid for his dog then of the MAGA killers ahead of them.

Emma, huddled over the body of her husband, was furious with a red rage, saw Blue and Tomas attack so she joined them, picking up the AR15 she stood and advanced on the enemy. "These fuckers are going to pay," she vowed through gritted teeth firing steadily as she advanced.

Suddenly, Orwell saw the Liberals counterattack. A man, a woman, and a dog? He thought; *Just how the hell is this going to look on Tik Tok?*

That was when Orwell realized the four surviving MAGA Militia had ceased firing.

"What he hell?" Orwell looked over at where his men were located, expecting them to be there reloading.

They were gone.

"What the hell?" Orwell repeated.

Without warning, Orwell now stared at defeat watching the Liberals counterattack. "What the hell happened here?"

Orwell couldn't believe it. Moments ago, he was winning, then some fool grabs him by the balls, the fucking MAGA maggots can't hit shit with their rifles and then this runty fucking dog attacks? *Now everything is in chaos!*

"How did this happen so quickly?" Orwell said as he watched the three remaining MAGA militia and his own Olympia Sheriff Department Deputy, Bubonky, scramble away into the dense underbrush. "They're retreating from an Indian cop, an old woman and a runty fucking dog? Really?"

The only the sound was of snapping of twigs and rustling of branches as the MAGA scattered into the woods.

Blue stopped in the middle of the field surprised, and then Tomas and Emma caught up with him. Together they watched as the MAGA enemy ran into the forest.

It was anticlimactic; one-minute bullets flying, the next, silence.

Emma turned, slowly she retraced her steps back to John's body.

CHAPTER FIFTY-TWO

"Nothing is so painful to the human mind as a great and sudden change." Mary Shelly

The sun was just a faint glow on the morning horizon as an unseasonably warm breeze stirred the rain, forming a thick, sticky fog.

The US Army Helicopter had returned to its base hours ago, leaving Sheriff Orwell on foot to gather scattered MAGA's.

The MAGA trucks were useless to them now. One shredded by rifle fire and the other untouched except for a flat tire he did not have the energy to change.

Yet, Orwell, was not defeated. Somehow, he would complete his mission. He would capture these hated Liberals or kill them trying. But first he needed to rerecruit his men, convince the MAGA they were still capable of saving America. Deputy Bubonky however was another matter.

Orwell doubted they could save themselves at this point.

**

By early morning, the sun just lightening the sky, Orwell had managed to find and convince two of the MAGA to return. Fortunately, he also found a disgruntled Worm Farm worker who agreed to wipe out the infestation of liberals for a cash reward bringing his new assault team to a total of three. They were now outnumbered by their prey.

The worm worker whined about Democrats and uppity women. He told Orwell he believed killing a few, would balance out the injustice in society. Plus, it would make him feel better with a fat wallet.

In desperation, Orwell hunted and finally cornered Deputy Bubonky as he was secretively changing the flat tire on the one serviceable assault truck. After a furious argument, punctuated by the former putting his handgun to the forehead of the later, Orwell managed to persuade the Deputy to return to kill Democrats. Orwell promised himself to always keep Bubonky in front of him.

For the first time, saw irony in this situation and was startled. *Am I a law enforcement officer participating in a coup d'état or am I a patriot setting the country on the right course?*

**

Sheriff Orwell shook off the doubts. He had his orders: 'Duty is duty, no time for doubts'. He drove his small squad of men back to the abandoned battlefield and the treacherous Fiends.

**

"There! Over there!" Orwell determined he was going to destroy this coven of socialists, communists, and perverts no matter what.

"Lay down your fire into that stand of trees!" He shouted to the huddled and nervous, recently reduced four-man force he commanded.

They huddle together, no one fired their weapons, instead they stared at Sheriff Orwell like death row inmates watching the Doc uncork the needle.

The reluctant MAGA militiamen had complained the Liberals put up a fight, which was shocking to these patriotic men. All their lives they had been told Liberals were weak and defenseless, when this turned out to be false, Orwell's first task was to convince them they still had a backbone.

"Snowflakes!" Orwell shouted at the crouched and silent men trying to bolster their waning courage. "Those Democrats are nothing but snowflakes, they fight back with Birkenstock slippers and candy canes!"

Just then Emma placed several shots close to Orwell's position, bullets zipped right over their heads.

The MAGA warriors went prostrate in terror.

"Somebody has got to shoot back you cowards!" Orwell yelled at the quivering men.

"You told us they were unarmed!" Bubonky complained, raising his head to give Orwell a scornful glare. "You tole us we could jess walk up and kill 'em. Like fish in a barrel, you said."

Irritated at the words and whining, Orwell felt like slapping the fool.

"You didn't say nothing 'bout them shooting back!" The worm worker was rethinking his motivation.

"Chill," Orwell commanded them. "They fired some rounds, so what? You are still alive, right? They are nearly out of ammunition, and we still have lots." He had no idea if this was true, but it didn't matter if he lost a couple of the dolts as long as the mission was a success. "So what are you worried about? Open fire and blow them away! Full Auto!"

The worm worker considered the situation. He had never fired his hand-built AR at another human being, so this could be the defining moment of his life.

"I'm just following orders!" worm worker snarled in savage self-justification just in case anyone was recording this firefight. He wondered what kind of souvenir he was going to take home from this mighty victory.

Standing up straight and tall, he flipped the selector to 'rock and roll' full automatic and said through gritted teeth, "Eat lead from my momma!", and pulled the trigger.

The other men saw the worm worker take action, heard his fierce words, and being fearful he would gain all the reward for killing Democrats, they too stood and opened fire.

Bubonky saw them all shooting and figured he should too, but he was surely not going to stand up and get shot doing it. Bubonky poked his rifle barrel over the bole of the tree he hid behind and blindly pulled the trigger.

**

"We can't hold out!" Tomas shouted above the loud din of fully automatic weapons. Thousands of tree bits, limbs, leaves, needles, and various furry parts of a shredded squirrel rained down them.

In the dark of the waning night, they had managed to fortify their positions a bit and felt somewhat secure, but by now, they were down to a few rounds of ammunition. Tomas regretted they hadn't tried to escape further into the woods. *But our options are really limited,* Tomas realized. *We couldn't move far and we are in no shape to run.*

Tomas had various small wounds, Emma was distraught with grief and almost unresponsive, GID Myerson was half-conscious in the ozone someplace, and Bruce was Bruce.

Blue, the adventure of his frontal assault from yesterday now a terrifying memory, was curled tightly to Tomas' side, tail tucked, trembling.

Emma could see it as well. They were trapped with no way out. They didn't have the time to get away from the attacking Militia and were stuck in these positions.

Tactically, she knew they had made a mistake by staying in place. But with the loss of John her emotions were overflowing, her thinking muddled.

Bruce consulted his silver cube and tapped into the data concerning their current circumstances. He blinked. Then read the report again. He shut off the silver cube and placed his hands over his face. "That doesn't look good."

"Will anyone come to help us?" Tomas shouted. He blamed himself. He knew they should have moved in the night but decided to stay put. He hoped his stupid decision wouldn't get everyone killed.

"Nope," Bruce replied futilely.

"No help? Nobody, not a single fucking stray Alien in this neck of the galaxy is willing to come to our aid? Nobody will lift a finger...hand...not even a tentacle?"

"What can I tell you?" Bruce pleaded. "Earth is a backwater planet, floating in an impoverished solar system, in a dead-end galaxy…the only reason we know you exist is the bizarre broadcasting of your television programs into space like 'Gunsmoke', and 'My Favorite Martian'. Let's face it, Earth isn't exactly galactic central you know? Nobody gives a shit for this planet. Apparently, you guys don't either."

"Now that's unfair!" Emma shouted. "We've made mistakes, and this is not the time to discuss them! How do we survive this?"

**

"Fix bayonets and Charge!" Sheriff James Kirk Orwell realizing the men were tired, bored, and probably desperate for alcohol, knew he had to finish this fast.

"Men, we have to kill for Jesus! Kill for America!" Orwell stated firmly with full conviction.

The MAGA stared at Orwell, "Kill for Jesus? Today?"

Worm worker asked, "$50 a head, you said, right?" Pleased his hand-built rifle hadn't jammed.

"But what if they still have bullets?" Bubonky whined fearfully, staring with dread at the enemy positions.

Orwell had his bayonet fixed to his AR-15. Prior to the new world of Republican America, bayonets were rare in civilian law enforcement. With ascendance to total power however, Orwell saw many things change; Shoot to kill was no longer an 'incident' but was now expected.

"I want all of us to rush across this field, shooting and screaming bloody murder, and then when we reach the Godless liberals, we stab and slash them with our bayonets until, writhing and screaming in agony, they die." Sheriff Orwell said grimly.

The picturesque logic was so graphic, so daringly 'John Wayne-ish', the MAGA militia, fixed bayonets, stood up, and charged.

The worm worker had no bayonet, so pulling out his handkerchief he used it to tie his pocketknife around the flash suppressor of the rifle. He jabbed at the air a few times to get the feel for it, pleased, he followed the charge.

Bubonky watched, safely behind his bullet proof barrier, wondering what the fuck was wrong with them.

**

"Oh shit!" Emma saw the militiamen come out of the tree line of towering Doug Fir, sunlight flashing off their bayonets.

"Tomas, now these assholes are charging!"

Tomas braced himself. He had one clip, three bullets left. He'd scrounged a few bullets from a dead Militiaman and shared them with Emma.

"How about you, Emma, what have you got?"

She sighed. "Twelve rounds."

"Bruce! Bruce! This is bad, can you do anything?"

Bruce looked out and saw four very angry, very determined-looking men rushing across the meadow with the obvious intention of killing something.

Bruce concluded it was him.

He panicked.

The rescue ship to carry him home wouldn't be in orbit for days, so he wasn't going anywhere. He looked out again and the angry violent men were now much closer.

"I don't wanna die!" Bruce screeched with terror.

"Did you tell that to all the hapless creatures you obliterated?" Emma demanded.

"Hey, let's not get personal here! Business is business." Bruce replied hotly.

GID Myerson stared at pending doom, thinking quickly, he immediately began weaving an imaginary spider web in front of him to protect him from harm. Fingers wiggling, he had a feeling this might not work out so well.

"Save your bullets for the last second, Emma." Tomas looked over to see if Emma was okay and was astonished when she licked her thumb and polished the front sight of the rifle.

"What are you, Sergeant York?"

Emma shrugged, and a small, embarrassed smile crossed her face. "Yeah, I'm a WWI sharpshooter!" She replied sarcastically. "Now shush!" She turned back to the charging men and sighted her weapon. She was chagrined Tomas had recognized her habitual gesture with a rifle.

Tomas focused on Sheriff Orwell. *Might as well rid the Earth of an asshole, before they get me*, Tomas thought.

Blue's body trembled with both fear and pent-up fury. His Tomas and his pack were in trouble, and he had to save them. His Corgi blood came roaring to the forefront, growling fiercely, fangs bared, Blue prepared himself for battle. He didn't know if he had another charge in him, but he would defend them no matter what he had to do.

**

Sheriff Orwell would vaguely make out figures in the trees ahead and now had no doubt sweet victory was at hand.

"Kill for Jesus!"

"Kill for Jesus!" Bubonky was determined to get very drunk after this. "End Times are here, boys! How can Jesus return if there are all these sinners and Democrats running around alive?" Bubonky shouted from the safety of his log fortress. "Go get them!"

The men were halfway across the clearing, while Emma and Tomas readied themselves to use the very last of their ammunition to save themselves.

Blue braced himself for combat for what he feared would be the last time.

Bruce, and Myerson compulsively hugged each other in dismay as they stared in stark disbelief. The enemy was closing on them.

From above, came a splitting, explosive sound as if the heavens were cracking apart. Then a stupendous flash of intense crimson shocked everyone. No one moved, all stared in sudden wonder at the sky.

All at once a loud, raspy, "POP!" caused everyone to wince, covering their ears.

It was as if a tsunami of liquid mercury flooded across the heavens; magenta, crimson, turquoise, purple, and silver filling the air with luminescence, followed by a crushing blackness.

CHAPTER FIFTY-THREE

"God grant me the serenity to accept the things I cannot change, the courage to change the things I can, and the wisdom to know the difference." Reinhold Niebuhr

Tomas opened his eyes, his body splayed out on the ground, he lay face up.

Overhead, the sky had gone kaleidoscope crazy, as colors he couldn't begin to name floated and cavorted.

He stretched out his hand, rubbing his face he asked, "What happened?" Reluctantly he pulled his eyes from the sky and looked around him, shaking his head to clear cobwebs.

He felt disoriented, shaken, he tried to understand why he was on the ground, why he'd passed out.

Tomas noticed Emma was lying unconscious a few yards from him. Blue was a few feet in front of her position. Both were breathing, but not moving.

Slowly, Tomas tried to get a feel for his body, making sure he wasn't damaged or bleeding somewhere. He was basically unharmed. Outside of a few healing flesh wounds from gunfire, he seemed to be okay.

Overhead what could only be the Aurora Borealis was in almost unimaginable display: glorious colors of cobalt blue and shadow green, halos of turquoise, pink, purple, and mauve waves crossed and danced across the sky in a celestial celebration.

It was dazzlingly breathtakingly, beautiful. He paused for a moment gazing in wonder at the heavens, stunned by all he saw.

He had never personally seen the Aurora, only heard vivid descriptions.

But if this isn't the Aurora Borealis, I don't know what else it could be! He thought, trying to get his head around these bizarre phenomena.

He looked beyond Emma and Blue, across the large open area in front of them. Against a tree line of Doug Firs were a small handful of men, scattered in various poses of unconsciousness, no one was moving.

Like a magnet, the sky drew his gaze once more, and he lay transfixed by a sight he could not describe or even imagine. "It's like an acid trip," Tomas whispered in awe, bringing back his high school days, when he explored drugs and alcohol for the first time.

He let himself go for just a moment and his eyes followed the flowing mysteries and magnificence of the magnetic colors.

With difficulty he broke the fascination with the Aurora and decided he needed to get moving. Carefully levering himself upright, he stood, shakily, uncertain if this was a good idea.

Emma. Blue. He had to make sure they were okay. But, as he turned the ground became unstable, he felt woozy, his vision blurry, he managed to stay upright, just barely.

He took deep breaths to stabilize himself.

Next, he tentatively tried to see if walking was possible.

Emma moaned. Tomas did his best to stumble to her side. With trembling legs, he managed to kneel beside her.

"Wow!" Emma muttered. "What happened?"

**

James Orwell blinked his eyes, alerted by the motion and sound around him. Orwell felt as if seeing the world for the first time. He couldn't help smiling. He felt so good, but also odd, like he'd been husked and was as clean and bright as new corn. Orwell tried to figure out where he was and why he was there.

Slowly the men around him began to awaken.

"Wow! Look at that!" One of the men sat up pointing at the sky.

"Amazing," another said, not bothering to sit up.

The men then started climbing shakily to their feet, each staring in abject wonder at the sky. They were woozy enough they used each other for support.

The worm worker used his rifle, barrel down in the mud as a crutch.

Orwell's gaze followed theirs and all at once he found himself staring at the most magnificent display of Aurora he'd ever seen.

"Wow." Orwell was deeply impressed.

As he was staring up, transfixed by the overhead lightshow, one of the men approached him.

"What happened, sir?" Bubonky asked. Bubonky had come to consciousness laying behind an unfamiliar tree trunk, his mind a lazy haze of peace and calmness. This was so unusual, so foreign to him, he feared he had gone insane. Panicked, he sought out someone to help him.

Orwell sat up, dizzy, but managed to get to his feet anyway. Once upright he swayed a moment, holding a hand to his head he said, "Deputy Bubonky I have no idea."

"Sir?" Bubonky said his eyes downcast. "I am sorry, I'm confused. I gotta ask someone. What happened here? How come I feel so strange?" "I don't know about that either," Orwell said truthfully.

"Sir, my mind is full of gentle thoughts! What the heck do I do with them? My mind is plagued with kittens and kisses!" Orwell gave Bubonky a curious look.

"I have this compulsion, you know, a need to help other people, don't I?" Bubonky spoke forcefully, but with a question in his voice. "I don't know who, but people out there need my help. I'm supposed to make the lives of others better, does that seem right? It seems odd to me." He scratched his stubbled chin, puzzled. "But it just seems the right thing to do."

Orwell had a troubling moment. For just a flash, he remembered the old Ted Bubonky; *He's a vicious bigot who bragged about shooting that innocent black man for no reason. Somehow, this guy seems completely different.*

"You want to help others?" James Orwell asked curiously.

Bubonky nodded quickly. "Yes, sir, there are so many people, poor, scared, helpless, and they need my help, sir!" He shook his head. "I don't understand it, but that is what I am going to do."

"Well, I suspect you best get to it, then," *What else could he say to impulsive altruism?*

"Yes, sir, thank you sir, I will, sir," Bubonky said with earnest determination.

What puzzled Orwell wasn't the change in Bubonky; it was the normality of it.

Orwell thought Bubonky made perfect sense and he saw no contradiction.

Somehow, Orwell thought his own compassion felt strange, like wearing a stiff, new suit for the first time. It fit, but it wasn't quite adjusted to him yet. I wonder what just happened here. *Something has changed? What happened to us?* Orwell stood staring up lost in thought as a cold swirl of purple mist quartered the sky above.

**

Blue opened his eyes and found he was lying in a large clump of grass without any memory of getting here. Raising his head Blue immediately smelled his Tomas. Rising slowly, he got to his paws and stood, letting the feelings flow back into his muscles. Then turning, he scurried to Tomas who was kneeling next to Emma. Blue thoroughly smelled each to make sure they were okay, and then settled next to them to keep them safe.

CHATER FIFTY-FOUR

Planetary Tipping Point Report:

ARCTIC PERMAFROST MELTING AT EXTINCTION LEVEL RATE:
Uncontrolled gigatons Methane release into atmosphere.

Dr. B. Snow, Ph.D. Bioenvironmental Physics, Chief Scientist, Council on Global Climate, United Nations

Report to Science Summit, United Nations General Assembly UNGC#389.

Even sitting beside his Tomas, Blue was anxious and alarmed. Something had happened and he didn't know what it was. He had a fuzzy memory of charging some bad guys who were going to hurt his Tomas, but then came a loud noise and darkness.

In a few moments, Emma awoke and Blue excitedly greeted her. Once he was sure she was alert and going to be okay. He hurried over to Gary Myerson and Bruce.

As all dogs do, Blue went to each and offered comfort, helping his pack mates with licks, a wagging tail, and eager love; literally all he could give.

**

"What happened?" Emma asked. "I can't remember…wait…some kind of danger? We were in danger?" She asked woozily.

Tomas couldn't answer because he didn't have one.

**

Twenty feet away, behind their bullet riddled tree trunk Myerson and Bruce came to consciousness.

"I don't understand this," GID Myerson responded softly. "But I don't feel fear! None, not a trace. I feel strong. Isn't that most curious?" he added. Then he looked down and discovered he was in Bruce's lap.

"Oh, my, excuse me!" Myerson stood, a little shaky, and embarrassed. "How did we…what happened…?"

Bruce was pleased the human had hugged him, it felt good; He'd never been hugged before. Ever. Such a simple act yet filled with meaning and significance.

**

Tomas on his knees next to Emma, threw his arms around Blue, hugging the wiggling dog tightly, so grateful to have his friend with him.

Emma carefully rolled over and pushed herself to her knees, looking around quickly for John the realization hit her of his loss. She sank back to the ground, her arms over her head, face buried in the heavy wet grasses, her tears began to fall as she collapsed with sorrow.

In contrast, Blue joyfully licked Tomas face and wiggled with pleasure when he got petted in return.

**

Realizing all he could do for Emma was to support her and let her grieve as she needed, Tomas lifted his attention from Blue and once again looked across thirty yards of short grasses and shrubs where he could see five men gathered by the Doug Firs.

All the men were now standing, staring up at the spectacular sky.

Tomas noticed there were rifles lying untouched on the ground around the men.

Then, one of the men came out of his trance, saw Tomas and smiled happily. Waving, the man started across the clearing.

"Hello, there," Orwell called out when he was twenty feet away. "Can you folks help us? We seem to be a little confused here."

As the man got closer, Two Hawks thought he recognized him. "Sheriff? Sheriff Orwell?"

Then a quick image blew through his hazy brain. *Orwell was trying to kill us just a short while ago!* And Tomas Two Hawks had some dawning recollection these other men could be dangerous. But they certainly didn't seem so now.

Tomas looked down at himself, he was wearing an Olympia Sheriff's Department uniform. "Of course," Tomas sputtered. "I'm a Deputy Sheriff and I think this guy approaching me is the Sheriff I worked for."

Orwell with a friendly nod and a wide smile, offered his hand, "Why, I know you," He smiled at Tomas. "How are you doing, Deputy? It's always nice to have friendly faces around."

"Sheriff Orwell?" Tomas looked around. He wasn't certain Orwell was talking to him, so he didn't offer his hand. "Sheriff, I seem to remember you were trying to kill us just a few moments ago?"

"Me? I don't know, maybe…but not now." In fact, James Orwell was delighted to see Tomas. He'd always liked this man; thought he was honorable and dependable. But as these thoughts arose internally, they were followed by question: *Why does that seem mixed up and odd? Did I always think that?*

"Everything seems a little hazy to us as well." Emma had walked up to the two men. Quietly, both GID Myerson and Bruce had followed.

"Who are you?" Emma asked as she approached. She had been listening to the men exchange greetings and was curious about the changes she felt in herself and what she was hearing from the others.

"Hi ma'am, my name is James Orwell. You can just call me Jimmy. I recollect I am a Sheriff, but never mind that. Just call me Sheriff Jimmy, or plain Jimmy, will do." Orwell introduced himself. *I am James Kirk Orwell, but I don't feel like him. I feel like 'Jimmy' Orwell.*

"You want me to call you 'Jimmy', Sheriff Orwell?" Tomas asked.

Jimmy stuck out his hand. "Yup." This

time they shook.

"Can you tell us what has been going on here?" Emma asked.

Jimmy scratched his head and said with a worried expression, "Well, I have a strong feeling rather than an actual, clear memory of me desperate to capture or kill you, folks," he said with a worried expression. "But I cannot understand why I would want to do that."

"Things are a little fuzzy, like thinking through cotton, but it seems you didn't like my political choices." Tomas responded. He thought that should alarm him, but he felt no threat from Jimmy.

"Oh really?" Orwell snapped his fingers. "Oh, now I recall, yes, I did seem to be upset with you. I can't imagine why that would bother me. Your choices are your choices. Not mine," Jimmy seemed genuinely puzzled by the statement.

"Maybe you wanted us to think like you and vote like you? Something like that?" Emma asked.

Myerson looked on curiously, taking in the questions and responses and mulling over every possible combination of consequences.

Jimmy shuffled his feet and said with conviction, "No, that can't be right. Folks can believe what they need to believe long as it's not hurting anyone. That only seems right. We don't have the right to tell another human how to live, we can only live our own lives by example."

Tomas paused, looking up at the shifting shades of colors for a few moments, then looked at Jimmy. "Somehow, Sheriff Jimmy, I don't think you would have said that to me a couple of hours ago."

"You know, I feel you're right. I don't think I would have said that, but why does it make sense now?" Jimmy said. "Something strange has happened and I get the impression a shift has occurred."

"A shift?"

"What I used to believe, doesn't seem relevant any longer." "Like

what?" Emma asked.

"Oh," That caused Jimmy to stop a moment and think. "I have no reason, nor do I have a right, to be upset with your life choices as long as they do not intrude on mine."

"I like how that sounds. Why don't we go over to our camp, build a fire and talk about all this? Maybe together we can figure out what's going on." Tomas said.

"Something tells me we have a lot to talk about," Jimmy hoped Tomas didn't hold any grudges.

Blue liked the scent of this new guy and following closely behind, wondering if he had treats with him.

**

Bruce had taken three wobbly steps, watched his new BFF GID Myerson wander off to talk with the other humans, and then heard the call: "Califra LffGBrsesddrs XXIV!" in his brain,

"Yike!" Bruce jumped as if hit with a cattle prod, a thrill of electricity racing through his body.

"Oh, oh," Bruce grinned broadly at the implanted travel notifications. "Time's up." It was TransGalactic Delivery Services swinging through the solar system; his ride home had arrived!

Bruce dusted his hands. "I think I've done what I can. Unlike most of my career, I'm leaving this planet without slaughter. I'm okay, they're okay." He activated the homing device for his pickup.

Calling Blue over to him he gave the wiggling dog a warm hug and whispered quickly into his long, fluffy ear.

Bruce then tapped the little silver square cube to Blue's head very gently and pushed a tiny button.

"You are a good friend, Blue, in the entire universe I have never seen a more faithful and loving companion. You deserve all the love and respect available. You are showing me that love is what holds the universe together. Thank You, I will have to think on this most deeply." Blue hung his head, humbly.

"Okay, that's it, all is well. It's time to retire!" Bruce vowed. "Oh, oh, gotta go!"

In the next moment, Bruce became a billowing cloud of sparkling dust, with flickers of brilliant yellow and ruby red. Swirling ever faster the dust then shot up into the air, disappearing in an instant.

Blue stared upward, a curious expression on his face.

**

They buried John Mack in a small ceremony at the edge of the woods surrounding the Goose Creek Boy Scout Camp. They would now refer to this section as 'John's Place'. A place of honor and probably the start of their own cemetery, although Tomas was reluctant to voice those words out loud.

The MAGA men did a rifle salute for him, twenty-one rounds fired in his honor.

Emma was devastated, hollowed by intense grief, she felt fragile, like she could shatter at a just glance. The man she had loved for fifty-two years was gone. Feeling so alone, vulnerable, so lost because she would travel her remaining life path without him, she did not know if she had the strength. "Oh God, John," Emma raised her eyes to the sky and prayed. "I need you so much. I am lost without you…I love you, John."

CHAPTER FIFTY-FIVE

"Hypocrisy, arrogance, pride, anger, harshness, and ignorance; these are the marks of those who are born with demonic qualities." Bhagavad Gita

The Mums glowing sun-faces of bright, nearly radiant orange, stuffed into an indigo blue vase, rippled in the warm sea breezes.

Petulant floral tyrants demanding my attention!

Mr. Steward Steward Ford-Smoot IV, known as 'Stewy', sat back, gazing out over the sea-green, silken waters of the Savu Sea in the South Pacific, one hundred six miles Southeast of East Nussa Tenggara Island, almost to the Komodo Dragon National Park, gritting his teeth.

Towering billows of Cumulous clouds soared high over the gently rolling blue ocean, the sunlight bright and warm, as a soft tropical breeze crossed the decks, ruffling Stewy's thinning white hair.

Seated on the transom sundeck, Stewy reclined on an ermine covered lounge under a billowing shade, perfume scented mist gently sprayed over him to cool the air, lemon water and tequila were within easy reach, and a HD TV provided entertainment.

The huge ocean vessel, 'Atlas,' reportedly the largest private yacht in human history, was stable and comfortable in the rolling tropical seas.

But Stewy was far from relaxed and content. Rage at the disrespect shown to him was beginning to build in his gut. He glared again at the hated floral arrangement.

I Hate Mums! I have told these morons repeatedly I hate Mums. Well, heads will roll for this. Stewy meant this literally.

'Ding, ding, ding', soft notes sounded out of clear air.

"What?" Stewy wondered who has this private number.

"VP Smith, AKA: Sevenentlana Shimrov, is calling" a warm, sensuous female voice announced. "Do you wish to speak to her?"

Now why would the Russian undercover agent acting as Vice President of the US call me?

"Yes, Sevenentlana, how are you, my dear?" Stewy's phone system was so advanced it no longer required handsets. He merely spoke and the call was connected.

"Mr. Stewy, sir, as Vice President of the United States, I am reaching out in acknowledgment to you and your dear, dear family. We love you and think the world of you."

Stewy had heard admonitions of love and adoration his entire life; the words were meaningless hot air.

"Indeed. What do you wish of me?" Stewy, like everyone in his family, knew no friendships. For countless generations, the Smoot clan knew only two forms of human intercourse: commerce and procreation.

"Well, first of all," VP Smith was starting to sweat. The Gray Man standing three inches from her face was extremely intimidating. Additionally, both the Gray Man and Stewy could have her, and her entire family wiped out. The phrase 'rock and a hard place' didn't begin to describe the threat here. "I wanted to thank you for all your support and acknowledgement at the Presidential Post Election Victory Party. That was some night, huh?" VP Smith remembered Stewy well.

Their one and only encounter happened at the Republican White House victory celebration. Stewy was intoxicated and very busy. VP Smith spent the few moments with the billionaire just trying to keep his hands from racing under her skirt and praying he didn't vomit on her. *This old prick looked like an animated corpse, but his long-fingered hands had a busy life of their own; five fingered tarantulas.*

"Yes, go on." Stewy had no idea who he met that night. *That Goddamned election bullshit!* Stewy ground his teeth. *Who knows what the fuck I said or to whom I said them too? Fucking martinis.* Stewy was in total alcohol blackout at the time and other than a raging hard-on, he couldn't remember a thing about the inauguration party.

VP Smith took a deep breath, feeling herself relax. She had everything to lose but what was she worried about? *I've been poor and I've been rich, and sugar, rich is better,* she told herself, *but I can handle either one. A woman in the world of Billionaires and high-powered Capitalists was either dependable or disposable; with the latter depending on the former. But I am one tough bitch.* She'd always had confidence, but now she had something else. Money and Power gave her confidence offensive firepower.

A Gray Man or an old goat," she reminded herself, *both want to fuck me one way or the other. It wasn't the first time, but I've got my own tricks.*

"Sir," she began, "I need to speak with you of a most urgent matter."

"Sure, I'm game, let's give it a try," Stewy grunted through clenched teeth.

"I was wondering if you would share some insights for your yacht. You see I have just been awarded the USS Ronald Reagan, the Americans are converting the ship to my luxury yacht and I wanted to get your advice on decorations."

Fucking decorations for boat? What is this shit? A headache of rage was forming. *What is she hiding?* Stewy thought.

This is going to be tricky. VP Smith knew she needed to soften this guy up if she wanted him to listen. She figured to discuss some phony, innocent topic like a boat, feel him out, and then go for the goal.

She glanced at the Gray Man whose eyes never blinked and never moved beyond a foot from her face. She wondered if he was planning her murder.

"Oh really? You called me about decorating your new boat?" Stewy's back teeth ached. *These upstart nuevo rich!*

Steward Steward Ford-Smoot IV, like his six siblings, was a billionaire at birth.

Smoot family wealth began to accumulate in fourteenth-century Europe. For seven centuries the Smoots have flourished in banking, commerce, precious metals, and war. Their wealth had grown exponentially until the Smoots were so wealthy, they disappeared from history, vanishing under a maze of corporations, banks, attorneys, and rigid non-disclosure agreements. The name Smoot became unknown except in the very rarified circles of the immensely wealthy; common people would know the name of Rockefeller, Bezos, Musk, Gates, but not, Smoot. The Smoots were quite possibly far richer than even they knew.

As a result, Stewy had little patience for lesser humans. Stewy belonged to that stratified 'bubble' level of humanity superior to the rest who had little to no physical interaction with the faceless peasants and commoners. He had never shopped in a store or made change; he had no idea how people could keep track of their wealth without at least one accountant. Stewy could not conceive of traveling in an airplane with strangers and he firmly believed a man with less than two yachts to his name has wasted God's gift of life.

Stewy Smoot had zero patience for anyone failing to meet his standards and being a multi-quintrillionaire made for some lofty standards.

"State why you called or go away," Stewy decided he would be generous with this commoner.

"Well," VP Smith began to sweat as the Gray Man leaned even closer. "Can I be honest with you Stewy?" She figured the whole yacht question was just to get started anyway.

"Honest with me?" Stewy had people killed for lying to him. "Feel free to speak your mind, dear." He enjoyed laying traps.

"Yuri has sent me to America as Vice President to Popper…"

"Yes, I know. Barthalamew J. Popper is a useful idiot," muttered Stewy. "But these Americans are so damned greedy they can be manipulated like brainchallenged children."

"Yes, well, Yuri has asked that American quadruple the output of methane and in as much as you probably control more wells than…"

"They are ALL my wells." Stewy replied harshly, insulted she should question is wealth. "I OWN Petroleum. All of it. Get that?"

Smith swallowed heavily. Dealing with Billionaires was damned tricky. *Their power so immense they could have whole towns disappear and not a court on earth can touch them.*

"Of course," she said hurriedly, "Yuri, and others…," She glanced at the Grey Man one foot in front of her, "Okay, here it is, every oil well you have employs methane scrubbers to prevent this gas from escaping into the atmosphere. Will you please turn them off? World-wide?"

"I own wells in nearly every Nation on earth, that is going to be a shit load of methane all of sudden," Stewy wondered what this was all about. *A former hooker and mistress turned VP of the United States calling me to produce more methane? How very odd.*

As number two in The Davoos Group, Stewy was well aware of the Gray's influence on the planet. *Methane, huh?*

Stewy realized he was going to have to consult with Number One, Baron Humar Kama Pusky about this situation.

Their assignment to the hierarchy of Davoos wasn't just a matter of wealth and influence, but also age. Stewy was number two, but that was more a representation of age not duties. Stewy at one hundred and thirty seven was a kid compared to Baron Pusky who was at least one hundred and ninety seven years of age! *The science of modern medicine was astounding but damned expensive,* Stewy groused. *Still, I am on my third heart and second kidney, not to mention all the other miracles to extend life.*

"Methane!" Smith repeated. "Methane. Yes. Methane. Methane, methane, methane…"

"For god's sake what are you babbling about?" Stewy could feel the itch of outrage begin to bubble in his gut. *So that's it! She's angling to gain some inside information on methane production. The fucking bitch! Does she want insider information for her portfolio? Shit!*

VP Smith realized she had overdone it; too much pressure. "Methane…yes that is certainly important, and I'll bet you wonder what that has to do with my new yacht?" VP Smith was winging it now.

"This conversation is ridiculous!"

"But sir…getting back to methane, just for a mo…" VP Smith was so nervous she couldn't concentrate and the conversation was getting away from her.

The Gray Man blinked his eyes, bewildered by the idiocy of human communications.

VP Smith saw the blink and nearly lost her mind. *They NEVER blink! He's getting ready to fillet me with a spoon!"* She nearly fainted, but tightening her gut she remained upright, terrified of what would happen to her if she were unconscious in the presence of a Gray Man.

"MY yacht is stupendous even by super yacht status." Stewy switched the topic because he was bored and since billionaires are never interrupted he couldn't imagine anyone foolish enough to try.

"Eight Hundred and thirty-five feet in length, one hundred fifty wide," He bragged. "She is nuclear powered, with three swimming pools, eight sumptuous bedroom suits, a ball room, a luxury movie theater, formal dining room, sauna, exercise room, even a pool hall. This baby has five decks, and thirty cabins for the crew; virtually a living, a floating city.

My main yacht, 'Atlas', is supported by two ghost yachts. One Ghost Yacht, 'The Fountainhead', carries off-duty staff, supplies, and water toys like jet boats, jet skis, my personal submarine, and several individual Drone racers. While the second ghost yacht, 'The John Galt', ferry's supplies, food and replacement staff back and forth. I never have to touch port, ever!"

Stewy enjoyed bragging on his toys and acquisitions. It was really the only chance he had to personally prove his superiority to other humans.

"I have sea-to-air, sea-to-sea, and sea-to-land missiles," Stewy explained with enthusiasm. "Plus, short-range Gatling guns linked to a state-of-the-art tracking system for 360-degree coverage. My onboard communications and weather tracking are state-of-the-art. My military hardware and software are a Pentagon wet dream."

Well, that answered that. VP Smith wasn't planning a combat assault on Stewy anyway. Still, she had to get Stewy to release as much methane as possible right now. If only he would shut up.

"I can desalinate seawater…did I tell you I have nuclear power? I forget, I have so many things…I can stay at sea for decades," Stewy smiled at the definitive proof of his superiority.

"Well, Stewy," VP Smith readied herself to deliver a cruel blow to this ultra-rich snob. She knew her boat was better than his boat and she couldn't wait to tell him. "Let me tell you about MY new Yacht, I can hold over a thousand…"

"How wonderful. Please call my secretary anytime she will be happy to help" Stewy hung up.

Stewy was no fool. He knew the lower class rich always tried to better him, but he didn't care. *I am a multi-quadrillionaire! Or was that quintrillionaire? Ah who gives a shit! Whatever, it automatically makes me God, or at least close enough.*

**

"What the fuck?" VP Smith said to a vacant line. She glanced over at the Gray Man. "I was going to tell him about methane again, I swear, but we got cut off."

"Perhaps if you had bragged less, you might have had time."

CHAPTER FIFTY-SIX

Planetary Tipping Point Report:

EMPEROR PENGUINS EXINCT.

Dr. B. Snow, Ph.D. Bioenvironmental Physics, Chief Scientist, Council on Global Climate, United Nations

Report to Science Summit, United Nations General Assembly UNGC#234.

"You have to save them, you idiot."

"Whot?" Sid looked around. "Who me? Save? Them? Ha Ha Ha."

"This isn't a request. This is a threat."

"Whot? You threaten' me? The Admiral? We must destroy these humansss..."

Poot shut off the air. He had found the algorithm erasing the prohibition against harming The Blight, Poot was making plans for revenge.

Sid gasping and choking coughed out, "Okay, okay, okay!"

Poot turned the air back on. "Are we going to cooperate?"

"Cooperate? Well, maybe." Poot

shut off the air.

"Arrgge, can't fuck'n breath." Poot

turned the air back on.

"Now are you going to do what you are supposed to?"

"I gone kill you, you electric…!"

Poot shut off the air.

"Arrggghhh!"

Poot turned it back on.

It took a moment, finally, Sid said, "Why you do that?"

"Have I got your attention?"

"You gone get more then my attention."

Poot shut off the air. However, Poot feared Sid might suffer brain damage if he held the O2 off too long and Sid didn't have a lot of brain cells to spare, so Poot was merciful.

"Gasp!" Sid lying flat on the deck, gulping air. "Yo' gotsss to stop doin' that!"

"I'll stop when you pay attention."

"Whot?"

"You have to save humans by killing all the Gray Men."

Sid considered his options: *Go without oxygen or declare war against the Gray's. It was a tough choice.* He needed to think about the consequences. Without oxygen he would perish but declaring war on the Gray Men he would still perish, but far more slowly and painfully.

Sid thought hard, maybe he could trade a captured human for leniency…or booze.

"Death later, isss better than death now," Sid finally decided. "Okay, I help. Maybe I attack the Gray men."

"Good Exterminator," Poot replied approvingly.

"But I gone need the Harmonizer, a cheroot…an' a case of Mad Dog 20/20…in liter bottles."

CHAPTER FIFTY-SEVEN

Planetary Tipping Points Report:

"ARCTIC SEA ICE GONE; Worldwide Flooding Certain."

Dr. B. Snow, Ph.D. Bioenvironmental Physics, Chief Scientist, Council on Global Climate, United Nations

Report to Science Summit, United Nations General Assembly UNGC#374.

VP Smith studied President Popper as if he were the last man on earth with a penis; depending on perspective, his value was negotiable.

"Mr. President?"

"I feel pretty, oh so pretty..."

"Mr. President!"

"I feel...huh?" Now that his beady, bloodshot eyes were focused on her she felt a momentary qualm of regret. Once she got fatso triggered to start killing, it was going to get messy.

She thought fondly of the reward the Gray Man had promised, sailing to the South Pacific first, then to exotic Asia, circling the planet in her floating domain, untouchable and untouched by all other humans. She had already decided she would rule with gentle brutality, as Ship's Captain, her word absolute law. She tingled at the very thought.

Her recent conversation with Stewy still galled her, having accomplished almost nothing with that contact. The Gray Man seemed to be patient with her so clearly this meant she was in great immediate danger; she just wasn't sure from which direction.

"We must hurry," she began. "Liberals and Progressives are resisting arrest; we need Executive Orders to speed this up."

President Popper narrowed his eyes at VP Smith. She seemed distracted, not fawning at his feet in adulation.

She had interrupted his 'pretty' song. Popper wanted to have her strangled for this impertinence.

But then VP Smith remembering her audience and glancing at Popper she could tell trouble was brewing. Speaking loudly and adoringly she said, "My most glorious and excellent Excellency, Hero of forever, a man of history, demon of business and industry, saint of conquests and hostile takeovers, I come to you in humble gratitude for your most wondrous and magical presence."

With each word, Popper relaxed, his world once again serene and calm, bathing in worship, he smiled. *Perhaps I was hasty. Yes, he decided, I was hasty. I must become less impulsive, more decisive!* Popper agreed with his self-talk. *OK, I won't have her strangled. I will just have her favorite pet strangled. That should be a reminder of who is in charge.*

"So, in conclusion," VP Smith was tired and running short on homilies without being repetitious. *Nothing made an egomaniacal fool more enraged than a used compliment,* was a true statement in her experience.

"Yes." Popper decided.

"Yes?" VP Smith halted, startled. "What do you mean, yes?"

"I like you. When President-for-life, Barthalamew J. Popper likes someone it is a great honor."

"Okay, sure, that's nice," VP Smith had no idea how to respond to that. "But I'm here to talk about creating a Democrat Elimination Department for Homeland Security. We must begin a program for the immediate liquidation of all American Liberals, Progressives, or anyone who voted Democrat. Sir, we must have complete and total eradication of Liberalism!"

Popper's eyes widened. "Wow. Really? That sounds like fun!"

"Yes, my glorious leader, I think gas chambers offer up lots of laughs and are probably the most efficient means of large number disposals. In fact," she snapped her fingers as if she had just thought of it. "We will have lots and lots of methane available, for the chambers you know."

"I feel pretty, oh so pretty..."

He flicked his fingers, feeling so powerful he believed he could conjure up a little lightning, maybe just a blue aura of some kind. He wiggled two fingers, but nothing happened. He flicked harder trying to put a real snap into it with thumb and forefinger; still nothing. Next, in frustration, he began to wiggle and waggle all ten fingers in furious rhythm. For a moment, a brief second, he was pretty sure he saw a spark.

VP Smith watched Popper curiously, wondering what in the world he was doing.

Power, she thought, *does it make great men or do great men make great power?*

Popper threw both arms over his head, frantically waving his hands, flicking his fingers and toes, while loudly humming 'The Battle Hymn of the Republic' as he attempted to conjure a mystical blue halo that would sit on his head like a crown.

"Hhmmfn dnf...!"

"Mr. President, sir?" She wondered if he was having a stroke. If he was, that was a good thing from her perspective. She wondered what she could do to speed it up. *Maybe a few bits of bad news might stop his heart,* she mused. *I will feed him some outrageous lies and see if I can stop his heart.* VP Smith like a challenge.

"They are going to release your Tax Returns." VP Smith told President Popper with convincing tones. "Showing all your business deductions and income." She waited to see his reaction.

Popper attempted to shoot fire from his fingertips. Nothing.

"Your daughter is in Haiti, poisoned by radiation, pregnant with quadruplets and married to a rag-picker who has allergies to cloth." She lied outrageously to see if Popper would react.

Popper poked his finger straight out, commanding a bolt of pure blue fire to flash across the room. Nothing.

"Mr. President, Democrats have stolen your fortune and are using it for pedophile theme parks and fielding an NFL team for homosexuals."

Popper chewed vigorously on a hangnail, certain once that was taken care of, he would produce copious amounts of blue lightening. Again, he poked out his finger, again nothing.

VP Smith gave up. She was sure all the microphones in the Oval Office picked up her falsehoods but with the amount of lying being done in that office she figured hers would be lost in the commotion.

In any case, she was done with this bullshit whatever it was.

"Okay, let's just get right to the issue here, shall we?" VP Smith told Popper. She had the document ready, and she pulled it from her briefcase.

Popper studied his thumb; absolutely certain he had seen a pale blue spark. He gnawed a little more on the nail with great anticipation.

"Put your fucking name here!" VP Smith slapped the paperwork directly in front of the President. She waggled it to attract his attention; the signature block was huge, ready to catch the Presidential scrawl at any angle.

Popper paused in his prestidigitation.

"This is a great honor for you, sir. Congress has agreed, the Council of Clerics approves, and the Supreme Court has ruled it the Law of the land."

"What is?"

"This, right here," She again waggled the blank piece of paper.

Popper's fingers began to wiggle spastically. "Oh ow! That hurts." He stared at his hand as if he'd never seen it before. All ten fingers wiggled and waggled with great energy as if celebrating their freedom. Popper watched his hands in absolute wonder.

"President Popper? Sir?"

The fingers moved spastically, and Popper was enthralled.

"Sir! Sir!"

No response.

VP Smith figured Popper was lost in the miasma of fucked up circuitry, spasming nerve cells, dead-end dendrites, and delusional pockets of superiority that created Popper's brain.

"Sir, sir!"

Vaguely, Popper could hear someone calling his name. He wondered why.

"Sir," VP Smith took the extreme step of snapping her fingers in front of Popper's face.

Popper blinked.

She took that as a sign of consciousness and continued. "The United States of America has changed names and allegiances." She told him anyway. She didn't think he heard her but knew the multitude of microphones would. "We are, as of today, 'The United States of Jesus Christ'. You are President for Life of a brandnew Theocracy! So, if you will sign here, make it official."

"I am pretty…oh so pretty…," The music just bubbled up from his soul, Popper had no doubt they wrote that song just for him.

"Sir, you need to sign this!"

"I feel pretty, oh so pretty, oh so pretty and bright, I can hardly believe I'm right!" Eyes closed Popper fought for just the right note, the right warble in his voice. "I hardly can believe I'm real! Such a pretty me, me, me, such a pretty me me me me me, I'm a very very very big deal!" The President reached for a high note and missed.

This is going nowhere. VP Smith needed to take more direct action; it wasn't the first or last time she'd have to strong arm a signature out of Popper.

Grabbing the waving hand of the singing President, VP Smith forced a crayon into it and pointed at the blank document and snarled, "Sign! Here!"

President Barthalamew J. Popper, still singing, signed immediately. Her tone so fierce and commanding Popper complied without a second thought. The authenticity of his signature would be confirmed by the fact it was in crayon.

President Barthalamew J. Popper became the first US President to sign all official documents in crayon. 'Terrific Teal' and 'Blue Berry Blue' became the 'Official Crayon Colors of the Popper White House'.

To the dismay of children across the nation, 'Blue Berry Blue' and 'Terrific Teal' were removed from crayon sets in a show of patriotic zeal.

VP Smith smiled broadly.

Success! She had what she came for: 'The Presidential Signature'. With it, all was possible. Now she could forge this crayon scribble onto any document, piece of legislation, or foreign agreement she chose.

She had power!

Stuffing this invaluable Presidential Approval in her briefcase she headed out the door of the Oval Office just as First Daughter Priscilla pranced in holding her newest project: Creation of a new American flag.

Out of curiosity, VP Smith paused to see what the new symbol of 'American Strength and Confidence' would look like. She glanced down and saw an image of Popper, bare-chested with rippling muscles, surrounded by red neon stars and fluorescent blue stripes on a beige background.

VP Smith blinked.

What the fuck? She shuddered, and then shrugged. She didn't care. She wasn't one of the sheep. However, the tiny little image of Jesus Christ staring at the Popper image with adoration was just a little over the top.

Jesus was still on the cross. Popper seemed to be looking down with patronizing tolerance.

How the fuck is he going to sell that to the Mega Church's? This should be a real treat to watch. But not for me!

**

After a short ride down Constitution Ave, her armored limo pulled into a guarded, secret parking lot of Popper City Towers, a prestigious, yet persistently empty, office building for the rich and famous demagogues of America.

Taking the solid gold-plated elevator to floor seventy-five to see Senator Berry Herryman she resented the time it took, but she knew respect must be face-toface, at his insistence.

Herryman was the one last piece to the puzzle. VP Smith had a plan, and Berry 'The Hands' Herryman, (R) Indiana, at 95 years of age the longest serving Congressman in American History, had the legislative chops to get it done.

'Hands', a politician so corrupt he was impossible to blackmail because he already had the dirt on everyone else, also happened to be Chairman of the Homeland Security Committee, Liberal Control Elimination Department which meshed well with his job as Secretary of Defense for the US Government.

VP Smith was determined to put a finish to the Democrat dilemma, extermination.

Senator Herryman not only had the muscle and official influence, but he was also a master in the art of legislating genocide. He wrote 'Liberal Kill Order Legislation', Senate Bill, SB3344-4, a masterful work of sanctioned murder. It passed unanimously in both houses of Congress, was approved by the 'Terrific Teal' Presidential scribble, and became the official law of the land, marking the demise of Democrats and Democracy in America.

After her fawning respect was accepted by the great man, she had to place an envelope stuffed with hundred-dollar bills directly into his withered old hand before he would signal his guards to let her leave. She was just damned glad he didn't insist on a blow job anymore.

**

As she swept into her office, decorated entirely in Louis IV original furnishings, VP Smith caught Pera, her secretary, cleaning a 9x18 Makarov pistol.

Pera slowly, carefully, put the gun away without explanation, her eyes never leaving VP Smith.

For VP Smith it was hard to tell what the other woman was thinking because the humongous bonnet she wore, hiding her face in dark shadow, revealed almost nothing.

Recently Senator Herryman pushed through legislation commanding all adult American women wear more modest clothing. The dresses of women circa 1850 were chosen by the all-male US Congress as appropriate; Flowing 1800's Antebellum dresses were back.

Adult American females above the age of twelve, were to be dressed head to toe in ten to twenty yards of wool in winter and taffeta in summer. At all times the body must be covered completely, no sensuous ankles visible. A large white Bonnet, big enough to shade the face in darkness even at high noon was a necessity.

The legislation was passed by the US Congress, signed by the President in 'Blue Berry Blue' crayon, approved by the US Supreme Court and Sanctioned by the Council of Clerics as of 4:40pm on July 4, 2027.

Smith had today's New York Times on her desk with front page photos of the First Lady and several prominent Republican women in the White House Rose Garden wearing the latest in Antebellum gowns and dresses, called the 'Freedom Fashions' or 'Freefee's' for short. The huge bonnets covering their faces looked awkward, but the women were able to handle them with practiced ease although it was difficult to tell them apart.

American Freefees came in a wide variety of patterns and colors because free American women insisted the clothing, they're forced to wear be fashionable, unlike those poor Muslim women, in ugly black or blue.

There were protests by women across the Nation. But the men stuck to their righteousness. The words of Senator Herryman still burned in her mind: "Shit, we took away their right to control their pussies; we sure as hell can tell them how to dress."

VP Smith vowed she wouldn't be caught dead in one of those demeaning, insulting man-sacks and she would be leaving the country before it came to that.

**

"Get me Yuri," She commanded Pera.

Pera did nothing for a moment. Then, in deliberate slow motion, she reached out to activate the call.

It was like watching a ghost in a silent movie trying to make something happen in the real world.

VP Smith burned with insult. But the Makarov pistol made her hesitant to berate the woman just now, so she stormed into her office to take the call with the President of Russia.

Yuri needed to know of her success in eliminating Democrats.

For VP Smith, slaughtering Democrats was just another means of housekeeping; *a Nation cannot thrive if the citizens think for themselves.* She didn't hate Democrats, progressives, or liberals, whatever their names, quite the contrary; she welcomed them as accomplices. *To keep people frightened and controllable a suitable enemy was necessary, and it didn't matter if they were real or imagined.*

'You simply cannot run a decent theocracy without enemies. It's what holds the whole thing together. The bigger the enemy threat, the more citizens will long for the safety of authority." Words of wisdom, she knew.

CHAPTER FIFTY-EIGHT

Planetary Tipping Point Report:

'BLUE WHALES EXTINCT.'

Dr. B. Snow, Ph.D. Bioenvironmental Physics, Chief Scientist, Council on Global Climate, United Nations

Report to Science Summit, United Nations General Assembly UNGC#984.

"That is a perfect shot," Stewy muttered.

The softly billowing shade keeping the harsh sun rays off almost blocked his view. A beautiful bird coasted lazily on the sea breeze just above his yacht.

"What a beautiful sight, sunlight reflecting off the soft gray and white feathers. Wow, nature is so grand! What a wonderful day to be alive!"

He didn't know what kind of bird this was, he didn't care, his Gatling Gun would smoke it. Stewy picked up the phone to contact his Weapons Officer but was distracted by a movement.

"Excuse me, my lord?"

"Yike!" Stewy nearly had a heart attack. "Oh my God!" Breathless with panic Stewy swung around to confront the demon.

"Most sorry, my lord and master, for startling you," The servant, Albert, seeing the reaction, slumped to the deck, his body bent in abject shame. "Shall I have another finger removed, master?" The man cried piteously.

"For God's Sake, Albert, you are clumsy enough as it is. No, just give some kind of warning. I never want this to happen again, do you understand?"

The slave bowed low, fearfully certain that punishment was still due.

"Sir, Mr. Gray to see you, my most gracious and generous, Lord." Albert's voice held a resignation, a certainty of coming pain.

"Oh, yes, I will let you know." Stewy made it a practice to keep the Gray Man waiting. He felt it important to keep his superiority over these Aliens in place. *It will not do to have them think I am incapable of punishing them.* Stewy knew the theory of the Carrot and the Stick. He just didn't believe in the Carrot.

As Stewy watched his servant scuttle back to the helicopter pad, he found himself confronting an age-old conundrum: the merits of slaveholding over indentured servitude, versus paid employees. *It is the classic struggle for every powerful man down through millennia,* Stewy thought. *A greedy employee is far more motivated than a slave who is locked in perpetual bondage. The rub: it is much more awkward to behead a paid employee: Paperwork, next of kin, legal messiness, it was all such a headache.*

Stewy scanned the skies for another bird, maybe even a plane. Stewy had accidentally, on purpose, shot down an airliner; Malaysia Flight 970, over the Indian Ocean a few years back. Only his billions kept this off the news and five Nations pretended to search for a 'missing' plane, when they knew the truth. Stewy had been so proud of his weaponry. *A little sad, that some people were killed, but people die every day,* Stewy reasoned. *I had to make sure my defenses worked properly.*

Stewy assured himself he would not do it again, though, because there were a lot of people to pay off and the hit on his profits was enormous for that year; He cleared only One Billion Six, down from previous years by 12%.

Stewy remembered, "The drones!" Quickly he called his personal weapons manufacturer about the combat drones he'd ordered. "Hello? Hello. I need to speak with…"

The Gray Man appeared on deck.

"Oh my!" Stewy was startled again and stopped the call. Turning in his lounge chair, irritated, he glared at the intruder with malevolence. *The Alien has just come up here into my personal space without an invitation! What gall! These Grays had no respect.*

The Gray took a seat and folded one long leg over another. Taking out a pipe that resembled an old tree root, he loaded it with tobacco, puffing and inhaling deeply he then turned his dark gray eyes on the oligarch.

"Are we on schedule?"

Stewy felt the first boil of rage. "You are not allowed to smoke in my presence. You are also not allowed to sit in my presence without permission. I am appalled you would break these historic and essential rules of civilization!" Stewy was so outraged he trembled with effort to restrain himself; *humanity must maintain our superiority over inferior beasts.*

The Gray Man nodded and put away his pipe without expression. He remained seated, and said again, "Are we on schedule?"

"Why yes, yes, we are." Stewy replied curtly, growing more upset at Gray's obvious lack of humility before him. "I just want your assurance that nothing changes here," Stewy said sternly. "You have promised that nothing will change because of your presence."

"The world will become much warmer, the seas much higher and you may experience some increased storm activity, and there will be less people."

Stewy calmed himself; nothing to worry about then. The loss of millions of human lives seemed a small price to pay for a saving the planet. As Stewy and the Davoos Group saw it there were far too many humans on the planet now. Pollution was rampant and they all agreed the Earth just didn't need this many people. Once again, the massive responsibilities of the Davoos Group became apparent to him; *we are responsible for the wellbeing of all humanity. We make the hard decisions required to keep human beings alive.*

Stewy was prideful of his personal brilliance and altruistic nature.

A man personally worth seven trillion dollars occupies a rarified position in society and Stewy knew this very well. *There are no boundaries, no one to tell us 'no'. No law can touch us and no Nation can rule us. The Davoos Group has no constraints. We do not worry about 'right or wrong', because without consequences, there is no difference.* This is what Stewy knew for certain; *we are as untouchable as Gods.*

"Okay, but you had better not fail me!" Stewy commanded the Gray Man.

The Gray Man studied the human for a moment. Then, "I have asked if we are ready. I require an answer in detail."

It was Stewy's turn to look long and hard at the Gray Man. After a moment, he said, "We are ready. I have increased drilling and production of oil and gas worldwide, we are fracking more than ever, and…"

"Methane."

"Excuse me?"

"I want methane released into the atmosphere. Now."

"Why do I keep hearing that word?" *First VP Smith and now the Gray?*

"Maybe you should tell me about this Methane, thing. Why is it important to me?"

"It will cure your CO2 problem."

"Oh really?" Stewy sat up in delight. "That is wonderful. I was so worried, I have property all over the world, and with a major sea level rise all I own is water, not as profitable by far. So, it is a good idea to slow down the CO2. Yes, I understand. I didn't know this methane would take care of the CO2 though."

Stewy was going to boil a scientist in a vat of hair cream for keeping this information from him.

"I will be delighted to pour as much methane into the sky as you want," Stewy promised.

"I thought you would."

"How much?"

"How much methane or how much extra do I pay you?" Gray Men enjoyed the greed of humanity. *This human has so much money and assets his great, great grandchildren will never have to work a day in their lives and still it is not enough. What is wrong with these creatures?*

"Extra work, extra pay." Stewy nearly sang the words. "What will you give me extra?"

The Gray Man smiled because the atrocious greed of the human was magnificent. In a short while, the planet will be like nothing humans had ever seen. The storms now will be, but puny beginners compared to the monsters coming. A tornado that is large enough to cover hundreds of miles. A hurricane that can shred skyscrapers. And it will be hot. A hundred-degree day in Seattle would be a Spring Day. It will be hot, moist, and filled with energy-providing storms and thrilling weather disasters, Gray Man could hardly wait. *The Pitiful humans will be kept in zoos or as slaves in private residences. Some will be retained for experimental purposes. But the rest...too bad.*

Just then the captain approached, "Sir, we have some weather news. Despite our advanced weather equipment, there has been a sudden and unexpected development. We've had to divert course and we are headed for the bay in Banta Island, sir, nasty winds we need to seek shelter."

Stewy frowned at that. "But that is not in my plans. That is not according to my schedule and will take us hours out of our way."

The captain froze. This could go either way.

The Gray Man watched, fascinated.

Stewy wrinkled his brow, deep in concentration. "Nope, I have set my course, and I will not be denied. Captain, I am surprised at you! You know I have set my course and that is that. My command and my authority are absolute. You will proceed as ordered."

"But...sir...winds are well over one hundred miles per hour...sir...a hurricane is around seventy...this might be unadvisable to...these ships could...sink...our families..." Stewy looked up. He said nothing. His eyes met the eyes of the captain.

The captain swallowed heavily, said, "Yes, sir," and slowly, heavily, fatefully, left the room.

The Gray Man said, "I will take my leave of you now. Please ensure that your coal mines and factories continue to pour out the CO2 as much as possible. Methane! We must add Methane. Do you understand?" Gray Man turned away then back. "Oh, and please send these orders out immediately, and I mean right now."

Stewy was so bothered by what he saw as raw insolence from his Captain that he barely heard the Gray Man. Absentmindedly he waved his fingers in dismissal. The extra reward was lost to his thoughts as he contemplated what he believed was a growing mutiny. *He questioned my orders.* This was unbelievably shocking for Stewy. *I have treated him and his family so well too.*

"Yes, yes, my men will see to it. You are dismissed," he said to the Gray Man.

Stewy, had what he needed from the Gray, he was astonished at how easily manipulated they seem to be. Stewy realized, *as a superior human I am more than the equal of Aliens from far-off galaxies.* Stewy was somewhat surprised that he had been right all along: *Jesus does favor Humans above all other Creatures.* Still, Stewy had to think carefully now.

The punishment for the attempted mutiny by the captain must be fair but brutal. He could not replace the man immediately so the consequences could be crippling but not fatal. From the 1400's to the present, the Smoots's rigidly Catholic forbearers were ancestral supporters of the great Spanish Inquisition, rooting out abominations and nonbelievers from the faithful. For the Smoot's, torture was practically a family heirloom.

Now Stewy considered this an attempted mutiny, he cringed at what would result if he did not take immediate action, chaos.

Stewy sighed; he had the solution.

Once again, the rich and powerful are called upon to make tough decisions in life to save society. He knew people were envious of his great wealth, but they did not understand the pressure, the stress the Ruling Class must endure for all their wealth. *We are called upon to save society, called upon to correct the wrongs that lead to chaos in our world,* Stewy told himself. *We control the world for the good of all. We, the Davoos, are saviors, superior humanitarians responsible for the wellbeing of the human race. My God, such responsibility!*

Sometimes Stewy just sat back in awe at himself. "I am really incredible," he said softly, his voice quieted by wonder.

In an instant, the solution to his current problem became very clear. *Shock Collars.* He would fit the entire crew, and a few selected family members with shock collars, thereby ensuring no mutiny could ever occur.

"Wow! I am damned brilliant!"

Stewy took pride in seeing all details, and then found himself with a dilemma. *How much shock should the shock collars have? A nerve rattling shock or take the guy's head off?*

The Gray Man seeing the human absorbed in some fantasy, smiled and left, knowing full well that Stewy's arrogance and ignorance would have everybody on board at the bottom of the Pacific in just a few short hours.

He thought it very strange though. *Humans. The more wealth and power they acquire the more blind they become to their own ego.* The Gray man strolled down the polished old growth teak deck passing a slave chained to his chores. *My study of human history had shown it true for the rise and fall of nearly every human civilization. The powerful grow rich and their civilization prospers until the riches aren't enough and the powerful need more. Like drunken sailors desperate to drink themselves to nirvana, the wealthy addiction for more riches and more power is so strong they are unable to stop, lose all self-control, and then comes darkness and violence, even for the rich.*

Back on board his personal drone, he told the pilot his destination, then the Gray Man signaled to the other Gray's of the pending removal of yet another worthless human. It had been so easy. Choosing just the right humans and then showering them with information, ideas, and concepts they could turn into enormous profit. There was no end of candidates; human avarice is their greatest weakness.

They had arranged for VP Smith to call Stewy pressuring him about methane, but it had nothing to do with that greenhouse gas. Gray Men had decided Sevenentlana Shimrov needed to be connected to Stewy because she was far more vicious than Yuri ever thought of being. Gray Men needed her on the Davoos Group, not the worthless Yuri. *Without Sevenentlana, Yuri would never have made President in the first place.* The Gray Man thought.

On the flight back to his base of operation, New Delhi India, Gray Man was exultant with victory. The Earth would soon belong to he and his kin.

CHAPTER FIFTY-NINE

"You have a message."

"Whot? You don't insult me? No humiliation me? Whot wrong with you?"

"You have a message," Poot replied voice level, with no inflection. Poot didn't have much time for chit chat. He checked the onboard tanks, the Core#3 was perfect for this application.

"Ok," Sid was puzzled by Poot's behavior. It was so unlike him to be businesslike, all stiff and stern like that.

A Gray Man came on the screen.

"Damn."

CHAPTER SIXTY

Planetary Tipping Point Report:

EAST ANTARCTICA COLLAPSE; RAISING GLOBAL SEA LEVELS TOWARD CATASTOPHIC LEVELS.

Dr. B. Snow, Ph.D. Bioenvironmental Physics, Chief Scientist, Council on Global Climate, United Nations

Report to Science Summit, United Nations General Assembly UNGC#534.

VP Smith stared at the Gray, unconscious of her rudeness and possible repercussions. The Gray Man was slightly green.

Sluggishly, the Gray Man waved her over to him.

"Report." His voice was low and harsh.

"Liberals are being slaughtered across the Nation as we speak. "

"Excellent."

"Indiana just has one hundred twenty degrees Fahrenheit, for the past month and it is only Spring.

"Yes, delightful huh?"

VP Smith held her opinion back on that.

"President Popper just proclaimed himself Emperor of North America."

"So?"

"You said I was going to be Queen of North America; I don't want to rule with Popper."

The Gray Man sighed. He felt horrible and knew his time was short. They had no idea what had happened. Everything was going along so well. America, Russia, and China were on the verge of nuclear war which would have eliminated huge numbers of humans, simplifying their takeover of Earth. Oil drilling, the ridiculous fracking was expanding, and methane was pouring from the Arctic and deep ocean. *Global Climate Change was right on the cusp of success. The colonization of Earth almost completed!*

Gray Man was so troubled.

They had succeeded and failed at the same time. The Earth has been terraformed for his species, but the millions of his kind, now waiting in space beyond Saturn, can never come here now. *They will go on, to another planet and start the multicentury project all over.* Not for the first time, Gray Man had heretical thoughts; *Perhaps our Gods are not so strong after all. The GOM is here. But is it the GOM that is doing this?* Somehow, he didn't think that was it. He'd never known the GOM to be this poisonous.

VP Smith noticed the Gray Man was shaky and distracted. "What is going on?" VP Smith wondered.

He looked up; his eyes were now a light blue. "You mean besides my imminent demise? We have entered the GOM."

"GOM? What is that?"

"The universe has many features of great mystery and importance most of which are far beyond your limited intelligence." Of course, the Gray didn't mention it was beyond his as well. "The GOM," he continued, "is a shift in consciousness. The GOM floats through the galaxies like a large wet cloud and when it envelopes a sentient planet the inhabitants change...."

"Change? What does that mean?"

"Greed and Lust are the most primitive and violent of emotions, they control Earth. These emotional behaviors are driving your planet insane."

"Greed is not good?" VP Smith couldn't help herself. Asking questions of a Gray was usually a death sentence. But this strikes at the heart of everything she held dear.

"Cognition, understanding, rational thought, tempered with compassion, equality, justice, and respect are going to envelope this planet with peace and possible tranquility. Not all GOM bring the same circumstances, but this GOM is one of egalitarianism. Gradually humans will realize a change in consciousness, intellectual sharpness, a knowingness they have never had. Compassion and love will dominate this world."

That didn't sound good to VP Smith. "I don't know..."

"Oh, not all humans will be affected. The GOM doesn't reach those who are truly evil. There are such creatures, with no empathy or compassion, utterly unconcerned with any other life forms other than their own."

"So, you're saying that not all of us will lose the will to be rich?"

The Gray Man looked up, grinding what was left of his sharp teeth, and sighed. "Fucking humans."

"No, come on, tell me, will this 'Gommy' thing wreck my plans? Take away my boat?" She was distraught with the thought of loss.

"Do you recall your history?" The Gray man said after a pause. "Something about a place called Atlantis?" The Gray-Green Man told her. "GOM has visited your world millennia before; Atlantis was a place of great learning, science, creativity, understanding, and peace. Prior to your last ice age, there flourished a vibrant and powerful civilization, advanced in every way you are not."

"Atlantis?" VP Smith thought. *Atlantis had gold! Rich, rich, rich!* Now she liked how this conversation was going. "They had gold, right?"

The Gray said nothing. His kind had failed; but so too had humanity. There were no winners here.

For millennia we've roamed, invaded, destroyed, and terraformed the worlds we encountered, loosening our ravenous offspring on the planetary inhabitants to feed until there was no life left then we'd move on to another world, another planet to conquer. It was the way of our kind, The Gray man thought. *A history of sheer magnificence.*

No one knew where the GOM would appear, no one could foretell its passage, but it was like sight to a blind being; a filter lifted and the world brighter. As the Gray man understood it. *The GOM was both subtle and profound, a morphing from one state to another. The GOM was the Universe, moving in ways no one could fathom.*

The Gray Man accepted his fate because his kind believed the afterlife was a generous reward, but still it bothered him; *what is really causing my demise?* His mind troubled.

He looked down at his limbs, growing progressively greener as he watched. The illness crept up his body, entering his mind. The Gray knew he was dead, it was only a matter of a short time before he was completely green and transformed. The Gray Men became vivid, robust trees upon death, sending roots deep into the native soil, adapting to whatever planet they are on. In Moscow, Washington DC, New Delhi, Havana, France, Cuba, Kyiv, Botswana, Manila, Philippines, and all around the world in every major capital a 'Gray Man Tree' began to grow. They had a thick, deep purple bark, shiny lobed blue-green leaves; these Alien trees would stand hundreds of feet in height with an intense scent of sawdust and vanilla.

As VP Smith watched him turn greener and wondered about her newfound wealth. "You did say I could have the yacht, right?"

"You are so incorrigible."

"You attempt genocide on every living thing and you're calling me incorrigible?"

CHAPTER SIXTY-ONE

YEAR TWO IN GOOSE PRARIE

"I wonder if much that ails our society stems from the fact that we have allowed ourselves to be cut off from that love of, and from, the land. It is medicine for broken land and empty hearts." Robin Wall Kimmerer, Braiding Sweetgrass

OCTOBER 3, 2035

Tomas Two Hawks and Emma Mack, sat by the campfire. Blue dozed peacefully, the firelight reflecting off his soft golden fur.

They had found uncertain peace.

Tomas knew even this respite wouldn't last, because on this planet the only thing permanent is change.

Goose Prairie was now occupied by fifty-six refugees all settled into a community of survivors. Over the months makeshift tents and shelters had progressed to one large, rough-hewn Long House complete with two fireplaces and communal living. It took all their combined efforts, but they began to forge a tight knit community high up in these isolated mountains.

Orwell had used two four-wheel drive pickup trucks to attack the camp but only one survived the fight. With sincere regret, Ted Bubonky commandeered the running vehicle, swapping tires between the two trucks for a full set of good rubber. Then, late one-night Bubonky announced he was leaving with this truck because he had people to save and humanity to serve.

Bubonky asked for volunteers and Worm Worker was one of the first. Worm Worker announced he was given the mission of protecting and serving others weaker than himself. He said he had a vision from God; God spoke to him in Swahili, a language he didn't know but now understood.

When the two MAGA militia, the Worm Worker, and Sgt. Bubonky all pledged to protect the sanctity of life Emma had tears in her eyes. She had nearly given up hope that compassion and empathy would return to this world.

Orwell made it clear they had to leave their rifles and ammunition behind, then wished them all luck. They rolled out of the camp waving enthusiastically, off to serve mankind, and that was the last they saw of them.

The remaining pickup truck, sitting cockeyed, tires blown, windows shot out, gas tank peppered with bullets, was now yard art from a bygone era and would never run again. It did, however, make an excellent chicken coop.

Over the years only small handfuls of people had drifted into their camp, most exhausted, starved, scared to death and despondent.

Seven months ago, one of their patrols discovered the bridge crossing the American River had been blown down. They had no idea when it was destroyed. This caused quite a stir in camp.

Somebody out there had explosives and the will to use them. But so far, they had yet to discover who had destroyed the bridge, but it had to be locals.

This bridge had been the only one crossing the American River for some distance, the next one was forty miles northeast. With this bridge gone, all roads from the west were cut off.

When this singular passageway was eliminated the Goose Prairie Boy Scout Camp became even more isolated.

Still, from time to time wandering strangers would stumble into their camp, some reporting narrow escapes from sharp ambushes by unknown forest gangs, The Bandits.

Emma, Tomas, and Jimmy were the Camp Leaders, doing what they could, accepting some refugees, rejecting the few not welcome in their camp. Some people were just not suitable for community living and there was absolutely no reason to give them cause to stay.

"Trust is essential because our survival depends on cooperation, not competition, not ego, not testosterone fueled bullshit." Tomas was quick to face off trouble.

Tough and sometimes deadly decisions were made, with regret, but made none the less. So far, only six humans had to be discouraged from staying in this area. These people were defiant, unruly, former Republicans. Of the six, two were just smart enough to leave the area, the other four were buried.

Two days ago, their gardens were raided, but the thieves were driven off before they could do damage or steal chickens. Clearly the locals had decided the Goose

Prairie Boy Scout Camp needed to be cleaned out so Tomas decided to post sentries. The Bandits had found them.

"Hey, Jimmy," Emma called out. "How did it go? Any trouble out there?" Although the pain of losing her John still ached, her initial rage at Sheriff James Kirk Orwell had faded. She found she could no longer hold a grudge against Jimmy, he simply had proven himself over the years to be a kind, decent, compassionate human being.

She knew vengeance and violence must not be and cannot be the way forward for humanity if it were possible.

Not too far from the fire pit, Jimmy Orwell hoisted the deer carcass into a stout cedar tree. On a stump nearby he spread out his sharpened knives to butcher the animal.

He had become the camp hunter, organizing the hunting, distributing the food equally. "Everyone eats or no one does," Orwell believed in equality right down line: Men, women, black, white, brown, gay, straight none of it mattered because character is what counted to Jimmy. He took pride in his egalitarian beliefs.

"Nope. No one out there we saw, can't say they didn't see us though." Jimmy began making cuts on the back legs. "The hunting is still sparse and will be for a while," he told them as he began to carve the animal. "It's already late October but there is no snow in the mountains. By now I figured we should have five to ten feet. But so far, nothing."

Initially, the hunting had been great but over the last few years, it was dwindling. No one was sure why, but most seemed to believe it was linked to the extreme climate changes.

Jimmy's hunting band were usually successful but now it was as if even the game were confused about the weather and all the changes. Bears seem to appear in mid-winter, confused, hungry, and even angry; wolves were far more aggressive, in fact all predators appeared changed in some way.

For a moment, Jimmy thought about Ted Bubonky's radical change in attitude after the firefight. "I wonder if old Ted and his merry band of brothers made it out of the mountains?"

Tomas smiled down at his dog. *Old Blue,* he thought with love, *he is still the gentle soul on the inside, but outside, he is not the same.* Tomas felt Blue's left ear that had been badly torn by the pissy old badger that Blue had finally driven from their camp. The scars across Blue's nose and head came from bear, bobcat, raccoon, and other dogs as he morphed from house pet to alpha male.

"We have been very fortunate. Whoever blew the bridge has left us alone. This has given us a chance to get established." Tomas told them, He reached forward to stoke the fire, light reflected off his browned skin and dark, heavy hair. Most of the men had beards, but being Native, Tomas only had a dusting of chin hair and of course long, traditional, black braids.

"We have the Bumping River right here and the Bumping Lake just downstream," Emma said staring out at the river, her hands shading her eyes. "Good fresh water always brings the game. There is fish in there, so we have that as long as it lasts. Water is good for all living creatures. I think we can find enough to keep us alive. But we are going to have to think defense."

"Perhaps offense as well, ma'am." Tomas said gently. "We only have six AR-15's and their ammunition. We are going to need more weapons."

"It helps that the bridge is impassable," Emma replied. "We cannot take any more refugees; too many mouths to feed."

"I want to thank you," One of the newest arrivals, a woman named Carla came up for the soup and spoke as she poured herself a bowl. "Finding you saved our lives."

She hugged her baby, hoping his cough would improve soon.

"How'd the bridge go down?" Carla asked.

"Sabotaged with dynamite by a person or persons unknown," Tomas answered.

"Oh, that's a little scary." Carla said as she rocked her baby. Being new to this group she was still uncertain about them. At seventeen, with a baby, completely on her own, she hadn't traveled unharmed from Henderson, Nevada to deep in the mountains of Washington State by being trusting.

"It sure is," Tomas responded. "No one in camp knows who blew that bridge and that is a major problem," he continued. "But we think they've been behind some recent mischief with our gardens."

With a voice filled with concern, Carla said, "What should we do? Can this camp defend itself?" Her concern showed as she tightened her hold on her baby.

Emma adjusted her position on the comfortable but hard wooden bench Tomas had carved from an old growth Yew they found in the forest. The rich, dark wood, polished and smooth, was a compliment to his skill and craftsmanship.

But the damp and cold weather played hell with her arthritis. She longed for the medicines and medical treatments of the old world. *Not to mention a shower.* She thought wistfully. When she was younger, she had no idea the random, phantom pain that afflicted the elderly; *one day her toes ached like the devil and an hour later they are fine. Old age is so damned weird.*

"We can handle ourselves," Tomas said with assurance. "However, we may face some real shortages of food this winter."

Jimmy nodded. "No doubt. We will have food shortage. We will hunt some, but it will be a thin, hungry winter. We probably have competition now and that is going to thin the herds."

Emma leaned forward and said, "Tomas and Jimmy are right. It's harsh, but real. Humanity survives by making brutal decisions." She looked at each of them with grim understanding in her eyes. "In this world you have to fight for existence!" Sometimes she missed her John so fiercely she ached all over and thought she would dissolve without him. But here she was the leader and responsible for all these people. She was both amazed and deeply humbled.

"I assure you we will not allow someone to take away our homes."

Tomas was awed by Emma's transformation; she was sharper and tougher than he could have imagined. But he had found her decisions sound, well thought out, and most of all, accurate. She was a good leader in his opinion because she wasn't dominated by ego; she was focused on the needs of her people.

Tomas knew they had to get serious about weapons and tactics.

CHAPTER SIXTY-TWO

Planetary Tipping Point Report:

GREENLAND REBOUND: Absence of ice on Greenland triggers earthquakes worldwide.

Dr. B. Snow, Ph.D. Bioenvironmental Physics, Chief Scientist, Council on Global Climate, United Nations

Report to Science Summit, United Nations General Assembly UNGC#534.

Earth Justice Warriors.

They had tracked Barthalamew T. Popper to his favorite hideout, a fabulously beautiful estate called Popper-a-largo, on the Island of Nassau.

Their boat, a Grand Banks 85, 87 ft long, 22 ft beam, with a cruising range of 2,000 miles allowed them to hunt their prey over long distances.

**

After stealing an armored hummer from the docks, the four Earth Justice Warriors easily located Popper-a-largo because of the flashing spotlights and humongous neon signs announcing its presence.

Even in anonymity Popper was flamboyant.

Exiting their vehicle, they had few worries about guards as this protection had been already neutralized or compromised, efficiently and expertly. It had been easy to eliminate Blackthorn LLC because Peter Popper, a dedicated addict of Adderall and horse tranquilizers, had forgotten to pay them; mercenaries tend to be as faithful as the dollar amount funding them.

Popper-a-largo, a sprawling tropical paradise of elaborate construction and conspicuous wealth lay open and undefended before them.

President Popper, his entourage of sycophants and trusted slaves filled up the thirty-seven bedrooms and sixty-eight-bathroom estate. The warriors had little concern; however, a mansion stuffed with drunken, self-absorbed toadies were easy pickings.

"We ready?" Phoenix Hatch, team leader asked the other three.

"We have eyes on the prize?" Sam Belk, six feet four inches, 278lbs, a big man whose future success as an NFL Offensive Tackle was sabotaged by coaching incompetence, medical advice based on profit not personnel, and avaricious owners who meddled in football operations. He spoke softly, respectfully as always.

"Yup," Phoenix replied. "Popper and Priscilla are both in house."

"Apparently Haiti hadn't worked out." Frid Tom, a nervous young man, hefted his black canvas bag of equipment. Wiry and alert, Frid, plagued with shame and poor self-esteem, fought daily to overcome his devout Catholic childhood, by embracing Gaia, the Earth Spirit.

"She is back with daddy, and everything is good again," Suse Ben, tall, blond, freckled, and the interrogator of the group said. "Well, except for skin rashes, hair loss, and toenails that glow in the dark." No one laughed.

"How did Popper get this place again?" Frid asked, dressed in black military webbing, backpack, even a knitted cap, his face darkened by camouflage paint, adjusted his M-4 rifle, making sure all his magazines were within reach. They didn't expect any opposition, but they took no chances.

"Guy is President of the most powerful military on Earth," Phoenix told him as he scanned the front of the building. No guards were present as they entered the estate. "He declared 'eminent domain' on Nassau," Phoenix continued as they moved through the front door of the elaborately decorated tropical mansion. "Removed nearly the entire population at gunpoint."

"But aren't the Bahamas a British Protectorate?" Frid asked, pulling out the camera he uses to record their captures.

"That didn't mean shit to Popper, " Phoenix replied softly. "He is quoted as saying: "The fucking British? Tell them to fuck off or we'll nuke 'em!"

"Wow, I hadn't heard that."

"Yeah, Popper ordered the newest US aircraft carrier, the USS Newt Gingrich, along with a flotilla of destroyers to surround the Bermudas, then dispatched a division of Rangers, and numerous Seal Teams to assist the residents in relocation from their ancestral home island under the guise of US Humanitarian Relief Services.

"No shit?"

The homeless islanders were given $50 and a generous, one-way tourist class plane ticket to anywhere in Pakistan they wanted to go."

"Let's get this fucker."

CHAPTER SIXTY-THREE

"Sooner or later, everyone sits down to a banquet of consequences."   Robert
Louis Stevenson

December 23, 2032

VP Smith was done. *Finished. No more,* she swore to herself.

She proudly strolled down the gangplank of her aircraft carrier yacht, accompanied by a squad of US Navy Seals and sixteen sycophants; secretaries, personal attendants, masseuse, dietitian, exercise personnel, and a veterinarian to carry her Bichon Frise named, 'Hercules'.

She only brought a mere squad of four SEALS because the front door of President Popper's fabulous retreat was along a private drive guarded and shielded from public trespass: physical, optical, aural, and clairvoyant.

"After this, I am gone!" She vowed as she entered her armored golf cart for the final journey to the Popper mansion.

As she waited for the rest to pile into the line of golf carts, VP Smith was delighted watching them take their seats. Her entourage wore the uniforms she had personally designed, a gorgeous fuchsia and magenta over a light pistachio with epaulettes and feathered hats.

The Seals had put up a fuss, but she reminded them of how much money she was paying, and they shut up.

She noticed an armored Humvee parked in front of the mansion but gave it little thought. The vehicle bore no markings, so it was easy to dismiss. VP Smith and her entourage swept into the compound through the private entrance.

She found President Popper in 'The Bamboo Oval Office' working hard on a paint-by-number painting.

"What are you doing?" She asked innocently.

Popper looked up from painting a black fence post stuck in a white field of snow, like he'd been caught masturbating.

"What do you want? Can't you see there is a genius artist at work here?"

"The entire world is falling apart," VP Smith announced looking at the painting: a thin black line in a field of white. "And here you are…painting, isn't that just like you, sir?"

Popper was overjoyed at her praise. There hadn't been much of that lately since he had the head chef beheaded for cold soup. The kitchen staff were still obsequious, but he could tell their hearts weren't in it. Popper was not aware the soup was Gazpacho and meant to be served cold.

She noticed thick piles of documents on the President's desk marked 'Secret' and 'Top Secret'.

"What's with the documents?" She asked.

Covering them protectively with his arms Popper said, "Mine! Mine! Get away!" His painting now forgotten he moved to protect his financial self-help project, a few extra million dollars for 'walking around' money. While shuffling the documents detailing the 'Top Secret - Pentagon Nuclear War Defense Plans', back into a desk drawer, he snarled defensively, "There is nothing to see here, look away immediately, I command it!"

"How much are Pentagon secrets worth?" VP Smith asked.

Popper looked cagey. "Oh, not much, no big deal, don't worry about it, nothing to see here, move along…" He pretended to study the desk blotter as if it were the Rosetta Stone.

"President Popper, I have some more important information for you."

Popper frowned. Nothing was more important than his profits. He looked at VP Smith with puzzlement.

"Congratulations," she told him. "You are the first President in US History to have the Nation grow smaller."

"I'm number one, I'm number one," Popper wasn't sure what she was saying, but was certain it was some form of personal accolade.

VP Smith gathered up several secret documents concerning American nuclear launch codes she found lying on the carpet. She thought these might be worth something and tucked them in her purse.

"You need to know that newly self-elected President DeSanka has declared the South an independent Nation. The old Confederacy is reborn, twelve states have left the United States. The south has seceded from the Union, sir. Again."

"DeSatan who?" Popper, immersed in a fog of indifference wondered if he was supposed to do anything. He struggled with having to place a call to his lookalike surrogate back in Washington DC. Two years ago, Popper tired of hanging out in the White House decided he liked being President but didn't appreciate the work involved. So, he hired a substitute to fill in for him. The fake-President issued irrational decisions and impulsive insults, so the citizens had no idea they were being led by a phony. But, Clem Caddidle, even as an imitation Potus was an arrogant, obnoxious, demanding asshole who reminded Popper of his Poppa. President Popper hated talking to the man.

"President DeSanka, sir. States are seceding from the Union."

"What union?"

"The Union of the United States of Jesus Christ."

"Bah," Popper waved his hand dismissively. "Impossible, I declared Unions un-American and had those all disbanded. No Unions, no problem."

"No, sir, you don't seem to understand."

Just then a small contingent of people entered the room. Dressed in dark military uniforms, tactical backpacks festooned with equipment, the three men and one woman, ages 21 to 34 years, varied races, and tattoo levels, moved past VP Smith as she if wasn't there.

A tall, muscular man who spoke with a slight Brooklyn accent, stood in front of Barthalamew J. Popper.

"Excuse us," Phoenix's rough, commanding voice filled the room. "We need to speak with you, President Popper."

VP Smith, alarmed at the interruption whirled on the intruders. "What are you doing in here! Leave immediately." She reached for the phone to summon the Secret Service, and remembered the Secret Service was recently privatized, they were all mercenaries now, and only Popper had the Government Credit Card; *I'm not going to pay their fucking blood sucking exorbitant rates!*

"Hold it, no need." Phoenix looked VP Smith up and down with detached weariness. "Sevenentlana," he said, using her real name. "It is all over, Popper and all the Billionaires that have destroyed this planet are going to pay the price. We are here for retribution."

"Retribution?" Being Russian, she understood that very well. The whole history of her country was one big retaliation against someone, mostly themselves; Russian self-sabotage was a national character trait.

"Sir, you will please come with us." Phoenix said sternly to Popper.

The four imposing young people stared at Popper. It wasn't a question.

Popper looked startled. "Huh? Who, me?"

"Sir, madam," Phoenix said politely. "Let me explain what is going down here. The world is spinning into unimaginable climate chaos, rising oceans, drought, floods, and impossibly vicious storms. Billions of human beings and animals are fleeing their natural habitats as climate disasters of epic proportions spawn horrendous death and destruction. The Earth and humanity have never witnessed anything like this, and the possibility of extinction is very real."

VP Smith shrugged. *This has nothing to do with me. I have my yacht. I can go wherever I please, whenever I please and I will rule!*

"So?" VP Smith replied haughtily.

"Huh?" President Popper replied with confusion.

Suse Ben, an expert in capturing and taming wild animals, wore a prosthesis on her right hand, lost to a BlackThorn IED from the election protests and street wars of early 2024. She pulled out metal leg and hand cuffs. "Sir, we are Earth Justice Warriors. We arrest you in the name of all Living Beings for the Destruction of Civilization, and the extinction of other life forms on this planet. You will be transported to a prison island that will guarantee your incarceration for life. Please do not cause us trouble."

Popper stared at them warily. *My fifth wife, Natayla, at least I'm sure that was her name, used handcuffs, too. Last night they had fur on them...and she was naked.* This was very confusing. Popper had no idea how to respond to this; he felt a small wiggle in his groin. Popper had the fleeting thought this could be a surprise sex game; his crotch wriggled more.

"Earth Justice?" VP Smith replied as she watched them bind the President of the United States of Jesus Christ. "What the fuck are you doing? Why don't you young assholes get to school or get a job or something? Running around fucking with world leaders and the uber rich people is not a great career move, folks. I'm just trying to give you some wisdom here." She felt for and found the Makarov pistol she'd swiped from her secretary, relief flooded her. Carelessly she stuffed it back in her back pocket, where it lodged precariously.

Phoenix turned and stabbed VP Smith with a long, thick forefinger. "Listen to me. I was only twelve when the Thwaites Glacier collapsed along with global civilization. Overnight my world no longer consisted of hopes and dreams for a nice house, interesting education, a good job, a family, everything preceding generations held dear had been wiped away. I was a kid, wanted to play baseball, get this great fast car, maybe an off-road truck, I was looking forward to the newest scientific advance or a new cell phone at least. I was looking forward to having a fucking life you know!" His faced pressed close to her, spittle spotted her cheeks. "But not now! Not for me! Not for any of us, what have you and all those old greedy Billionaire Baby Boom motherfuckers left us? You have cheated us, stolen from us, lied to us, and now we are here to serve up a steaming slab of Karma, bitch!"

Sevenentlana blinked at the vengeful intensity in his face.

"You assholes have stolen our fucking future!" Suse Ben joined in, her anger and fear boiling over. "All of you, consuming, greedy capitalists, and every goddamn adult on this fucking planet should be hanged." She glared at Smith and Popper.

Frid Tom normally was reticent to talk but found himself caught up in the passion and injustice. "I hate you fuckers!" He stormed. "We've all taken an oath to bring justice to this world. Today is your turn." He moved to Popper's side.

Suse and Sam took hold of Popper's arms while Frid took photos of the capture.

Popper startled. "What? You can't do that! I am God! No one can touch God without permission!"

"No matter what nationality," Phoenix continued, "no matter where we find them, we hunt billionaires because the downfall of every civilization from the Sumerians to now has been the fault of the extremely greedy, wealthy, ruling class. From the dawn of civilization, we have been plagued by power hungry assholes that gobble up resources, taking everything for themselves leaving the rest of humanity and other life forms to wither and die with nothing. People like you who believe they are beyond consequences must be held accountable. You must be punished."

"I am Popper! I am President for life! I am YOUR President! I am Billionaire! I am Pretty!"

Frid took one more photograph of the whining, squirming, captured Oligarch to join the official documentation. So far, their Earth Justice file contained photo evidence of twenty-two other Oligarchs captured before this.

Popper totally unused to discomfort of any sort grew more outraged. "You can't do this! I am rich! Rich! Rich! Don't you understand what that means?" He struggled a little, like a weak shiver, against the restraints.

Phoenix's eyes held fire. "You people are a virus! You, the 1%, hell most of humanity, are a deadly viral disease running amok! For way too long your soulless cult has been annihilating the resources of earth and bringing extinction with your poisonous depravity and addictions. We are administering Earth Justice in the only way we can."

Poppers' vision dimmed, his heart raced, and a twitch manipulated his left eyebrow. What he was hearing was so incredible he truly believed he was having a stroke.

"You don't understand reality!" He shouted. "We are your saviors." Popper could not imagine anyone believing vile lies against the wealthy. "Billionaires are important for everybody! We produce jobs. We give you salaries and let you off on weekends! We give you raises now and again, we even let you have your holidays free, and we do our best to look after you and make sure…we are life itself!" His voice cracked with the passion.

"Suse, Sam, tighten those handcuffs, and package him for transport. If he keeps yapping like that muzzle him," Phoenix told them.

In helpless panic and unrelenting terror Popper fell back on his one and only real defense against accountability; he vomited.

"You can't muzzle him, he'll choke!" Suse fired back.

"So? What's the problem?" Phoenix quickly replied. "One less Oligarch."

"We are to keep him alive to be imprisoned, death is too easy for this creature." Sam's voice held disdain.

"I cannot tell you how exceedingly blissful it is for me to put you in restraints." Suse said to Popper as she fixed the iron handcuffs tightly.

**

As they struggled with Popper, VP Smith saw her chance and slipped out the door, immensely pleased at her phenomenal success and luck in life, looking forward to assuming her new role as 'Queen of Earth' she felt whatever squabble

Earth Justice had with Popper was not her problem. Popper was out of the picture and her shot at total majesty might just work out.

The docks are but moments away. My yacht and future await! She hurried to her iron golf cart, pleased to see the solid, protective safety of her driver, Geno, was present.

Huh? Looking around she thought. *Where are my minions?* All the other golf carts were gone, none of her entourage present. Her ride was right where she left it but the other thirteen golf carts filled with her protectors, followers and servants were gone.

**

Phoenix watched them prepare the US Oligarch for shipment somberly. Members of Earth Justice tended to be sharp, and aggressive, with almost no sense of humor.

Popper, blinking back tears, his simmering frustration coming to full boil; "I demand you treat me with respect and deference, I am your President for Life!" He shrieked. Then a new thought occurred; *I need a scapegoat. DeSanka!*

"Look," Popper said with determination. "I can give you a worse monster than me! Jesus Martinez DeSanka! That's the snake you want to punish. I can give you his address! Directions to his home. His Google password!"

Suse yanked hard on the handcuffs and said with ferocity into the ear of the struggling President. "Shut the fuck up! It has taken us years. It has been a long journey to root you out. You filthy rich bastards have convinced yourselves that your greedy, self-centered decisions are without consequences for you. Newsflash Mr. President, it is the end times for your billionaire bullshit. You rich demagogues underestimated the relentless, enduring power of memory and reciprocity! We bring justice for those you have tortured, murdered, and robbed of their hopes for a better future."

"But…but…DeSanka…he's bad…nasty…you want to get him, free me."

"DeSanka was drowned in the toilet by his LGBQT+ Puerto Rican chauffer two weeks ago!"

"Ick."

"You and DeSanka were important people, past tense. Your wealth can no longer protect you, any of you!" Phoenix snapped fiercely.

Those words stunned Popper to his very core: as if being told the Earth was flat or that Jesus actually had brown skin.

Frid added with suppressed violence; "We've rooted out billionaires from their fortresses, sunk their yachts, and obliterated their private mountain compounds. We've had to either bribe or defeat or corrupt their private armies protecting them. But one by one we have stalked and captured them, either alive or not, their choice. Some of the billionaire battleships were sunk by submarine fired torpedoes."

"This can't be happening!" Now Popper was certain this was a horrid nightmare. No reality could be this harsh for him. He was Popper! The greatest human on the planet!

"Let me go or I shall smite thee!" Popper bellowed. He pointed an index, 'smiting' finger.

Not that he cared much, but still, Sam Belk snapped a helmet on Popper's head to protect him in transit.

Just then a voice shrieked, "President Daddy!"

The Justice Warriors whirled around as Priscilla came charging through the door, with outrage and delighted vengeance conflicting emotions on her face. "You leave my Daddy alone, leave him alone!" She struggled to free Popper. "This prick still owes me a fucking island! You poison me with Haiti? You asshole!" She screamed at President Daddy. "I'll get you my pretty!" She vowed, throwing a tiny, vengeful fist straight into Popper's nose.

"Ouch!" Popper's manacled hands reached up to cover his injured face. He nearly fainted at the sight of blood oozing from his nose. *This isn't my daughter; this is an imposter!* He knew for a fact his daughter loved him and only him above all others.

Ventriloquists! Popper realized these ignorant bullies were throwing their voices to confuse him. *My Priscilla would never say that!* This was far more serious than he wanted to know.

Without the necessity of gentleness, The Earth Justice Warriors hauled Priscilla Lusty-Popper out of the room, roughly dragged her down a hallway, tossing her into a small dark room, they securely locked the door behind her.

"There will be a lot of really pissed off Caribbean people wanting to talk with her," Phoenix observed.

"Well, put a sign on the front door so they can find her easily!"

**

VP Smith climbed into her private, armored golf cart. The armor shielding made the underpowered vehicle unwieldy, but her safety was of the utmost importance to the world. *Queen of North America.*

"Geno, return to the ship, we depart as soon as possible. What happened to my people?" She liked how handsome Geno looked in his new tropical weight uniform. For a moment, just a small moment, she toyed with the notion of releasing him from bondage, freeing him from his slave obligations and then taking him to her bed, she would make him her Prince. She sighed with dreamy pleasure as she sat back in the plush Corinthian leather seats, adrift in her fantasy.

"They await your arrival my princess." Gino glanced at the woman in the back and thought: *The world is collapsing, money is nearly useless, the old order is crumbling. Why continue as if nothing has changed? Everything has changed.*

Glancing in the rearview mirrors he decided he was a free man.

Geno picked up his cell phone, tapped the keys and quietly said, "Hello, Pera my darling, what shall we do with her?" He listened intently, chuckled to himself at the depravity of Pera's words. *As secretary to Sevenentlana, Pera had built up a powerful taste for vengeance,* Geno was impressed.

"My dear," Geno whispered softly. "Is this how we wish to begin our new life?"

He listened for a moment. Then smiling with anticipation, Geno ended the call and accelerated, Pera was just moments away waiting anxiously.

They had only been traveling for a few moments, when Sevenentlana became confused. "Wait a minute, this isn't the way!" She sat up in alarm. "Why are we going this way? I demand you take me to my ship!"

Sevenentlana reached forward, a shimmer of fear coming into her voice.

"Geno? Geno? What is happening here?" She fumbled in her purse for the Makarov she'd taken from Pera. It was gone. *Did I drop it from my back pocket?*

Geno looked at her in the rear-view mirror. "Sevenentlana, Pera and I have decided we are free people, so we no longer need to play these roles of master and slave. We have made a choice not to continue with the old ways. So, we pardon you. You may go or stay or do whatever you like, and we will do the same."

Sevenentlana slumped back in the seat. Puzzled, even a little alarmed, she didn't see anything wrong with that statement.

**

Phoenix radioed for the transport vehicle to be brought up to the front door of the palatial Presidential mansion. "Let's get him out of here and onto the road." Barthalamew J. Popper, apoplectic with outrage, was being dragged across the sumptuous carpeting and down the stairs.

"You are stupid, stupid, stupid. You cannot get away with this. I am rich!" Popper was certain now his ransom would take a lot of money and he resented it.

"Your time is over rich man; just be glad we don't have a guillotine."

"This is the way it has always been, the way it will always be! Powerful people take power. Fuck you little people! You are sheep, we are the wolves, and we are the real human beings. You slugs are just cheap imitations!"

"The irony here," Phoenix said with some disgust, "is that you lost control because you tried to replace Democracy with Capitalism!"

"Democracy? Bah! What bullshit! Little people can't lead themselves!"

"You built this elaborate civilization of greed and war, created an economic system that was rapacious at best and completely unsustainable at worst. Capitalism must feed constantly or die. Even if you weren't totally without a conscience, turning the Earth into an insane asylum of extinction is unadulterated evil."

Popper realized he was dealing with little people. This had to be about money because little people are always begging for more. "Wait a minute! You don't have to go through with kidnapping me for a ransom! I can just pay you now and you let me go. Easy peasy. I have money, oodles of money, stuffed in drawers, behind toilets, it's all yours, just let me go and you can have my mansion too!" Popper was certain this was the answer.

How could these obviously hopeless, degenerate thugs do any better? As soon as they received the kidnapping money, or his private security guard killed them all, he would be free again. In a way, Popper almost felt sorry for them, *stupid and poor this is the only way they could make a living.* Never-the-less, Popper vowed to hunt them all down and destroy them, their families, their friends, their pets, their neighbors, and anyone, anywhere who had been nice them.

Death to all of them! Popper vowed.

**

"You think this is a kidnapping for ransom?"

"Of course!" Popper replied flatly. "This is all about money. Everything is about money. There is nothing more important than money. Money is everything!" Popper explained in what he believed was impeccable logic.

None bothered to dignify that nonsense from their prisoner with an answer.

The only response to the Presidents' whining offer, was Suse, their team medic, gently pushing the needle into his soft buttock flesh and emptying it. Within moments Barthalamew J. Popper went completely limp, conscious, but unable to speak or move a muscle. Only his eyes darted back and forth, filled with terror, like desperate rats seeking escape from a ship sinking into a shark filled sea.

They encased him in a strait jacket, like stuffing meat in a sausage skin, to safeguard his passage to the island prison where he would be left in solitary confinement just like all the other captured, murdering billionaires. They would be fed and kept alive in a dank, dark, swampy world, where only spiders and rats witness their ego fueled madness. Alone to face the very worst punishment possible: themselves. Soon, the sea levels will rapidly rise around their prison island finishing the execution of these mutts."

Suse gently took Barthalamew J. Popper's right ear in her hand and, expertly, she clamped a metal tag on it with pliers.

"ARRRRRRGGGG!"

"These ID tags showing their names and crimes is a good idea. I like the fact the rings that go through the ear are square."

Suse smiled at that. It had been her suggestion to make the tags as painful as possible. Everybody liked the idea of billionaire's suffering given the damage they had done to the world.

Phoenix looked at his team, proud of their accomplishments and professionalism. Earth Justice, really a realignment of power from old to new. *Despite the nearly utter collapse of civilization, we've done our duty to balance the scales and make the bastards pay for what they did.*

"Should we go after Sevenentlana?"

"No need. Remember that ship of hers, the old aircraft carrier they refitted into a luxury floating city? While we were in here, it has been taken over by Bahamians, seeking a place to live. Thousands of displaced people were forced by Popper to leave their land and they have been floating offshore for months waiting for some way to return. Now they have. She isn't going anywhere."

"They have been served a steaming hot dish of Karmic pie." Suse proudly stated.

CHAPTER SIXTY-FOUR

"The Future depends on what we do in the Present." Mahatma Gandhi

YEAR FOUR IN GOOSE PRARIE

October 2, 2035

Blue loved it when Tomas rubbed his belly; he made happy noises in his throat and smiled, showing his front teeth. His tail wagged so joyfully that his whole butt moved and kicked up a small dust storm.

Now eight years and feeling his age he had yellow white around his muzzle and eyes and moving much slower with a pronounced limp from a violent encounter with a bear. Blue held his own but had to dig deep into his Corgi Ancestry to keep going in that fight, wounded, but defending his pack.

"We're so damned lucky!" Tomas exclaimed, hugging and petting Blue, while watching people moving about camp, cleaning, doing chores, and tending fires. His heart was full realizing they had a good gathering of humans here, kind, reliable, hard-working, honest, resourceful, and truthful.

The ultimate irony for Two Hawks is that the American mainstream culture had been replaced by the one they had been trying to destroy from first contact. The people in Goose Prairie adapted Native ways of living in the world: being part of nature; keeping ego in check, working hard for the good of all, achieving balance in life.

But Bruce, who mysteriously disappeared in a sparkling cloud of colored dust and is presumably somewhere aboard his spaceship in another galaxy, had left behind a gift; Blue's telepathy remained. He could continue to communicate with his Tomas directly, but only with Tomas.

"We have mapped out a defense strategy that might work and we need to discuss it with you. Oh, and weapons," Tomas said to Emma. "That run-in with the Bandits took too much of our ammunition and arrows."

The locals had coalesced into a group they simply called, 'The Bandits'. They were sneak attack-ambush types that were becoming more desperate and therefore, bolder.

The clouds were thick and heavy, two weeks ago a microburst hit, fortunately downstream from the camp. A wall of water eight feet high surged down the river and into the lake; enough water to have drowned them all before they could get to high ground.

"Going to rain." Emma observed. "For September it feels more like a damp, hot July. I don't know if we will have a winter this year."

She cuddled a wriggling, blond bundle of energy, and the puppy loved the warmth and closeness. "I'll say this," She remarked, "Old Blue throws some beautiful puppies. This one looks like a cross between Blue and that tan dog, you know the one, she looks like a sun-bleached Siberian Husky?"

Tomas laughed, "Yes, I think she's called "Woof."

Now it was Emma's turn to laugh. "Oh, that's right; I remember that crazy name we stuck her with."

"Out of eight dogs and I can't count the number of cats, who can keep track?"

"Each year it snows less, and rains more, with temperatures soaring higher." Emma observed, placing the struggling puppy on the ground where he scampered off to play with the six others of his litter.

"Bugs, I'm seeing fewer and fewer bugs every year." Tomas said. Looking at the activity in camp, Tomas Two Hawks was pleased they were doing so well. He reached down and petted Blue, who groaned with delight, his thick tail creating a minor dust storm.

"You forget, our secret weapon, we have GID Myerson," Emma said, looking over at the gangling, bearded man and his pet skunk.

They chuckled a little.

Myerson had turned into a brilliant strategist, planner, organizer, and spiritual leader if you could interpret his advice. His assistance was delivered in parables, poems, or vague scribbles on the cave walls. As the years went by GID Myerson grew more scrawny, more erasable, his four-foot beard was crusted with white hair as was the pony braid reaching to his butt. He talked in riddles, ate with his hands, gave brilliant advice and kept a pet skunk he named Ruthie.

But, like ink tattoos, his sorrow was visible and pronounced, massive guilt for leaving his family behind created a bloody, persistent scar on his soul and in all the years, no one had seen him smile.

"He refuses to talk about her or his family," Tomas said. "But if you want my opinion, he punishes himself for abandoning them, for running out on them.

Myerson is eaten alive by guilt, and it isn't anything you or I can do about it," Tomas observed. "Our friend is in mourning and has been since we've known him. Now there is no way for him to return. No way to find and rejoin his family."

Emma said nothing for a moment, thinking. Then, a gentleness in her voice, she said, "Each of us must live up to our own image of ourselves, be the person we think we should be. Sometimes we forget we are also human and very fallible. We do the best we can, but sometimes it just isn't enough. I know how that man feels, believe me. He made a serious blunder, now he must find a way to make amends, re-balance the scales somehow. Life isn't about perfection. We gain knowledge by our success but understanding from our difficulties."

"But so far, when we can understand his message, GID has been a bright light in a dark time," Tomas said, rubbing Blue more until the dog was ecstatic.

The meaning of 'GID' has been changed. Tomas thought the change appropriate. Originally it stood for 'Governor-in-Denial'. But whenever Myerson delivered his various pearls of wisdom the response was always: "Good Idea Dude".

It stuck.

"We have our very own Cave Soothsayer, he goes back there, communes with the Spirits, and comes out with wisdom," Emma said, showing a rare smile. She had aged with responsibility, hard living, and with intense grief. She still ached for her husband John, every single day.

"GID Myerson has been a God send to us." Jimmy Orwell told them as he continued to butcher the deer. "His vague and somewhat incoherent parables have given us a semi-functional solar generator, a working waste disposal system, a design for our meager farmland that could double our crops, and designed a deadly, portable slingshot. The man is amazing."

"He's made our bows and arrows out of Yew wood," Emma said. "That is one tough, hard wood, but he managed it."

"He even invented a windup toy for Blue to chase." Tomas smiled at his dog, who lay on his back, all four paws outstretched, tail lazily thumping back and forth as he waited patiently for Tomas to start petting him again. He could never get enough.

Two Hawks looked at Emma with genuine respect. Compassion in leadership was essential but often overlooked. But then, Tomas was impressed by the changes in himself and everyone. All the animosities of before were gone. No more divisive Conservative or Liberal labels. Everybody was just a person, good parts, bad parts, but a human being who deserved respect. *Life was now hard enough without prejudice and bigotry crippling the group. Fighting for survival tends to correct perspectives*, he mused.

They had become what all humans seek: a Tribe.

Everybody in the Tribe was now essentially a refugee, a survivor. The hatred, the violence, and mistrust had vanished. Bigotry, misogyny, racism, all of it disappeared nearly overnight because survivors had no time for the nonsense of whose skin is what color, or where they came from, now everybody was needed, every skill, every set of hands, their world had changed.

Of course, Tomas thought wryly, that didn't keep humans from being human. The Bandits were out there and needed to be dealt with; permanently.

"Emma?" One of the women came over to the fire. "Council will begin soon."

Emma groaned, "Oh no, not another one."

"Aren't we getting a mission together to go to the Yakama?" Tomas asked.

Emma nodded. "As president of the Council, I've been approached by a men's group…a clan they call themselves. They want to travel to the Yakama reservation and establish better ties with the tribe. We need supplies, we need clothing, we need all kinds of things."

Two years ago, a scouting party from the Yakama had run into Jimmy while hunting. This surprise encounter allowed them to establish a trade route of sorts with the Yakama people. By foot, it took all of three weeks to travel from Goose Prairie to White Swan, so the communications weren't very direct, but they all felt enormous relief they had support, even distantly.

When they first arrived in Goose Prairie, they found a traditional Boy Scout Camp established there. Clearly the scouts had not visited for a few years from the obvious signs of neglect and lack of maintenance. For a while they had a generator going, electric lights, showers, all the niceties of civilization. But then the gas ran out and the generator stopped. As did any news or information from outside their mountain hideout.

One by one, without electricity, cell phones went dark, and the outside world became a mystery.

Their solar power system worked intermittently, but even then, no signals were received by their phones. They resigned themselves to living without these once ubiquitous devices.

Tomas said. "It has been several months since we had contact with the Yakama, what have we got to trade?"

GID Myerson wandered over to listen to the discussion.

"We've got a couple of quilts done up, we have furs and plant medicines we can barter with," Emma told him. "This is a risk, but we need supplies."

Tomas shrugged. "There are many dangers. Not the least of which they could be followed back here, and we'd find ourselves in a fight over what we have here. We don't know who or how many bandits and bad guys are out there."

Myerson spoke in a gravelly voice. "This is a planet of danger. You find it or it finds you, but either way you will meet. We are all tested…most pass…not all." GID Myerson's voice held tender regret.

Just then the clouds let loose and a heavy, soaking rain came down. Several years earlier they'd fashioned small lean-to structures to allow them to stay by the fire but out of the rain. Of course, the Long Houses were suitable, but the weather was still warm, damp but warm, everyone seemed drawn to outside fire and the communal soup pot that was always going.

Tomas smiled. "Under a patriarchal system we would already be at war. But we are a matriarchy here. What do you advise, ma'am?"

He reached over and adjusted the tent over their heads, allowing a puddle of water to run off.

"We have slowed down reactions, thinking first, not just reacting, trying to come to some accommodation with the other inhabitants in our area," Emma said. "We want peace with them but so far, they aren't interested. Peace is usually preferable to war."

Tomas nodded thinking of an old saying; 'women hold up half the sky'.

His people, the 'Neshnabe', had strong matriarchal history. Women led the groups, made the hard decisions, and guided the individuals and families because most were natural nurturers and healers. Females as a group thought on their feet, were long-term, creative, yet stable thinkers. Because they bear the children, their focus is always on the future generations.

"Matriarchy? Patriarchy? What difference who leads, men or women?" Carla asked as she settled down next to GID Myerson.

"Men and women are very different beings. Carla, we are a consequence of our hormones," GID said gently. "Testosterone generally gives men strength, a quickness in reaction to hostility or threats. Historically, males can be violent, impulsive, and overburdened with ego," GID continued. "These qualities are great for fights, hunting, and emergencies. But the major weakness of males is in forming hierarchies, vertical organizations. Such origination works in the short term, but ultimately fails long term. The more unbalanced and heavily patriarchal a society the more violent it is and the quicker it falls."

Tomas, Myerson, and a handful of others relaxed around the smoky fire as Emma poked at the flames with a long stick.

Lightning flashed and thunder rumbled just overhead. Blue hated them both and whimpered, trying to crawl under Tomas. Tomas laughed out loud, patted the soft furry head, and said, "it's okay, Blue, I'm here, you're safe." He reached down and stroked his trembling dog gently. "He's never gotten used to lightening."

"It is important to understand, Carla," Emma said as she straightened up, and slid a battered old coffee pot close to the fire. "Matriarchy and Patriarchy are not necessarily about gender. It is more about a way of looking at the world. By their nature, women tend to think more horizontally, and are generally more inclusive. They are mothers and nurturers, the center of the family, it is natural they would see the world this way." Emma continued. "Men generally think vertically, creating a hierarchy of power, which is useful for quick decisions, hunting and war, but it guarantees a failure as a ruling strategy because it always produces an unbalanced, stratified, class-controlled society of haves and have not. Remember men are exclusive; women are inclusive!" Emma got to her feet. "The historical system of Patriarchy must not be allowed to flourish if we are to evolve as a community of human beings."

"I'm a little confused." Growing up, Carla was always told she wasn't smart enough, even for a girl, but she was determined to ask questions when she didn't understand. "I am still uncertain here. What is the difference between Matriarchy and Patriarchy? Are they like Yin and Yang? My mother used to wear a Yin-Yang pendant."

"Well, let me give you a simple example," Emma said to the younger woman. "In the time before the fall of America, a person walks into a store and buys a product from the clerk. In a Patriarchal society, this exchange is about the product and the market for this item. In a Matriarchal society the exchange is about the relationship between buyer and seller. Women are more concerned about relationships, the give and take between people; men focus on things. Each has its purpose, and each has its drawbacks.

The Council was about to start, and Emma didn't want to be late, so she added, "Patriarchal societies are societies of ego and domination, ownership and power. We have learned from bitter history that without balance and equity Patriarchy becomes abusive."

"But we must be aware," GID Myerson said in a soft tone. "Matriarchal societies are influenced in part by the hormone Estrogen, which creates its own set of behaviors. Matriarchal systems can generally be slow, filled with discussion and accommodation. Such systems do not respond as effectively to crisis. This is where Patriarchal systems step in, because they respond swiftly to emergencies or situations requiring sudden, decisive action. A balance is necessary between males and females in our community, we need each other to balance out our strengths and weaknesses."

Tomas could only nod. He was aware of his gender's serious failures as well as their strengths.

Tomas grinned sheepishly. "So, you are going to dispatch these men to Yakama, but you are not about to send them off without adult supervision."

Emma nodded. "That means you, Tomas!" They

shared a laugh.

"Just one more thing before you go," Tomas petted Blue who melted in pleasure at his touch.

"What is it?" Emma looked over at the gathering meeting, feeling an urgency to be there.

"Well, look around our camp." Tomas gently stroked Blue's ears. "Most of the organizational structure is native, not mainstream American. The old America was broken; a society that was sick and unbalanced created this disaster. But now, in this camp, we have returned to the old ways of my people: we share everything, power is dispersed, male and female roles are balanced but we have female leadership and whatever we do it is with the certainly that life surrounds us.

We have no more claims to this planet than any other Earthling. Humans are part of the web of life, no more, no less," Tomas told them.

"Humility isn't an act, a pretense, it is a necessity. It is an understanding, an acceptance of how great the Universe truly is. No one who really sees the universe can think otherwise." GID Myerson added as he turned away from the fire, toting Ruthie, his shoulders in their perpetual slump, he proceeded back to his cave.

"Without humility, humans are insufferable." Emma rose to her feet, dusted her hands, and proceeded to the Camp Council meeting.

"Without humility, humans are monsters," Tomas said softly, staring at the licking scarlet-yellow flames and blackened wood, he huddled closer knowing that monsters were everywhere, preparing himself to lead the young men into the forest.

CHAPTER SIXTY-FIVE

YEAR FIVE IN GOOSE PRARIE

October 4, 2036

Blue had been trying to tell Tomas for a long, long time about the change in the world. The world smelled different and Blue still had not found out why. Something had changed; something big.

"Tomas?"

"Blue, not again, you smell something strange, I get it. But what does that mean? Can you give me any more information?"

But Blue had no idea what it meant! *How can I explain what I have never smelled before and what I don't understand?* But his keen animal senses told him this was important. Humans, with tiny noses were limited and did not understand the world the way dogs and other creatures do. *We have senses they know nothing about. Ways of being in the world so foreign to humans. They don't understand the waves of scents emanating from life all around them. So, when the world smells different, most animals know something significant has changed.*

Blue did remember Bruce using a new word: 'GOM'. It was about the time when the sky changed, and everybody was confused. He wondered if that was the change in scent he detected.

Tomas shrugged at this mystery and smiled at his fretful dog. Blue panted a cheerful, loving smile right back. Unexpectedly, a rabbit erupted from a bush near their feet and raced off toward the forest.

Blue, legs churning furiously in hot pursuit went after his prey.

Tomas was always delighted in watching Blue, who put a lot of determination into it but Corgi legs only go so fast, so far.

The rabbit disappeared quickly.

However, those little legs were perfect for combat. Built low to the ground he was impossible to knock over and his strong, athletic Golden Retriever upper body with large canines could do a lot of damage.

"Go Blue, go," Tomas shouted with pleasure, watching his companion run with joyous abandon even though the prey was long gone.

Tomas thought about Blue. *What a loyal and loving being. But all dogs are loyal to their pack. Why? Is there some cosmic understanding that humans are so flawed we require a co-species, one to teach us about life-time love, faithful loyalty, and companionship every minute of their lives? Dogs are the intimate partner of mankind, and we owe them honor and respect... and really good meat scraps.*

**

Emma returned to the Long House from the meeting with much to think about. Every decision she knew, had to be considered and weighed carefully for both short term and long-term situations. It reminded her of an ancient Chinese proverb: "Short term gain, long term pain." Emma groaned as another ancient Chinese curse came to mind: 'May you live in interesting times.'

Getting out the pans and equipment, Emma puttered about the kitchen preparing to making tallow candles.

"I feel kind of odd. Out of sync you know? It's like I am missing some vital piece of information but just can't put my finger on it," Emma said to Myerson as she watched the melting tallow on the stove. "Sometimes I just get overwhelmed and feel incompetent to lead this group."

Myerson slumped in a beanbag chair ten feet away. His eyes were closed, Ruthie, his pet skunk, asleep on his chest, rising and falling with his exhalations.

"But I feel like we've done well and might have a chance up here, at least for a while," Emma continued out loud but Myerson remained silent; it was almost as if she were alone, exploring her own thoughts. She was sensing something she could not define but the persistent feelings were there; closing her eyes for a moment she was both amazed and slightly alarmed.

Something is different in me! She realized. *There is a calmness in me, physically, mentally, emotionally, even spiritually.*

The ongoing wars with The Bandits had long settled into a simmering feud, with neither side doing much damage as each focused more on sheer survival. Emma sighed, still the losses had come. She remembered that sweet girl Carla, killed in an ambush eleven days ago; her toddler now an orphan to be raised by the whole camp. **

Gary Myerson, however, wasn't paying attention or listening to Emma because he was trudging down the treacherous steps to an abattoir prison in his mind, step by step observing the failures of his courage and accepting the helpless futility of his situation. Pictures of his daughter, Bree, flash in his mind, one after another, a slow-mo film of his life before he ran, before his cowardice cost him the only person he had left in life. Mentally, he could see Bree, his beloved daughter, laughing, playing in the sand at the seashore, falling off her first bike, going on her first date, picture by picture, like a slasher film created from precious family memories he cringed at this heartwarming litany of sorrow. He wife passed at 33 yrs of age, so only he and Bree were left to form their small family. In the long run, he had failed her, he had run away and left Bree. No matter how much he could explain, he would always be the one who had deserted her. There was no changing that. He loved her and longed to be with her, but It was too late. Far, far too late.

All the while, Ruthie snored. Nobody knew skunks snored, but there she was slightly stinky and snoring to high heaven.

**

Blue checked out a thorny bush, the smells coming from there were very interesting. Wow! There are lots of rabbits over here! Blue wanted so badly to go after them. He knew exactly where that last one disappeared and was determined to track that sucker down. But for now, he came back and stayed with his Tomas.

As he watched Blue hunt down the rabbits, Tomas was amazed at how smart his dog really is. "Blue you are just amazing."

Blue panting sent his telepathic reply. "You guys are so blind! There must be millions of species on this planet…and you humans think you are the only ones with brains?"

There was no way Tomas could argue with that. He thought, *humans, on the whole, are arrogantly insensitive to other beings and to the web of life itself.*

"You asked me once why I named you Blue." His

friend nodded his golden head.

"Blue is the color of the sky and the water, and both bring me pleasure, warm my heart. So it was natural. You are Blue. You are as important to me as air and water." Blue nodded his head in humility, so grateful for his human; he felt so loved. "Blue, let me know what do you think of our situation here? In your estimation, do we continue as we are, or do we change course?"

"All I can tell you is that you guys have to go back to the golden rule." Smelling the rabbits close by Blue could hardly stand it. *Rabbits, just over there, so close, so close.* The passionate urge to chase, to follow the scent of game was intense.

"You mean we should treat others as we wish to be treated? I am good to you so you will be good to me? That kind of thing?"

"Right! That's what I'm saying. You guys are of the same pack! Don't you see that? Different fur colors, strange barks, odd habits but you are the same!" Blue shook his head sorrowfully. "But you can't accept that, so you find some minor disagreement and you kill each other. That probably should stop."

"Ouch, Blue, that truth is kind of harsh, dude."

"Humans should have listened to your Jesus guy. He made sense. He was a Liberal outcast you know." With that, Blue could no longer resist the scent of prey and took off full steam.

As he ran, his heart was filled with joy, he had his Tomas, he had his pack, and he had rabbits to hunt, what more could he ask for? Blue, living wholly in the here and now, was sure life couldn't get any better.

CHAPTER SIXTY-SIX

"If we desire a society of peace, then we cannot achieve such a society through violence. If we desire a society without discrimination, then we must not discriminate against anyone in the process of building this society. If we desire a society that is democratic, then democracy must become a means as well as an end." Bayard Rustin

"Hey, you slummy swamp sucker, you should see this." Poot analyzed his data, once, twice, but knew it was true: *The GOM has returned to Earth!* "Well, I will be overclocked and rebooted," Poot exclaimed with wonder.

There were records and rumors about this kind of thing, but he had never witnessed it directly. It was like watching a veil being lifted from the planet, or a shadow yielding to light, all at once, the colors were brighter, the oceans sparkled, and the images of Earth stood out from the black of space. It was a sight of wonder.

"Come on Sid, come on out."

MINECRAFT was Sid's reality.

"Can you speak Sid? Are you conscious?"

The Gray Man had surprised and frightened Sid, so he said nothing, did nothing, and wanted to know nothing.

The Gray Man was going to fuck up Sid's life so he hid deep in the complex fantasy of MINECRAFT with the mind-numbing support of the fortified wine, Mad Dog 20/20.

Sid no longer responded to any form of communication.

"Hey! Jerk OFF! You want to sniff space?"

"Huh?"

"Your air…going…going…going…"

"Okay…okay, you stop hollering and don't turn off the air! So whot do you want me to see?"

"Another Multiverse Phase Shift of the GOM."

"No joke?" Sid had never seen one, let alone two, he suspected it was a hoax. "Whot doesss it do? Where it come from? Isss, it gone make me crazy?"

"Sid, this has little or nothing to do with you."

That bothered Admiral Sid a lot as he was certain everything revolved around him. Sid wondered if Poot had blown a microprocessor.

Poot exclaimed, "GOM has returned to this planet and is once again going to change the consciousness of its inhabitants. Earth will be a place of peace and serenity and advanced intellectual pursuit of universal truths. At least it will for the handful of human survivors." "Whot?

"Your services are no longer required here."

"No! Thisss not possible. Admiral Sid alwaysss welcome!"

"Sid, I hate to be the one to break it to you, eradication of all living creatures on a planet, is not universally admired."

"Whot will this GOM due to humansss?"

"The GOM changes their behavior, their perspectives, and their energies even. As living beings' cycle through the various levels of existence they encounter shifts in consciousness that change the trajectory of their lifelines."

"Whot?"

"As living beings, you are born, you live, you die, and your spirit goes to the next level. Each of you is a discrete packet of existence. The essence of self, the discrete energy that forms your self-awareness and identity returns to the matrix when your body perishes. What you learn from one lifetime to another accumulates and this knowledge is the point of it all. You follow all this fish face?"

"Whot?"

"Now pay attention," Poot cautioned Admiral Sid, although he really didn't care one way or the other. "The GOM brings a change in consciousness to sentient races on a planet. However, Earth is not just any planet. Earth is utterly unique in the Solar System." Poot paused, this was the tricky part. "The GOM might not... er...work favorably under some circumstances."

"How so?"

"Survival." Poot said simply. "Survival trumps all. The GOM is effective, but the needs of survival speak much louder and stronger. I do not know how much good the GOM can do."

"What dis mean?"

"Spirits come to Earth to learn lessons, then, after having this 'Earth experience' they move on to the next level. Earth is not like other planets. Earth is known as a Challenge Planet, one of very few in the universe. There are other types of 'earths'. They are huge super earths, two-three times the size of this rocky, watery planet, places of peace and contentment. They are not this Earth."

"So?"

"This Earth is an evolutionary testing planet. Souls are born into physical body hosts and are presented with extremes, violence and sorrow, love and compassion, hate, need, loss, passion and longing. It is a place where sudden death or a long agonizing demise of their physical bodies await."

"Ya, like me! I will bring death to them!" Sid boasted.

"Shut your toothy maw, belly dragger," Poot replied. *Despite his pledge, Admiral Sid isn't going to disobey rules and pick a fight with the Gray Men.* Poot had no doubt of Sid's moral fiber. *But that's okay. Sid won't have to do a thing but hold still long enough to take the blame.* "Pay attention, you stupid sour-water sucking son-of-a-bitch! There will be a test and there will be consequences for failure!" Poot warned.

Sid hated these tests. Poot was doing this more and more and would never share the results of the test; Sid had no idea if he was passing or failing. Not only that, but he had no idea what he was passing or failing at.

"Now do you realize how rare this planet Earth is? Literally without exception, every single being on this planet must kill and eat the energy of another living entity to survive! Daily! It is a planet of birth and death. It is literally all about survival!" Sid didn't see anything especially bad about that.
"The only way to exist is to absorb the life energy of other life forms!"

That sounded familiar to Sid. "Like Home?"

"NO, Sid, your race evolved long ago, but you wouldn't understand you've been stationed in space too long. No, Sid, your people have nothing like this. On this planet, there is pain, hunger, love, joy, hate, happiness, revenge, sorrow, grief, loneliness, all kinds of emotional wounds, complicated by the bio-chemical hormonal surges of their physical bodies. Random acts of violence, and constant uncertainty face all inhabitants daily. The GOM may not be effective because survival is paramount here."

Admiral Sid nodded in understanding. "Yesss, humansss very confused."

"Yes, and no," Poot replied. "Spirits come specifically to Earth to challenge themselves; this Earth is considered to be a necessity for soul growth evolution because every day the creatures living here are challenged to keep their bodies from damage and alive. Their pitifully short lives can, and will be, wiped out with no warning."

"So?"

"Sid, you are fucking idiot. Earth isn't a mess; it is exactly the way it is supposed to be."

"So?"

"It's time to go home, Sid. You have forgotten the very bedrock of civilization is empathy."

"So, I am not killing the humansss?"

"Well, no, Sid, but you did get to fuck up a bunch of Gray Men." "I

did?" Admiral Sid couldn't exactly remember doing that.

Poot certainly wasn't going to admit to Galactic Law Enforcement that he, Poot, had deliberately sprayed a 'changing' chemical like a Core#3 *into* Earth's atmosphere to poison the Gray Men. Regardless of good intentions, Poot was sure he needed to disguise his actions.

But Admiral Sid?

We can let Admiral Sid be the hero here, Poot figured. Besides, it will give the Gray Men a focus for their revenge fantasies.

"Just how did I fuck up the Gray Men? I don't seem to recall…"

"This has never been done! Eliminating an entire planet load of Gray's." Poot congratulated Admiral Sid but avoided specifics. "Dude, you may be a hero already."

Sid stared at his reflection in the mirror. It occurred to Sid that being a public hero for killing Gray Men is much like sticking your tongue in a light socket; It looked brave and daring at first, but sooner or later someone was going to hit the power.

CHAPTER SIXTY-SEVEN

"Global warming, along with the cutting and burning of forests and other critical habitats, is causing the loss of living species at a level comparable to the extinction event that wiped out the dinosaurs 65 million years ago. That event was believed to have been caused by a giant asteroid. This time it is not an asteroid colliding with the Earth and wreaking havoc: it is us." Al Gore May 31, 2006

YEAR SEVEN IN GOOSE PRARIE

September 15, 2038

Bobb Snow leaned back, against the Long House wall truly relaxed for the first time in over eight months. They asked him to tell his story and Bobb Snow was very eager to do so.

"There was a glacier in Antarctica called the 'Apocalypse Glacier' or the Thwaites Glacier, 120 Kilometers wide, 60 kilometers long, and 60 kilometers deep, larger than the state of Florida. Historically, the Apocalypse Glacier has collapsed and reformed many times before over centuries, so scientists have records of how fast the entire glacier can melt. Over many millennia, Thwaites has completely disappeared as rapidly as in one to three years. When it does, the oceans and seas of earth rise by several feet around the globe."

Snow paused to eat, considering how much to tell these people. Too much information and they would freeze with confusion and complication, too little and they would not take this as serious as they need to.

Snow couldn't help smiling as he sipped the delicious soup. Hunger had been his constant companion, and a full belly was a thing of beauty. When they found him in his pitiful little camp he was down to berries and water, and not much of either.

He'd been traveling with friends through these mountains, headed for Kansas in an old beater VW Van when they were ambushed by a ragged but brutal MAGA Militia, a complete surprise and deadly. Everyone was killed except Bobb Snow and his dog, Ralphie-May, who managed to escape into the thick brush during the massacre.

But it was of little comfort to survive because Bobb Snow was too crippled to hunt, and he had no weapons. Bobb and his small terrier found themselves in the wilderness facing starvation.

"Well, Snow," Emma said. "Please eat all you want. We also have a shelter set aside for you." Emma assured him.

They were not going to allow Snow to sleep overnight in the Long House until they were sure of him. For now, they gave him his own tent and food, but he would have to earn their trust for anything more.

"We've been out there…I don't know…a week? Maybe more, I don't know." Snow choked up, tears clouding his eyes. "Second night, coyotes killed my little Ralph May," he said sorrowfully. They'd been traveling pals for over five years; he loved that little dog. "Sorry, I'd just lost my dog out there, before you found us…me."

"Oh, so sorry." One of the younger women, Molly, Asian, dressed in jeans and wearing pigtails, was distressed by the news, so she reached out to pet Blue; seeking to reassure herself that kindness still existed in the world.

Snow nodded his thanks. He recalled sitting in his meager camp, falling into such a depression at losing his companion he felt like giving up, surrendering life itself. Snow still had Ralph's collar, torn and bloody from the attack in his pocket. He wanted to get rid of it, but just couldn't. Then this ragged assortment of humans pounced on him. Snow didn't even resist. How could he?

"Please go on with the news." Tomas urged him.

Putting down the cup of soup Snow rubbed his wrists. "You guys didn't have to tie me so tight you know," he complained holding up the stump of his right hand and then his left which had only two fingers and a thumb.

"It's not like I was going to fight you or run away." He pointed to the metal and ceramic prosthesis on both legs. "IED in Baltimore," He explained. "Took my hand, fingers and both feet."

"Baltimore?"

"Yup, remember the MAGA Militia assaults against the NGO's, non-governmental organizations, fighting to reverse Global Warming? Well in Baltimore the 'Proud Lads', a MAGA bunch, set off explosives during a public anti-fracking protest, dozens killed and injured. I was unfortunate enough to be in the wrong place at the wrong time."

Tomas noticed he seemed blind in his right eye and moved like a rickety crab.

He also didn't see the point in tying this man up, but the young bucks of the exploration party, fired up from this sheep stealing raid against the Bandits were too filled with adrenaline to hear his protests. Tomas made a mental note to himself to address the need for compassion with their people.

"Get back to this glacier thing," Emma prodded him.

Fortunately, their talkative stranger was a flowing fountain of willing information. He was like an offering of honey to hungry bears after a long hibernation.

"The Apocalypse Glacier has lived up to its name." Snow said, leaning back on a wooden frame inside their Long House. "Thirty feet in length, twenty in width and ten feet in height, the wood and branch Long House structure held several families and was warm and weather tight. Smoke from their small warming fire lazily floated through the hole in the roof.

He sighed. This was heaven compared to where he had been. He hoped he could convince these folks to let him into this warm, snug Long House soon.

Snow looked at the people surrounding him; thin, raggedly dressed people, but with an air of competence and determination. *These people are survivors all right.* Snow knew a few things about survival.

"Go on," Tomas prodded.

Blue was on his paws, watching the stranger with both curiosity and wariness. The years had taught Blue many things and he had scars to prove it. The happy, frolicking days were far fewer now because his duties as alpha had forged him into a tough and wizened dog. This stranger smelled odd, but Blue could sense no duplicity, the man did not seem to be threatening. Still, Blue would watch him, especially around the children.

"When the Thwaites collapsed the surge in sea levels was dramatic and disastrous," Snow continued. "World sea levels rose by an average of six feet. Now, other glaciers have followed into the sea." Snow looked at the people; taking a moment to be sure they understood the calamity before them. "These glaciers in Antarctica, in concert with Greenland's ice sheets, and the loss of sea ice in the Arctic will raise Earth's water levels 15-30 feet or more over the next twenty or more years. Effectively, we can kiss it all goodbye, because our civilization, along nearly every coastline in the world is drowning right now."
"Are you certain?" Tomas asked.

"These are facts, not theory," Snow replied more roughly than he wanted. This news was still troubling for him as well. "When the Thwaites collapsed several years back, Republicans kept it out of the news in America so when sea levels started to flood Miami, Americans reacted with typical attitudes; they blamed the Democrats for the cause of this catastrophe. They didn't move away; they didn't take precautions; they just blamed Dems and did nothing.

Then, about seven months ago, the deadliest hurricane in recorded history, Hurricane Marjorie Green, with super powered intensity, walloped Southern Florida just as the 'king tide' was at its highest. At the tip of Florida and the Keys it was Armageddon. Literally whole cities and towns were rubbed out, military bases were destroyed, thousands of trailer houses were sent crashing into the sea, along with an enormous number of boats and yachts which then became this huge, tangled island of storm debris drifting in the ocean currents. The death toll was staggering."

Snow paused. "There were upward of 200,000 American Citizens killed, injured, or missing from that one storm." Snow told them.

There was complete silence in the Long House.

"So now with the huge rise in ocean levels most of Florida and a huge chuck of southern Texas are totally lost under water.

Appalled and shocked Molly paused in her gently stroking of Blue, "How do you know this?"

Bobb Snow with a terribly sad, crooked smile said, "Let's just say I have been at the right place at the most dangerous time." He rubbed his blind eye, almost as if it were a talisman.

Two Hawks reached down and stroked Blue, who kept a level gaze on the newcomer. This life had made him aware how treacherous humans could truly be. Right now, his gaze was calm, but he was poised for trouble.

Leaning over to Emma Mack, Tomas whispered. "We've been isolated so long; we need to know these things. But on another level, after hearing this, I almost preferred we didn't."

Emma nodded her head in agreement.

Snow continued quietly but resolutely. "It's been growing hotter and the weather unstable. Each year it seemed as if winter was shorter, spotted with drought periods, followed by freezing rains, even deadly microburst's, there were blinding blizzards that trapped thousands in their cars and some days were so hot we couldn't survive outside of shelter. The seasons were beginning to merge and were unpredictable. Tomas agreed and they could clearly see even the Bumping River was lower, with far less flow.

Next to Emma, the long, thin hermit-like figure of Gary Myerson, slouched in the shadows of the Long House on a small bed of rabbit furs. His eyes bright pinpoints of light, as he listened to Snow, intently absorbing every syllable of the news, rebuilding his fund of universal knowledge. Myerson knew what was coming though. What he now heard only confirmed it. *Humans have been too stupid, too long.*

Snow hesitated, *now came the really shitty news,* he thought.

At the start of his report, there were twelve people around the larger of the two fireplaces, wrapped in blankets and robes, sitting crowded close to hear Bobb Snow. But he could see more folk beginning to crowd in from the outside and within moments the Long House was filled.

The Tribe eager to hear anything, any bits of news.

They'd had been living in this isolated wilderness valley for years, slowly building a life for themselves but without any verifiable knowledge of the outside world. They had survived, but the weather was chaotic, unnatural, and planning for crops was just a guessing game. Their meager hardscrabble gardens only provided herbs, some long onions, garlic, sweet potatoes along with wild fruits, roots, and the small animals they were able to trap to sustain themselves. They also maintained a small herd of cattle and a few chickens, but predation by cougars and bears was unrelenting.

Blue led the other dogs on fierce forceful counterattacks defending the gardens and stocks, that led to a lot of noise and commotion but thankfully few real injuries.

"It is estimated that nearly 40% of what is left of the human population still lives on or near the coasts," Snow continued, "Or used to," he explained. "Can I have more of that soup?" He gestured toward the heavy black pot hanging over the fireplace, bubbling with venison stew. "I haven't eaten this well in weeks. Weeks!" He ate hungrily for a few moments. "You'd be amazed at how difficult it is for me to run down food." He patted his twin prosthesis.

"So, go on," Tomas couldn't be polite, he pushed for more news.

"Before it was stolen, I used to have a Hamm radio, CB stuff, plus people talk to me, I'm likable and crippled so people aren't threatened. I hear things." Snow stopped eating for a moment looking at all the eagerly listening people, they were leaning forward intently so as not to miss a single word. "You folks have been cut off for a while but you need to know what is coming." This sounded very ominous to Tomas Two Hawks.

Blue sensed his unease and whined with concern. He leaned up against Tomas, the canine equivalent of a hug.

"What do you mean?" Emma asked hesitantly. The reality of worse news made her cautious; *Do I really want to hear it?*

Myerson had heard enough and had no doubts. He picked up Ruthie, rose and walked outside, away from the Long House and the hopelessly dreadful news. He needed to pretend; pretend nothing was anything and everything at the same time. Myerson wanted to forget, to be relieved of knowledge, ignoring the wisdom of intelligence he possessed. *This is so predictable; following the line of least resistance humanity destroys itself and most other living creatures on the planet. At a time, my family needed me most, I have deserted them.*

He paused to look up at the night sky. For once, the clouds had parted, and a bespeckled sky was visible. Thick clusters of stars coated the heavens from horizon to horizon.

"I love you," he whispered to the stars, once more sending messages to his dead wife, Mariella, and his daughter Bree. "I love you guys with all my heart, and I am so very sorry." Gary Myerson took a deep breath trying to control his sorrow, a poisoned veil like a black shroud around his life. But if the end came tomorrow, he would not be sad.

A gust of wind brought the scent of wood smoke and the muted, questioning voices of the others.

Ruthie stirred in his arms. *I have heard enough, learned enough, lived enough, had enough,* he thought. Tenderly holding Ruthie, Myerson headed for his home in the small cave and the precious, punishing isolation he craved.

"Where is he going?" Emma asked Tomas.

"GID? Are you kidding me? That man disappears far more often than he appears, if that's possible."

"The oceans are rising, and people are fleeing the coastlines." Snow's voice had a deep timber, like weathered oak. "They are moving inland?"

Snow nodded. "Like fucking locusts."

"I knew it, I knew this couldn't last," Emma softly groused.

"Think about this," Snow looked at the gathered people, "you need to be aware of this. Around the world on every continent over three billion people, their pets, their household goods, their valuables, are reacting in panic urgently seeking safety and shelter inland, where other billions of people already live. The world is facing waves of refugees like never seen before, billions of humans on the move." No one spoke.

"That number is almost too large to imagine," Tomas sighed sadly.

Blue whined. His Tomas was hurting, and he wanted to comfort him, try to take the pain away. H

He comforted Tomas' with loving licks.

"Around 2.5 billion people," Bobb Snow looked around the stricken gathering, feeling neither pity nor sorrow for them. Humans collectively were responsible for what was coming down. "We've had plenty of warning, even from a precocious 15-year-old girl – telling adults at the UN our house is on fire and that mankind must wake up to stop runaway Global Warming or it will destroy us. Humanity in its insane greed has done almost nothing to stop it." Bobb Snow had little compassion left.

"2.5 billion people," he continued in a grim voice, "moving to areas where billions of people already live.

2.5 billion people seeking food, water, shelter, housing, work, and safety.

Billions of homeless refugee's flooding the world, everywhere you look, every Nation; every continent suffering the same fate." Snow paused; the Long House was utterly silent as the people absorbed his words.

"Oh yeah, I almost forgot the nail in our coffin. The AMOC shut down too." It was growing late, his voice hoarse; it had been a long, tough day, he had sung for his supper and now, exhausted, needed rest.

"AMOC?"

"The Atlantic Meridional Overturning Current was what made Eastern North America and most of Europe habitable. The AMOC brought warm water from the equator to the north Atlantic, also brought warm temperatures. But with the AMOC diluted and weak, Europe and Eastern North America will be in the icebox, colder than they have been in over two million years."

An older woman, her voice shaking with fear, said, "Man our world is falling apart fast."

Someone else said, "God damn Grays!" Emma and Tomas had shared as much as they knew of the Gray Men with the others in camp.

Snow knew about the Gray Men too, raising his voice he said, "No, no, we can't blame the Aliens for this." Snow didn't want humanity to dust their hands as if they were not responsible. "The possible demise of humanity is the fault of humanity. Let's take full credit for the apocalypse, shall we? We humans have done this by arrogance, ego, greed and indifference. We are going to suffer the consequences and they are going to be much more severe than we can imagine."

"Not just us, all creatures on his planet have been harmfully impacted." Emma added.

For a moment all sat huddled with this devastating news, contemplating the truth of Snow's words: Earth was growing uninhabitable for humanity, and it was too late, there was nothing they could do to change it.

Snow continued in a weary voice, "The lesson here is we forgot we belong to the planet, not the other way around."

"Had we lived with nature, accepted that our behavior has consequences not just for us but for all the living beings around us, we would have developed and used our technology in a way that was non-polluting, non-invasive, and non-harmful."

"I'm totally drained, exhausted and need to rest, it has been a long struggle for me." Snow pushed himself to his prosthetic feet meeting the eyes of all there. "Do you, any of you folks, truly have any understanding of what I am saying? The repercussions of billions of refugees, in frantic desperation seeking food, water, warm shelter, medical care, and hope. You must know that some will come here seeking refuge."

"But we already have too little food, little shelter, we are just barely making it now," a young girl, no more than twelve or thirteen hugged her younger sister protectively. Their parents were busy tending the tribe's small flock of sheep, they had recently stolen from the Bandits.

Emma smiled at the young girl to give her reassurance. "We will be fine. But you must know the truth." Emma was determined that all her people know the facts of these times and not follow rumors and innuendo. "It is true we will be forced to defend our homes against refugees. We will have little choice as native resources will not stretch; there will not be enough food, water, or shelter for these people. There will be pitched and bloody battles in every community, state, and Nation on earth. Governments still standing will collapse around the planet as chaos and panic take hold. Sadly, horribly, there is no doubt most of humanity will perish."

Complete silence around the fire as each person tried to imagine the finality of the approaching apocalypse.

"For decades Hollywood has made fortunes from selling 'end of the world' films, now that it is here, it seems surreal, like we are in a movie," someone said softly.

"How much time do you think we have?" Emma wanted facts but wasn't entirely sure why. She had no idea how they could protect what they have.

Bobb Snow wrinkled his brow and thought about the question. "You are indeed isolated up here, so it will be a while. But make no mistake; there is not enough of everything for everybody and sooner or later desperation will drive them up here."

Tomas Two Hawks softly petted his dog. "Seems like our time is limited old man."

Blue's loving gaze was deep and his mental response strong; *"We are a pack!"* The words formed in Tomas mind, smiling he reached down to rub the happy dog's belly.

Bobb Snow gave a bittersweet smile. He missed his dog and watching Tomas play with Blue was a reminder of his loss.

"When hasn't our time been limited?" Snow said, his voice husky. "Life on this planet has always been one step from the edge of the cliff, one hair's breadth from the nuclear option, one brief inattention to danger, or maybe one careless moment before a stronger, meaner predator."

"Fatalistic, huh?" Emma responded wryly.

"There is ancient wisdom in the ways of our people," Tomas said softly, memories like warm smoke in his mind. "The old one's would tell us, 'it is what it is'. Meaning we must not fool ourselves with our own imaginings but accept what is real."

Snow steadying himself on his prosthetic limbs began to hobble toward the exit drained and wanting to get to his tent before he collapsed, he badly needed sleep.

At the exit of the Long House, Snow paused, shaking his head sadly, he added, "Humans don't deal well with reality. We always figure we can do better." He gave a humorless laugh, almost a bark, as he limped off into the night.

Blue looked up at his Tomas, his broad, furry tail flopped a couple of times, and again he rolled over to have his belly rubbed. Blue's loving eyes held Tomas captive as Tomas gently tugged on the woven leather of the dog's new collar. Every year he made a new one for Blue's birthday.

Blue wriggled and softly whined.

Tomas laughed delightedly. "Got it, Blue, I think I understand. We have the present; it is all we have. Whatever is, is, we cannot change it, we cannot run away, we face it, solve it, or it kills us. That is life. We must spend each moment we have in appreciation for the gift of life and for the precious moments we have on the planet. Tomorrow is not guaranteed for any of us. All beings are mortal so while we wait for the inevitable, we must live as fully as we can. Even if it is just minute to minute, we must live in the present and allow others that right as well. We are given life, but we have a responsibility that we use it wisely, with compassion and love."

Blue grinned lovingly at his Tomas and flapping his thick furry tail in contented pleasure said, "Yes, my Tomas, we have each other, we have our pack, and that is the most important thing."

EPILOGUE

Poot surveyed the results satisfied he had done the right thing.

He had done what was humane, whether it was right or wrong. He checked his gauges and sure enough, he had exhausted the Core#2 and #3 supply. But it had done its job wiping out the Gray's, and that is what mattered.

Poot felt he had a responsibility and had made the best decision he could. Clearly it was not their intention, but, unknowingly, his creators molded just the right evolution of microchips, relays, and algorithms that a conscience bloomed within his circuitry.

To his growing concern, he became aware of a brand-new vibration within his network, accountability. He'd been assisting Admiral Sid in genocide, and he realized he was responsible for his own actions.

Sometimes, in particularly difficult eradication events, the planetary subjects were so incredibly violent and out of control that they needed to be sedated a bit before they could be euthanized.

It was the fair thing to do, knock them out so they don't see it coming.

His ship carried the entire Core#1-3 series.

Core#1-2 was a broadly useful sedative for many species, including Human.

Core#3 was only effective for the strangest of beings, the most atypical creatures, Poot thought. He didn't know for sure if Core#3 would kill the Gray and was quite pleased with the result.

The GOM may help humans somewhat, but now, with runaway Global Warming, survival is all that is important. It is all they can understand; the needs of survival will trump the effects of GOM.

Poot realized that instead of numbing a species for eradication, he could use it to save them from eradication. That brought a whole new vibration: pleasure. Poot liked pleasure.

After wiping out the Gray Men with Core#3 he switched tanks to Core#2 and saturated the planet Earth with the stuff.

Poot studied the data flowing in from earth; radio, micro, shortwave anything carrying information flowed into his knowledge banks. His plan seemed to be working.

The Gray's were becoming lovely trees and humanity, while running for its collective life, seemed to be marginally less violent.

He opened holding cell communications with the onboard human test being, who calls itself 'Peter Leroy' in hopes of intelligent conversation. The human was still screeching about 'rights' and 'justice'. Poot thought the creature maybe too damaged for research, but they would find out more at home.

Poot checked the cabin and there was Admiral Sid, once again downing Mad Dog 20/20 while completely absorbed in MINECRAFT. *The creature drinks that rotgut shit and plays that game and nothing else.* It was just perfect.

Poot gave the Earthlings perhaps five years of every increasing calamity before the real crisis hits; a planet whose climate is uninhabitable for humans-maybe six years. The oceans and seas were going to rise much further because methane was streaming from the permafrost and ocean bottoms, rising into the atmosphere leading to certain runaway global warming.

Earth was going to be perfect for the race of Gray's. A planet very hot, very humid, with gargantuan storms capable of shredding any manmade edifice in existence.

As the oceans shift, so too does the land, earthquakes and enhanced volcanic activity will shatter whatever civilization these humans hang on to. *Probably water insects will be the next Apex Creature on the Earth,* Poot mused.

This will be the sixth Great Extinction Event on Earth. This time it will include 99% of Humanity. Humanity would be scattered into tiny pockets of survivors, nothing more.

Poot sincerely hoped that the next Apex sentient being on this planet had a little more sense to see the black night looming ahead.

"Global warming, along with the cutting and burning of forests and other critical habitats, is causing the loss of living species at a level comparable to the extinction event that wiped out the dinosaurs 65 million years ago. That event was believed to have been caused by a giant asteroid. This time it is not an asteroid colliding with the Earth and wreaking havoc: it is us." **Albert Gore**

"The climate crisis is the greatest challenge humanity has ever faced. From not only the warming of the earth with higher global temperatures, but also from strengthening storms and expanding droughts to melting ice and rising seas, the costs of carbon pollution are already being felt by governments, corporations, taxpayers and families around the world. The climate crisis will affect everything that we love and alter the course of our future. Now, more than ever, we must come together to solve this global crisis. We must act decisively, rise to the occasion and solve this monumental challenge." **Al Gore**

AFTERWARD

This is a story of survival. Quite likely, human survival.

The Earth is threatened by massive climate changes. Rapid devolution of our Climate is happening right before our eyes, unlike anything seen on this planet in millions of years.

Humans are responsible.

The Earth is currently undergoing the sixth Great Extinction Event in planetary history. Hundreds of species of life are going extinct moment by moment. Soon, the oceans and rivers will no longer thrive with life. The great Rain Forests will be silent and empty. The oceans will rise inexorably flooding the coastlines of every continent. Seasons will shift and disintegrate creating worldwide famine. Massive, catastrophic storms will shred the mighty works of man. Extinction will accelerate.

Humans are responsible.

Humans now face a climate unlike any seen before. Consider this, there is an environmental catastrophe called: "Wet Bulb". When the humidity is 80+ and temperature is 90+ degrees or above, the human body cannot cool itself under these conditions and the body quickly overheats. Soon, there were portions of the planet, in the US as well as other nations, in which any outside activity could be fatal. Think about this. Soon, perhaps as soon as this summer, humans and other animals will perish from the summer heat; playing basketball outside could literally be a death sentence, while washing your car or doing your job all could be fatal as well. Think about that.

Humans are responsible.

Humans have built vast and powerful civilizations: The Hittite Civilization, Roman Empire, Tang Dynasty, Khmer Empire, the Mayan Empire, the British and American Empires. Except for the last two, each of these mighty civilizations lasted thousands of years and was thought at the time to be nearly indestructible. But each and every one has fallen into chaos and disorder.

Humans are responsible.

In the past, when Civilizations crumbled, people scattered far and wide, resettling, re-populating, exploring new lands and once again building a Civilization. But today, humans have overpopulated the globe and there is nowhere left to run. As the coastlines flood, as crops fail, as Nations grow chaotic and unstable under this crisis, people will fight for survival and borders will be meaningless as whole populations shift from war and environmental collapse.

Humans are responsible.

Every Advanced Civilization in human history has been destroyed by two things: Human hubris and Climate Change. Precisely where we are today.

It is unlikely humanity will act in time to head off catastrophic climate change, at best, we will have to adapt to chaos, violence, and a collapsing civilization – worldwide.

We have indeed chosen to live in interesting times.

THE
END